I0691841

the
'idiot spy'
(the series)
book eight of ten

diamonds + gold
divided by
cash
=
treachery

c. benjamin lattimore

diamonds + gold divided by cash = treachery
Published: March 2022
Printed in the United States of America
ISBN: 978-1-7334945-7-1

DISCLAIMER: This is a work of fiction. Names, characters, businesses,
places, events, and incidents are either the products of the author's
imagination or used in a fictitious manner. Any resemblance to actual
persons, living or dead, or actual events is purely coincidental.

a lattidreamer™ publication
© C. Benjamin Lattimore, 2022

to my amazing wife, Marisa—
your commitment to my obsession is phenomenal!

ACKNOWLEDGEMENTS

my children, Christopher, Monica, and Courtney--my grandchildren, Isaiah, and Desmond. A heartfelt expression of love to my older sister Mary E., and my younger brother, Darryl A. Yet again, and again, and again, venerate regards to Maurice Cheeks and Reginald Wilkes.

lots of love ethereally to, Mary Alice, Walthro M, Barbara Ann, and Walter Eugene. To my friends, Gordon Gant, Joseph Bongiavanni II, Monique Gorham, Rahsaan Stevens, and my newest guardian angel, Mrs. Marjorie C. Cheeks.

CHAPTER ONE

At 0400 hours, the smooth ride turned into a harrowing experience that appeared to be headed straight for Hades. The starboard engine lights came on, and the plane suddenly began to drop out of the sky. Although the port engine operated effectively and could deliver the plane to the ground safely, its important gauges began to rise. Everyone on the plane was alerted to this problem as they felt the sudden descent of the aircraft.

Carla scanned the gauges and saw several problems and began to calculate what needed to happen. At 25,000 feet, she guided the plane into a deep descent, to cool the engines and blow any debris out of them. At 15,000 feet, she began to pull back on the yoke to slow the descent. At 12,000 feet, the plane appeared to be in a freefall, and all was lost. At 9,000 feet, she and the co-pilot began to fight the descent force and employed the power assist option to meet their needs. At 5,500 feet, as the plane headed towards the ground at over 600 miles per hour, Carla calmly pulled hard on the yoke and hit four switches above her head. There was a roar, a rumble, and a sudden burst of energy in the wrong direction. The starboard engine started, Carla engaged the flaps, and threw the throttles full forward. The aircraft engines blasted forward and began to climb slowly to higher altitudes. Although the plane sputtered, its forward revelations kept it on a targeted ascent. Carla thought that the fuel was contaminated and began to query the co-pilot about the fuel that was used.

As the plane began to naturally ascend into the air, people began to lessen their grips on the armrests, each other, and their legs. Asiram, crying, said to Zanthius, "I love you so much, and this might have been the end of our lives and the children. Please tell me each day you love me if you love me. Life can be so short.

CHAPTER TWO

"So, my brother, how the hell are you feeling? That was a close call, and thanks be to God that Courtney was there. Do you realize she has been there for all of us, and we sort of treat her as a matter of fact? Not only has she saved our asses, and many others, on the other side of the equation, she has taken lives, against her oath. Everything does not have to be a group decision. Why can't you and I just publicly thank her for her family, her husband, and her critical services? She certainly saved my ass and yours as well, what's wrong with us acknowledging it?" Jilkes asked.

"How do you be thinking we thank her? We could give her a car, or buy her a small boat, or something that be personal and just for her. I don't be thinking we buy her a ring or something like that. I would hate to have to bury the Sarge. By the way, you would help me, if'n he came a calling for me, wouldn't you?" John Lee inquired.

"John Lee, I love you and will always love you, but if we go getting the Sarge involved in something that will make him jealous and stupid, then we're all dead and gone. Do you remember when he went against those guys when Jong was injured. Shit, he didn't have a rock and Mr. Man waltzed into their camp and put a hurting on them. He is a force greater than any we have faced. I suggest we give Courtney a personal gift, but nothing that gets either one of us an ass kicking by the beast."

Jilkes dropped his head into his lap and began to cry. John Lee immediately asked, "What be wrong with you? I've never seen you cry like this. Did I say something wrong? Are you mad at me? You be sick or something?"

"Can you shut your dumb ass up for a minute, and let me breathe, I'm flustered. I have been hit, you have been hit, Brown, Bernstein, Chakes, and the Sarge, and many others. I'm getting tired of killing people and having people try to kill me and you have felt that stinging pain. We had our differences at first and it took an ass whupping to bring you in line. I'm afraid the next time you or I get shot, it will be our last time, and that bothers me. I mean no one, and I do mean no one, until we met our wives, was more protective of us than we were of each other. I watched your back, and you had my back—we had the rest of the guys backs as well—a perfect union. Now, I feel we're getting old and have started to make too many mistakes, the kind that get you killed. I would be extremely violent if something happened to you."

There was a moment of silence and John Lee attempted to look away and cover his emotions, but yelled, "I love you so much, man. I be worrying about you as well." With tears running out of his eyes and down his cheeks, he said, "I be liberated. I love him, and he loves me."

John Lee paused for a minute and asked, "What be different in this here deal? I be done always love you and you be done always love me. What be different?"

Jilkes, with tears streaming down his face said, "I think it's more about our mortality. I would truly be crazed if something was to happen to you."

"Yeah, well I already be crazed thinking about it. We need to be having this here shit, come to an end. How about you and I go hunting for that freaking conejo by ourselves?" There was a stillness that turned the tide of their discussion.

Jilkes said, "I'll be damned, the answer was in front of us all of the time. I know we suggested that years ago, but this time we need to put a plan together and just do it! We need to do and be who we were over in the Nam. We need to forget our responsibilities, assume another identity, and hunt that son-of-a-bitch down. We do like we did in the Nam. Here, we became too civilized. We know how to play that war game, but we were afraid to do it amongst civilized people. We need to have a drink and talk to the Sarge before we head back home. You be an amazing moron, my brother. All we need to do is listen to your wisdom and interpret what it means. You're one brilliant imbecile, and genius all in one, if I can mix the two together. You're one astounding human being, and I love you so much. Let's have this exact conversation with our leaders."

# # #

Later, John Lee and Jilkes began to work themselves into a frenzy in the back of the plane and woke up a couple of the babies with their emotional outbreaks. The Sarge looked backed at Mallory and decided the two of them needed to figure out what was going on with their star pupils.

Mallory was first to reach the back of the plane and he asked, "Is everything alright with you two?"

Jilkes proclaimed in a loud voice, "Hell, no! We're tired of shooting and being shot at. We need to conclude this charade and place the Sarge's cousin in hell with his friends. Our approach has been backwards from the beginning and John Lee hit the nail on the head. Go on, tell them what's missing."

The Sarge arrived and heard the words, "what's missing". He asked, "What's missing, and why are you two back here firing up like you're about to go on a hunt?"

Jilkes said, "Sarge, because that is exactly what we need to do. Go on John Lee, tell him what's missing."

John Lee sputtered for a moment, but finally announced, "We trained liked fools over in the Nam. We ran each day, we crawled in mud and shit, we walked and ran all day, and now we be moving like we be in motorized chairs. We need to go on the hunt for that there cousin of yours. We need to train like we did in the Nam, where we didn't think we would come back, where we were scared, and where we found each other. I mean we be done got soft in this here rich man's life. We be fat and eat all kinds of foods when we should be training and getting ready to enter hell. He will kill us all, including them there children, or we be doing the killing. I say we be getting our Nam attitude on and go hunting for this asshole even if we have to enter the gates of hell you be talking about Sarge."

There was absolute silence and evaluation of John Lee's remarks and those sitting in the back of the plane had their curiosity aroused. Bernstein, Brown, Montomie, and Chakes walked to the back initially. They were followed by

McArthur, Gladstone, Jong, and Whitmore. Whitmore said, "This sounds serious and final. Damn I didn't find a wife yet."

In the back of the plane, the Fab 10 + 2 assembled and the Sarge gave them the skinny of what John Lee had said. As the Sarge faced forward, he saw Larry, Zanthius, both Juans, and Mike standing in the aisle. He motioned to them to stand down. Mallory said, "John Lee is absolutely right. We need to get over this luxury shit, and go into the sewers looking for his ass, or he will forever be our nemesis."

The Sarge put the conversation on hold and walked past the guys to where Zanthius, Larry, both Juans, and Mike were standing. He apologized to them for discounting their input but indicated to them this was an old Vietnam squabble that they were trying to resolve. He decided to invite them to the rear of the plane to hear what was being discussed.

As the group reassembled, Ava, Courtney, Monica, and Asiram noticed the men were all in the back of the plane. Courtney stood up first and said to Ava, "I wonder what all that testosterone is talking about in the back of the plane."

Asiram turned around and said, "We should go back there to hear what the bodies with two brains are discussing." As the four women headed for the rear of the plane, the Sarge made a repugnant gesture that he would remember for the rest of his life. He held a finger in the air as if he was telling Courtney to stop. When she saw that signal, she said to the ladies, "He must have lost his damn mind. He held up a finger as if we're children at a damn traffic light, and for us to look both ways before we proceed. Oh, hell no! Ladies, if you're with me, then we have officially put certain aspects of our anatomy on strike and on layaway. We shoot, we kill, we cook, we clean, and my husband is going to raise his damn finger in the air for me to stop! Oh, Ben Beckmire, I hope you remember what that rose smelled like, because you my friend, will have to use a lot of Vaseline to make that trip to the other side."

Ben Beckmire realizing exactly what he had done, yelled, "Oh shit, I just pissed my wife off. Sorry, guys, I must go and beg the woman I love to understand something that was unintentional. Shit, if the rest of you have women out there, I suggest you go and suck up to them. I know four people who are going to be tyrants."

Mallory asked, "Who are you talking about?"

"I'm talking about Ava, Asiram, Courtney, and Monica."

"How did you get my wife in your mess?"

"You know the group that bonds first, and the others just follow the leaders. Well, those four ladies are going to be the cause of a lot of 'lonely, rub my legs, but don't you dare touch the goods', nights," the Sarge said.

"What on earth did you do?" Mallory asked.

"I simply held my finger in the air to indicate we were busy and, knowing her, she's going to make me pay for that for a long time. Her eyes turned blood red in a flash, and she is going to kick my ass. Damn, it was instinctive, but it didn't mean what she is going to manifest it into. She is going to say I pushed her in public, or I disgraced her in the presence of her friends, or I simply openly flirted in front of her. Whatever makes her the happiest is the one that she's going to go with. Damn, I wish I could erase a single second."

John Lee said, "You best be going up to the cockpit and telling that there captain you need to make an announcement and apologize to that there wife of yours in front of the entire group. You be needing to squeal like a pig and tell her it was one of them there weak moments when you thought you were in charge. I think if you said it like that, then you might only get one leg broke."

Jilkes said, "You need to do what he said because I was planning on having a long night of love making with my wife when this thing lands. If they follow Courtney, then you have sentenced us all to a sexless existence."

Without uttering another word, the Sarge walked to the front of the plane and opened the cockpit door. He told the captain he had to make an announcement and needed the intercom system.

Two or three minutes later, he profusely begged for forgiveness from the woman he loved and told her the episode in the back was about things they did in Viet Nam that were atrocious and vile. He told her and the other women, that the men recognized how important they were to their defense, offense, and general mental health, and there would never be another meeting without the presence of the women. He stated his men had a lot of blood on their hands and there were thousands of souls roaming around hell waiting for them. The Sarge exclaimed, "Our final rendezvous is with a family member who makes sense of the devil. He is unlike any person you have every met or known. He is the devil in an assumed body. He would kill his own mother if she got in his way. He is capricious, lascivious, demented, deadly, and the most dishonest person you will ever encounter. Thankfully, they destroyed the mold after he was created. He is the same person that strapped our babies in those suicide vests in the mid-west. Now, I must admit, the Fab 10 +2 have committed some dastardly acts. I also must admit my son Larry, is equal with me as well when it comes to doing harm to people. I'm letting this cat out of the bag because we are about to face our most formidable challenge. John Lee brought it back to basics when he said, "we be living that rich life and done got soft". Soft is what my cousin expects and, therefore, I'm asking my wife, my sons and daughters-in-laws, my daughter and son-in-law, and you, my extended family, to join us in becoming the renaissance of the fighting machine that we were in Vietnam. My cousin will slaughter for pleasure and, therefore, we want to change the course of this event and hunt his ass all the way to hell, if need be. We have defended our family well in the past, but now we have to aggressively seek out the son-of-a-bitch that would blow our babies to pieces."

There was silence initially, until Courtney rose from her seat and walked up to her man, and he fell to his knees. He said, "I live for you and my extended family. Some of the things we did over there, was off the charts. I just didn't want you to hear any aspect of that other life we lived. Please forgive me for waving you off with my finger. I immediately realized I had made a life ending mistake with that simple action. I love you more than life. Please forgive me."

"Ben Beckmire get off your knees and give me a kiss. That was so uncharacteristic of you. I felt something big was stirring. Honey, I took the high road, but I wouldn't try that shit again, if I were you, my lover."

"Oh, honey, that behavior will never manifest itself again. I can assure you of that."

Asiram looked at Zanthius and said, "I've noticed you're beginning to get a few handles around the midsection. You and I are definitely going to join this program."

Monica rose from her seat and said, "Before we start running and doing things out of character, I suggest we all undergo a physical examination to make sure we're all capable of walking up three flights of stairs and carrying or pulling, another human to safety. We need to plan our routine, and in fact, we all should have blood work done when we get to St. Thomas."

The Sarge asked, "Why blood work?"

"You're married to a doctor, my fearless leader. Ask her why."

The Sarge whispered into Courtney's ear and said, "You know my guys don't want to know what's wrong with them. They're like me, afraid to know what's around the corner. Perhaps we'll skip that part."

Courtney took the microphone from the Sarge and said, "Big, bad, Ben Beckmire is balking on the blood work. Ladies, do we have to employ the headache routine to make sure these guys follow up on what they suggested which is getting into fighting shape?"

Asiram yelled, "My man is going to do that, and more, or he'll be sleeping with the kids for the next month or until he realizes we all need to know the unknown about our bodies. Are you ladies with me in holding back on some of that nighttime entertainment they seem to like?"

Jilkes said to John Lee, "The Sarge has just ruined my chance of working hard tonight with my wife. She's been trying to get me to see a doctor because I sometimes feel a little dizzy. I keep telling her it's just because when I wake up, I jump out of bed rather than easing out of it."

"I be hearing the same thing, but I say to her, John Lee Jr. be healthy and strong, so John Lee Sr. be the same way— healthy and strong. She usually turns away and mumbles in that there language of hers."

The Sarge recaptured the microphone and said, "Monica is correct, and at our age, we need to know what limits us and if we should be taking a pill, or something, to help."

Asiram yelled, "You people don't seem to mind taking the stuff that begins with a 'C', and the other one that starts with a 'V'. If we equate everything to the part of nature that excites you, then I think we'll have a hundred percent participation."

Zanthius looked at his father and said, "I'm just her husband. Her mouth has its own brain, and it's separate. In other words, we're in."

There was common consensus that prior to entertaining an exercise regimen, the members of the group would submit to a physical at the local hospital starting in one day.

The Sarge pressed Courtney on the notion of "is it better not to know than to know"? He kept saying, "Suppose I have some incurable sexually transmitted disease or something. Do you think I want to know about that?

Courtney said, "Mr. Man, if that's your issue, then you're already dead and the cause of death will be 'his wife injected him with a combination of household ingredients'. Death was swift but painful."

"Honey, I'm being serious."

"Then, why of all things to die from, you pull death from bad sex?"

Jong walked up the aisle and said, "Perhaps we should plan on staying on one of the other islands? I'm sure he knows where to find us. Perhaps we should stay on St. John at Caneel Bay. There is a lot of privacy there."

"Jong, there is a lot of privacy at 'The Sanctuary' on St. Thomas."

"Boss, perhaps we need to change our location for a few days and try to act like the proletariat or a company having a planning meeting in an exotic environment. We be obvious— private plane, vans picking us up, people catering to us, and knowing who we be."

"I'm getting your drift on this one my brother. Don't the Rockefeller brothers have some sanctioned land over there?"

"Sarge, I don't know much about the Rockefeller brothers. I only know that there is a private place over there where movie stars such as that Travolta guy, Danny Glover, that soccer player Maurice Cheeks and his friend, Reggie Wilkes who played for the Dallas Cowboys, go and hang out."

"How do you know so much about this place and who stays there?" The Sarge asked.

"You need to read the newspaper more often. It gives you a lot of information about people."

"I need Sue Lyn and Darryl here. Can you place a call and see if they can visit for a few days? You can send one of the planes in Miami for them. Also, can you call Mr. Carter and tell him we want to move our headquarters to St. John after we all submit to a fricken blood test?"

Jong asked, "Sarge, are you afraid to find out if you have any bad bugs in you?"

"You damn right! Aren't you? I know you would rather just fall off a cliff as opposed to someone telling you that you have an incurable disease caused from eating watermelon. I know we're old, but John Lee and Jilkes hit the nail on the head—we need to get on the offensive and kill that son-of-a-bitch before he hurts someone else in our group. You know in the Nam; we had no boundaries or restraints. When we went on a mission, we did what we had to do and that is what we need to focus on here and get our ladies to try to comprehend a modicum of what we went through and why we trained so hard. I want to move in the house that is almost finished being built. I don't want to keep looking over my shoulder, I want to look down the block and see which one of my friends want to race me in a wheelchair."

"Mr. Sarge, have you noticed only the men who have wives are the ones most desperately in need of reduction?"

"I told Courtney the other night that I was getting fat, and she told me all of the married men were gaining weight and the single ones remained buffed. I started to comment on that fact, and the look on her face discouraged any excuses. I think when we land, we head straight for the hospital to have blood drawn and if all is well with all of us, then we begin a rigorous training routine."

"Sarge, reality says rigor is a matter of the mind. Not mind over matter, but the mind recognizing that matter no longer has rigor. We can push hard and hurt ourselves or push smart and work our brains. We should focus on mind exercises much more than physical ones. In doing so, we refresh old thoughts and clear away old doubts because of age. We practice Tai Chi, practice breathing correctly, and other ancient techniques that strengthen the mind and the body. In the Nam, we didn't need it because we were afraid most of the time and acted on instinct and adrenaline. Here and now, my liege, we must use more brain power to conquer our enemy. I will and can show our people how to use what they have to the maximum."

# # #

The captain came on the intercom and said, "We are forty-five minutes away from sunny St. Thomas. Sorry about the temporary loss of one of our engines, but as you can see, we were in control of the situation from the start. There are many probable causes for that inconvenient moment, but I will reserve comment until I have received an analysis of several issues that may have caused that problem. Anyway, we'll be on the ground in a few, you know the drill, exercise it, and check your neighbor. Also, I have contacted the manufacturer of this aircraft and told him that we needed a loaner immediately in case we have to leave in a hurry."

# # #

Fifty minutes later, the plane landed safely in St. Thomas and the group was anxious to disembark from their favorite jet. Zanthius said to his father, "Dad, when a plane has a problem, I think you should rid yourself of it. What are your thoughts?"

"Son, we've already discussed that notion, but you can't move this many people on commercial airlines without a problem. Jong is on it because we have concluded we need a different configuration with all of the babies that the flood gates released."

CHAPTER THREE

From the airport, the entire group was transported directly to the hospital in St. Thomas. Each person filled out paperwork and listed Dr. Courtney Beckmire as their primary doctor. The liquid called blood, was extracted from everyone of age, and a basic physical exam was conducted. When you're a significant donor to a hospital and build a wing, some benefits should be assigned to you—one being anonymity.

# # #

Two and a half hours later, the group arrived at Red Hook by a series of cabs, where a boat was waiting to transport them to St. John. Mr. Carter's son accompanied the group along with a few other trusted employees. The young Mr. Carter approached Mr. Beckmire and hesitantly said, "The management wouldn't accept my card because it has a limit on it. I told him we would bring a new card or cash. Is there any way to accomplish that, or did I make a huge mistake?"

Ben Beckmire signaled Jong to join him, and when he arrived, Beckmire said, "My trusted friend's credit card couldn't secure space here because we have a limit on his card.

Please make sure that issue is corrected before we leave this place."

Jong said, "Michael's card has a limit, but 'The Sanctuary's' does not. I believe this is the best process, and I think Michael understands why there is a limit on his card. His dad has full access, and the bank recommended and sanctioned this idea. Michael understands what's going on."

"Michael, what was your day supposed to be like?" The Sarge inquired.

"We have a wedding at 'The Sanctuary' and it's pretty big," Michael replied.

The Sarge looked at Jong and said, "Our business model needs him back at 'The Sanctuary'. I don't want him here with us."

Michael said, "Mr. Beckmire, this wedding has all three properties involved and will create a lot of good will and future business opportunities for all of the partners."

"Why didn't your father say this when we asked for assistance?"

"Mr. Beckmire, you are his partner and my boss. We're here to satisfy you guys and gals. My dad believes you're an angel. After I had the agreement assessed, I concluded that you people are bad businesspeople, or people who clearly try to help people help themselves."

"Michael, I have a broader question for you. Do you have anything we could use to start a fire?"

Michael looked at one of the workers and whistled. Hiraldo stood up and pointed to a canvas bag. Michael said, "Not enough for everyone, but one in two will have coverage. I also have six friends here who will be camped out with communication devices and who will discuss the comings and

goings of anyone approaching the resort. They are
strategically placed and know how to use the kitchen
equipment that I gave them."

The Sarge said, "You and your father are big time in our
books. Here's a question for you. Suppose and just suppose,
one of your guys wanted to sell us out and collect a bounty?"

"That is a reasonable question and/or concern. Let me say
the people who are over here, are individuals that I trust—
family. I made an employment opportunity for them, and they
know how we roll. Violation of that opportunity would be a
death sentence. In other words, we would spend every dollar
that we have, to find a traitor and behead him or her. Mr.
Beckmire, you, and your group have done some magnificent
things on this island. I especially appreciate what you did,
because you returned my father from the asylum to reality, and
turned him into a productive, respectful, and honorable man.
He, nor the others, are braggadocios, but are politely grateful,
that you and yours showed up on the scene. My father is now
kind and considerate of my mother and has moved her into
management. They talk, and not fight. I saw them sitting by
the water laughing together. In other words, this is all huge on
this small island. You have helped in many ways, and you
know my commitment exceeds my words."

"What does that mean?" Jong interrupted Michael and
asked.

"Jong, you remember the person who assaulted a certain
sister, don't you?"

"Oh, yeah. Sorry, Michael."

"When this thing gets to port, stay on it and head back and
do our business," Ben Beckmire stated.

"Mr. Beckmire, we have a go-fast boat trailing us just in case you wanted to see what we were doing at 'The Sanctuary'. It'll get us back in fifteen minutes, plus, my dad has taken control and is involved in every aspect of the wedding. I mean him and the other guys who hated each other, meet every week over food and drink to discuss how to grow 'The Sanctuary'. These are things that you can't put a price tag or a loyalty sticker on. We all got your back."

"I don't know whether to believe this mess, or to think that it's because we're such good people. Anyway, tell your man to leave the bag and I'll pick it up," the Sarge stated.

"No, no, Mr. Beckmire. Leave the bag and someone else will get it and deliver it to you. We got this. We have our people dispersed and, according to them, there are no known strangers congregating on St. John. When it's time to leave, give me a call and I'll come over and collect the hardware. I can't stress enough--we got your back, and we got this issue. Also, the operative identifier for my people is 'rum punch'."

Ben Beckmire hugged Michael and said, "I need you free and clear and not caught up in some mess."

Michael whispered in his ear, "We all be in some kind of mess. But it be a mess we choose to help and not one to hurt someone unless they be done messed with our people."

"That be a lot of messes, Michael. Anyway, I need you to head back to the other side of the island and help your dad. By the way, where is Ms. Viola?"

"Mr. Beckmire, she be on the main island making gallons and gallons of Rum Punch."

"Oh, shit, I don't like that. Let me get four of my guys and we'll head back with you to secure her."

"Mr. Boss man, I have four ex-Navy Seals working with her and guarding her every move."

"Is my man Chakes there as well?"

"Mr. Beckmire, your people don't break protocol unless they speak to you. Now, Ms. Viola doesn't believe in protocol and will never ask permission, as long as she is her own woman. My people are armed, and a few potentially dangerous looking characters are being held in customs for some minor infractions. Unless it's an inside job, she be very safe."

"One last question. Tell me about your Navy Seal friends. How do you know them, and can you trust them?"

Michael's head dropped, and said, "I trust them with my life because I was once one of them, until I was set up by a now deceased Sergeant who blew marijuana on me and had a female companion swear, that I attempted to rape her."

The Sarge looked at Michael and thought about how easy it is for a young African American male to be targeted, tricked, and seduced into failure. He shook his head and said, "I'm trusting you when you say, 'you got our backs'. It usually goes beyond a simple saying and ends up with people having to make life altering decisions. Can you and your people make that choice regardless of the outcomes?"

"Mr. Sarge, I've already made that decision, and those people with me won't think twice because they know I'm straight up and will burn a city for them."

"How did you guys achieve such loyalty for each other?"

"They knew I was being railroaded, and never turned their backs on me. Each one of them married for the wrong reasons, and the wrong person. I took them in, and they've been on the outskirts since day one, watching you guys from afar and making sure my dad was covered. They were the first responders to Ms. Asiram being dragged across the sands. I told them to stand down, and to only act if the culprits reached their vehicle."

Michael paused for a moment and finally said, "It was only recently, my dad realized that the reason we kept showing more food being consumed but less revenue, was because I was feeding and housing my friends. I know he knew it, but he would never acknowledge it because my dad is a true man and friend. I like to think that we're as tightly woven as your group is, but we've not been battle evaluated to the degree that I think you and your people have been. Listen Mr. Sarge, they won't be in your way unless someone attempts to do harm to one of you under our watch."

The Sarge looked at Michael and considered a few options but said, "I may have some light work that needs to be consummated. Do you think you and your people can dissolve a few gang issues over where Ms. Viola lives? I think we put a hurting on them, but new leadership arose and is apparently as fierce as the old group."

"Mr. Sarge, I would like to assess the situation with my people and get back to you with a prescription. We know the people running the new game but have stayed away from them because we don't like to be visible until a corrective action plan is necessary to be enacted."

"Michael, I like that philosophy. I'm going to talk to my people and see if we can engage you and your friends to do some soft work for us. Do you or any of your friends mess around with drugs?"

"I must admit, we've all smoked weed. We all need a chance to prove we can do work, especially serious and confidential work. We have no leaks in our pipes, Mr. Sarge. One of us likes weed more than the rest but give us the chance to have a serious conversation with him--he's either in or out."

The Sarge asked, "Would you and your people agree to submit to random drug testing?"

"Mr. Sarge, I'll make that call and have them meet me at the hospital when we get back and begin the screening process."

The Sarge looked deep into his eyes and asked, "Why do you want to get involved with a group of people who the entire world would like to see demolished?"

Michael looked at the Sarge and his eyes began to water. After a moment of thinking about the question, he announced, "I believe in Robin Hood, Mr. Beckmire. That guy and his merry men, showed up at a dilapidated joint on the water, befriended an old man who had lost all hope and the will to live, and who had a bank that was about to take all that he owned. Robin Hood and his gang made a deal with that old person that stated, no matter what happens, the old fella would never lose his property, and all losses would be assumed by his investing partners. Now, Robin Hood and his people aren't obtuse. They have a smart lawyer who constructed the relationship, not only with that old fella but with others. I need Robin Hood and his gang to further invest in this island and give me and my guys an opportunity to provide security, cleanup, and revitalization services to the communities on the island."

The Sarge threw his hand out to shake Michael's and found a deserving, strong, and serious handshake waiting. He said, "I will champion your cause. We don't invest in violence, just solutions to it. Show me you can do that, and I will attempt to get you positioned. One more thing. We talked about the needs of 'The Sanctuary'. I placed a significant amount of trust in you on that one. Somehow, I need you to have a meeting with our partners at 'The Sanctuary' and get your people placed. Stop stealing our food. Tell them I'm asking them to find opportunities for these guys once their paperwork has been reviewed and approved by the group—not by me, but by our partners. If your guys can pass the scrutiny, then I will create jobs for them and have them as our ultimate security when we're here. Just one more thing. Michael, if they're not right, then don't risk your future on them. If they like the weed, then we don't have a place for them in our organization. Don't bring any potheads into my community. Are we clear?"

CHAPTER FOUR

After being on the wonderful island of St. John for seven days, a beehive of activity was in progress each day. The men tried to out-run the women, but that was like the beginning of a wet dream that was never consummated. On each outing, the women proved to be in better shape (younger), more athletic (younger), mentally more responsive (younger), sexually more aroused after working out (younger), consumed appropriate foods for endurance and long-term health (younger) and at night were looking forward to a stimulating conversation that led to a sexual encounter (younger).

The men on the other hand, at night wanted to go to sleep (older), drank beer and other spirits (older), accused their partners of being overly stimulated (older), sexually consumed (older) and that they needed to invest in a drug that slowed down their metabolism.

The Sarge after taking notice of the aftermath of their joint workouts, realized his guys would have a beer, or a drink along with their steaks and ribs. The women would consume salads, yogurts, salmon, beans, and other healthy foods.

On day nine of their joint training, the Sarge told the men they were an embarrassment and that the women were making them look like butlers instead of warriors. He forbade them to drink after working out and the eating of meat of any kind, was prohibited until sanctioned.

Later in the day, John Lee decided he was going to complain to Jilkes. When he approached Jilkes who was talking with Chakes and Luana, he said, "I be thinking the Sarge done lost what mind he be done had. He now is acting like our diet manager. We can't eat meat unless sanctioned by his holiness."

"You know, John Lee, you're the one who had the grand vision of us being like we were in the Nam. You know, run ten miles with a full load and then run another ten miles back to the gym to lift weights. You asked for it and I don't want to hear your big country ass whine because if you look at that thing you've started to carry around, you might just back-off and forget why you came over here in the first place," Jilkes said.

Chakes asked, "Did he really ask the Sarge to take a different approach to training?"

Jilkes replied, "He had an epiphany and wanted us to be like we were in the Nam and hunt down the Sarge's cousin, rather than have him launching countless attacks on us. It was a great idea at first and one that I endorsed. However, my ass is in a sack--every part of my body hurts. It's the type of hurt I don't mind because it has brought us together once again. Now, that's amazing. Look at all we've been through and what rewards we have enjoyed. He and I met two fantastic spies, we seduced them or they us, we married them, and we both had little guys by them. We're rich, we've been shot, and it's time to move to the south and enjoy being slum landlords to the group. I just love what happened in boot camp, many years ago. And in front of you, Chakes and your bride, I will once again say, I love him so much because he has been there for all of us and especially me."

John Lee's eyes watered up and he fought back the tears until it was impossible to do so. An emotional eruption happened, like a volcano spewing ashes into the sky. Jilkes hugged him and said, "This is why we have to find and conclude that guy. If not, we'll always be vulnerable to his attacks, announced and unannounced. In the war, we followed instructions. Here we still have a chain of command, but I think it's up to you and me to hate this guy enough to figure how to destroy him completely."

# # #

Jong and Mary Alice sat close enough to the water so that their feet would be immersed into it. His phone rang and when he answered it, the caller said, "One of my clients ordered a new jet but it is seven seats shy of his newly calculated requirements. I'll take your jet in trade and offer you this one for, shy of $5.2 million."

Jong replied, "Send me the specs and pictures of the layout. Once I see them, I will confer with my bosses, and we might make you an offer. Our captain is going to call you because we lost an engine on descent. Consequently, we're not sure if there is a lot of confidence in your products."

"Have your captain call and send me the computer tapes, so we can analyze them. As I said, I'll take your jet, give you a brand new one with a new configuration for $5.2million, and the deal is done."

"I cannot commit to anything without my leader's permission. Once again, send me the specs, and I will propose it to my people. I must inform you of one thing--my employer is not happy with this current product after experiencing an engine failure. We are literally stranded because we are fearful of flying on that plane, ever again."

"I will also talk about compensation for that once we analyze what went wrong with the engine. This new plane is the same vintage, but with different engines that are stronger. The layout was for a basketball team that upgraded in the middle of construction because they added a psychologist, therapist, and other staff that they felt their team needed. Each player was designated a certain amount of leg room and this configuration would have decreased that space and caused anarchy among the team members. I promise you, once you see and test this plane, you and your people will be biting at the bit to own it or lease it. This deal has only been offered to you and you're the only people who know about the change of aircraft and its availability."

"Once again, send me the pictures and I will float them, but you have to consider some price reductions based upon our recent experience."

# # #

At the St. Thomas Airport, a Delta Airlines jet made its final approach to the runway and the crew gave out explicit prelanding instructions to the passengers. Once at the gate, four men from different seats in first-class rose, retrieved their bags and exited the plane. At customs, the men were summarily allowed into the country without any problems. Each man engaged transportation to 'The Sanctuary' in separate vehicles.

The men arrived at different times to avoid suspicion and/or the perception that they were there together. Immediately after arrival, two of the men asked the same question, 'where can I meet nice, clean, locals who are interested in having some fun and, perhaps, earning some money'?

This information was relayed to an acquaintance of Ms. Viola. After hearing this information, Ms. Viola told her friend it appeared odd, but was grateful for the information and the diligence in which it was relayed. She also asked her friend about the status of her daughter and her son who she was attempting to get his prison sentence reduced. Ms. Viola told her she may be able to help him if he's willing to help himself by telling who supplied him with the weapon?

Michael on the other hand, knew these guys were fishing and using the wrong bait. The only other person at 'The Sanctuary' besides him connected to the group, was Ms. Viola and she turned out be an invaluable asset.

When the men asked for rum punch, they acted as if this was their first time meeting, Ms. Viola said, "You guys seem like you should know each other. Have you ever met before? It's that style of clothing and dress that be giving you guys away. Tell the truth, are you members of the same fraternity or something like that? Where you be coming from?"

The assumed leader said, "You are so observant, but a little bit off course. I've never met these guys, but the front desk did tell everyone checking in today that the best rum punch on the island was made here and by a woman by the name of Ms. Viola. Is that your name?"

"I guess they been done exposed me again. Man, I be Ms. Viola and this here rum punch be the best on the island. I no brag about it, but it is the best on the island. My mother, her mother, and her mother's mother, kept this formula in their heads for years, man. It might end here because my granddaughter be too smart to deal in rum. She be one of them lawyer types, always suspicious of encounters."

"Where is she now? We, I'm sorry, I meant, I'm looking to purchase some beach front property, and I will need a good lawyer to help guide me through this thing."

Ms. Viola turned to one of the other men and asked, "Why're you here, to buy beach front property as well?"

The guy literally spit his drink out and said, "That's some potent punch. No, I'm not here to buy anything. I'm here hoping I'll walk up on some rich woman, and she'll find me attractive, and perhaps invite me home with her to keep."

Ms. Viola said, "Well, there be many of that type down here looking to make a connection with an attractive man. A lot of them like to have, or own boy toys. If I had to guess, I be thinking you guys are looking to end that thing called nine to five and catch a fat rich woman and enjoy her spoils. I personally think if you've got it, flaunt it. I'm serving my punch at a party tonight near Sugar Loaf. It's a mixer, but I don't know you people and you can't invite strangers in unless they've been screened."

The guy that looked in control said, "What does the screening entail?" Ms. Viola, making things up as she got deeper into the conversation said, "Everyone has to have a medical exam and blood test. You can't be walking in on blue-bloods without having been checked."

The guy who assumed a leadership role said, "I would like to attend a party like that to see if I fit the bill, but I'm not interested in being examined and having blood drawn."

"What happened to your beach front property notion? I'm just kidding."

"If someone wants to buy me property because I compliment them, then I'll save mine and see how far I can ride their boat."

# # #

Meanwhile, Michael was sniffing around with his customs associates and making general inquires to a couple of his mates about the four individuals. He was told their passports had been altered and were fake and was advised not to get mixed up with them.

Michael promptly called Ben Beckmire and told him there were people of a suspicious nature who had altered passports in their possession and were being followed by customs officials. He also told him Ms. Viola was trying to get them invited to a private party.

Beckmire said, "Tell Ms. Viola that a small group of us would like to attend this event as well, and could she arrange it?"

Beckmire saw Mallory and said, "I'm going to do some recon work tonight, who should I take with me?"

"I suggest you take the usual suspects. Any of the ten we trained plus any of the newcomers. Oh, your nephew and Sue Lyn are here as well. I guess we want to put them in charge of that new money we happened upon."

"They're family, right? They're going to get it on soon, or they already have. The first thrust is going to make a baby. That boy is loaded for bear down there and she's as ripe as a Jersey tomato. Let's give them this chore and see how they manage it. We'll see how they develop a business model and lines of accountability that can sustain any attack by auditors and the IRS. Let's first challenge them with retrieving the booty in the billabong. I need to call Hutang and tell him the people we want to handle their funds have just arrived, and that I need a couple of weeks for them to figure out what's at stake. Mallory, those diamonds had size and clarity to them and that gold, well gold is gold. I want the entire group to meet with Darryl and Sue Lyn and explain to them what is expected of them. I don't want to be the only one measuring our future leaders."

"Sarge, we're clear on the details about what we want them to do. Why don't we all head over to St. Thomas tonight and make an evening of it. We always eat at our place, why not try something different?"

"Can you arrange a meeting between the group and the kids? It's important that everyone buys into this and has an understanding about what can be expected. Now, I mentioned to Darryl about handling finances and, if I know him, he's going to be as knowledgeable as any one of us. He's anal like that, and she's always going to try to stay in tune with her man and his mindset. Insofar as food is concerned, we eat at our place because our food is excellent, and we know who oversees it. I think it would be a good night, but what do we do with the babies?"

"Sarge, I suggest we take everyone for an evening out. Some of us drift off to the place and see if there is any strength to those fellows with altered passports."

"Okay, you call Michael and ask him if he can get a private launch to pick us up and be on standby to bring us back. Before we do anything, I want to meet with Darryl and Sue

Lyn and let the group run them through the grinder," the Sarge said.

"I'll set up the trip and then I'll establish a time for a meeting and the interview," Mallory said.

# # #

It was three in the afternoon and the sun was turning a lot of bodies different colors. In the restaurant at Caneel Bay, the group assembled and the Sarge indicated that they were going to go to St. Thomas that night to do some recon work and socialize. He spoke of other sundry items and without any indication said, "I called you people together to discuss and question the potential investment strategies my nephew and Jong's niece have considered for those assets we placed under the protection of the 'Great Saltie'."

He looked at Darryl and Sue Lyn and said, "Hey guys, this is how it works in the real world. Give it your best shot and let's see if you listened to me when we had the initial conversation about handling funds."

Darryl hesitantly stood up and said, "I love my uncle, but I think he could have given me a little more information and time to prepare for a discussion. Listen, Sue Lyn and I think you guys have done a marvelous job with your assets and probably could have made another $500 million to a billion had you allocated your resources more smartly and against everything you hear on television."

Asiram yelled, "That statement seems a little cocky for a guy who has less than a million in all of his accounts."

Darryl looked at Asiram and said, "I wish we, or I, had a million in an account. I'm my uncle's nephew. We're from a place where things are always in flux. My uncle casually mentioned to me and Sue Lyn that he may want us to manage funds for Hutang and his people as well as figure out ways to assist all the Aborigine villages in Australia. But to your point Ms. De Lombardo, I think Sue Lyn and I have done a quick study and have produced ways, rules to employ, sanctions to acknowledge, and simplicity to express the handling of those assets in the billabong that are being guarded by a relative. Technically speaking, other than my uncle, Zanthius, and Larry, none of you could fly back to Australia and retrieve those assets from the billabong. I, also can achieve such a feat, as well as move the assets into financial institutions that relate to gold and precious stones."

Sue Lyn interrupted Darryl and said, "We've also calculated the net return on bullion, but have yet to value the diamonds because it's a market that is influenced by size and stupidity. We've arranged for a legitimate precious metal dealer to oversee your investment on the gold side of the equation. We're waiting for a certain movie star to offer his fiancé a brilliant rock at a significant price, and then we'll explode the market with larger, clearer, and more costly diamonds that will sell to a certain niche."

Darryl paused her politely and said, "We flipped coins to see who would deal with what. I'm on the gold side of the equation, and she has sold a product on the open market that has not been seen subject to the hyperbole that preceded the display of it. Ms. Asiram, on the gold side of the equation, bullion is measured and valued on a different basis. There is an international market that buys and sells it daily. Now, I must admit, we are new to this game and, I must say, we've spent a vast amount of time attempting to understand trends, markets, market makers, value, timing, and the economics of investing in each item. I feel like we know more than the experts and that is a cause for alarm because I should not have a feeling that I know all there is to know about the buying and selling of gold."

Zanthius said, "Darryl, we're related, and this is your first dive into this ocean. I think, you need an advisory board, but I think there should be a certain amount that you can make decisions about without oversight."

The Sarge said, "Zanthius, my initial consideration for these guys was to manage the funds that we promised Hutang and his people. I didn't think of having them relate to us as well, but it makes sense."

"Dad, I frankly don't know a lot about what they're talking about, but if we put in place a board or oversight group to sanction their moves, then we at least know we had a part in the play and agreed to the fact that it was X rated."

"Uncle, it would be insane for us to operate without oversight. With Mr. Hutang, its different because he's in a place where they don't have banks, they trade with pebbles, garments, and as a matter of fact, our actions could corrupt an entire eco system. They have been doing business the same way for centuries. Okay, suddenly we come in with electronic banking, and more assets than they've ever known. Abruptly and unexpectedly, you have changed an entire culture and a way of life. Can his people handle a strong financial future?"

The Sarge said, "Worlds change so fast, and their culture is something I never considered. They don't have banks, or other financial institutions, but they manage to buy, sell, invest in debt, and have unwritten notes of agreement. I never thought about it, but when change is slow and deliberate, it can foster and teach new concepts. You think about it and let me know how you would proceed with this one."

"Uncle, you've asked a lot of me and Sue Lyn and I'm not sure we're capable of supervising the kinds of assets that you guys have."

"Nephew, you and Sue Lyn are two smart cookies. Learn to play the market with a conservative platform and you'll learn how greed kills. I have an old friend in LA, who is a make-up artist, and probably one of the best in the field. Unbeknownst to people, he has billions invested in a variety of things and has agreed to take on two neophytes to help an old friend. I told him you would be there in three days. So, nephew, take your girlfriend out, have fun, and be prepared to leave here in two days. Oh, and by the way, I'm going to have to kill her father unless you decide to take this relationship to another level."

"Uncle, I was hoping to speak to you about that in private, if possible, because we're in trouble." Beckmire excused himself and wandered out of hearing distance from the group and asked, "What the hell do you mean by that?"

"Uncle can I just tell it like it is?"

"You'd better tell me something or my friend will cut your throat and I won't be able to do a damn thing about it."

"Uncle, we have not technically made love. She has learned to pleasure me with her hands and mouth, and I have learned to do the same."

Darryl's head dropped and Ben Beckmire said, "Don't you dare drop your fricken head. You were man enough to do things against the wishes of everyone and you held your head high like a peacock, so don't drop it now. Tell me the rest of the problem."

"On occasion, she would let me rub my member on her special part until I enjoyed an orgasm. Often, I would shoot my load in her navel, but I stayed too long in the area of concern and shot my seminal fluids at her zone, but not in it."

"Hold up! You expect me to believe that bullshit? Is that the best you can do?"

"Uncle, I swear to you, I have never had the pleasure of penetrating the woman I love. There have been many occasions, but I have never placed my member inside of her. I've had it in other places, but never in her vagina."

The Sarge looked at him in a scornful manner and said, "So, what's the problem? If you've never penetrated her then why is there concern?"

"Uncle, that was the first time I had ever felt that way and I shot an awful lot of my sperm right at her zone. She is now two weeks late for her cycle."

The Sarge looked at his nephew and said, "Why couldn't you aim at the ceiling? What made you want to aim for that place?"

"Uncle, I wanted to place it all in her and run away. She begged me to insert it. We found fifty ways to get around the no copulation rule. Each time we tested our will and our respect, but we got closer to violating the rule, but without doing it. I'm concerned that what I did, indirectly exposed, and impregnated her. I so much want to be a father like you, but I don't want to disrespect her father and show people my word is lifeless and useless."

Ben Beckmire thought about all of his adventures and walked over to Darryl and placed his arms around him and said, "Nephew, when you give your word it's like saying no matter what, you will honor your words as a man. I knew you two had beat the odds and found ways to express human nature without violating the key ingredients of your conversation with her father, uncle, and me. All three of us are not stupid, however, I am beginning to think that you are. Whether she is pregnant or not, I recommend you send that jet I let you use back to DC and ask her father and mother to come to the island because your dumb ass has an announcement to make, and you would love for them to be present when it is made. You boxed yourself in when your aim failed you and you spit fire at the place where life begins. To be so smart, nephew, I think you missed a grand aspect of life."

Darryl dropped his head again, Ben Beckmire slapped it, and said, "You want to be a lover man, then be it. Just don't hang your sorry head down around me or I will slap it off your shoulders. You had the world by the balls, why not her stomach, or chest, or face, or mouth? Why on earth would you put a million of those things in a place that is obviously ripe and receptive? Now, that's why I call you stupid."

#

Jilkes saw the Sarge and asked if he had a minute. The Sarge asked him what was up, and Jilkes said, "I think you need to let me, and my boy go hunting alone for your cousin."

"I can assure you I will never allow a maverick operation to proceed unless I'm in the front. What on earth brought this on?"

"We want to go south and live in a community and not have to worry about a sick person visiting us in the middle of the night. With your permission, I would take, Brown, Bernstein, Mike, Larry, and John Lee. You would have your main force with you, and we would be like a, ah, suicide force. Let us go and track him down and bring his head to you in an ice bucket."

"I love the idea, but that's not how we roll--we are a team. I can't let you guys go roaming around looking for an elusive target. That just doesn't make sense."

"We had a larger strategy in mind, and that was to leave John Lee and me around the DC area after we had a vicious fight between us," Jilkes announced.

"That's even more ludicrous because my cousin knows that I love you guys and that there is no way in hell, I would eject you from our group. He would see through that and use the knowledge to attack us based upon our weakened defenses. This is the concluding chapter in this long saga, and I need all my people near and alert. As a matter of fact, I think he has four of his people scouting out the area as we speak. They're going to a party that Ms. Viola is fixing rum punch for and I'm sure she and Michael will deliver them to us. Let's deal with them first and then try to develop a strategy that keeps us all close and safe. I know you people are tired of this mess, and so am I. Without you my friends, me and mine would be dead. I need one more push from everyone, and then we'll sit back and take turns buying beer and having cook outs."

CHAPTER FIVE

It was 0200 hours when a fast boat roared in the calm blue waters behind the huts where the group was staying on Caneel Bay. Michael and two of his friends, were accompanied by four completely inebriated individuals. Their wallets and other personal possessions were in plastic bags so that they wouldn't get wet.

On the beach, an anxious John Lee, Jilkes, Mallory, and Larry waited patiently. Each man was pushed off the boat. Upon hitting the water, they felt helpless and panicked as they struggled to reach the surface without swallowing too much water. The salt water, and the fact that their hands and feet were bound, sobered the men up, to a degree. They were rescued by Michael's people.

When on land, they were still coughing and attempting to catch their breath. John Lee said, "This here ain't the continuation of that great party you people probably just left. This here party can be called a necktie party, but instead of a tree, I'm going to use the water. Now, my African American friend is going to ask you questions that must be corroborated, or if that word be too big for you, answers have to be the same amongst you people."

Jilkes looked at the assumed leader and said, "You look fit, strong, angry, and too much for one of us old men to handle alone. So, I'm going to save you for last and march you over to the other part of the beach. Now, I'm sure you know that we're old people trying to survive, and your employer wants us already dead. Oh, who was your passport man? He did a sloppy job and now you got the customs' people chasing your ass as well."

He looked at Michael and asked, "Where are those guys?"

Michael said, "I gave them the night off, and left them at the party."

Jilkes said, "Oh I see. So, these guys are ours to do with what we want?"

"Insofar as I'm concerned, they were involved in a boating accident," Michael stated.

"Well, ain't that just dandy," Jilkes announced.

He continued by saying, "Okay, guys, these are the rules. One of you will be randomly chosen using a crude system to illustrate our resolve in knowing what you're doing here, who is your employer, and where he can be found? Now, the one chosen as the chase boat will be summarily gutted from his small head to his big head and I must let you know, we're experts at opening a body. This ain't going to be a good day for anyone. I frankly can't stand the sight of blood, but these other guys are like fricken vampires. That big old country looking guy, has done nine, to his credit and has taken a bite out of a victim's heart before it stopped beating. I personally think the number is eight because I'm sure that lady was dead before he bit into her heart, but that's a story for another day. Okay, let's get this party under way. I'm going to walk over there and write a number in the sand. If that's your number, then you'll have to die in a hurry so the others will know we don't want to waste a lot of time with this matter. Okay, I'll be right back."

Jilkes and John Lee walked a few paces away and bent down on their knees. Jilkes wrote the number three in the sand. He returned to his captives and said, "Okay, I've written the number in the sand and now you guys have to select a number."

Jilkes walked to the assumed leader and asked, "What number do you select?"

"I select the number that says, 'screw you'." Without hesitation, John Lee unsheathed his mother of all blades and slammed it into the guy's foot. The guy attempted to scream, but Larry rushed to his side and gagged him. John Lee withdrew the blade from his foot and the blood gushed out.

Mallory took a towel and wrapped it around the guy's foot and said, "You must be the new 21st century, kind of stupid. Why would you tell the man that? Now, if you would like to see how pain works, you're at the right show. We've caused a lot of pain and you were tagged by the master."

The guy was approaching the shock window when Jilkes said, "You picked the unlucky number because you didn't follow the rules. Who sent you here, and where can that person be found?"

"Don't know what you're talking about. I don't know these people."

Jilkes looked at him and said, "So, how did you all wind-up getting passports from the same bad printer? Did you all just wander down an alley looking for an original Monet, but instead purchased a Latilessvangoe? Come now, we're not that stupid."

"Sir, I don't know these people and my passport is legitimate." Unexpectedly, John Lee quickly drew his blade, and stabbed the man in his other foot. Larry expected a reaction to the lie and positioned the gag to muffle the sound once John Lee's knife penetrated his foot.

John Lee said, "I'm going to gut you and eat your heart in front of you before you die. Take a minute and think about that image. Tell another lie and I'll show you how good I am at my trade."

Jilkes said, "Larry, can you get another towel to stop the bleeding? And, Larry, I hope you're using gloves."

After slowing the bleeding, Jilkes said, "It's your move. You want to live or die? Your feet are a mess. Let me know and I can make your choice happen."

The other three men looked at the blood saturating the sand and knew the day would be long for them as well. Suddenly the assumed leader said, "I need medical attention. You're going to bleed me out."

John Lee asked, "You want help? Then tell us who sent you here and where that person can be found?"

"How can I trust you?"

Jilkes inquired, "Hell, how can we trust you?"

The guy looked sincerely at him and yelled, "I'm in fricken pain. We were sent to canvas your hideaway here. He's in San Antonio and is gathering a strike force of elite individuals. First question on his list is, 'do you have a problem killing women, children, and babies?'"

"He actually, asked that? What did you people say to that? Don't lie. If you lie, I'll cut your damn foot off."

"We all swore to his creed. He's offering a huge sum of money for your leader's head. He has promised two million dollars for the man who severs his head."

"My question remains, but I guess it was answered. You will kill us, our women, and our children."

Jilkes, acted like he was possessed. He walked in front of the man and proceeded to snatch his Adam's apple out of his throat. The others watched in horror at what was left of the man as he slivered into unconsciousness, and then death. Jilkes looked at the other three and said, "If you don't have anything important to offer, then my friend is going to gut you like a pig, and buddy, he's damn good at it."

John Lee surveyed the group looking for the weak link when he saw that one of the men was praying. He looked at him and said, "What be the prayer you be saying over my child after you kill him?"

He slammed his huge knife into the man's neck and began to twist it on impact and said, "You fucking hypocrite. You come to kill our women and children and you got the nerve to pray to God. Well, let me finish that prayer for you. God, please forgive me for killing this piece of shit."

Mallory eased over to Jilkes and whispered, "You need to get him back on the reservation. He has strayed far away, and we need to end this soon."

Jilkes moved quickly to where John Lee was standing and said, "You can't just kill people before we've had an opportunity to interview them. I think you've made your point, now let me, Mallory, and Larry handle these two. Why don't you take a walk back to your hut and have a drink, I'll join you once we've gleaned as much information out of the remaining two as possible. You take a walk and chill out my friend. Oh, by the way, that was some serious shit you did back there. I'll call Michael and tell him we want to go bottom fishing real soon."

John Lee began to walk away, turned around abruptly, and made an aggressive move at one of the remaining guys. He then said, "If you gonna kill my wife, son, and my friends, then I'll gut you like a pig and filet your ass at the same time."

Jilkes said, "I'll join you in a few. Let us handle this."

Mallory said to one of the men, "If you think he's off the chart, wait until the quiet guy over there goes to work. I suggest you people sell the farm or suffer a ghastly death. That guy is sadistic beyond your wildest imagination. My name is Mallory and we all served in the same unit in Vietnam, save a few of our group. In Vietnam, we killed a lot of people. Now, how should we proceed with this interview? Should we cut one of your dicks off and then interrogate the other dude with the dick? I know, how about we decapitate both of your dicks, and perhaps we'll get a straight and/or crooked response?"

A deep voice said, "None of that will be necessary. This was my mission, I failed, and when I get back, I'm good as dead anyway. Let me say, your man is way off the reservation. I had a couple of guys like him in the Nam. Oh yes, I was in the Nam for six years. I know who you people are and what you did for our country. The two men you killed were not real soldiers, they were mercs and they were from Columbia. He has hired jungle fighters, urban fighters, mountain fighters, and every other kind of specialist you can imagine. He is hell bent on seeing your leader's head in a basket."

"You just lost two of your men. What kind of leader are you?"

"Those were not my men and I had nothing to do with their demise. I suggested a different strategy, but they insisted on trying to mix business and pleasure. I told them that the senior citizen was too cunning and sharp, and we should avoid her at all costs. That lady threw out an invite to a party full of rich women who were allegedly looking for companions and they all saw a two-for-one deal. Is she one of yours?"

Mallory said, "A not too recent acquisition, but a steady hand when you need one. You know you can't go back."

"If I survive your torture, then I'll have to go back. They're holding my wife and they say they have people following my daughter on campus with a termination notice if I failed to deliver certain information."

"Are you on the level or is this some hyperbole to attempt to escape the hangman?" Mallory asked.

"At this point, I don't have a lot of resources to rely on to assist me with my mess. I will say this, as a fellow Nam vet, I ask you to give me any consideration possible."

"Wow, that's like a pirate being caught by other pirates and then requesting a 'parlay'. I will ask you to be honest and tell me who is holding your wife, and where? You said that people were following your daughter. Where is she? And finally, why were they making you do this against your will?"

"They're not only holding my wife, but his wife as well. He and I were trackers and I guess we were considered some of the best in the Nam. I also heard your man was pretty good, even though he's not Native American. Anyway, we've been to your place in Virginia and have laid out a strategy for future engagements. We went to your places in the South and realized the locals love to shoot strangers. We visited your place in middle America and gave it an assessment as well.

Our last charge was to visit here and make an appraisal of this place, but not on St. John. St. John is isolated, and a retreat would be terribly compromised. Listen, we've been marking time with those assholes. We heard who you were, and everything about this mission was against our code. We needed the money because other people were trying to force us out of our homes so that they can build a damn pipeline. When we found out it was Beckmire's group, we backed down and told the handler we couldn't go up against former vets from Nam, and especially this group. That's when he told us he understood and secretly, proceeded to kidnap our wives and, indirectly, threaten our children. We didn't have a choice at the time."

Mallory said, "Is there any way we can corroborate this story?"

"Listen, we are from Minnesota and people are trying to throw many families out of their homes. We needed the money but couldn't pass the first test."

Mallory asked, "What was the first test?"

"It was, do you have a problem killing women and children. We independently, wrote, no can do."

"I so desperately want to figure a way around not ending your lives, but I don't have a lot of faith in what you say. What else can you give me?"

"I can tell you the man in charge is one sick human being and he has hired a lot of people to end, what he's calling, the 'Family War'."

Mallory asked, "How long will he be in San Antonio?"

"I'm not being smart, but we aren't some of his confidants. We were hired to track and plot an engagement against you at all of your known hide-a-ways."

"Where were we the most vulnerable and the least?"

"Your place in Virginia is strong and can apparently face down intruders from mounted, but un-manned guns. We did not mention that in our report. Your place in the Midwest is open and you can spot people coming from miles away. It also helps that you have listening devices deployed all over the place and that the entire town thinks you people are untouchable. In St. Thomas, we don't have a clue because our newly departed associates wanted to come here and try to score. The problem with this place is, if you're caught with a weapon, they put you under the jail."

Mallory studied the man's expressions and decided that he was on the level. Larry got closer to the other captive and asked, "You don't say much, do you?"

The guy looked at Larry, sized him up, and responded, "No need for everyone to speak. He speaks for me."

Larry asked, "Where are you from?"

"Like the man said, we're from Minnesota."

"Which one of you is supposed to check-in?" Mallory asked.

The quiet guy said, "That would be the first guy that died."

Larry asked, "Do you have a plan to get your women back?"

The other guy said, "We hadn't had much time to focus on that. I guess they must know by now, something didn't go as planned."

"If we let you go, will we one day have to face the barrel of a gun being held by you, like in the last *Planet of the Apes* movie?" Mallory asked.

The quiet guy said, "We don't work that way. We need to figure out how to rescue our wives. Listen, we told him that you were most vulnerable in the Midwest. He was once there and should know how that worked out for him. He will probably recommend this thing happen in Virginia because that place is a gun-toting state. You will never face us in battle, and you have our word on that."

CHAPTER SIX

The Sarge pulled Chakes aside and questioned him about the actions of Ms. Viola and told him he did not want her involved in their work on the front side of the equation, and only when there was a direct threat to her or the children in her charge was, she to act. He told him he was happy that nothing happened to her or them, but it was too risky for her to get involved in their work from the beginning. This could have gone bad for all of them.

Chakes told the Sarge that he spoke with her and tried to explain to her that we don't have rogue actions conducted by any member of the team. He told the Sarge he thinks she understood but thinks she's a better spy than the rest of them.

The group stayed and worked hard on St. John for seven days and nights. The men conducted three training sessions per day and a night jog in the sand and around the beach. The guys were getting their second wind and were feeling the effects of good clean living. The women did two sessions per day and looked amazing. Although most of them were younger than their spouses, they were definitely in better shape than their counterparts.

# # #

Once on St. Thomas, the group continued their healthy living and exercise routine. The men had reduced their time to run a single mile from fourteen minutes to twelve. Their combined goal was to do a ten-minute mile. Courtney suggested they stay at the twelve-minute mark.

Surprisingly, the blood work each person had when they first arrived on St. Thomas showed few maladies. Three of the men bordered on hypertension, two had elevated sugar levels, and one was diagnosed with Rheumatoid Arthritis. The women were within all the normal ranges, and none needed medication or remediation.

The Sarge put out the word, that at dinner, the group would vote on where it would head next. Larry and Zanthius had discussed the fact that the guys needed time to exert and recover, and that they weren't doing it well. They went to their father and Larry asked, "Dad, can we have a solid conversation with you about our assessment of where you and your people are physically?"

The Sarge rolled his eyes and asked, "Can it wait until later?"

Zanthius butted in and said, "Probably not, unless you want to prematurely bury a couple of them."

That statement got the Sarge's attention, and he said, "Let's do this."

Larry began the conversation by saying, "Your guys are in great shape for their ages, but we think they need to back down from some of the strenuous running and jogging that you have them doing. What we've noticed is that most of them don't recover well after working hard which could be an indication of something more serious. We recommend you negate the artificial parameters, and at a minimum, keep the goal around a mile in fourteen, but preferably in the fifteen minute range. Now, you only have two people who are really in shape and that's John Lee and Jilkes. Now, they could meet your goals, and perhaps even better it, but they're a different breed. Those two will never forget where they came from and how hard they had it as children. They will always be hungry and worried that someone is going to try to take food off of their plates. Dad, in other words, you're pushing your people too hard, and their love for you will probably kill them at the rate you're going. You yourself, don't recover well. I know you've lost probably ten or more pounds in the past week, but you need to drop another ten to twenty and let that coffee go. It might be best if you tried green tea for a change," Zanthius indicated.

The Sarge looked at his two sons, and said, "I thought conditioning was the key to feeling good and living longer."

"Dad, it is, but your guys aren't marathon runners, they're older men who fought in a war that most people don't even remember or know what it was about," Zanthius said.

The Sarge dropped his head and quietly asked, "Do you two remember?"

Larry said, "You picked me off the streets and gave me a view of a world that I did not know existed. I want you to live as long as possible, but you must do things in moderation. You can't just decide to get in shape. You must plan on figuring out how you're going to do it, at your stage in life. We both know you're a beast, but some of your guys are showing signs of wear and tear."

The Sarge stood up and said, "Thanks, guys. I'll address this tonight at dinner. You know sometimes, you need your children to set you straight. Group hug!"

# # #

In the gym, the Sarge saw Gladstone, McArthur, Montomie, and Whitmore, they were all pumping iron. He walked over to the group and said, "When are you guys going to take a partner?"

McArthur asked, "Wow, what's up with that, Sarge? Do you think we're spending too much time together in the gym?"

"Naw! I just worry about you guys and everyone else. I think I've been pushing you guys too hard lately in preparation for hopefully, our final battle with Diablo. He's apparently staked out our places and has designed attack routes and angles. You know none of us are as young as we used to be."

"No shit! When did that epiphany come to your mind?" Gladstone inquired.

"I guess you guys just want to work out. I'm sorry to bother you."

He turned to walk away and Montomie said, "We're sorry, Sarge. What's up?" He looked at the four men and said, "My two sons told me I was pushing you guys too hard and that your recovery times were too long which indicated you, or we, are getting older, or that we are old. Their concern is genuine, and it made me think about what this was all about. Listen, I love you guys. Our being together has sparked a new energy in me and has confirmed that sense of brotherhood we will always have. The truth of the matter is, we are getting old, and I selfishly never want us to part. I mean, this has been the greatest trip a person who doesn't do drugs could ever be on. I've found that ultimate high, and it's all consuming. I don't want this to end, and I never want us to be more than one hundred feet away from each other. Now, those are things that I'm wrestling with because I love you and I know there is the possibility that some of us won't survive Diablo's next attempt."

Whitmore who rarely has anything to say, said "Sergeant Beckmire, it is our pleasure to follow you to hell and back. If some of us don't make it back, then we'll have a shit load of memories. We salute you, Sarge. Squad; attention!"

At dinner, Mrs. Carter had concocted a seafood dish freshly caught in the waters outside of 'The Sanctuary' that she cooked in Spanish olive oil and seasoned with spices from the earth. Surprisingly, Courtney stood up and said, "May I have your attention for just a moment. Please, for just a moment."

John Lee stood up and yelled, "The Doc is trying to talk. How about a little quiet?"

"Thanks, John Lee. I want to take this opportunity to thank each one of you for coming to the aid of my husband, Ben Beckmire. I've had personal interactions with each of you on one level or another, and I have never thanked you for helping this amazing man--my husband. He loves you all so much, I wonder why he married me."

Courtney's eyes began to water, and she said, "I just needed to thank all of you for helping my husband, and my best friend."

The stillness in the room was incredible until people started realizing their own mortality and started to cry. There was not a dry eye in the restaurant, other than the children who didn't know what was going on. At their table, the Sarge hugged his wife and told her how much he loved her. He then motioned to Mrs. Carter to serve the meal.

The Sarge said, "Most of you don't know Mrs. Carter, because Mr. Carter was being a jerk for a while. The young woman in the corner is Mrs. Carter, who prepared this scrumptious meal for us from the bounty of the earth and the sea. I'm also happy to let the group know that the jerk, Mr. Carter, has asked Mrs. Carter to help him manage the business. In addition, their daughter, the CPA, and their son Michael, who we all love and appreciate, will provide additional services to our group on a contractual basis. Just one more thing, my wife expressed a series of emotions and thoughts that I've neglected to say, but I will address them all after your bellies are full of this wonderful concoction. Bon Appetite!"

The group enjoyed the meal so much, that Mrs. Carter ran out of the dish. She apologized and confirmed, "I assure you this won't happen again."

Mr. Carter said, "FYI—next week, the other two properties are hosting a sorority from the states. They are called the Deltas. Each room in 'The Sanctuary' is sold out. Your rooms are always yours unless you're not going to be here."

Jong stood up and said, "I think it's safe to rent our rooms as well. Even if we had plans on being here, it's necessary for you to show a profit and while we pay you on a discounted basis, if at all, you need to always have control over 'The Sanctuary'. Michael, do you agree?"

"Mr. Jong, that was going to be the subject of a meeting with you later, but I thank you for allowing us to fully occupy 'The Sanctuary'. This is great news, and the other members of our team will surely appreciate this information. Once again, we thank all of you for trusting and believing in us."

The Sarge stood up and said, "Any other announcements? If not, I've had a piece of paper and a pencil placed in front of each of you. Listen, Michael and Mr. Carter have essentially kicked us out of our rooms for the coming week. We need to decide on a location. We're not creating new destinations, we're only considering the places we currently have houses or businesses; Virginia, Alabama, Spain, the Midwest."

Ava stood up and said, "It's so wonderful in Valencia this time of the year. I guess Juan and I will vote for Spain."

The Sarge stood up and said, "Ava, it's a silent vote."

After everyone wrote their preferences, the Sarge said, "I had a conversation with a few of our colleagues today and, I must say, it was enlightening. Eleven of you worked with me in Vietnam. Two of you tried to enhance the poor ones and got us into a war with the mob. Since then, people have tried to kill me, my wife, my son's mother, to illustrate to a son, who I didn't know existed, that they wanted whatever it was he had in relationship to the Carbon Factor formula. Please stay with me for just a moment. Eleven people showed up to defend me, my wife, my son's mother, and have been with us and watching our backs for close to three years. Many of you have met your soul mates and some of you are still looking. I say to those in waiting, good luck with that.

"I've lived a charmed life with people who love me and I them. However, my problem is, I don't want it to end. Those eleven guys have been the source of my sanity, inspiration, and my reasons for trying to help people to help themselves. I must admit, we've done some despicable things for our country, but in the interim, we've been true and loyal friends. I personally, never want this adventure to end because it keeps me and the people I love together. This has been an amazing saga! And, yes, I want to gut my cousin from his midsection to his brain, but I also don't want to see my friends in a hospital from gunshot wounds, or for any reason. This has been the most incredible journey I have ever been on. Again, I don't want it to end."

The Sarge paused, looked around the room and said a silent prayer. He then said, "I don't want to see anyone else get hurt trying to protect me and my family. I want to send you all to your respective homes and handle this matter on my own. If something was to happen to anyone of you, I would be devastated."

A stillness fell over the room, but was broken when John Lee said, "I be wanting to go home and enjoy my family. I can't do that knowing one of mine is being methodically hunted by his cousin. So, anyway, what you think you be saying ain't gonna be happening, so you might as well talk about where we go from here."

As the individual slips of paper were totaled, the vote was unanimous—two more weeks on the Island, then a quick trip to Spain, and then an all-out hunt for Diablo. The Sarge said, "I guess you all think alike because this is a helluva place, but we have to see if we can go back to St. John because we're interrupting the reservations at 'The Sanctuary'."

Michael walked over to where the Sarge was standing and whispered in his ear. The Sarge looked at him and smiled.

He said to the group, "Well, it looks like the Carter family are great planners. Our man Michael just informed me he had courtesy reservations for the group at the same place. That place is expecting a large group in two weeks, and they have asked Mr. Carter if he would host a group and treat them like royalty. So, there you have it. We'll stay a week or so over there and then come back here before we leave. Is that alright with you, Mr. Carter?"

"That would be fine with us. It'll also show we're always at capacity and that means we'll probably get written up in the Islander paper."

"The last thing we want to be is squatters. You're running a business and making money for us. We don't want to spend the money you make us, on us."

#

After dinner, Mallory told the Sarge that two of the people who they interviewed were put in this thing because his cousin had their wives kidnapped. He told the Sarge that he knew it sounded like a story, but the guys apparently were over in the Nam and knew the kind of work they did. He asked the Sarge if he would spend a few minutes with them because I thought their problem is larger than their being involved in this stakeout mess?

"What do you mean?"

"Sarge, I need you to spend five minutes with these guys and tell me if you think they're legitimate."

"Where are they?"

"Michael has them on ice in the old freezer."

Mallory nodded to Michael, and he quietly left the rear of the room and joined he and the Sarge.

The Sarge asked, "Won't they freeze to death in that unit?"

"Naw, Sarge. It's an air-conditioned room that me and my dad use to disappear."

When the three men arrived at the freezer, one of Michael's guys said, "I fed them. They eat like they don't have a bottom to their bellies."

The three men walked into the freezer and the two Native Americans jumped to attention.

The Sarge asked, "What is that all about?"

"Sergeant Beckmire, your pictures and your deeds are a part of the stories we tell our children. We call you the honorary Native American even though your people are from Australia."

"How do you know where I'm from?"

"The entire fighting world hears the stories of you and your men, and when they were inducted into the military. You people have been on the run so much your stories have been embellished."

"Why should I let you two guys leave here alive when I know you came here with others to hurt me, my friends, and my family including our children?"

"We didn't pass that test. We were in the Nam like you, but we did more finding active tunnels and outlets as well as tracking elite units. We crossed each other's paths when you people first arrived in the country. We made fun of your guys running and training all day. My friend and I were forced into this position. Your family member made us evaluate each property you have and tell his head henchman which one was the most vulnerable. We told him that Virginia was the most vulnerable, but we intentionally left out the fact that the machine pistols are controlled from afar. We told him in the Midwest, you could see them coming from a mile away, but it is also the most conducive to attack. We did not tell them about the machine pistols or the long guns in the Midwest. Listen, he has our wives, and he knew we needed the money because his people are trying to displace us and build a pipeline through our community. They're trying to bankrupt us and force us to leave. The crooked politicians are in their pockets. My people live on three thousand acres and they're trying to get rid of us in any way possible. I told your man that we would never bear arms against you if you let us go. Our fight is more than this family feud. We have an entire nation that is being systematically displaced, so that a large oil company can run a pipeline."

"If you go back, my cousin is going to know you were compromised because two members of your group were eliminated. He's a savage and he will kill your women just for the hell of it. You're working with a sick human being."

"What do you suggest we do? He's in cahoots with the land grabbers and he will bury our wives in the surrounding fields. What do you suggest we do?"

Mallory said, "This is the very thing we fought against out west. They need our help."

The Sarge turned to him and asked, "Mallory how many fights can we engage in at the same time? Don't you think I want to help these guys who, by the way, came here to kill us. Dah!"

# # #

After considering the initial information from his captives, the Sarge looked at the two men straight on and asked, "Are there any other main characters, other than my cousin? Who are the people trying to steal your land? Do you have names and addresses? There are a series of things we could do, but we need to know the actors, the people behind the scenes, and those who make things happen in your town. If you can assemble information that we can use to confirm your information, then individually we can target the group that's targeting you. At that point, we can help you out of your mess. I'm sending my nephew and a friend's daughter back to DC. I can change their trip and send them to Minnesota, but you my friend would have to forfeit your entire family if anything happened to my people. My question is, can I trust you and will you give us adequate information to make a difference in your hood?"

"Sergeant, you don't know our names. I'm called Windom and he's titled Earther. These are our true names, not the ones given to us by the people who conquered us and enslaved us to alcohol and other drugs. My American name is Elton and his is Kenneth. On our children's lives, we swear that what we told you is the truth."

Beckmire said, "I'm going to send my nephew and my associate's niece back with you. My people will get you out of here under an assumed name. We will land in a friendly airport in Maryland, and then continue to Minnesota. While you're traveling, we will make the necessary reservations and get you guys set up with a make-up artist. You have a short window to work with. Get me as much information as you can about where they're holding your women and who are the carpetbaggers involved in trying to run you and your neighbors off their land. I mean the bankers, and everyone else we need to roust. If you give me, and mine, enough information, we can come for a day and clean up the banking, carpetbaggers, and form a partnership where we liquidate all liens against your property. You will own ninety- five percent of the land and we will own five percent--that's to make it legal. We'll shake them down, pay them their fees, and run them out of town. You must stay hidden until we have enough information to fly from this paradise to fricken cold-ass Minnesota. I once had a woman there that I was in love with. I just remember how cold it was. Can you find out where they're holding your family members?"

"Sarge, we can't fly commercial."

"I wouldn't expect you to try to fly commercial. We have several planes and the one that you're going to leave on is almost now solely designated as my nephew's and his wife-to-be. I know he wishes that were true. We'll get you there, and me and my people will come for a day and try to clean it up. We are good people that help people. Please don't try to take advantage of us. The penalty is beyond your comprehension."

"Oh, you mean you'll let that big crazy guy with the over-sized knife go to work on us?"

"Naw, he's really trying to gain status. We have seven others who make his work look like child's play. Oh, and by the way, for every job we do to help people, we place a contract on you and your family, just in case there is a double-cross in the theatre. It's standard practice, nothing personal."

"Can I ask you a question about your motivation?"

"We're motivated by helping people to help themselves. Each person in our group is rich and vested in many lucrative ventures. We don't like carpetbaggers, and we don't like people who try to steal from the rightful owners of this land. My clan began in Australia in the outback. We have a property in the Midwest where carpetbaggers tried to scam farmers out of their land. We ran them out of town, endowed the farmers, and they should never need to embrace crooks to salvage a bad crop season. Life is short, sweet, and full of hurdles. We try to eliminate the hurdles. No one should work hard their entire life and have someone just steal their property. Not fair, and we don't like playing unless it's fair."

The two captives spoke in their native tongue for almost a minute and when finished, the talkative one said, "The stories are true that our elders tell. You and your people are our 'birds'. They talk about strangers flying in from the sun and correcting the imbalance that is currently plaguing our people. Timing is everything and you will become legend amongst our people, as well."

#

Later, the Sarge summoned Darryl and announced, "You'll have passengers going back with you on our jet, and Mallory will give you full details about what you'll be doing for the next few days. In addition, I need you to schedule a visit for the parents of Sue Lyn to the islands after we handle this issue in Minnesota, where you'll eventually head after landing in Maryland. I need you, Nephew, to begin to think out of the box in more ways than the one that dictates your carnal desires. I need you and Sue Lyn to be smarter than the people you have yet to meet, if that makes any sense. People are scoping us, and we need to have every asset available when we need it. Your passengers might just be able to offer us refuge for a few days. You never know, but I need you to check it out and let me know if we must retreat, would this be a good place to fortify our position and regroup? This final saga is going to crisscross continents, states, cities, and towns. I'm afraid we're going to have a lot of casualties. I will need you to make independent decisions for the good of the group. Please don't let me down."

"Uncle, you've scared me beyond comprehension. What on earth are you talking about?"

"I'm talking about your uncle who wants us all dead, and who has hired more mercenaries to make sure it happens. Your Uncle is the devil, Diablo, the anti-Christ, and a million other names that signify evil and death. He would rather kill you than say hello. He will come to you with a proposition that will give you an opportunity to own all that we have and to become the first trillionaire. Your life is going to change within a millisecond, and you'll have to save your head or forfeit it for the good of the group. The choice will be yours, but remember, a lot of Aborigine people and others will suffer greatly if you make the wrong decision."

"Uncle, how do you know this? You're scaring me."

"Yes, that is the intent of this mission. You like the planes, you like the unlimited credit card, and the hundred-dollar bills, that you have plenty of. You will have the opportunity to save yourself or sacrifice your family and your heritage. It will be an easy decision and you'll make the right choice. By the way, after you told me that Sue Lyn may be pregnant with a little Beckmire, I forgot to congratulate you.

Although, you'll have to explain to her father exactly what happened in terms of you shooting your load on her zone, but not in her zone. You'll have to convince him of that. I sincerely, wish you good luck with that horseshit."

"Uncle, that's the honest to God's truth. I've never penetrated Sue Lyn. I swear to you."

"Nephew, I'm not the one who you'll have to convince. I can only give you what our spirits give me. They're not connected to you and your earthly sexual pursuits. However, if I were you, I would craft another story. The one you continue to exclaim has so many holes in it. I, however, do wish you luck. You know in their culture this is a serious offense and a total sign of disrespect. In the hinterlands, they can summarily execute those who deflower females without asking permission or suggesting a dowry. Good luck with that horseshit you want to express."

"Uncle, I swear to you on all of our ancestor's graves, I've never penetrated Sue Lyn. I so desperately want to, but I made a promise and we've held our end of the bargain." Darryl's eyes began to swell, and he broke into tears.

Ben Beckmire asked, "Why are you crying?"

"I'm crying because you think I'm lying to you. Uncle, ask Sue Lyn and she will tell you the same thing. I love her more than life, and rather than embarrass her and dishonor you after making a pledge, I'll figure a way out of this world."

Darryl started to walk away and that booming voice of Ben Beckmire said, "I did not give you permission to end our conversation, or for you to turn your back on me, and may I remind you, it was committed by you as a sign of disrespect."

"Uncle, I'm trying to be a man and make the right decisions. However, I need the one man whose respect and trust I so desperately need and fight for, to believe in me. No matter how much it hurts me, I will never tell you a lie and what I've said about that situation represents the absolute truth. I've never penetrated the person I love."

"Darryl, Son, I believe you and, as a matter of fact, I was making fun of you. What makes you a man is the fact you gave your word to avoid a specific act and you, and Sue Lyn found ways around it without disrespecting the specific edict that was handed down. I simply applaud your resourcefulness. Never turn your back on a conversation unless it's aggressive. You're a Beckmire and you must know that I love you and I'll always have your back if you don't do stupid. Beckmires don't do stupid. Come here and give me a hug."

# # #

Late in the afternoon, Jilkes asked John Lee if he wanted to take a run? John Lee agreed, and, on the way, they picked up McArthur, and Gladstone, and then Brown and Bernstein, followed by Chakes and Montomie and then Jong and Whitmore. The Sarge saw them as well as Mallory and they joined in. Running towards them was Michael and his crew. They were running flat out and probably only Zanthius, and Larry could come close to their pace. As they passed the group, and continued on their way for fifty yards or so, he turned around and yelled at the Sarge, "You mind if we run behind you guys and catch our breath?"

The Sarge said, "I used to like you, Mr. Showoff. Why so fast and far?"

We've increased our time by two minutes and decreased our distance by three miles. We used to do a lot farther and faster, but we're getting older."

The Sarge said, "These old guys used to run ten miles at a relatively fast pace, carrying an extra forty-five pounds without stopping. When we first started training like that, they complained their assess off. One day over in the Nam, it seemed like the entire Viet Cong army was on our asses, and we must have run more than fifteen miles at a strong pace."

Michael said, "With forty-five extra pounds on you?"

The Sarge smiled and exclaimed, "No, Michael! We dropped all of the bullshit and just kept the guns and bullets."

The Sarge nodded at Mallory and signaled for him to retreat to the rear. When he got to the back, the Sarge said to Michael, "We don't know your guys, and we don't do well with strangers. I have a simple question for your guys. Can you keep my people safe while they're on this island without me and mine having to carry weapons at every juncture?"

Michael said, "Mr. Beckmire, you know their story, and I'll put my life up for each of these guys. They've had some tough times. We've all had some tough times, and these guys were living wherever I could arrange. They don't do drugs, we all drink a little, but they're basically in hiding from bad marriages. As I said to you before, we could be a good fit for you here and I think we have eyes and ears everywhere on St. John. I just need to make this official and try to get them some rent and food money. I've been stealing food from 'The Sanctuary' to feed them. I've also paid for some of the provisions, but it gets a bit behind based upon what my dad can pay me."

"Hold up. I thought we made a deal with you?"

"You, kind of, sort of, maybe thought you did, but it wasn't consummated."

"Let's have a meal when we get back and work out the details with Jong. I thought you were made whole by us after you had to do some fish feeding of a convert. As a matter of fact, you went fish feeding two more times for us, if I'm not mistaken. Okay, let's talk when we get back and let's see if my people think your people are loyal, trustworthy, and will make the sacrifice if necessary."

As the group was about to make their turn-about, in the distance they could see a group of women running towards them. It was suggested they run a little farther and a lot faster. As the group got closer to the women, Asiram yelled, "Hi, Honey, Hi, Daddy-in-Law. See you guys later."

The Sarge stopped in his tracks and saw a couple of women trotting really slow behind the younger crew. It was Courtney, Ava, Monica, and a pregnant Luana. Courtney yelled, "Just trying to make sure our pregnant lady doesn't overexert herself."

The Sarge turned to Mallory and said, "I've seen it all. Courtney in a running outfit and sneakers. I must admit, she looked tight in that outfit. When did Monica begin to run?"

"Sarge, that's as new to me as the French language. I didn't even know the woman owned running shoes. Damn, I'm going to have to talk to her. I'm so proud of her, but who has the kids?"

"I think it's reading time with Marisa and Mary Alice. Those two have formed a bond that's really cool."

# # #

At 'The Sanctuary', Mallory suggested they go up on the hill to one of the other places and have a conversation with Michael and his friends.

When all parties arrived, the Sarge said, "I've invited two of my guys who are going to tell everyone else, and then there are going to be another ten people to show up."

Approximately, ten minutes later, Jilkes, John Lee, McArthur, Gladstone, Jong, Montomie, Brown, Bernstein, Whitmore, and Chakes entered the restaurant and positioned themselves near the Sarge and Mallory. Three minutes later, Zanthius, Mike, Carlos, Juan, and Larry waltzed into the place. The owner picked up the phone, called Mr. Carter and said, "I think there's going to be a huge fight in my restaurant, and your son is going to be involved."

Mr. Carter said, "Naw, no trouble there. They're just going to interview my son and his friends. That new item you developed as a starter; now might be a good time to load them up with it and see what they think. That group is very discerning and picky, not my son and his friends, but the rest have acquired a fine dining sense. By the way, you guys have been busy as shit. Is it our price structure? The next time we meet, we should discuss it. If you're charging a significantly lower price than we are, and if we lower our prices based upon where you are, we might start false competition. Something I think we should discuss."

Larry stated, "I guess me, my brother, Carlos, and Juan, didn't get the memo. What is this meeting about?"

The Sarge said, "Son, I have no idea where these people came from and how they knew we were meeting with Michael and his people. I guess everyone wanted to take a walk and get away from the direct relationship with the beach."

Zanthius said, "Dad, can you tell me who your new friends are, and what is their relationship to our group?"

"Son, Mallory and I came here to have a talk with them, but it seems like the entire group wants to talk to them as well. I guess that's how we roll. Perhaps the best way to get started is to figure out who they are, what are their strengths and what can they provide us. Are they reformed, or recently released criminals, retired priests, or what? Michael, we know and trust you, but who are these guys?" The Sarge asked.

# # #

Michael, for the next half hour spoke about himself, his propensity for loyalty, and his associates' skill set. He admitted they were light years short of skills that Beckmire's group had amassed, but iterated they were good at what they do and perfect at keeping silent under a pressing code.

The Sarge studied Michael and his crew and thought to himself, "hell, I'm sending my nephew and his lady to Minnesota, why not have these guys go and do an assessment and perhaps do some strong-arm work".

As Michael continued to rant on about his team, the Sarge unconsciously interrupted him and said, "Are your people mobile? Can they travel to Minnesota? I mean can they travel in the next thirty minutes?'

Michael looked at him and affirmatively stated, "We're mobile and ready to go."

The Sarge said, "Michael, I need you here. I need your people to do some reconnaissance work for me in Minnesota. Is that a problem?"

Michael looked at his crew and stuttered, "Ah, ah, ah, no, Sir. We can make that happen. Right guys?"

There was a silence that fell over the room and the Sarge asked, "Are you sure about that?"

"Sarge, when there is no comment, it means we're on board with the assignment. We have a chain of command that's much like yours."

The Sarge nudged Mallory and asked him to walk with him. He told Michael and his people he would be right back. The Sarge, once alone with Mallory, asked if he had any concerns with the notion of sending those guys along with Sue Lyn and Darryl. Mallory indicated it would be a great diversion if the word got out that they were in Minnesota doing some wet work. He felt there was a lot of mileage to be gained by having those guys go and at least get the details of who needed to be handled. He also indicated they should have Michael's team report to Darryl and Sue Lyn and take all their instructions from them.

The Sarge studied the idea and evaluated the pros and cons of the situation. He thought it was time for Darryl to handle a complex situation. He realized that Darryl and Sue Lyn were the architects of their new weapons systems in Virginia and in the Midwest. He told Mallory that Michael's guys, plus the two Native Americans would be a strong force to contend with. The Sarge also told Mallory that Earther and Windom would have to relocate their families until the coast was clear. He suggested they go back in the meeting.

Fifteen minutes later, the Sarge and Mallory met with Michael first and interrogated him fiercely. The Sarge asked if his guys were wash outs from the corps, psychos, or section eights looking for some comic book battle action? He and Mallory hurled insult after insult at Michael, who maintained his temperament and suggested they allow him to make the trip with Darryl and Sue Lyn. He contended each man was worthy of the opportunity and that they would rather die than fail a simple mission. Michael assured them that they would follow the established command and be loyal to the commander.

Mallory asked "Michael, suppose the commander is young and naïve and has no battle experience, would they continue to be loyal to him or her?"

"Mr. Beckmire, Mr. Mallory, I hope you guys trust me and find that I'm loyal. You guys have done some wonderful things here on the island and you have restored my father's belief in himself and probably reintroduced him to my mother again. I owe you so much, and I believe I've helped you guys out of some interesting situations. My guys are as loyal as I am and will not let you down. They will follow smart orders, but they will not run into a burning building looking for paper dolls."

Mallory and the Sarge laughed. The Sarge said, "Ask them to come in and let me tell them what's at stake and what actions I need from them."

# # #

The entire group assembled and the Sarge had everyone introduce themselves to each other. He signaled out Elton and

Kenneth, aka. Windom and Earther and asked them to give a summary of what's happening in their community and how they can help.

Thirty or so minutes later, everyone was aware of the major players, the company heads, the bankers who were bank rolling the eviction action, the private citizens who were interested in lining their pockets, and those who would do the enforcement work for the group.

The Sarge said to the group, "You will all be flown from here on one of our planes. But before we get to that logistic, I have one major question that needs to be answered. Darryl is my nephew, and Sue Lyn is the niece of my man Jong. They will lead this mission. If anyone has a problem with that, I need you to speak on it here and now."

The Sarge paused for a moment but didn't hear feedback from anyone. He said, "If there is a problem in Minnesota and it is a result of someone having a problem with the leadership, then we'll consider that action as insubordination and that gentlemen, will require me, and mine, to come to wherever you are, and make amends. Our amends are conclusive and life ending. I am not threatening anyone, I'm just saying, we're going to help Windom and Earther, but the leadership role is in the hands of Darryl and Sue Lyn. People don't make it hard on us, or yourselves. Are there any questions?"

Mallory said, "In the course of setting things right in Minnesota, it may cost us some money. Darryl will have access to funds to pay off the corrupt. I don't want anyone terminated unless there is a clear reason and/or you're in danger. While you're on the flight, you'll have time to consider all the little details. Windom and Earther, how much do you owe the bank and is it the bank that's leading the collection and eviction movement?"

Windom said, "There are eight families on the track of land that they're trying to seize. My people have held those properties for centuries. My father, his father, and his father's father were the original owners of that land."

Mallory asked, "Do you have any idea how much is owed to the bank and what was the premise that allowed them to try to shutter your places at the same time?"

Windom responded, "There aren't many employers in the area and only a few people own the factories. Within a week of each other, we were all laid off from our jobs. After two months of being unable to afford the mortgage, a letter came to the house indicating that we were two months behind in payment and that full payment of the mortgage would have to be made in ten days or foreclosure would be proceeded with. We're so strapped and under skilled in the plants, but we've been there for ten to fourteen years. It was kind of a planned strategic slavery. They own the businesses and saw this opportunity, and they wanted us out. Our salvation came when a man showed up and offered us money to survey your properties. Our names were given to him by one of our people. They told him we were the best at planning and executing an incursions and extractions. He failed to mention the name Beckmire." The Sarge and Mallory smiled.

Windom said, "I owe about fifty-five thousand on my property."

Earther replied, "I owe nearly forty-nine."

The Sarge said, "Any guess what the others owe and what kind of businesses can you guys develop for your people?

Okay, I'm getting ahead of myself. Any idea what the other six families owe the banks?"

Earther said, "We all owe about the same amount, between forty and ninety."

The Sarge said, "I wouldn't consider that the same amount. That's a spread of $50k. Anyway, Darryl, do you want to transfer the money or carry cash?"

Sue Lyn whispered in Darryl's ear, and he said, "We should have both at our disposal. We definitely should settle the mortgages with a bank transfer and have cash to save lives if we can't convince them to disappear."

Earther uttered sounds in his native language and Windom said, for all to hear, "Mother earth is not fully polluted, and some waters still run pure."

The Sarge asked, "What did he ask you and what's the meaning of your reply?"

"He wants to know if we're jumping from one set of crooks, to another. I told him that everyone is not a crook and that these people appear pure. I must ask you, what is the consequence of you paying off our mortgages? How will we pay you back?"

Mallory said, "That's a great question and one that happens through good deeds. We're not sure what we'll find when Darryl and Sue Lyn report back to us, but we're in the business of helping people—not trying to steal their land. We're like Robin Hood except we don't steal. Our businesses have been good to us, and we share when we can. We've helped people in Australia, St. Thomas, in the Midwest, in Spain, Vets around the country, and now, hopefully, in Minnesota. All we ask is that you never turn your back on a neighbor or a friend and help as many people as you can. In your case, it's going to get tough because big brother is going to come after you with all he has because you're in the way of him making billions from the pipeline. That is where our 5% ownership comes into play and spreads the culpability to us. We will hook you up with a few lawyers who can assist in your fight.   Do you have access to any attorneys in your community?"

"We do and they're willing to help, but it has to happen after hours and in secret. They represent the few companies that are in our community and who are probably a part of the scam."

"Maybe you need an independent legal organization, funded by outside monies and partnerships. We could hook you up with the American Civil Liberties Union (ACLU), and other community minded organizations and begin to approach this issue from a point of strength and exposure. Anyway, let's first determine how far these guys are willing to push the process. When they hear the Beckmire team is involved, they might just back down and find a way to include you in the process and perhaps offer to legitimately buy, relocate, or make you partners in the deal. Now, that would be ideal. You wouldn't, or none of those families would, ever be at the whim of a group of carpetbaggers. Anyway, let's see how this works," Mallory said.

The Sarge said, "I don't want to have me, or my people, come out there and bury a whole society." Everyone took notice of his eyes when he said that and realized they were on the right side of this fight.

Darryl said, "Sue Lyn and I are more technically oriented, but we occasionally do the detail stuff. We may look young and innocent, but we handle a significant amount of this group's money in terms of investments. Sue Lyn and I, also understand weapons and weapon systems. The two systems in Virginia and in the Midwest are our designs as well as a new modification we want to test in Virginia. We like doing battle from afar with the use of monitors. My uncle likes the gore and the mess. We're not opposed to doing the gore and the mess, but we prefer to convince our enemies how tenacious we can be, by using technology. Sue Lyn is my partner, lover, wife to be, and mother-to-be of my child. I know I don't have to ask you guys to be on your best behavior, or I'll personally throw you out of the fricken airplane."

Everyone laughed except Darryl who emphatically, stated, "That was not a metaphor."

The Sarge stepped up and said, "Okay, when do we want to get this show on the road? Oh, Windom and Earther, do you have any idea where your people are being held?"

"We know exactly where they're being held."

Darryl said, "Uncle, I was going to get to that on the plane ride and figure out the best way in and out. Earther and Windom, do your people have passports, just in case all goes bad?"

"We've never needed a passport."

The Sarge said, "If necessary, we'll move you guys to our Midwest farm until we clean up this mess. Darryl, if we must move them, then that means, me and my people are on the way there and we will kick-ass and take names later. Make it clear to all, if we come, we won't come with an olive branch."

He then looked at Michael and said, "Are you ready to turn your people over to my nephew, and his companion?"

"Yes, Sergeant Beckmire. My guys will now respond to those who are designated as the leadership."

"Okay, they're going to need some spending money. Darryl, what is the compensation for this job? Have you considered payment for these guys?"

"Uncle, until I see them in action and know that they can follow directions, I would rather give them spending money and assure them a plane ticket back."

The Sarge asked, "Are you guys okay with that arrangement?"

Michael responded, "Sarge, we're trying to join your band, and this will give us an opportunity to assure you that we can do some of the work while you guys stay back and play badminton."

"Fair enough," the Sarge stated.

After studying his nephew's face, the Sarge said, "Darryl, I want you out of there if this thing gets crazy. I want it concluded no later than a week from today. Remember you are to be a father and when you get back, her father is going to be somewhere waiting on you to hear how your words are lifeless. I know, Son, we'll get through this together. Anyhow, back to the group, will $5k for the week be sufficient?" Each man's eyes opened wide, and they nodded their approval.

The Sarge continued, "Earther and Windom, until this is over, we're going to place you on the payroll so that you guys will have something extra if we must move you out of there in a hurry. Remember, people, I want it resolved in one week. Do heavy lifting and keep the pressure on those crooks. I want it over in a week. Don't leave Earther and Windom's people there if you smell a rat. Also remember, the people stealing their land are not the same people that are holding their families. The shithead holding their families is Diablo, or my cousin. If it ain't right when you discover some of the facts, get the hell out of there, in a hurry. Windom, before you people get there, I need you to make alternative arrangements to get out of town if all goes bad. If the plan is compromised, then develop a strategy that will get my family and your people out of there. We'll have some small arms provided for you. Darryl, you know how to access them, right?"

Mallory said, "Remember, Windom and Earther, they think you met your demise on the island. Everything you do has to be done in a hurry. I have a make-up man who will meet the plane once we've determined when you're leaving. Darryl, he'll contact you."

"Remember, if it looks bad, then turn around and get the hell out of there. By the way, Michael, what are your people's names?"

"This is Jasper, that's Harold, he's Isaiah, and that guy is Desmond."

"Nice to meet you guys. Do you have any questions?"

Isaiah said, "No questions, but I want to thank you for giving us this opportunity to help as well as giving purpose to our existence. We thank you and appreciate everything. We won't let Darryl or Ms. Sue Lyn down."

Two hours later, the small group were on a jet heading for Minnesota with an interim stop in Maryland. The group huddled and discussed the details that Windom and Earther had given them. They also discussed the get out of dodge notion if all failed. Darryl suggested they take care of the money business first and see if that draws the cockroaches out of the woodwork. Windom thought he and Earther needed to secure their families first. Darryl apologized and agreed that the families were their priority. Earther asked, "How are we going to get back into the country?"

Sue Lyn said, "We're going to stop in Maryland where we have associates and then move on to Minnesota, and besides, it's called St. Thomas, and the U S Virgin Islands is a part of the good old, United States of America. By the way, is there anyone you can truly trust in Minnesota that can provide transportation? The other families that are being scammed; can they be trusted to help us?"

Earther was about to say something when Windom grasped his arm and said, "They're all our family."

Sue Lyn paused for a moment and looked at him and asked, "You're the chief, aren't you?"

"Why would you ask that question?"

"I believe you're the chief. Please answer the question?"

"I am the Chief, and my wife and his wife are being held captive, and we were forced to come here and scope out an attack on you people on the island. We gave false information on every property."

Darryl stared at Windom and asked, "If you were in charge, what would you do?"

The chief looked at him and said, "Only a wise man would ask a question like that when he's about to enter a place without any intelligence. I have a few recommendations, but I do not want to go against your uncle."

"Chief, my uncle ain't here, and these guys will agree with either you or me, but they should have an opinion or recommendation. Sue Lyn and I are not retarded, and my uncle wants to know if I will use all available resources prior to deciding. We don't know shit about Minnesota, other than the fact it's usually cold there. For everyone to come out ahead on this project, it requires that we all have input into the solutions and the strategy for engagement. I can't arbitrarily make decisions on an environment I know nothing about, and you guys can't commit resources you don't control. My uncle is crafty and comes from a long line of smart people. I on the other hand, where I was born, was ordained to do things that most mortals wouldn't consider possible. This is a learning experience for Sue Lyn, me, and for you six guys--a test of loyalty, creativity, and resilience. Isaiah, Jasper, Desmond, and Harold, I want your input, but I make the final decisions. Can we play by my rules guys, it's my ball?" As he looked at each person, they nodded their acceptance of the order of things.

## CHAPTER SEVEN

The jet landed in Maryland where each person was screened by friendly customs officials. Windom and Earther met the Sarge's makeup artist friend, and he modified their looks, dramatically.

The plane was refueled, and the small group made its way to Red Wing, Minnesota. They rented a huge 10 passenger van and proceeded to the area along the ridge where the carpetbaggers were planning to place extensions of a pipeline. As the van rode down Main Street, Earther said, "Something is wrong here. Our people are not visible. Something is happening, and I feel it ain't good."

Darryl said to Isaiah who was driving, "Let me and Sue Lyn off at the next corner and you guys proceed down the street. Let Desmond and Jasper off at the following corner and they can work their way back up the street. The rest of you guys continue up main street and park the van and remain in it unless we run into trouble."

As Windom and Earther passed shops they knew, no one was visible or working. On the other end of Main Street, two massive individuals appeared on the street and asked Darryl and Sue Lyn, what they were doing? Darryl replied, "We're touring my ancestors homelands. Why do you ask and who are you guys?"

"Our company has purchased a lot of land in this area for redevelopment. We own most of Main Street and all those small farms heading north. The town has been closed to foot traffic since people have been breaking into our newly acquired businesses and pilfering them. We, therefore, are going to have to request that you guys keep on your way."

Darryl said, "I can't imagine the elders selling sacred soil where our ancestors are buried. Where have our people gone?"

"Sir, I couldn't tell you that. All I know is we're here to keep people out until the lawyers finalize the transaction."

"Who are the lawyers?"

"Sir, I'm not at liberty to divulge that information." Darryl thanked him and proceeded towards the van.

When Darryl and Sue Lyn arrived at the van, Windom said, "I think I know where the people are and the prime suspect behind this robbery."

Darryl asked how many families owned businesses in town and was told that only three Native American businesses remained and that the others had been purchased years ago and were run by people from the East. He was also told that besides their wives, those people probably are holding others until everyone signs on the dotted line.

Sue Lyn asked, "Who is the person who will benefit the most?"

Earther said, "About three months ago, a fancy pants man spent a lot of time walking up and down the road until he had covered it three or four times. He was surrounded by a group of men and women, and they looked like mercs. They were all beholden to him, and from the bulge in their jackets, they were armed. He never spoke to anyone other than his people and if a local got too close, his people would divert them. He could be heard asking the same question over and over. He asked his people, "if not this route, then what are the options"? They would say, the only other way is beside the lake, and that can't happen."

Windom added, "After that, it became clear what they wanted and that's when the strong-arm tactics began. He was told by one of our people that Earther and I were the best trackers in the nation. One of his associates came to see me, and the next thing I know, my wife is missing and so was Earther's. As you know, the fancy pants man, we believe, is your uncle. Someone called him Walter. He was once seen talking with the ex-mayor and regional sheriff. I think we should find the ex-mayor and have a conversation with him. We should find the elders first and see what's going on and what kind of leverage is being used over them. We need to know what the people know before we go barging in and trying to rescue our women folk."

Thirty minutes later, the van pulled off the highway and onto a road that led towards the hills. Much truer to beliefs, the group pulled into a Native American village with makeshift huts made from brick but following the basic design of a tepee.

In what could be considered a community center, the group entered and were introduced to the elders who, unfortunately, were already reeling from early afternoon bouts with firewater. Windom asked about the relationships with the white man and what leverage they had over the elders.

One of the men stated, "It is a good deal, and one that will make our people wealthy."

Windom vehemently asked, "They have our women, and you're concerned about money?"

"Money will allow you to replace your home and move to a better community. We have worked out a good deal for our people and those of you who lived in Red Wings. Everyone will prosper, and your women are okay. No harm has fallen upon them," the man said.

"Where are they being held?" Earther asked.

"We don't know where they are, but we do know they're safe," the man responded.

Darryl introduced himself and said he was from a place much like this and the white man was trying to do the same thing to his people. He indicated that on his land, large diamonds were discovered. The white man tried to steal the land from the people by killing them off. Do you have any agreements from these people that we can review, and see if it makes sense for your people? This young lady is a seasoned lawyer with a large organization that funds the study of land misappropriation. Would you like for her to have a look at your paperwork?"

"No, our old mayor is looking out for us."

Earther exclaimed, "Of all the people, you select that racist son-of-a-bitch to handle our affairs! You think it makes sense to have people kidnap our wives, force us to plot a small-scale invasion, and then force us to sell our property so that a pipeline can run through our ancestral burial ground? The mayor was run out of office because he was caught stealing from us. What did he promise you people? What does he have on you? Did you sign any papers?"

"All papers and deals will be finalized in two days. You'll be able to buy a house anywhere in Minnesota," the man said.

"Where do you think they are holding our wives?"

"I told you, we don't know, but we do know they're safe."

"How do you know they're safe?"

"The mayor promised that nothing would happen to them as long as we did the work for that important man who was here," the man stated.

Windom said, "Let's get out of here. These guys don't have a clue plus they're drunk." As the group was leaving the community center, a car could be seen coming up the road. They ducked back into the center and lo and behold, it was the ex-mayor and the sheriff. Darryl said, "If we have to do butchers' work, where can we dispose of the bodies?"

Earther said, "We know of a hundred places that will never be searched. We can make them disappear." He then gave Darryl the 411 on the ex-mayor.

The ex-mayor and sheriff walked into the community center smoking huge cigars. The sheriff said, "Chief, everything is a go. All the papers are being prepared and will be ready for signature tomorrow. This calls for a celebration."

The sheriff reached in the bag he was carrying and pulled out three bottles of cheap bourbon. As he opened one of the bottles, Darryl and Sue Lyn entered the area from one of the adjoining rooms. Darryl introduced himself and Sue Lyn and said, "We're here to stop you from swindling our Native American friends."

The Sheriff asked, "Who the hell are you people and what are you doing on our land?"

From the shadows, Windom and Earther walked into view and the sheriff reached for his weapon. Isaiah from the rear, placed his pistol to the head of the Sherriff, and said, "That would be a life ending move."

The ex-mayor said, "You people have crossed the state line and are carrying weapons." He looked at Earther and said, "If I don't make that call, well, you know the rest."

Darryl looked at Isaiah and nodded. Isaiah pulled a Bowie knife from its sheath and threw it into the ex-mayor's foot. As he began to scream, Desmond tore a piece of cloth from a dirty tablecloth and gagged him. Isaiah, then pulled the knife from the ex-mayor's foot and looked at Darryl for guidance. Darryl looked at the sheriff and said, "Windom and Earther are missing their wives. Do you want to tell them where they are, or do you want to bleed out like the ex-mayor is doing?"

"I don't know where their wives are, and if I did, I wouldn't tell you dumb ass people."

Isaiah faked the sheriff out by pretending to throw the knife. When the sheriff jumped up, and as his foot came down, Isaiah's blade entered the man's shoe and went into his foot.

Desmond obtained trash bags and put each man's legs in them. Darryl said, "I don't like blood and violence, but I'm on a deadline. See, Sue Lyn and I are due back in school in two days and my uncle, the good one, not the one who has corrupted your souls, wants to see how we manage claim jumpers. In my hood, which would be in Australia, we would just take your ass to the billabong and let the crocs have a meal. Here, things I guess, follow more of a tradition and have protocols. Oh, Harold, put a tourniquet on the mayor and slow the flow of blood. He's beginning to look a little pale."

"Now, Sheriff, this can get really funky if you like. I prefer and propose that we conclude this violence and talk like gentlemen. You know, just like you and those guys in charge of stealing this land do. What say you?"

"I need a doctor," the sheriff said.

"No, you don't. You'll need a priest at the rate the blood is being pumped out of your foot. Here's what I'm prepared to do. I'll slow the bleeding and get you to the nearest hospital in the next five minutes, but you'll have to tell me where to locate Earther and Windom's wives, who the ring leaders of this mess are, and where I can find them," Darryl stated.

"You're just a punk-ass kid. Who sent you here? Don't you know we're professionals."

"No, the doctor you need and the lawyer you'll require, if you survive this interview, are professionals. You're a bad crook who got caught with his feet in someone else's jacuzzi. Last chance to tell me where their families are and who oversees this robbery?"

"Listen Sonny, go screw your little slant eyed bitch. I have nothing to say."

Darryl turned colors. He had never heard anyone refer to Sue Lyn like that. He said, "Why are you so disrespectful?" He turned as if he was walking away, pulled his weapon out, and fired a round into the upper most thigh of the sheriff. He then fired another round into his other thigh and said, "You may not apologize to her in this life, but I can assure you one thing, you'll never have sex again."

Darryl looked into the man's eyes and placed the barrel of his weapon on the man's genitals and said, "This is what disrespect will get you." The sheriff attempted to say something, but Darryl pulled the trigger and blew that part of the man's anatomy into oblivion. Darryl then looked in the man's eyes and fired a round into his head.

Darryl looked at the ex-mayor and said, "I'm going to remove the rag from your mouth, and the words that flow from it had better be the names of the perpetrators." He looked at Desmond and Harold who were surprised at what just happened and told them to wrap the sheriff up for delivery.

When Darryl removed the rag from the man's mouth the ex-mayor went on a rant that lasted ten minutes. He named bankers, lawyers, judges, city council members, investors, the elders, insurance brokers, and mobsters. Sue Lyn told Darryl the ex-mayor was excreting a lot of blood and that he should consider getting him to a hospital.

Darryl said, "I'm going to get you to the hospital at the request of my lady friend. Prior to getting you there, you will call a press conference and divulge every single person you've mentioned. Now, I know you think they can protect you, but Mr. Mayor, for you to remain alive, especially after witnessing me shoot your friend, I'll have to take a million-dollar contract out on you and each of your family members. And Buddy, in this part of the world, that will go a long way. I need you to print the names you mentioned on this piece of paper. Don't leave out a single person. Tell me exactly what the purpose was for calling in loans fraudulently, conspiring with banks, loan officers, as well as employers, to terminate all people who worked for them, who lived along the desired track of land. You go public or we'll go first, and we have the resources to apply to this problem. You see, what you did to Earther and Windom, we've seen done to other people around the world and we have designated a large part of our budget to help them and to secure them. Instead of trying to steal the land from them, you should have invited them to the table to discuss options rather than talking to a few drunks and keeping them supplied with whiskey. However, first, where are their families?"

"They're being held at the county jail."

"What are they being held for?"

"They're being held for suspicion of solicitation," the mayor said.

Earther started at the mayor, but Darryl jumped up and intervened. He said, "Please, let's just retrieve your people and get the hell out of this place. I'm not feeling that this is the kind of place you can lay around in and be a hero. In the morning, we're going to go to the bank and pay off all the loans for all the families along the track. If some families want to stay there, that's on them, but they won't have to worry about jerks like him stealing their land. We're also going to open an account that helps protect your sacred land throughout time.

"Windom, I need someone to reach out to all of the people and get them at the bank first thing in the morning, so we can clear all of their debts and get their deeds in their hands."

He looked at the mayor and said, "Mr. Mayor, you've just switched sides and you can't go back unless you want to end up like the sheriff. Speaking of the recently departed sheriff, Mr. Mayor, if I were you, I would block all visions of what you thought you saw for your sake, that of your wife who you hate, and those two boys that you adore. I must make the call because you might try to get righteous on me. If you think you can get protection for ten years around the clock for you and your sons, then you can tell me to kiss your ass on camera. However, if that's a problem, then I suggest you follow the script I've laid out and we all might survive this saga. The sheriff, I'm hoping, will never ever be found. Perhaps we can lead a trail out of town with some young harlot and let the wife go from there. She will be happy with the missing person idea because we heard she was involved with that young deputy. This is the perfect retirement plan, plus an insurance policy that will make her sleep easy at night, not wondering about her missing husband."

Darryl looked at Windom and Earther, and said, "Let's go and get your people. Is there anything in your homes you cannot do without?"

Windom said, "My memories are in my heart and my mind. I need to get my wife."

"Mr. Mayor, I'm going to get you to the hospital, but you need to make a call to any reporters you know. We have called two that the tribe knows, but we need white people to report on this as well. Harold, I need you and Desmond to drop the mayor off at that hospital down the road and call Isaiah on his cell. We must blow this location and sleep in the fields. Earther, find us an outdoor bedroom? Tomorrow, people, we make your ownership of this land unquestionable, as the mayor explains to the people of Red Wing the plan, the people, the institutions, and everyone else that is involved in this nefarious scheme. Mr. Mayor, I need you to call your wife and tell her you've had an accident and to meet you at the hospital. Since you believe in kidnapping, we'll hold her for a while to make sure you don't get cold feet. In addition, I'm going to put a bid on the internet for your two boys under the title, 'General Contractors Wanted'. I can assure you a select group of people will know what that means especially after I list $000,000. To the dark and dirty dwellers, that's a shit load of money. I hope I'm getting through to you that we are resolved to end this thing one way (Darryl looked at the sheriff's body wrapped up) or the other. Clearly a choice that's up to you. To show you that we're fair, we'll get you and your family out of here to a place where they can begin all over again—Australia. Your choice, my friend."

"How can you get us out of the country?"

"You're going to control where you have the press conference and we'll control the exit route, through lakes, and back roads that you and your people don't know much about. You should have spent time talking to your neighbors, rather than plotting against them. Earther assures me we can get you out through some rough country. Don't worry about money, where you're going, you'll learn to live off the land and to provide services to people. Eventually, you might show remorse and earn your way into our business model, but I assure you, no one will come looking for you or yours where I live. Listen, the town is going to be closed for a while and it won't be your goons patrolling it and running people out. It's going to be the very people you tried to displace, who'll be in charge and not two or four old drunk men who call themselves elders," Darryl stated.

Sue Lyn's phone rang, and it was Ben Beckmire. He asked to speak to Darryl. After a few words of caution, Ben Beckmire asked if there was a problem relating to the people in charge? Darryl told him that the ex-mayor and sheriff were the leading characters in front of the action with a slew of crooked politicians, bankers, investment institutions, and rich white people. He told his uncle that the sheriff's foot was impaled by Isaiah's knife to show resolve, and that he was eventually terminated.

Ben Beckmire said, "Darryl, I need you and your people to get out of there now. You can't go around killing people, especially law enforcement."

"Uncle, he was corrupt and a disgrace to his badge. We have the situation under control and Michael's guys, who are now my guys, are tenacious and follow instructions. They're protective and good at disposal. Earther has a place where he swears no one will ever find the remains of the guy. The ex-mayor has decided to right his wrongs and go public. I'm going to get him and his family out of the area and into my hood. Is there any way you can send the third plane in the fleet, it's such a long ride? How much should I give them in cash to make the journey? I can't leave them here. They'll all be dead by tomorrow evening. I want to send them to my home, humble them, and let them help out."

There was a deadly silence on the other end of the phone for over a minute. Finally, the Sarge said, "Nephew, I gave you a man-size job to oversee, and it seems as though I'm trying to second guess your judgements. May I speak with Sue Lyn for a minute?"

Darryl gave the phone to Sue Lyn and the Sarge instructed her to distance herself for this conversation from Darryl.

Once she had distanced herself, the Sarge asked, "Sue Lyn, has Darryl gone off the deep end? Is he summarily terminating people and feeling almighty?"

"Oh no, Sergeant Beckmire. I am proud of his decision making and how he includes people in the process when he is uncertain. He is protecting us with escape routes, timetables, and methods of deployment if we come under attack. In other words, my man is managing his business."

"Wow, thank you for that bit of information. Let me speak to my nephew and, Sue Lyn, keep him grounded or I'll send his ass back to the billabong."

"Sergeant Sir, he would make you proud. He sent a message, a strong one and now people are turning on each other and the path is in sight for total reclamation of the properties. Now, the thieves will have to deal with the Nation, and they will become chief partners in the land deal. It's brilliant, and he has manifested each part of the deal and will pay the balances first thing in the morning. We're going to reclaim the wives and get the hell out of here asap," Sue Lyn announced.

"You're confident that all is being managed properly?" The Sarge inquired.

"He's using one of the plays from your playbook," Sue Lyn stated.

The Sarge thought to himself, "these kids are too damn smart". "Thanks, Sue Lyn, may I speak to my nephew?"

Sue Lyn handed Darryl the phone and the Sarge said, "Nephew, this is your game. You can't leave those people there or send them home. I'll have Jong call Sue Lyn and send the other plane in the next two hours so that it can be there at your disposal once you've played your final sonata. Nephew, please keep yourself and your people safe. Always, take care of your people. How many people will have to be extracted?"

"Uncle, let me call you back on that. Give me a few minutes and I'll get back to you."

# # #

Hours later and with a good plan in place, the ex-mayor was at the hospital, a larger plane was on its way to Red Wings, and family members had been called to the hospital expecting to find an emergency in place. Instead, their loved ones, and two dogs, and one cat had been corralled for a long journey.

Earther and Windom had extracted their wives from the corrupt police station where they were being held. Darryl wasn't sure how long it would be before they were discovered and decided to give the police a combination of things from the bush that would leave them unconscious for over thirty-six hours.

Windom's wife indicated that the blonde deputy touched her in places reserved for him. Darryl didn't know of the admission and, therefore, was blindsided when Windom went into the cell and began to beat the man mercilessly. Darryl and Isaiah entered the cell and attempted to pull the man off the officer, and it took a blow to the kidney from Earther to stop the attack.

Darryl screamed, "What the hell are you doing. I didn't authorize you to do that. Are you now working on your own without my input? What's going on?"

"That guy touched my wife in places kept for me."

Darryl yelled, "And, therefore, you placed another beef on top of the problems we already have? I can't assume the risks that come with you. You've placed us all in danger and have compromised this entire mission."

"What would you do if he had assaulted Sue Lyn?"

"The same fricken thing you did, but I would have told those in charge what I was about to do. Listen, my uncle has taught me one thing, and that is people can't operate independently if they're a part of a group. You went out of bounds, came back in, and assaulted an officer of the law. We have a significant issue behind us and now you've put one in front of us. The one behind us will never be unearthed, hopefully. So, I'm left with the mission of deciding the fates of two men. I don't like violence, but I will employ it. You've forced my hand and I must now terminate these two people which will broaden the investigation and eventually catch up to us. You can resolve this issue by confessing and, therefore, covering the group with immunity. When in a group and you go outside to do a deed, then you're no longer a part of that group, especially if it wasn't sanctioned by the group."

Windom looked around the room at those who were present and realized that they came to help him, and he had just defecated on them. He looked at his wife and walked over to her and said something in a language that Darryl and the others didn't understand. She nodded, and he turned away. Windom said, "I've violated rules based upon emotions and, therefore, I must stand tall and accept the outcome."

Darryl said, "Forget all that macho bullshit, I just need to know that you'll never, ever, go it alone without consulting me, your handler and friend. I would cut his head off if he touched Sue Lyn. But this is a group and I've been appointed leader. I assure you my uncle is going to measure us on every level and following instructions is huge on his list. He's going to ask us to detail what happened and if you try to cover up this thing, you're done. You will absolutely and completely be discharged from the circle. This happened, and we must acknowledge it. Windom, don't do no dumb shit again, or I will personally conclude your non-complying life."

CHAPTER EIGHT

At 0900 hours, Sue Lyn, Darryl, Isaiah, and Desmond entered the bank that held the deeds to the properties of the accompanying families and demanded to see their loan documents. They were told the timetable had passed for negotiating a new loan and that payment in full was due on all the properties.

Sue Lyn looked at the woman and said, "How much do they pay you to destroy people's lives and dreams? The way you look, I wouldn't think it's very much. I'd like to see the balances for the following properties." She gave the woman a list of the properties.

A bank executive interceded and said, "I'm sorry, but judgement has been passed on these properties. Is there anything else we can help you with?"

Sue Lyn proclaimed, "As a matter of fact, yes! I need the number to the banking examiner in this region as well as the Securities and Exchange Commission, along with the FBI, CIA, State Police, and the Attorney General. We want to make settlement on the properties on the list that I gave you and you're denying us the right to do so."

The executive looked at his options and realized that a lot of people were going to go down in this deal and that he didn't want to be one of them.

After an hour of locating documents and making calls, the executive provided all eight loan documents, and Sue Lyn handed him her American Express Card. When presented with the card, the executive said, "You're not going to be able to pay off these balances with a credit card."

Sue Lyn said, "I want to pay off each loan with this card. Let's start the process and see how far we get."

Forty-eight minutes later, eight properties were settled and presented with a zero balance. Sue Lyn said, "I guess American Express is larger than the people who control this bank. That was our primary issue, we'll be back with a secondary offer in a few weeks, meanwhile, some of you might want to obtain some slick, New York style lawyers, to represent you in court. Thank you and have a wonderful day!"

The group left the bank, got into the van and Isaiah drove down the road. He pulled off to the shoulder after a few minutes and everyone in the van cheered.

Darryl said, "Sue Lyn, you truly know how to manage our business. Your father, uncle, and my uncle, will be pleased to learn of your performance."

Darryl reached over and kissed her and said, "I love you so very much."

Several miles down the road, a red pick-up truck approached from the opposite direction, it was Earther and Windom. They immediately made a U-turn and followed the van. Windom called Darryl and asked how it went and was told that his property is free and clear and that there were no liens on any of the eight plots of land. Darryl said, "If I were you, I would call my uncle and tell him on behalf of your family and friends, you thank him or something like that."

Windom said, "We're going to overtake you, so just follow us."

Twenty minutes later, the pickup truck pulled off the road onto what seemed like land without a road. They made their way through small creeks, caverns, and finally pulled into a hollow area surrounded by small mountains.

When everyone got out of their vehicles, Earther said, "This is too good to be true. What will we owe you and how can we repay you?"

Darryl looked at the families that owned the eight properties and said, "My uncle, Sergeant Ben Beckmire, almost ordered the demise of Earther and Windom. He listened to their plight and how they got pulled into this never-ending battle with his cousin. My uncle and his associates are good people and always have strings attached to everything that they do."

Heads dropped and Earther said, "I told you this was too good to be true."

Darryl said, "I believe my uncle talked to you about a percentage that left you in control of your property. The 5% allows us to operate on your behalf. Now, would you like to know what the strings are?"

There was silence and he said, "The strings are simple. Every time you see a person in need, you should try to help them. If you find a homeless person, you should try to give them shelter even if it means opening your home to strangers. My friends, those are the only strings attached to what has happened. We did good by you, and you must do good by others. Now, some of you might want to go home, but I don't advise that until we've cleaned up your town. Once the mayor exposes his comrades in the morning, Earther and Windom, your families will have to board a plane that should be landing about now and head for the security of my home, because my bad uncle is going to come looking for you and your family. Get your children out of here asap and be prepared to leave with only the clothes on your back. Sue Lyn is going to give each of you a $10,000 debit card. Now, those of you who are left, I strongly suggest you stay in these hills. I would not suggest that you go back to your homes. As a matter of fact, get in touch with your family members and have them meet you at the airport where there are lots of cameras. Don't go home for a picture or your dog. We'll find someone to collect the pets in a day or so. If you go home, you will probably be murdered after the ex-mayor exposes his comrades. Go to the airport, park your vans in front. We'll have you board the earliest flight leaving Red Wing. We'll route you to the west coast initially and then you'll board a commercial flight to my home. I will not tell you where my home is because of security reasons. Do any of you have passports?"

A man who had not been properly introduced said, "We all have passports and all of the sacred papers that we own. That is all we have along with a few dollars."

Sue Lyn said, "Listen, if we get you out of here safely, your lives are going to change significantly. His uncle and my uncle will be there to assist you financially. You will own the rights to that pipeline because the only other option is to build next to that lake, and that ain't going to happen. Your homes as you remember, will probably never be visited by you again. We'll have someone pack up your places and put your things in storage, out of town. Listen, the bottom line is that you guys

are going to become very, very rich, and I'm talking hundreds
of millions of dollars. That pipeline can't divert east or west
without costing billions of dollars. We have a smart team of
lawyers who can help you. Do you have any Native American
lawyers you trust, and if so, discuss this amongst yourselves
and let us know down the road? I just want to echo Darryl's
caution to you that these are some very bad people. Please do
not go home, go to the airport and we'll get you out of here
safely."

CHAPTER NINE

The sorority sisters checked out of the compound in St. Thomas which made 'The Sanctuary' available. Darryl thought it would be easier to get his group to the Island first and then bring them back to the mainland then out to the Midwest or Virginia. He knew that for full safety, Australia was his best bet. In total, including children, the final number of people being displaced was 40. When Darryl realized the total number, he asked Sue Lyn, "Can we accommodate this many people in 'The Sanctuary'?"

Sue Lyn said, "We should head for Australia because I'm not ready to tell my father I'm pregnant because your sperm was aimed at my love zone, even though you never penetrated me. He'll hate me for a day or so, but he might try to kill you. My dad is somewhat of a madman when it comes to me."

"Honey, I never violated my promise to him. I got excited and tried to aim for your stomach, but I lost all consciousness and shot my best load upon your amazing zone. I am so sorry, but I'm also happy because we're going to have our own child. I, after trying to convince your father and uncle that I've never penetrated you, according to the rules that were laid out, will deal with them one-on-one in a manner that is respectful, yet humble. Oh, shit, we could have you examined by a doctor who could confirm you've never been penetrated."

Sue Lyn yelled, "Stop! I'm no virgin. I had sex when I was 13."

Darryl looked at her and said, "Okay! Is there anything else you want me to know?"

"I love you, but I don't want you to be 'tricked' into a marriage because of a fetus," Sue Lyn responded.

"Okay. How about getting into a marriage because you are loved, admired, pregnant, and wanted by a very unassuming individual. I love you and I'm ready to be your mate, husband, friend, a father, and lover until the day I die. Is that enough to sway you to my side?"

Sue Lyn ran to him and hugged him tightly and said, "I must tell you what happened and then you decide."

"Sue Lyn, I can't control the past, any more than we can control the future. The past is prologue. I'm only interested in consummating a relationship with the woman I love. Hey, no one knows me like you do. No one respects me like you do and, furthermore, I don't give a hoot about what people say or think. I love Sue Lyn and hope like hell that she loves me."

# # #

In sunny St. Thomas, the Sarge, Jong, Michael, and Mallory were deep in conversation. The Sarge said to Jong, "That jet is not going to be big enough to carry forty people."

Jong replied, "Sarge, I didn't send our jet, I rented a charter from the people who supply basketball, football, and baseball teams with planes. According to the timetable, it should be arriving in the next thirty minutes or so. I'll call your nephew and tell him to get those people together and get out of there. If those mob types are involved, they're going to probably want to make an example of someone. Have you talked to Darryl or Sue Lyn about where they're going to take them?"

"I have not. Logically, I would think he would bring them here. But I would also hope that he knows that this place has been discovered by my cousin. Let's let him make decisions and see how far they can do this task without us intervening," the Sarge recommended.

The Sarge then turned to Michael and asked, "Have you heard from your people, and if so, what's their take on what's going on?"

"Sarge, my guys follow commands. The only thing they've asked or talked to me about is borrowing some money."

"What did they do with the $5k that we gave them?"

"Darryl never gave them the money. I think he forgot, and they didn't want to ask him about money. They prefer I load up their debit cards with $500 each. Sarge, I have about $1500 in the bank."

"Damn, what do you do with your money?"

"Sarge, my dad hasn't really increased my salary."

"Michael, didn't we have an agreement with you?"

"You did Sarge. I guess it hasn't hit accounting yet."

The Sarge looked at Jong and growled. Jong announced, "Too many deals that I don't know about. And when things go wrong, you blame me. From now on, you must include me in everything that requires payment."

"I will, my brother, and I'm sorry. Now, can you send $100k to Michael's account and call Sue Lyn and tell her to remind Darryl to pay his people?"

# # #

Later in the day after all the funds had been transferred, forty family members, Earther, Windom, and six strangers boarded a rented jet. It would fly from Red Wing, Minnesota to Wyoming to get passports for those who were without them. It would refuel in Los Angeles and then make the journey to Sydney, Australia. Prior to the plane taking off, the local news was broadcasted throughout the plane. It showed the ex-mayor in some non-descript place, reading a statement to the Attorney General that indicted himself, businesses, politicians, mobsters, lawyers, and judges. After reading his statement, he limped behind a curtain and entered the rear of a van that would take him to a plane that was heading to the west coast.

When the ex-mayor entered the plane, Windom jumped up and headed in his direction. Darryl calmly said, "If you touch him, this plane will not leave the ground and you'll have to fend for yourselves. Follow my instructions or leave the plane."

Earther grabbed him slightly by the hand and whispered something in their native tongue. Isaiah stood up and said, "We're in this boat together because we have a common enemy, it appears to me. What happened yesterday, is prologue."

Sue Lyn clapped her hands and said, "Some of you have passports, and others don't. This is going to be a tricky ride and I need people acting like they love each other. If we leave you here, you will be hunted down like wild dogs by the mob. The ex-mayor made his confession and things are going to start like a down-hill roller coaster ride—fast. These feelings will pass, or we will have problems. All the properties are secured in your names, and you have your titles. If nothing else, be thankful that people can't steal your property, and that a helluva lot of people are going to go down from this attempt to swindle you out of your land. Once this thing is in the air, have a drink and we'll figure out how to co-exist."

The ex-mayor was isolated with his family in the rear of the plane, but there seemingly was a budding relationship that would create a problem or be a blessing. One of the mayor's sons caught the eyes of one of Windom's daughters. They attempted to act as if they were antagonistic towards each other until the ex-mayor's son Daniel stood up and yelled, "I'm in love with Mysteir, Mr. Windom's daughter and she loves me."

The ex-mayor stood up and asked, "What the hell are you talking about?"

"Dad, I've been, fortunately, and secretly dating Mysteir for over a year and I want to marry her. Mr. Windom, you, and my father can either sanction the relationship or miss out on two people who love each other. We will leave this plane right now and take our chances, but I'm not going to let hatred, racism, and some disgusting deal keep us apart. Get with the game or we're out of here."

The ex-mayor said, "Sit your ass down, and shut the hell up."

"Really Dad? I make an announcement, and you tell me to sit my ass down. I'm a man and she's a woman, and we will not be treated like children. If that's your answer, then we're out of here and don't try to contact me."

The ex-mayor's wife whispered something in his ear and told him that if he didn't sit his ass down, that she too was going to miss this ride.

Windom looked at his daughter and said, "So, this is what you've been doing at the library. I'm happy you found someone with big enough balls to publicly state his emotions. I'm happy for you, my darling."

Darryl yelled, "Are we good? Can we get out of here?" There was no reply which signaled to him that everything was kosher.

Just prior to giving the pilot authorization to take-off, Darryl's phone rang, and it was Jong who asked, "What is your course of action?"

Darryl said, "Mr. Jong, so nice to hear from you. Do you want to talk to Sue Lyn?"

"I know her phone number. What is your plan?"

"Mr. Jong, we've loaded the families on the plane, along with one of the perpetrators of the scheme. I've decided to head to the west coast with an interim stop in the Midwest to get a few passports, and then home. This way, my family can protect all of them, and they can learn to leave the past in the past. I would be remiss if I didn't tell you that your niece is expecting a child, and I'm the father, although by default. It's a long story and by the time you guys see us, we'll be legally married. Hello, hello, I can't hear you." Darryl hung up the phone and signaled to the pilot to get them out of there.

Prior to take-off, Daniel said, "I would like for Mysteir to sit next to me. Is there a problem with that request?" There were no comments made and her father secretly winked at her and gave his blessing.

CHAPTER TEN

A significant number of hours later, the rented plane, stopped in Wyoming and addressed the passport issue. Later, the flight would stop in Los Angeles, refuel for the long ride to Sydney, and eventually land in the Northern Territory.

# # #

Almost a day later, the beleaguered group woke up and realized they had traveled halfway around the world. There was complete ambivalence throughout the group because the initial connection was to figure out ways to kill the Beckmire clan, and now they were amongst his clan in a strange land, with strange people, customs, and animals that they had never seen before.

On the other side of the world, Jong had the difficult task of calling his cousin to inform him that his precious baby girl, was pregnant, but not through penetration. He also informed him that by the time he saw her again, she would be a married woman. He told Jong that he wanted to be there when his daughter marries that pirate. He also asked Jong how a person can become pregnant from anything less than penetration, and

Jong told him that he would let his son-in-law to be, explain that one.

His cousin called his daughter and told her he forbade her to marry without him and her mother being in attendance. She commiserated and forced Darryl to forget about marriage in his land where the customs were different, but the meanings were symbolic and pure.

The members of Michael's team prematurely gathered and appointed Isaiah and Desmond as their mouth pieces. Isaiah asked, "Darryl, do you think I could have a word with you?"

"Of course, what's up?"

"Me and the guys are short of cash. Actually, we're not running short, we're on empty."

Darryl froze for a moment and realized he had not attended to business in relationship to the men who were assigned to protect him and Sue Lyn. He yelled, "Oh shit! Isaiah, I apologize for not placing you and the team ahead of everything else. I got carried away with our ability to extract everyone from that place with minimum exposure and casualties. Do you guys have bank accounts or debit cards?"

Isaiah went on to tell Darryl that they're poor people and live paycheck to paycheck when they could get one, and that by the time it got processed, it was empty, and service charges were placed on the accounts.

Darryl laughed and said, "Get the other guys and huddle around because I want to tell you guys something."

A few minutes later when Jasper, Isaiah, Desmond, Harold, Earther, and Windom were all together, Darryl said, "I like the way you do business and I know, anyone of you could lead this group because, after all, I'm slightly younger than you guys. However, it's my family and they have elected me. Let me say this and I'll never mention it again. If you do as you're asked and carryout assignments efficiently, you will make a shitload of money and that, I guarantee you. Between her uncle and my uncle, you guys have a chance of joining a team that looks out for its people. Watch my back, protect my woman, and our new friends, and I will make sure you'll never have to steal food again. How much do you need, or better still, these debit cards are balanced to $5k. Do you need more than that until we get situated and open accounts for you guys?"

Isaiah asked, "So, this card is worth five thousand dollars and all I have to do is go to any bank machine and ask for money?"

"Not quite that simple, but close enough. You'll have to enter a four-digit code, which will be indigenous to you, to retrieve funds and check on your balance. I wouldn't suggest that you take it all out at once and walk around with $5k in your pockets. Someone might try to take advantage of you. Listen, when we get to my home, we're going to go shopping first thing and buy you guys some real clothes for a real place that can be unforgiving if you don't know what you're doing or where you're going, or what is a safe to touch and eat, and, what is not. I'm figuring it's going to cost about a grand a person, so we're looking at spending about $5k on clothes."

Desmond asked, "What about weapons?"

"Long guns and shotguns are okay, but if you get caught with a pistol then you're facing a long jail sentence. We have rifles and shotguns, but we also have pistols for you guys when we're moving quickly."

The captain called Darryl and said, "I have a news feed from Minnesota that concerns your people. You want me to broadcast it?"

"By all means. Let me give them a heads-up."

The news was graphic and showed people of stature including judges, politicians, lawyers, and bankers, being summarily arrested, and led from their palatial homes into the back of police cars. The newscaster said that a warrant was issued for the sheriff and ex-mayor who had been seen leaving town in a black SUV. Police and state troopers were on the lookout for them and their families. The newscaster also stated that according to bank officials and records, the eight families whose homes were located along the path of the proposed pipeline had disappeared as well, with the deeds to their properties. He also said, those properties were going to be worth millions upon millions of dollars. He even floated the notion that they should never sell their land but lease it to the highest bidder.

In the back of the plane near the shitter, the ex-mayor and his family sat quietly. His son was in the middle of the cabin with Mysteir, and they were happy they no longer had to hide in the shadows of the library and church to communicate with each other. She told him she was proud of the way he handled his father and how he asked her father for permission to date her openly.

In the front of the plane, Darryl was about to have a staff meeting when he realized that Windom and Earther were not present. He walked back and asked Windom, "Can you and Earther attend a meeting, so that we can decide whether you want to be fat rich guys or rich guys who help people and stop the kind of thing that almost happened to you."

Windom said, "We'll be right there, Boss."

When the two men arrived in the front of the plane, Darryl said, "I'm suggesting you guys hide out for the next few months in my home where I can protect you from any fallout until we're sure we have all of the culprits in custody. It's going to take a while before you'll be able to realize any real benefits from your properties. I would not suggest you go and borrow against your properties, without checking with my uncle and his crew first. They're honest people and are the reasons the eight families will be able to see benefits for themselves, their children, grandchildren, and other relatives. However, this is not what this meeting is about. Me, Sue Lyn, and my guys will have to make our way back to the states in a few weeks or so. You'll have plenty to do while you're here and you'll be protected by animals, my people, and the 'Great Saltie'. I'm going to need your skills to help me, or us, find my uncle, the bad one. He's hired a significant force to make sure this time when he comes for us, the only person left alive will be him and his people. He will kill the children and the women last, but I assure you, he will kill them. He's also going to come hunting for the eight families. That deal had his signature all over it, and he is probably so mad right now he'll eat your heart if he comes across you. In Australia, there are many forces, much like there are in your hood. Evil is hard to manifest itself here once its meaning has been established. My bad uncle is unable to come home."

Earther said, "I feel like I owe you and your people a lot. We came to provide intel on you that could have led to your deaths. You spared our lives, paid off our loans, you smuggled us out of the country, and you gave us money to live on. This is unheard of. What I do challenge you on, however, is why you won't let me kill that asshole of an ex-mayor?"

Darryl laughed and said, "Trust me, I'm over it. How about you Windom?"

"I'm with you. He has no place to hide, he saw what happened to the sheriff, he knows the mob guys are looking for him and his family. He's harmless and not a threat to us. Killing has its moments, but he would be a senseless kill," Windom stated.

Darryl brought the conversation back to focus when he said, "If you help us catch and kill my bad uncle then we'll help you with your next mission in life and that's to help people help themselves. You won't understand it until you have more money than you can physically count, and you'll see people who will genuinely need your help. You'll know, and we'll let you join our gang to help the good and eliminate the bad."

Windom said, "Earther said it best, 'you helped us and we want to help you, so we're in'."

"This meeting was important because as soon as we disembark from this plane, people will send signals to my uncle about their perception of who is in charge. It's an old Aborigine game and strategy."

CHAPTER ELEVEN

In St. Thomas, the main force trained twice a day for an hour plus. In a single week, the Sarge had dropped ten pounds and looked more menacing than he had in a long time. Jilkes and John Lee continued to set the bar high in terms of strength and stamina. Larry, Zanthius, and Mike were still the fastest members of the group, but Bernstein and Brown were 1/2 minute behind their fastest time in the mile.

Around lunch time, Michael sought out the Sarge and told him that ten strangers, fitting the description of mercs, had landed and were all staying at the Frenchman's Reef Resort. He asked Michael, "Can you get any intelligence on them?"

"So far, what I know is they all have altered passports. What's up with that? People must think our officials hear are retarded. Our local customs officials are going to raid their rooms once they've all been accounted for. Seems like another surveillance or direct assault from your cousin. What I can't figure out is, why would he attempt to come to a place where the laws are so strict about guns?

"Sarge, do you believe in Samurai? It was said they all had long tubes with them. If that were the case, they would completely escape the gun issue. I'm concerned, Sarge, I know you know how to handle your business, but these guys might be the real deal. You might want to have your people add the .380s as a part of their wardrobe."

"Michael, this is exactly why I didn't want you to go north with my nephew. I told you I needed you here and look at the intel you have given me. Is there any way to extract one or two of them from their hotel?"

"Sarge if I had my crew with me, it would be an easy process."

"What if I sent you with my crew? Do you think you could get us in and out of the property with a couple of these guys?"

"Sarge, who would you send?"

"How about John Lee and Jilkes with Gladstone and McArthur watching from afar?"

"I don't know how you work, but if that's your choice, then I'm okay with it. I assume we all should pack. What's your take on that?" Michael asked.

"My guys will always have a weapon on them. I need you to watch them and learn. They are precise. When they commit to an action, it's done with the full force of their wrath, no second guessing. Just watch them and learn. Don't be afraid to ask them questions."

"Sarge, are your people really that good, or are you all having flashbacks from yesteryear?"

"Michael, I could put those two up against your entire group and they would come out on top. They can smell shit from ten miles away, and hear noises that the average person wouldn't hear, and see things that impact our missions. Your people probably would not hear, see, or smell shit until it was pulling the trigger on their asses. Watch these guys, learn from them, and more importantly, listen to their chatter. It could save your life. Let me summon them. I suggest that you carry as well. I don't know the mission of those arriving on the island and, therefore, anything, and I do mean anything, is possible."

"Sarge, do you mind if I ask you a question about your team?"

"You may ask, but I'm not guaranteeing a response."

"What made them so fearless, destructive, and resilient?"

"Son, when you're thrown into an event that is called a 'Police Action', and in the end, 58,000 people are dead, you want to make sure that you're not in that body count. My people were scared, they didn't know or trust each other, didn't like each other, and literally, wanted out of the unit. Once they learned that they needed each other, the dynamics changed for the good, although, it took a fight between Jilkes and John Lee to solidify the group. John Lee called Jilkes the "N" word and Jilkes pulverized his ass. He beat John Lee into submission, but John Lee thinks that he beat Jilkes. He was delusional for a while, but Jilkes, on our runs, wouldn't let him fall behind. They built a bond that one might consider demonized. If you attempt to assault one, then the other would do dastardly things to you. Their bond is the strongest sign of love that I've ever seen between two men. You insult one, then be prepared to feel the wrath of the other. You hurt one, oh, geez, you had better leave mother earth. My own guys won't meddle in their conversations."

"That tight, eh?"

"Michael, I'd rather tell Jesus he was wrong than get in the middle of their squabbles. I mean it's just that serious."

"Thanks for the heads-up. I will study them and, hopefully, pick up some pointers. We never had your kind of experience and deployment. I've heard so much about you guys, I'm not sure what's fact or fiction? I mean like, you entering the enemy's camp and killing eight guys without a gun because you were out of bullets. If I consider all the hyperbole, you people must have killed over a thousand people, and that ain't possible."

The Sarge looked at him and said, "Rookies count, real men try to survive and keep their friends safe and sound. I wouldn't put too much credibility on rumors about us, but I will say to you, when we die and go to hell, there will probably be more than a thousand souls waiting to torment us. That number is not even conservative. Anyway, apparently, your boys are doing okay with my nephew, and they're beginning to bond and make headway. He took Windom, Earther, and their families, along with the members of the other families that share those rich lands, to Australia. There he could provide maximum protection until the people who need to run the pipeline, make a real and incredible offer to them, and I do mean unbelievable, in the hundreds of millions of dollars. Those guys are going to be left there and even that ex-mayor will be used. We need some new laws passed for the Aborigine and, he's not a total jerk, he does know how to argue a good case. We checked his background before we decided to spare his life and found out that there might be some utility in keeping him alive and taking him to Australia. Get with Jilkes and John Lee and prepare to extract a couple of those guys."

#

It was 0315 in the morning when three of the ten men staggered back to their hotel rooms. Unbeknownst to the group, the customs authorities had seven of their group in custody. The other three were easy targets and were easily subdued by tranquilizers darts. When they were being transported to a place near 'The Sanctuary', John Lee woke up one of the guys with a broken stick of ether and said, "Boy, you be fucked up. You know where you be?"

The guy looked around and tried to make sense of his surroundings, only to realize that his friends were out like a light. He tried to speak, but his words were confusing to him as well as John Lee and the others. Jilkes fallaciously asked, "What brings you people to St. John?"

John Lee flatly stated that they were on St. Thomas. Jilkes looked at him and John Lee uttered, "My bad."

Jilkes looked at the guy again and asked, "What brings you guys down here and who sent you with those bogus passports? Now, before you answer, I got to tell you about the consequences of telling a lie. If you lie, he will cut some part of your body off. Now, you might think it's a part of your pinky finger, or something small like that, but I'm here to tell you that the butcher likes to cut away a man's procreation area first and then work small. So, here are my questions. What's your mission? Who sent you? Are there others on the way? Now, can you answer those questions truthfully, and will the others corroborate your story once we separate you guys and begin our disembowelment shit?"

The groggy guy stated, "I don't have the foggiest idea what the hell you're talking about. Who are you people, and why are you holding us? We're with the government and we're here on official business."

"What's your business here?"

"We have specific information that someone is trying to set this place up as a terminal for illicit substances. Now, before this goes too far, I suggest you find a way to revive my friends and tell us who the fuck you are. We're all agents. What's your status?"

Jilkes asked, "Is there any way you can prove that?"

"Asshole, I don't have to prove a fucking thing to you. We represent the United States of America Government and have credentials to prove it. I sincerely hope you or those people from customs, haven't blown our cover based upon doctored passports? You and your people have just conspired to disrupt an investigation by the United States Department of State. In other words, you're in deep dodo! Who on earth did you think we were, and who the hell is on your coattail?"

Jilkes said, "Shut the hell up. I have to make a call and ascertain what we do with your bodies."

"Really? Please tell me what the rest of the government is going to do about bringing justice to people who killed their agents?"

Jilkes walked away and called the Sarge. He told him they may have made a mistake and that these guys work for the government in an interdiction capacity.

The Sarge inquired, "Do you trust me?"

"Why on earth would you ask me a dumb question like that. After all we've been through?"

The Sarge exclaimed, "I need you to follow my orders! That's right, my orders. I need you to turn around and go back to where that slick tongue person is trying to baffle you and shoot him in the damn foot. Don't talk, just blow his foot off."

"Sarge, are you sure?"

"I gave you an order, soldier. I will not repeat it."

Jilkes yelled, "Yes Sir." He walked back into the room and withdrew his weapon.

The guy who was tied up said, "I need to make a statement."

Jilkes said, "Too fucking late, hustler." He shot the man in his right foot. He listened to the man's screams and said, "You know what, I was beginning to believe you and that makes me sad."

John Lee walked in and placed his pistol on the guys left foot and said, "You hoodwinked my friend. This is going to hurt." He shot the guy in the left foot and said, "You be starting to bleed out."

He looked at Jilkes and said, "Let's both shoot him in his knees at the same time. We ain't never did that before."

"Stop, please stop." He yelled. The noise and screams woke up the other two guys who looked bewildered when they saw the guys feet and knew they were in trouble.

Jilkes said, "I hope you remember the three questions I asked you. Because if not, we're going to place rounds in your knees."

"Sir, I need a doctor."

Jilkes said, "Wrong fucking answer!" He pulled the trigger. It was no longer aimed at his knee; he placed the weapon to the man's head and blew a hole in it. He looked at the dead man's companions and said, "I hate being hustled and this motherfucker had me eating his horseshit. Now, you guys have a choice, tell us what we need to know, or you'll end up just like that asshole—with a hole in your head. John Lee, you take that guy and question him and I'll keep this one here so that he can look at his friend before he answers me and realize that we don't play games and then we'll compare notes."

Twelve or so minutes later, John Lee came back with the person he was questioning. He saw Gladstone, McArthur, and Michael who threw his shoulders in the air to suggest he was concerned about the gun shots he had heard. John Lee looked towards Michael and said, "They got the message—one dead and two to go!"

Jilkes asked the guy who he was with, what was the most important thing to him on earth? The guy told him that it was his two sons. Jilkes asked, "Then why are you playing this merc game. You know your President is considering having mercs complete the war in Afghanistan. Did you have any idea who we were and what we've done? Did anyone tell you we've killed more people than the plague?"

The guy told Jilkes his youngest son needed an experimental drug for arthritis, and he needed to figure a way to obtain it. He told Jilkes he was without any health insurance since the current President repealed parts of the Affordable Care Act, better known as Obama Care. Jilkes asked him what drug would work the best for his son and was told that Embrel or Humara were the likely candidates. Jilkes told him he would spare his life and provide health care for him and his family if he could find a way to pinpoint where the mastermind of this event was. The guy looked at Jilkes and asked him who is the hustler now? Jilkes told him he could make that happen, and more importantly and currently, not waste a bullet on his head.

John Lee returned with his captive and said, "I like this guy. I don't want to kill him. He gave me some credible intel, but I'll leave it up to you. Your man be smarter than the dead man?"

"He's light years ahead of that guy. Where is Michael? I think it's fish feeding time. Now, insofar as you two are concerned, this is going to be a really touching moment. I don't know how you explain your actions, but we're going to let you guys live. I'm also going to give you a number to remember. You have an option with the number, you can use it to help us manage an assault, or you can destroy it. If we encounter you again, your fate will be worse than meeting the devil in a poker game. You will never see those you love again, or you might be able to stand over our bodies and ask, "how you like us now"? I'm looking for a little humanity, the same sort of thing that we're offering you. Give us a drop or a half bottle but give us something if you can without endangering your own lives. You must make up your own notions about your friend. All we can say is he's dead, and we'll see him in hell when we get there."

One of the captives said, "I'm not sure about the authenticity of this comment, but I overhead someone say the final assault will be conducted on the island. I walked by a room and the person who uttered those words never saw me. I know what I heard. I am thinking they're going to rain their fire on this place. Can I substantiate that? I can't. I just know what I heard. Oh, and by the way, there was only one goal— eliminate anyone and everyone associated with your group. That was accentuated and specifically spelled out and defined. It meant every living person associated with your group."

Jilkes said, "We've heard that before and watched him place suicide vests on our children. The one problem is that we're going to be the aggressors. He can't deploy everywhere in the world."

The other captive said, "He won't have to after he completes his ownership papers of those diamond mines in Australia."

Jilkes and John Lee both looked at the guy intently, and Jilkes asked, "What the hell does that mean?"

"Apparently, the leader has or will have ownership of diamond mines in Australia. The surviving members of the assault will have the results of what is called, in what I consider medieval times, a tontine relationship meaning the more people that die, the more substantial the insurance payment or ownership becomes to the survivors. It's an English thing, but more financial advisors and insurance companies are investigating the utility of the notion."

John Lee asked, "What is that there tontine?"

Jilkes said, "I'll explain it to you later. Trust me, it only works if you plan on killing your family, and if a child dies you name the new child the same name to make sure that you're still in the running. Listen, last man standing, gets all of the benefits."

John Lee said, "Now, that sounds like some really sick shit."

"I'm not so sure it is sick, but I do believe that in the past, it was the primary reason that people killed each other to move up the chain. I hear some large and respectful firms are investigating the utility of it, and large business schools are doing the math on the process to see if it's worth another experiment," Jilkes stated.

Jilkes looked at the guy who mentioned diamond mines and asked, "How do you know about diamond mines in Australia?"

"Mr. Walter is a very convincing man. He's not paying us in paper, he's offering us shares of the diamond mines that were found on the land of his ancestors and according to tribal customs, he is, and his family are, automatically provided thirty-five percent ownership which gives him the ability to have a major say in the discovery, extraction, and elimination of the other members of the tribe. Listen, I'm trying to sell life insurance for me and him. I don't want my feet shot, and then a bullet to the head. I'm giving you information that I heard but can't attest to the validity of it. I would sell my soul if it would let me see my family one more time."

John Lee looked at him and said, "That's a mighty big and final option. If you be telling the truth, then I'll buy some chips for you. If you be trying to deceive me then I'll gut you from your dick to your brain and take a bite out of your heart before you die. Now, do you still want to sell your soul?"

"Sold! I, know what I've told you is the truth."

Jilkes thought about the mines and called John Lee into a huddle. He asked, "If we're looking for someone to hit us here, and we just unfolded diamond mines in Australia, where do you think the emphasis would be?"

"I'd be focusing on the diamonds. Oh shit, I see where you be going with this one. They done sent these here fellows down here to distract us while he goes to Australia and slaughters everyone including those kids. You be one smart African American and I just respect how you figure this shit out, and how you make me smarter by making me think outside of the bag."

"John Lee, it's outside of the box."

"Why you be trying to correct me all the time? A bag or box, what be the difference? They both supposed to hold shit. I be correct on this one, right?"

"Listen, I'm not correcting you. I'm just providing you with additional information to make your arguments and statements a little more precise. Most people don't understand the way you talk. Therefore, I try to make what you say a little more understandable. I'm not picking on your country ass way of talking. I'm just trying to interpret and translate your back-country language."

# # #

Jilkes called the Sarge and told him that after interrogating the two captives, he believed that there was going to be a massive strike in the Northern Territory.

The Sarge said, "I've been feeling an emotional moment that is causing me issues relative to the outback. Legally, he doesn't stand a chance to accomplish anything such as a take-over. I must check with Monica and Luana to see if they did due diligence. I need you people to make sure you leave no traces behind that will connect us, but the call on the people who remain, is yours. No unnecessary terminations."

The Sarge was drinking with Courtney, Monica, Mallory, and Zanthius. After digesting the information from Jilkes, he nervously yelled, "I need every person capable of firing a weapon to be ready to leave this place in one hour."

He looked at Mallory and said, "I've put my nephew and Jong's niece in jeopardy. Get us out of here in an hour, Corporal. I need you to do this. Those guys who came here are a distraction. My cousin is after the diamonds. He's going to kill everything and everyone in sight."

Zanthius entered his room and said to Asiram, "We're heading back to Australia."

Her head dropped, and she said to him, "I'm not going anywhere. I'm tired of running. I'm not going on this trip."

Zanthius slowly moved towards Asiram and said, "Okay if you're not going, then I'm not going. You're my wife and I must consider you. However, can you tell me what has you in such a funk?"

"Jackass, I think I'm pregnant again!" Zanthius let out a scream that could be heard all the way to Australia. He screamed for five minutes and when his father, mother, and stepmother turned the corner to their suite, and after Ben Beckmire kicked the door from its hinges, Zanthius yelled out of the window, "Asiram is pregnant! Asiram is pregnant! My wife is pregnant again!"

Courtney and Ava walked over to Asiram who was crying. Ava said, "Girl, I didn't like you at first because, as you'll learn, no one's good enough for your babies. I also watched too many James Bond movies where the gorgeous spy always seduces and murders her mark. I just want to say this, I'm so damn happy that you're pregnant. This is the best news I've heard in a long time, plus you saved his life on many occasions. I love you Asiram Beckmire De Lombardo." Ava started kissing her and began to cry as well.

Courtney said, "Hey, can you get out of the way so that I can get and give some love?"

The Sarge said, "Congratulations, Son!"

Zanthius pulled his father into the hallway and said, "Asiram said that she is not making the trip to Australia."

"Son, that is where your work begins. I need you both on the ground with me in the Northern Territory. I can't risk leaving you behind because you might be captured. Our strength is when we have our team together. You need to make this happen now because a lot of innocent people are going to be murdered."

The Sarge gathered Ava and Courtney and said, "I need you ladies to make things happen because I'm shy four of my men. Has anyone seen Jong?"

Courtney said, "Look on the beach and you'll find him and the wife playing in the surf."

"Zanthius, I need you to complete that mission, Son!"

After everyone left the doorless room, Asiram said, "Wow, I love those two ladies so much. They don't bite their tongues! They just say what comes to their minds. Listen, we're a team, right? I mean you and me, and I love you and hopefully, you love me. We're also a family, and our family has been called away, once again. I'm not clairvoyant, I didn't know how you were going to react about the news, and I went on defense in case I had to kill your ass."

"Asiram, I want as many kids as you think we can handle. We have a permanent extended family, and that means lots of babysitters. My dad was concerned but told me to get to work and fix this issue. Anyhow, we stay packed just like the rest of the group. We have plenty of debit cards and credit cards. I can't think of anything else."

# # #

When the Sarge found Jong, he said "We have a situation in Australia and your niece, and my nephew are in danger. My cousin used those guys as decoys to mount an activity in Australia where he'll kill every living thing. I need you guys on board with this. Is there a problem?"

"Sarge, we were just talking about how happy we both are that she's pregnant again."

"What? OMG! Asiram is pregnant as well. Anyway, we'll celebrate on the plane. Oh, is the plane ready?"

"Sarge, the plane is always ready, fueled, and with double pilots. Talking about planes, the new one will be ready in two weeks," Jong stated.

"Good work, my brother. I don't know what I would do without you guys. I mean I love you people so much," the Sarge said.

## CHAPTER TWELVE

On the long ride from St. Thomas to Sydney, Australia, the Sarge began to read the Economist newspaper and ran across an article that enraged him and made him sad. It talked about clauses in the Australian constitution that excluded Aborigines from the census. He remembered his grandfather telling him how so few conquered an entire continent. The basic principle for mounting the Queen's flag on a land was simple; if the inhabitants did not look European; did not use alleged proper utensils while dining, did not dress like Europeans, and could not speak the Queen's language or the other conquering tongues, then the lands were up for grabs. So, few Europeans conquered Australia because the Aborigines were tribal and wouldn't ban together to run the invaders out.

The Sarge flashed to modern times and thought how little had changed. Aborigines are trying to be mentioned in the constitution and acknowledged as the first Australians. He recognized that the Aborigines were only three percent of Australia's twenty-four million people. He knew that the Aborigines occupied Australia approximately 60,000 years before the British set foot on its soil. The article also stated that Aborigines were more likely to go to prison and more likely to die early in comparison to most other Australians.

As he continued to read the article, Courtney realized that her man was crying his eyes out. She turned to him and asked, "Honey, what's going on? Why are you crying?" He gave her the article and closed his eyes.

Mallory, watching the interaction, threw his hands in the air looking for an explanation from Courtney and she held up a finger and began to read the article. Halfway through the article, Courtney began to cry and by the time she finished it, the Sarge was fully asleep. She passed the article to Mallory who felt the pain and began to cry. He gave it to Monica who started to cry immediately. She passed it on to Zanthius, and Asiram who cried, who passed it on to Larry and Marisa. When John Lee began to read the article out loud to his wife she began to cry as well as Jilkes and his wife who could hear him reading the article.

Hours later, the Sarge woke up, lightly touched Courtney's arm, and whispered in her ear, "I love you so much." She smiled and he fell back to sleep.

# # #

The plane took on fuel in Auckland, New Zealand and its next stop was the Northern Territory.

When the plane arrived in the Northern Territory, it was met by customs officials. They boarded the plane and went straight to Ben Beckmire and asked, "Sir, can you come with us?"

The Sarge gave a signal to be calm to his people and everyone watched as the Sarge exited the plane in the hangar and spoke to another official. The three men talked for about five minutes and the Sarge shook their hands and apparently thanked them.

Once back on the plane, the Sarge said, "Jilkes and John Lee, excellent intel. Apparently, there was a large contingency of people who looked like soldiers that flew in on a charter this morning. The plane was searched and nothing out of the ordinary was discovered. They are staying in town, and the customs people are watching their moves. I need our plane moved from here. We're only going to have our small caliber weapons. My guys will have high tension bow and arrows, just like we had in the Nam."

John Lee yelled, "Oh yeah, this is about to get rural."

The Sarge said, "We have our bus, and on it, ladies, you'll have those light-weight automatic rifles and plenty of ammunition. I first, want our plane out of here so those people can't sabotage it. Once we leave customs, there will be several hundred people meeting us to provide protection. I want to put those NY style jackets on our children. I know it's a little hot, but I want them secure. Any questions? Oh, by the way, don't stray away from the group ever. We're family and this is how we're going to survive this mess—by always staying close to each other. I was also told that they have a new cave for us that is closer to the billabong, but on the other side. From this one, we will be able to see people trying to come and go. If they want to do surveillance, then they had better be aware of the animals. They don't know we're here, but it won't take a rat very long to let the world know we are here. It's only a matter of time before my cousin realizes that we're here. I must contact my relatives and prepare them for this adventure. Monica and Luana, legally, are we protected from a take-over?"

Luana stood up and said, "Not if there is no one left to contest the take-over. If he kills everyone on the board, in the corporation and shareholders of record, then we're out of luck and he's in the driver's seat."

Monica asked, "Why don't we register this thing on one of the exchanges in New York and let him try to steal it in front of the entire world?"

Luana looked at her and said, "That's a brilliant idea, but it would take months to file all of the papers and, by that time, his cousin could own the mines from attrition. I think he created a tontine."

The Sarge asked, "What the hell is a tontine."

John Lee stood up and said, "I'm going to let my smart African American friend explain it to you."

Jilkes looked at him, shook his head, stood up, and said, "A tontine is an investment scheme—it's a lottery of sorts. It combines the features of a group annuity and a lottery. The last person alive enjoys the benefits of everyone who participated. Your cousin, by liquidating the board, the shareholders, and everyone else, simply becomes the owner of the mines, by default. Each dying member's shares or investments will be inherited by your cousin if he forces them to sell him their shares. I don't know all the issues involved, but I do know that a group of universities are experimenting with the formula once again. From what Luana described, your cousin is operating like these mines are a tontine—last man standing gains ownership."

Luana stated, "That's medieval chicanery. I've heard stuff about that, but I still find it hard to believe people are that obtuse."

"Listen, I'm no lawyer. It seems to me, a rookie, this is the route he's taking," Jilkes stated.

Monica said, "He's not listed on any forms as an entity. His chances of completing this deal are minimal."

The Sarge exclaimed, "He's Aborigine! His family line is infused throughout all the tribes here. Any misstep in the legal filings will be an opportunity for him. He worked for the government of the United States of America, and from what I've heard and know, he has controlled senators, congressmen, and cabinet members. My cousin is not to be underestimated. He is Diablo, and you should never think that he can't do a certain thing. He's the master of evil and will try to kill each one of us. Jilkes, you and John Lee deserve kudos. You didn't back down from the lawyers. I don't know a damn thing about tontines and, therefore, I'm happy my people read. It sure as hell is going to make me read."

Luana stood up and said, "We'll read this stuff together. I'm not sure I understand it, but I assure you, by the time we get settled, I'll be an expert."

Monica said, "That's two of us."

# # #

No one bothered to call Darryl and Sue Lyn. However, they were aware that a Beckmire had landed. When the group arrived at their new camp, it was directly behind the billabong that housed the 'Great Saltie'. The Sarge inquired, "Nephew, how the hell are you?"

"Uncle, we're good and my team has proved to be thorough and reliable. Perhaps I should say your team?"

"No, nephew. These guys are yours. Also, that plane that you like so much, will be your new method of transportation, and, as a matter of fact, we should consider getting a slightly bigger one for you and your team. I will, along with some of my guys, do a follow-up interview with these guys. The world is not pink, grey, blue, or orange. I don't easily put strangers, in proximity of my family members. Your people know that and probably understand it. Anyway, how is Sue Lyn?"

"She's fine and learning to deal with her situation. She aches, swells, throws-up, sleeps a lot and eats like a giant person. Uncle, did you come here to check on our performance?"

"Nephew, you're a man and I don't check-up on men. Your other Uncle is alleged to be mounting an assault on the mines, the board, the shareholders, lawyers, and everyone else involved in them. He sent a force to St. Thomas to distract us, but Jilkes and John Lee were able to 'carve out' information from two of their captives who felt that it was best to be on the run than to be summarily dispatched like an associate was. We must rally our people and prepare for a major incursion. I don't know how they're getting here, but from what I was told, they will be here. The last time they tried coming by ship. Can you have someone check customs, the harbor master, and ascertain if any ships are scheduled in port soon and from where?"

"Uncle, I'll have it done. Did everyone come with you?"

"Yes, Nephew, the entire gang is here, including Sue Lyn's uncle."

"Is he pissed at me, and should I avoid him at all cost?"

"Not at all. Her father is going to find his way here before you marry his daughter and I suggest that you do not plan a ceremony until you've explained what happened and he has cogitated about that notion and has given you, his permission. You will not, and let me repeat, you will not go forward with any wedding plans until you have properly requested permission from her father. If you disrespect him in this manner, you will probably have to kill him, or he'll kill you. Your choice, but I assure you, I cannot enter the fray."

"Uncle, so he's coming here?"

"*Es Stupido*—it's his daughter. Plus, who do you think she learned how to develop weapon systems from? Anyway, nice to see you and glad to know that you're okay. I'm going to need you to instruct your people that while they're here on the continent, they will have several people telling them what to do. If in fact that's a problem, then make sure they're on the first thing smoking in the morning on their way out of here."

"Uncle, did Michael make this trip?"

"Nephew, Michael is not here. I'm grooming him to be our ambassador for the islands. Why do you ask?"

"I would like to have him as a part of my team. I don't see this thing ending after you gut my other uncle and I see our mission as an on-going one, as with Earther and Windom."

The Sarge looked at him and said, "I'll consider your request, but if I agree to this, when on the island, he's still my runner. Is that something you can live with, as you create your own personal army?"

Darryl smiled and said, "It will be a righteous one and based upon the principles and the teachings of Sergeant Ben Beckmire. Now, you can take that to the bank. You and your guys are my inspiration and I want to build the same kind of commitment and loyalty with these guys. Uncle, I'm no real leader and I worry that one day my lack of experience will get me in trouble and that is why I need a Michael, much like your Mallory to help me make the right decisions."

"You're truly a Beckmire. You're so smooth and cunning." The Sarge thought out loud for a second and then belted out, "Have him catch the first thing coming this way.

Tell him to use that debit card we gave him and to get here in a hurry. I have a feeling that we're going to need everyone that we know. By the way, have you ever heard of something called a tontine?"

"Uncle, it's for crazy people who want to outlast each other and benefit from those who die before them and become the last person to reap untold riches. It's still in practice in some countries but outlawed in the United Kingdom and a few other countries. The problem with tontines is that it makes people crazy to the point they begin to commit murder, and other heinous crimes such as slowly inducing heart attacks, strokes, and delirium, all under the guise of trying to eliminate their competition. Actuarial scientists are investigating the benefits of it once again, but under a controlled environment where people don't know who the other members invested in the lottery ticket are. Why do you ask?"

"Your other uncle has somehow got the facts twisted and is using the structure to articulate who the targets are. If we're not wrong, he is going to kill everyone connected to the mines and through attrition declare himself as sole heir. The problem he faces is that the motherload is in the billabong where there are Salties who have survived bullets and time. So, in my estimation, the 'Great Saltie' will be the last entity standing and he'll have to conquer him. The stones in the billabong are sizeable but pale in comparison to the ones in the cave that are buried under this land. Just suppose he attempts to remove those from the cave and begins a mining process to extract other stones, well his problem is that the cave will become a billabong also. This, my nephew will be an unconquerable moment in time. The 'Great Saltie' has surpassed all reasonable notions of existence. Unless your uncle thinks he is an aberration, then he is in for a rude awakening. Let's just assume that he kills us all. The stones in the billabong are probably not where we placed them. Besides, creatures that defy reality live in those waters.

"Uncle, from what I've discerned about my other uncle, it's not about bangles and baubles. He must best you in every metric. Uncle Walter has resources that are derived from the US Government, drug dealings, arms smuggling, blackmail, extortion, corruption, and a whole lot of other devious schemes. He doesn't have to personally confront you. He can say that you people are abusing and mind-screwing children and the whole world will want to drop a neutron bomb on you. Apparently, you're better looking and smarter than he is. His motivation is personal. Somehow and somewhere, you bested him in a mind screwing contest. Uncle, it's all about ego."

# # #

Meanwhile, Ben Beckmire and Darryl were discussing probable causes, several container ships had docked and deported several large storage units that were filled with people, guns, and ammunition. Australia was about to participate in a dance that would leave a lot of people dead, indigenous people rallying around those on the side of right, and the animals enjoying a buffet of fresh flesh, for weeks.

CHAPTER THIRTEEN

Sydney, Australia was witnessing a high count of tourists. Hotels were half-filled, bars were at capacity, but the strange thing about these tourists, was that they were mostly white men, and some rough looking Africans who looked as though they were fresh out of the bush.

Historically, the Aborigines were clannish and less likely to come to the aid of their fellow Aborigines, ergo this divided mindset was the reason why, so few Europeans, conquered the continent. They would not band together to fight the intruders. Even in the twenty-first century, this was mostly the case when it came to matters that impacted all Aborigines.

Word had spread through the music that a significant diamond discovery had been made and that there were people heading towards the outback for the purpose of confiscating the mines. People were flying into Western Australia, Sydney, Cairns, and the Northern Territory. Darryl was made aware of the high number of mercs entering the country and heading towards the Northern Territory.

Darryl said to Sue Lyn, "You know I love you, right? And you also know that I would never hurt you, right?"

"Okay! Honey, what's up?"

"I'm getting signals and information from the bush that there is going to be a huge assault on the mines. I'm afraid to go to my uncle and tell him about my premonitions, because he might think that I am becoming power hungry. I know he believes in the mysterious things that happen here, but I'm not sure he's going to listen to me."

"Darryl, your uncle needs you. He gave you command and control. He gave you access to millions of dollars. He gave you a group to support you and a plane. If you don't go to him, then I will. They're all planning for their eventual demise. Can't you see it? Listen, they've fought many a battle and landed on the winning side. They realized that it is time for someone to die and they're wondering who it's going to be. Your uncle wants to lead the charge and spare his people, but that's not going to happen. This is about being in the wrong place at the wrong time. According to the numbers that I'm hearing, a lot of people are going to die. Darryl, perhaps you or I, might be in that number."

"Sue Lyn, stop it right there. If we're righteous and obedient, then our fate will be painted by my ancestors. I must admit to you, I've seen my uncle meet his death and I've seen him surrounded in hell by thousands of souls attacking him upon arrival. My problem is that I don't know which uncle it is that I'm dreaming about. They both have dubious backgrounds."

"Darryl, I wouldn't agree with that. While both backgrounds might appear questionable, one has a nefarious history beyond repair, according to my father and my uncle. If you hesitate to discuss this issue and if it comes to pass, you'll never live it down. I know you have a lot of pressure on you with my father on his way here to kill you. I suggest that you gain allies and the most important one is your uncle. My father is not going to believe the circumstances of my pregnancy. He's going to kowtow, but at some point, he's going to try to kill you. Please keep your uncle and my uncle between you two. My father knows that I will never lie to him or color the truth. I'm hoping he believes me on this one."

"Sue Lyn, I'm not afraid of your father."

"My dear innocent lover--you should be!"

# # #

Ben Beckmire walked pass Darryl and motioned for him to join him. Wajickee was in place, as well as, Mallory, Jilkes, John Lee, Zanthius, and Larry.

Larry bellowed out, "I hope we're not going back to that apparition by the billabong. Dad, I'm still having nightmares of what I saw and how close it came to me."

"Son, that mark on your leg is a result of his tongue acknowledging your presence and accepting you as a Beckmire. When you see him, he's only going to look like he's forty feet or so. When adversaries come across his essence, it's an easy sixty feet. He's an enormous entity and if wronged, he will be the beast that no one wants to see let alone remember. The 'Great Saltie' is all that we are."

At the water's edge, Zanthius said, "There is a fortune in that billabong. Dad, does it ever dry up like most billabongs do?"

"Son, I'm not sure about this one? What say you, Wajickee?"

Wajickee seemed to be in a trance and said, "Is it possible for someone to fire a weapon with accuracy from more than two miles?"

The Sarge said, "With man's propensity to kill man, it wouldn't surprise me. Why do you ask?"

There is a man on a small hill with a weapon about two miles due south. I've sent some small critters to attend to him. How far should we set a perimeter if they can shoot that far?"

The Sarge said, "I would like to know when they're four or five miles out."

"Ben Beckmire, which one. Four or five miles?"

"Sorry, my friend. How about four miles out, but with warning signs when they first enter the Outback."

"It will be done. I would like to see the weapon that fellow has, please excuse me, and by the way, this billabong never runs dry."

# # #

Later in the morning, the sounds from the didgeridoo could be heard from various parts of the area which signified that this encounter involved all Aborigines. Each clan's instrument sounded distinctively different. On Walkabout, Wajickee found the sound very healing and hopeful.

When he returned from his walk, he also had the rifle that the individual had. The three men on reconnaissance, were bit by Redback spiders, one of the ten deadliest in Australia. Their bodies would, subsequently decay since most carnivores knew that the venom was toxic.

When Mallory saw the weapon, he said, "What on earth is that thing? Look at the size of the rounds."

The Sarge said, "From far away, they can pick us off like targets. We might have to rethink our strategy. We might have to take the fight to them."

Wajickee asked, "Why would you do that? They don't know the outback. They don't know the animals. They don't know the spiders or snakes and they don't know the dingoes or wombats. They don't know the bush, and it would be suicidal to attack us from the water. I think the bush can make enough noise to distract them. Also, the bees out here are as deadly as the spiders and snakes, and we have billions of them at our disposal. You must not forget your teachings, my friend. The good never fear the bush. The bad must fear all aspects of it."

# # #

Around lunch time, Michael and Sue Lyn's father stepped off the same plane in the Northern Territory. Sue Lyn's mother was too ill to make the long journey. Both men acknowledged each other but did not know that their fates would be dependent upon one another.

Sue Lyn saw her father and walked over to him and bowed. While she was asking him about his flight and other small issues, he saw Darryl. He brushed her aside and made a beeline towards Darryl, when Michael stepped aggressively, in front of him. Jong walked over to his cousin and began to lambast him. Darryl walked over to the three men, lowered his head, bowed, and in a perfect dialect, began to plead for understanding and pity. He told her father that he had never penetrated his daughter and that from them messing around his seed entered her fertile valley. He told him that he wouldn't believe the story if it were told to him, but that on his honor and his life, he swore that it was as he stated. He told her father that he loved his daughter very much and understood where she got all her brains and looks from. This horseshit went on for fifteen minutes when the father lowered his head, lower than Darryl's. A truce had been agreed upon and a price had been faintly mentioned for the untold embarrassment that Darryl had caused the family of Sue Lyn. When Jong heard the amount, he looked at his cousin and lit into him as if there was no tomorrow. His cousin looked at Darryl, and said, "Perhaps a simple token of your respect for me would suffice."

Darryl looked at her father and said, "I will let you name our child. I will let you visit him and us four times a year and in four different locations. You will also be able to come and visit anytime outside of those parameters as you wish."

The men looked at each other and Jong's cousin grabbed Darryl and said, "I think I got the best of the bargain."

While the men were walking through the airport to their transportation, Darryl asked, "What shall I call you after I marry your daughter?"

"You will call me, Father."

Darryl smiled at the thought and said, "May I start at this moment?"

"Yes, you may."

"So, Father, to change the nature of our interfacing, do you have any idea how to price diamonds, mine them, transport them, and account for them?"

"Son, why do you ask a question like that?"

"On this land, there are diamonds the size of rocks, that have been discovered. Now, I know that my uncle and your cousin have used you in many nefarious ways, and I promise that I will never attempt to corrupt you for profit. However, I will want you to assist me in creating the proper manner to provide all aspects of a mining event, from security, extraction, depositing, accounting, and reporting. Now, I know there are a hundred other steps between those basic things that I mentioned, and I would like you to assist me figuring out those intermediate steps."

"Son, where do you keep them now?"

"Oh, some are in the caves and others are in a billabong. I'll show you when we get there. Here's a secret, they're protected by a slew of mythical creatures called saltwater crocs and one massive one called the 'Great Saltie'."

"Son, I was enjoying our discussion until you, short of calling me a moron, insulted everything that I am."

"Father, ask your daughter and she will verify my story. Perhaps, your cousin will ask my uncle to take you to see it. I mean, I can show you, but only he can show you the 'Great Saltie'. Just like your people believed in dragons and mythical creatures; in Australia, the things here are beyond comprehension."

# # #

Two and a half hours later, Sue Lyn's father began to realize the enormity of the outback. He asked, "People actually live out here?"

Sue Lyn said, "Father, this is the birthplace of the nation. Before there was a Sydney, Perth, Brisbane, Cairns, and Melbourne, this land was occupied by the Aborigine people. It was easily conquered because the English saw that the natives did not dress like them, speak like them, eat like them, and use utensils, or worship the same deity. That is why the few conquered this continent. The pity is that the Aborigine people wouldn't band together to fight for their land. They stayed in their own clans until the British wiped them out, one by one, and made this place a penal colony. Can you believe that? A penal colony for criminals. Therefore, most of the people you will meet here who are not Aborigine, come from a family member who was charged with a serious crime in England."

"Sue Lyn, have you been taking hallucinogens? This is no different than anywhere else in the world. People are people, and everyone is looking for an advantage?"

"Father, an advantage here could be your dying by a spider bite, bee sting, or snake bite. There are animals so small and deadly that you probably would not believe me if I told you that. There are certain waters you can't go in unless you've been sanctioned. As an example, you can't go in that billabong behind those trees. I will tell you this, there are diamonds in that water the size of softballs."

"What, do I have to worry about some crocodile attacking me?"

"Father, if you want to leave this land alive, then I suggest you show little interest in the things that seemingly motivate you, and more interest in my marrying Darryl. Your indifference, in this land, will get you killed."

He looked at her and said, "I've survived worse and I'm sure I can survive this place."

Sue Lyn began to cry which attracted the attention of Darryl, who asked, "Why are you crying?"

Her father emphatically said, "She's a woman, that's what they do."

Darryl studied the words for a moment, lashed out and said, "Your daughter is going to be my wife and the mother of my child. She is not just a woman who cries. She is the savior of people because of her knowledge of weapons and strategies as derived from your teachings. However, in this magical land, you must learn to be humble, or your arrogance will make you suffer an extreme death. If I, were you, I would knock that Redback spider off your arm. There is no antivenom for its bite and, please, don't kill it."

# # #

At dinner, things began to heat up and various sounds and noises filled the night air. Darryl walked towards the huge fire and said, "Tonight, I'm going to officially ask Sue Lyn to be my wife. We have had all kinds of variations of making love, but we've never really made love, according to the covenants and the meaning of making love. I must admit, we've played in different ways, and apparently, one of the forms had things go swimming into a place I've never been. My uncle, her uncle, and her father find it hard to believe what I say, but as I stand here, I attest on my unborn child, I have never crossed the boundaries set by her uncle, my uncle, and her father. Also, as I stand here, I want to introduce seven new associates—Michael who just arrived, Isaiah, Desmond, Jasper, Harold, Windom and Earther. My uncle and his crew have sort of baptized me by fire, but they've also aligned me with Windom and Earther. They have other names, but those names came from another spirit and time that was disrespected. More importantly, this group is designed to learn the ways of my uncle's group and improve upon his and

Mallory's development of the Fab 10. He has indicated that these guys are a part of my group if they so desire. Me and my people promise fairness, equality, and swear never to reside on the side of evil for the sake of someone else's concerns. Oh, by the way, Windom and Earther will become extremely rich, as well as the other families that are blessed to own properties on the path of the pipeline. Much like you guys and dolls, who are rich, but continue to do good. Uncle, Earther and Windom have pledged their lives to our cause of helping people help themselves, and they promise to always remember what you and your people did for them. Uncle, Mallory, and the rest of your guys, me and my crew, salute you."

Sue Lyn's father began to clap slowly, and then frantically, with the group joining in. He stood up and said in broken English, "At first, I no believe his story about my daughter. His spirit is pure. His soul is at peace. I now like my new son, and believe him when he states, him never crossed the street on my daughter."

The Sarge, realizing that this conversation needed to move in a different direction, stood up and said, "Michael, you've brought us a way out of this mess, and you've bonded with my nephew and Jong's niece. We're old and tired and have been bouncing around all over the world and we want to sit on our porches and eat watermelon. There is a devil out there and he's related to me. His name is Walter. Walter will kill everything you hold dear. He once, strapped suicide vests on our children in the Midwest. I say all of that to say, we've done some mighty bad things. Me and this group have killed thousands of people and we're still alive. We have amassed a fortune after having a fortune. We are no angels and, sure as hell, when we go to that dark place, there will be thousands of souls awaiting our arrival.

"You will make more money than you can spend. You will be tempted by things and power. If you cross that road, one of us will pull your name and number and that will conclude your existence. If your heart is not pure, then please leave now. You and your guys have been on hard times, and we've studied each of you and your habits. To make this group honest and fit, you'll have to find five more and you'll know when you come across them. Some may be adversaries like Windom and Earther were, but when you examine their causes and reasons, you'll know they had little choice."

The Sarge took a drink, and said, "Sue Lyn, you have grounded my nephew. You love him, taught him, exposed him, and sheltered him. He has done the same for you. The two of you will be the new me and Mallory except, Sue Lyn, you won't have some of the anatomy that Mallory has. This battle is not going to be the last one. I'm afraid my cousin has employed a lot of people to meet their end for greed. Historically, this country has been conquered by the few because the original inhabitants wouldn't ban together to run a few Europeans from their land. Those few turned to hundreds, those hundreds turned to thousands, those thousands turned to millions and the Aborigines were decimated and relegated to the lands that the Europeans could not survive on. This fight within the next few days is about killing a lot of innocent Aborigines and placing my cousin's name and title on these lands that is totally, Aborigine. There are diamonds on the quadrants of this territory that is filed in the Land and Title Office. There is enormous wealth buried under its soil. There is no need for anyone to pick up a diamond and attempt to smuggle it out of here. Why would you do that? As a member of our group, you will be endowed with an annual stipend in the seven-figure range. What is here belongs to the Aborigine people and will help build their future, secure their mines, and improve the services to all Aborigines, all over the continent. I will personally eliminate any individual that attempts to leave here with unsanctioned tokens.

"Jong, you and your cousin, soon to be my nephew's fathers-in-law are as critical to our survival as is anyone of us are. The weapons systems in the Midwest and Virginia are utterly amazing. I offer your family, my nephew, who is a person of impeccable quality, good lineage, integrity, and a solid Beckmire. This kid is as good as they come. He will love, honor, protect, and be faithful to Sue Lyn for all his breathing days. He will provide your family with three beautiful children who will look different, but who will be smarter than most computers. This I can promise you, and I will take the entire group down to the billabong to meet a descendant of the original Beckmire clan. In Australia, everything isn't as it appears. There be monsters here!"

Jong in his native tongue said to his cousin, "This place is truly weird. Don't wander away from the campsite and don't go anywhere alone. It's imperative you say something to the Sarge and compliment him on his fine speech and his wonderful nephew."

Jong's cousin stood up, bowed, and said in his native language, "Your nephew is dung shit, and if you weren't such a big bully, I would kick his and your asses. Also, your sons looks like girls, and you all stink."

Jong stood up and translated the discourse and said, "Your nephew is a wonderful human being and I admire you as a leader and you all have such a pleasant aroma about you. May peace be with us all."

The Sarge knew Jong was talking shit because he laughed throughout the whole translation. When it was said and done, the Sarge said, in Spanish, to Jong's cousin, "En otro situacion. Te hubiera metido mi pie por el culo."

In perfect English, Jong's cousin said, "Good luck with that adventure."

# # #

The wedding ceremony was off the charts for the area. Only Ben Beckmire and Darryl knew Wajickee was a spirit. He recounted the many struggles of the Aborigine people and their inability to thwart the onslaught of the Europeans. He blessed the union of Darryl and Sue Lyn and said, "The tears I shed are not from me, but are from the 'Great Saltie'. He too once loved beyond tradition and is empowering this marriage with his full spirit. He wants to acknowledge this marriage by the billabong and with a special gift for the bride. Please follow me to the edge of the water. If your spirit or soul is not pure, please do not touch the water. I will say this once again. If your spirit or soul is not pure, please do not touch the water."

At the edge of the billabong, Wajickee summoned the' Great Saltie'. He led Sue Lyn and Darryl into the water, up to their waist. Jong's cousin asked a slightly disrespectful question of Jong, who replied, "All you think you know will be dwarfed by what you learn and see while you are here on this continent."

Wajickee summoned the spirits of several Aborigines and from beneath the depths of the water, large saltwater crocs rose surrounding Darryl, Sue Lyn, and Wajickee. Her father started yelling, but was silenced by his cousin who said, "Don't draw attention to your evil self."

After a few chants and the sprinkling of water upon each of their heads, they were officially married. As they exited the waters, in the background, everyone witnessed a giant Saltwater croc breach the water and make a wake. It was the 'Great Saltie'. As usual, those who are blessed to view him are in awe of his size and agility. After all, legend has him clocked in at over 250 years old.

At the feast, the dingoes and other indigenous animals began to sound an alarm. Wajickee said, "The animals are restless tonight. Foreigners are in the outback, and they're being stalked by our friends. Nothing or no one will interrupt this magnificent wedding."

CHAPTER FOURTEEN

As the night began to turn into day, Darryl and Sue Lyn were still making it happen. He told her about the wonderful euphoric feeling he experienced each time he reached his zenith. Sue Lyn told him that she had never ever experienced the emotions, feelings, and the almost unconscious feeling she had when she reached a climax.

However, her father would not sleep for two nights. He was filled with nightmares of the beast that breached the water. He felt it singled him out and was out to get him. When Jong saw his cousin in the morning looking nervous and scared, he said, "I know you didn't try to find those diamonds."

The man was shaking and looking around as if something or someone was stalking him. He said, "That beast is trying to take my soul. I have to get out of here."

Hearing all and knowing all, Wajickee walked over to the two men and handed Jong's cousin a cup with tea in it. He said, "Your soul is confused and tormented. Confess to yourself and all will be well. Drink this and stay out of the sun."

Jong asked, "What did he mean about your soul being confused? What on earth have you done?"

The man ran towards the bush but was stopped by several spear toting Aborigines who said, "Mate, you no want to go out there just yet. Dingoes be feasting on spies."

Jong caught up with his cousin and said, "I need you to tell me exactly what you've done, or you might not get off this continent. Tell me!"

After many tears and threats of killing himself, his cousin confessed that he attempted to steal diamonds. Jong told him he would find him a ride to the airport and to never speak to him again. Jong also told him he was a disgrace to the family and that he should find his way back home and end his life.

Knowing all and hearing all, Wajickee sent a small present with Jong's cousin that would relieve him of all his guilt and sins. The small creature wouldn't bite him until he was far from Australia.

# # #

Knowing what they were about to do, Darryl walked out of the cave and took in a deep breath of air. He saw Isaiah and asked, "Are the guys up and ready for a little run?"

"Darryl, we've already been on a run around the camp because there was a lot of animal activity going on in the bush."

"Yeah, I heard the screams. Okay, I guess I'll have to run by myself."

Sue Lyn yelled, "I want to go, and I need to go."

Isaiah said, "Let me get Michael and we'll all join you. While we're out, we can collect any weapons that were left by those mercs."

"Good idea. There are seven assault rifles and pistols. We certainly can use them."

Isaiah asked, "How do you know how many people were out there?"

"I went on Walkabout and visited their place of hiding."

"What's this Walkabout stuff?"

"Oh, I see! I'm going to have to give you guys lessons in Aborigine culture and history."

As they left the confines of the camp, they saw Aborigines standing guard and enjoying the calm before the storm. They all acknowledged Darryl and congratulated him on his wedding. They also knew Darryl knew where to find the remains of the unfortunate people who were not from the bush. One of the Aborigines asked, "Hey Mate, you see those two fellas up on that ridge about nine hundred or so yards? Do you be wanting to 'ave' a conversation with them?"

"Naw, mate. They be scouting and trying to figure a way in. They be getting closer and closer. If they breach the five hundred yards mark, 'ave' the dingoes scare them back. They must be daft or something. I know they heard the screams last night. My people couldn't hear them because of the sweet sounds from the didgeridoo. Thanks, mate."

Desmond whispered to Isaiah, "There's a whole lot of crazy shit happening here in this place. I'm afraid to close my eyes and go to sleep for fear of some spider, dog, or croc, biting my head off."

Isaiah laughed and said, "You need a new religion my friend. This place is strange and if you don't have a belief system in place, then I feel you're pretty much dog meat."

"What is it you believe in?" Desmond asked.

"I believe that man is not as smart as man thinks he is, and that there are greater forces at work to offset the insanity that man does to man. I believe in spirits, ghosts, and everything else. I can't discount things I don't have empirical information about. I definitely believe in God, and if you don't, you had better start having faith in something or someone, my friend."

When the group came upon the remains, Darryl grabbed Sue Lyn and said, "Honey, you don't want to see this."

"Darryl, we've been married for less than a day and you're ordering me around already."

He looked at her, then at the bodies, and said, "Okay, suit yourself, but I can tell you it ain't pretty and it will cause nightmares."

Sue Lyn peeked at the shredded clothing and said, "Perhaps you're right, but I want to be fully invested in everything, including the killing."

She brushed past Darryl and screamed, "Oh my God! The dogs ate through their bulletproof vests."

"No, silly. The Wombats did that. Their jaws can crush bone." Jasper happened on the scene and turned around and began to regurgitate. Harold looked but turned his head and quickly moved upwind to avoid the smell.

Sue Lyn said, prior to throwing-up, "I'll always listen to you in the future, my love."

Earther, Windom, Darryl, Isaiah, and Desmond picked the useable equipment from the bloody remains. Earther said, "The animals here are fierce and have mighty jaws. Something bit and crushed this guy's entire chest cavity. What could do such a thing?"

Darryl said, "The animals here are different. They have the equipment necessary to survive in this environment.

They're not friendly, but they are respectful. The people who are here had no soul when they came here and, therefore, the animals feasted upon them. If an Aborigine died in the Outback, the animals would pick him clean, but would not kill him. Listen, this is not a friendly place for anyone who has bad karma. The beast in the billabong sets the tone and when he sends out a vibe—all the animals on the continent respond."

Darryl continued, "This place is magical and deadly, but forgiving, if in fact your heart is solid. I am a Beckmire, and as such, I have the liberty to transgress between this world that you know and the spirit world that is strongly represented here. On this very spot where we stand, there are enough diamonds to make each of us billionaires ten times over. The problem is if the 'Great Saltie' senses greed then your chances of enjoying or extracting them are one in ten. I know this stuff is here and I've known it existed, but everything here has its time and opportunity.

"My uncle is surrounded by a group of people who would do anything he asked. I'm hoping I've done the same in my selection process. As a matter of fact, what would you do with a billion dollars? Would you buy planes, homes, cars, boats, and jewelry? Or would you buy peace for the Earther and Windom's of the world or set up schools for the Aborigine people, and provide them with equal rights and representation in Sydney? Therefore, in that case, my uncle is filthy rich. He is rich in spirit and humility. He had the option of killing Earther and Windom because they came to spec out a plan to assault and kill my family. Earther and Windom witnessed the swift and horrible deaths of the other two guys who accompanied them. My uncle's people believed in the message they received from these two men. My uncle in turn sent me and you guys to secure their families and properties. He didn't ask for twenty percent of anything, although 5% allowed him to operate legally on their behalf. He didn't ask them to be beholden to him. He didn't ask for a thing. He recognized an imbalance, a greed syndrome, and knew he could perhaps help these two guys and their friends. My uncle and his people don't do this for money. They do it because it is the right thing to do."

Everyone was spellbound by Darryl's words and Isaiah said, "You know Desmond is unable to sleep because he's afraid of all that you've said."

Darryl looked at Desmond and said, "I've got your back and I assure you tonight will be a different experience. Your issues were complicated, but not un-resolvable. You're on a new path and it has been sanctioned by the spirits. Do not worry, tonight will be different."

Isaiah asked, "How old are you?"

"Does my age matter to receive your loyalty?"

Isaiah thought for a moment, and as he reached down to remove a pistol from the skeletal remains of one of the victims, he replied, "You're old enough to rescue me, my friends, remove us from stupid, and give us a picture of smart—a world of helping people help themselves."

# # #

At basecamp, Darryl saw his uncle and Jong and asked about the whereabouts of his father-in-law? Jong respectfully bowed his head and said, "An emergency came up at home and he had to leave suddenly. I got him transportation to the airport, and he was able to catch a flight home."

Darryl looked at his uncle, then at Jong, and said, "There are no fish in the barrel. Do you have another one?"

A perplexed Jong was about to say something when Beckmire interceded and said, "Excuse me Jong, I would like to have a few minutes with my nephew. Is that alright with you?"

Jong commiserated, and the two men walked out of the village and into the bush and beyond the normal boundaries of security. Ben Beckmire said, "I know you love Sue Lyn and she's a wonderful human being. You, my nephew, will have the awesome task of consoling your wife when she finds out he attempted to steal diamonds from the Aborigines."

"Uncle, you must know that I knew this all along?"

"Darryl, I just didn't want you to forget or deny it."

"I kept my part of the bargain and we never copulated. We've stimulated each other, but last night was the first time I ever got to do the work in the right place. It was unquestionably, amazing!"

"Nephew, that's a little too much information. I need you to be gentle when you express your knowledge of what happened to her father. There is a balance we need to maintain here to suppress our adversaries. You and your wife can tip the scale and create a massive disconnect. Please be careful with your discussion. She's as important here as you are, and I know you know this. Keep the balance nephew, and all will work out for us."

# # #

After lunch, Darryl asked Sue Lyn to take a stroll with him. He gifted her with an automatic pistol and an extra clip that had been retrieved from one of the corpses. He had one as well. As they strolled deeper into the bush, Sue Lyn said, "I think someone is following us?"

Darryl said, "It's just the guys providing security for us." He waited for a minute or so and found that Earther, Windom, Jasper, and Harold were following them from the rear, a few paces behind Michael. Isaiah and Desmond were on both sides of them. He said, "I don't recall inviting you guys to stroll along with me and my new bride. What's the deal?"

Earther said, "We just signed on to your leadership and we don't want you doing stupid and getting yourself in trouble out here."

Darryl proclaimed, "Really, Earther! You're going to protect me in my hood. Now, that's funny. Okay, gentlemen, show me how to get back to the village?"

Earther and Windom laughed, and Windom said, "We were two of the best scouts in Vietnam including that John Lee and Jilkes team. We laid down breadcrumbs to find our way back. We are good at what we do and when you decide to head back, let us lead you, my master."

Darryl said, "Let's head up to that tree over there and then I'll show you a cave we should use to thwart the soon-to-be attackers. I would like you guys to give me an assessment of the pros and cons of using this place."

As the group headed towards the tree and cave, Darryl motioned for everyone to hit the dirt. Approximately 150 yards in front of them were three Aborigines leading a band of gun toting mercs. As that group continued, one of the Aborigines stopped and turned his noise up in the air as if he was smelling something that was out of place. What he was smelling was Jasper's cologne. Darryl smelled it too and told him to wash himself in the dirt quietly. He told the group that the Abo got a whiff of the day cologne that Jasper was wearing. As the other group disappeared, Darryl said, "I need Earther and Windom to follow them on an angle. I want Jasper and Harold to keep an eye on Earther and Windom. Michael, Isaiah and Desmond, you guys will come with me and Sue Lyn. Do not engage unless your life is at stake. They have far superior firepower than we do, so let's treat this mission as one of reconnaissance."

When everyone returned to the basecamp, Darryl and his crew sought the Sarge. Darryl said, "Uncle, a group of mercs were being led here by three Abos."

"Watch your language, you know I hate that word."

"Yes, as do I, but those three Abos, excuse my language, were politely offering us up for a few bottles of booze. I will attend to them later, on Walkabout."

"How close did they get to us?"

"Earther said, three hundred yards of unobstructed territory. If they decided to flank to the right, they would have been upon us."

"Oh, I see. Let's take a walk so that you can see why I'm not concerned about that area. Darryl, did you not talk to them about that area?"

"Uncle, they surprised me on my walk with my new bride and they offered to protect us in my hood. I laughed but appreciated how we're beginning to bond and that we're acting as a group. Anyway, I neglected to explain to them about this area."

"So, a visit is in order!" The Sarge .

"Most definitely. They should know what makes up our defense system. I think our partners disappeared when those damn Abos led those people to our camp."

"Nephew, please refrain from using that word. I order you as an elder."

"Understood, Uncle."

Windom asked, "What does that word mean?"

The Sarge said, "It's like being called the "N" word if you're African American."

"Oh, I see," Windom said.

When the group approached the area where the mercs had accessed, the Sarge said, "This is the animal kingdom. In this area you have almost every brand of insect, spider, tick, snake, large kangaroos, dingoes, wombats, and deadly marine life. This is the only inland area of the outback where the box jellyfish survives. It's a function of nature, but this sea dwelling cnidarian invertebrate can somehow exist in these waters. You don't always see them, but their tentacles can be as long as ten feet and any slight contact with the body is deadly. There is no antivenom. Listen, people, this is a sacred place and we're sacred people doing good for mankind. If we were evil and if your soul was contaminated like a certain person who has left us, you wouldn't be able to survive in this area. All of these inhabitants would seek you out and terminate you. Australia is not St. Thomas or Minnesota--it is a place, where even Confucius was confused about it. It gives no quarters."

Isaiah asked, "Mr. Beckmire, please explain to me how all those names that you called can be defense against a group of armed mercs?"

"Did you come across the bodies of several decimated individuals today and did you see their condition? Anyway, that was a pure demonstration of Australia. You can't show up here and expect to conquer the land without knowing who the rightful owners are."

Desmond asked, "What's to prevent all those different things from coming in the middle of the night and doing us in? By the way, do you have a chart of all those things we should be wary of?"

"Son, faith! If you don't have faith, then you should leave this place."

# # #

Back at basecamp, the Sarge began to think about the question raised by Desmond—"do you have a chart of all the things we should be afraid of?"

Zanthius saw his father and straight on said, "I think our preparations are misguided. I think my uncle is trying to 'bait and switch', us. He knows we're here and, therefore, he is trying to make us think that the focus is on the mines and the billabong. The House of Records, I believe is his intended target. Dad, think about it. If the building is burned to the ground, the Aborigines will not be able to prove their ownership of anything. My uncle is going to burn the House of Records to the ground. People scoping us and showing up on our horizon, are just a mirage and a distraction. I feel it in my bones. My uncle is going to burn the House of Records into oblivion!"

The Sarge looked at Zanthius and smiled. He muttered, "idiot spy", eh! My children are the best!"

# # #

Ben Beckmire called for a general meeting of everyone who was in the camp, minus the children. Marisa and Mary Alice were assigned to secure the children and were provided with the necessary tools to do so.

The Sarge told the group about his expectations on the impending assault. He told them that the House of Records maintained all documents in paper form and if someone set fire to it, all of Australia, except for the rich, would have to provide clear documentation of ownership. He indicated he thought the assault would not be on the village, but on the House of Records, the stake holders, members of the board, and attributed the idea to one of his sons.

The Sarge began to feel stronger and stronger about his notions and decided to send local Aborigines out to convince those of record, as stakeholders, to leave their homes and seek refuge in the village. He was adamant about his convictions and knew that his cousin was running out of tricks.

# # #

His cousin had souls to sell but didn't count on the 'idiot spy', once again thwarting his plans. The emphasis was not on the village, but on those who were stakeholders to the land that held the massive collection of diamonds. Beckmire decided he would spoil all efforts on behalf of his cousin to steal the mines. He would end up sending Jilkes, John Lee, Darryl, and his crew along with Whitmore, Brown, Bernstein, and Gladstone. Each would be heavily armed with weapons seized from his cousin's people. He suggested each weapon be field tested and inspected, because he realized his cousin knew they were not as brazen as his people in terms of smuggling weapons into a no-weapons policy country.

Courtney walked up to the Sarge and whispered something in his ear. He looked at her and said, "Honey, I need you and everyone else here in case I'm wrong."

"Really, Ben Beckmire? If Walter is designing a distraction, and if you're correct, instead of attacking the village, he sends his forces to destroy the House of Records, I'm sure he's going to have more people, than the group you articulated, to foil his plan. I think we should put the kids on a skiff in the billabong and let Ms. Viola calm them and protect them. Honey, if you're right, and if this is the motherload for your cousin, he's going to send every living ass with a gun to the House of Records."

Asiram said, "Daddy-in-Law, I've been a good wife, and mother for too long. I'm getting bored. If the House of Records is based on a paper modality, then I'm sure that's where he's going to do his work. I'm with my mother-in-law, we need to figure out how to protect that place and, in the meantime, digitize as many records that impact this quadrant as possible."

A light went on in Ben Beckmire's head and he said, "That's the answer. Film as much of the history of this latitude and longitude to prove beyond any measure of a doubt it is owned by the indigenous Aborigine people. Girl, you never stop amazing me, that's why I love this group. You never know where your answer, inspiration, protection, or backup is going to come from. God has been good to us, and we've never taken advantage of anyone who was in need. We only help people to help themselves. Courtney, can you gather the people that I did not call on and get them to the House of Records with cameras, flash drives, video, and audio equipment. Honey, I think this is his real play and, if we're wrong, by the time he redirects his people, the village will be empty and the billabong free of crocs. Fortunately, everyone wins in that scenario. We're not here and they're not at the House of Records—no one dies."

Luana raised her hand to ask a question. When Ben Beckmire acknowledged her, she asked, "Is it possible that no one ever dies on either side? I mean, sometimes I hear casual conversations about death, and it bothers me because I know my husband is deep in the fabric of this group. Of course, he makes-up his own mind, but I certainly want to assist him when it comes to matters that impact his life or the lives of others. I know we kill the bad guys. I've done it and so has Ms. Viola. I'm not sure I like it, but for the good of the order, I found it necessary to pull that trigger. I guess what I'm saying, is simple. I don't like pulling the trigger and never had the need to pull one until I met this meathead and fell in love with him. However, I will execute any hostile force that presents itself against the ideology of the group, or any member. Not going soft, just don't like the idea of executing people."

The Sarge walked towards Luana and Ms. Viola and said, "You guys are more than important to us. You have brought a special aura to our group that was missing. Ms. Viola, you are captivating and smart and, Luana, you're a brilliant jurist that loves one of my guys, naturally. Me, and my guys, have served in the military where we were required to eliminate the enemy or be eliminated. We will figure this thing out. If you're having bad thoughts and dreams about what you've done then, perhaps, I can have my relative calm your apprehension and sanction what you've done to protect me and mine from my cousin. Please, I need your commitment and resolve. Any handicapping might cause one of us our lives."

As the Sarge turned to walk away, Ms. Viola said, "Mr. Sarge, Man, if you don't know who you be trusting, then I need to have a long talk with you. Me, and mine, along with everyone else here have paid their dues. We all be ready to protect each other. You don't have to stress and try to figure out if me, or mine, will pull that trigger again. Anyone who comes for the children is dead on arrival."

"Ms. Viola, I'm not second guessing you or Luana, I'm just trying to make sure we're all on the same page. I'm trying to outfox Diablo and that is a humongous task. I worry about everything and everyone because my cousin will kill us all if given the opportunity. Listen, I know you guys have shown your mettle, but I need everyone here to be prepared to go the extra mile. My wife has reminded me that a divided force is a susceptible one. What's your opinion on how we should handle the House of Records?"

"Mr. Sarge, Man, if I were you and in charge, I would put the children with me, Ms. Marisa, and Ms. Mary Alice in that there billabong along with them shotguns that we like. Now, you say that big croc is your family. So, you go and have a conversation with him and tell him we be sacred people and not to fancy us as a meal. Now, if you be doing that, then the rest of you can make your way into town and set up, you know, what it is you must do to keep people from torching the place. Now, I know you be a smart man, you know who the targets are, and, therefore, you've made arrangements for them to disappear in the outback. So, knowing that, I would just make my way to the House of Records, along with the local law types, and protect what is needed."

The Sarge looked at her and said, "Would you like to run this outfit?"

"No sir, Mr. Sarge, Man. You be asking me, and I be telling you, that there is no challenge to solid leadership. Now, Man, I follow you to the end because I love what you do and how you have made a new life for my two babies. No, Man, I be with you until the end."

The Sarge hugged Ms. Viola who said, "Not too tight tiger, I don't want to be making that pretty wife of yours jealous. Not too tight!"

## CHAPTER FIFTEEN

As day slowly turned into night, Ben Beckmire began to deploy his people in the area where the House of Records was. They were immersed in every conceivable venue that was near the House of Records and armed with small caliber weapons. The big guns that were captured were placed on roof tops that were five hundred yards or better away from the House of Records and were manned by Brown, Whitmore, and Jong from the front, and Bernstein, Gladstone, and Chakes from the rear.

At 2000 hundred hours and as the last remnants of the sun disappeared from the visible sky, four large tractor trailers made their way into town and stopped near the House of Records. It was an awesome view of precision, direction, and planning. It appeared to be a simple event, lay the charges and other accelerants, and sit back and watch history get burnt to the ground. The only problem to that simple event was the unknown and unexpected foes lurking in the shadows.

Courtney, Monica, Asiram, and Luana, were placed in what the Sarge and Mallory considered a support location and a safe zone. In reality, they were stuck in the heart of the mercs command center. The four women were in a room next to where the strategic planning was being consummated. The

Sarge and Mallory recognized where they had stationed the women and cursed themselves for the placement.

Mallory said, "What the fuck! What have we done?"

The Sarge was silent, almost comatose, and finally said, "I have to surrender myself to them. They're going to figure out there are women in the room beside them with little pistols. Damn, damn, damn. I totally fucked this one up. Shit, shit, shit!"

#

In the room, next to where the brass of the mercs were concluding their action plan as to how to obtain the necessary records and destroy the House of Records to show that Walter was the absolute owner, there was a slight commotion. Courtney whispered, "My husband would expect me to go out in style. I'm not going to be bullied by people who will hurt my family. Ladies, I'm going into the next room and shoot everything that I can."

Asiram looked at Monica and said, "I'm with her. I can't let her do this alone."

Luana looked at the group and said, "Hell, you only decided what I was going to do without you guys. If everyone is on track, can we disrupt this mess and try to save lives on both sides. There are eight people in there that seemingly have control over this massive number of people. I think we should go in there and shoot four or five of them and see how we end this siege for the diamond territory."

Asiram said, "Oh, my, we have a new wonder woman. Perhaps we should follow you?"

Courtney looked at Monica and it reminded them of a look from many years back when a person named Malik came into the restaurant to kill Monica and Larry. The two women rose from their hiding places and marched into the adjoining space.

Courtney announced, "You're evil, so I don't feel as though I'm violating the oath I swore to uphold." She pointed the weapon at a man's head and pulled the trigger. Asiram, Monica, and Luana filed in behind her and pulled the trigger on several targets. In the aftermath, six men laid dead on the floor and two were standing looking bewildered and perplexed. Courtney said, "Our husbands are out there, and if you think we're going to let you arbitrarily execute them, then you're wrong. Who is in charge?"

An older gentleman looked at her and asked, "I thought we were fighting against men? Why did you shoot me and my comrades?"

"Your wound is superficial. Slowly put your hands on your head, and if you even sneeze, you'll get what they got. There are two ways in which this event can end. A lot of people will die for a very evil person, or you can figure out a way to make your people surrender."

Everyone heard the gunfire and knew it was from small caliber weapons, the kind the ladies carried. Jilkes and John Lee made their way to within fifty yards of the building. Jilkes radioed the Sarge and told him they heard small caliber weapons fire but couldn't see who was doing what. He then asked the Sarge, where he had stationed some of the women and he was told that they were in the building where the gunfire came from. Jilkes told him that he and John Lee had disabled three guards and confiscated their weapons, and they would take a closer look. He also told the Sarge to tell the long guns that he and his boy were dressed like mercs.

Ten minutes later, they were on opposites sides of the building and peered through the window. Jilkes radioed the Sarge and told him there were bodies on the floor and that the women were holding two male captives.

The Sarge asked, "What did you just say?"

Jilkes repeated, "The women are holding two men hostage and are surrounded by bodies on the floor. Sarge, I think they did this on their own. I'm going to signal to them that it's us and try to gain entry without getting shot by one of them."

John Lee knocked gingerly on the door and said, "This here be John Lee and Jilkes. Now, we be wearing some of the mercs equipment, but we don't want to be shot by you ladies. Do we have your word?"

Asiram said, "If you ain't John Lee or Jilkes then you will be shot, and quite often."

John Lee exclaimed, "Asiram, this John Lee. Girl don't you be shooting us. We need to make a move before them fellas forces come looking for direction."

The two men entered the building and saw that the ladies had upgraded their equipment and weapons.

Jilkes asked, "What on earth happened?"

Courtney said, "Our ex-husbands placed us in here for back-up purposes and this is the place where the people were planning the fight. That guy who is slightly bleeding, seems like the one in charge. We heard them planning and decided we could end this without a lot of bloodshed, so we entered the room and shot six people. We were only supposed to shoot four or five, but I think Luana got a little anxious."

Jilkes radioed the Sarge and said, "Sarge, come in. You need to make your way to the building where you assigned your ex-wife."

He barely finished the transmission when the Sarge opened the door abruptly to the sight of several large weapons being pointed at him.

Courtney said, "Maybe I should shoot you for putting us in the place where they were planning the assault."

The Sarge looked around the room at the bodies and then at the ladies without saying a word. Mallory walked in hugged Monica and checked out the casualties. He thought he would find a timid and upset Monica, but what he found was a woman who was protecting all that was important to her. The Sarge looked at his wife and gave her a hug. He said, "Ladies, I had no idea they would pick this building as the HQ. Who are these gentlemen?"

The guy with the flesh wound said, "Sergeant Ben Beckmire and Corporal Mallory, it's been a long time. How the hell are you doing?"

Mallory looked at him but couldn't figure out who he was.

The Sarge asked, "Do we know you?"

"Oh, yeah! I blackmailed you people into going on several raids when your time was up. When your cousin sought me out, he told me you had aged poorly, you barely could walk, and your men were in the same shape as you. I see he lied, and I must admit, you people look formidable and much like you did in the Nam. Anyway, your ladies have conquered the fort, by themselves. They have summarily executed some of your cousin's alleged, exceptional picks. I have over two hundred fifty men out there who are equipped with our government's latest fire power. How many do you have, including these murderous women? Those people out there will not negotiate or listen to me plead for my life. Their contracts call for them to execute anyone who endangers the mission, including their commanders."

"Hold up a minute. I'm still trying to figure out who the hell you are?"

"Sergeant, when you and your guys were about to catch a helicopter out of the Nam for good, I made you go into the jungle in the rain, and your people took their pants off because of the noise they made."

Mallory inquired, "Permission to blow his head off, Sarge?"

"Stand down, soldier. We need him for the moment. Did my cousin truly describe us as you stated earlier?"

"That's the only reason I took the damn job. I remember what you did over there and how you did it. I remember how you and your boys were always selected for those one-way missions and you always came back, and in tack. We have film of you people doing extractions, assassinations, and that double bow action that fooled people. Listen, I was offered a cool million to come here and destroy the House of Records. Unfortunately, you people didn't fall for the souls he sacrificed in the outback. So how do you want to play this?"

The Sarge looked at the man, then at Mallory, and smiled. John Lee raised his hand and the Sarge was perplexed. He said, "John Lee, we're not in kindergarten? But what's on your mind?"

"Sarge, can you be asking him what his total mission was?"

"Damn, John Lee. You just asked him. But anyway, what was your full mission? Were you supposed to destroy the House of Records and then turn your attention to us?"

The man said, "My mission was to handle the House of Records. This asshole beside me had the mission of terminating you people."

Mallory said, "So, your sole purpose was to handle the House of Records and that was all?"

"My mission was to retrieve certain documents, authenticate them with the HR stamp, and then make it a quick and complete fire. I don't do fellow soldiers who served in the Nam. Now, this asshole here, who is also a member of several hate groups, offered his services for two million."

The Sarge said, "I take it you don't like him."

"No, not true, he's actually my son-in-law, who infected my daughter with HIV, which she transmitted to my grandson. He likes it both ways but failed to inform his wife about his proclivities."

"Does he talk?"

"He has signed an oath he will never speak to an African American."

"Mallory, you're white. Ask him if he has anything to say for himself?"

As Mallory approached the man, he spat on the floor. A clear sign of disrespect and a dislike of Mallory.

John Lee said, "Sarge, you think he'll talk to me?" The Sarge asked him to give it a try.

As John Lee approached the man, he spat towards Jilkes, the spit landing near his boots. John Lee yelled, "A, hell no." He walked behind the guy, pulled his snot rag out of his pocket, and gagged the man. He told Jilkes he needed some trash bags to make sure no one accidently made contact with his blood. He asked the ladies to retreat to the room they came from because he was going to amputate this guy's head."

The Sarge ordered, "Stand down John Lee. I think our option is the best. I would hate to infect the animals with this guy's blood. That's a nasty rag you have in his mouth."

"Sarge, that there be the thing I use to blow my nose and pick it with."

Mallory asked, "When were your people going to get paid and by who?"

The older gentleman looked around the floor and pointed to two of the corpses. He said, they have keys around their necks, and they were going to make two million for their parts."

"Where's the money?"

"Being protected by ten heavily armed mercs at one of the containers."

The Sarge looked around the room and saw what the women had done and asked, "Do you guys believe in magic? How about demons that control the snakes, spiders, lizards, crocs, jellyfish, ticks, wombats, dingoes, and roo's? What if I told you this place is full of magic and that my side could kill your side without firing a single bullet? I mean everyone who showed up in those containers and everyone who is here for the wrong reason is a target. My cousin will never get his hands on the diamond mines. They belong to the Aborigine people. You need to talk to your people and try to avoid a bloodbath because in the morning, the Australian Defense Force will be here in strength. I don't know what your boss promised you, but I can assure you your people will all die here and horribly. It's called the outback because if you don't know your way around, you won't get 'out or back'."

"Sarge, those guys aren't going to listen to me. Best I can guess is they'll all make siege on the container that has their payments."

"And that's where they will all perish. They must totally disarm, or they will be slaughtered. This is Australia and they're in the outback where old customs and rituals still manifest themselves. By the way, what is your name and last rank?"

"I'm the guy who led that raid on the VC compound with those arrogant Special Forces and Green Beret types." I'm Colonel Richard Hood."

Beckmire said, "I remember the mission. Those other guys wanted to go first, and you asked if they had ever heard of the *killing machine*? You were fair to us, and we'll be fair to you. Make the deal or they will all die."

The other guy rose to walk out with the Colonel. He said, "Keep this piece of shit here. I don't trust him."

# # #

As the main force gathered near the containers, Hood said, "So far, we've lost only ten to twelve comrades. Other than me, the other leadership team is dead. Embarrassingly, we were captured by four women with pop guns who didn't miss. Now, here's the deal. If we continue this mission to burn down the House of Records, it has been said that we will all die a horrible death. What does that mean? Well, it means that this place is not like anywhere else on earth and we will be attacked by all kinds of animals whose names I can't remember. Here's the funny thing, the guy leading the group is none other than Sergeant Beckmire. In case you don't know the name, he oversees the group called the *killing machine*. I was told they were old and decrepit but eyeing them I can only say that's not true. They have the help of the locals, animals, and the Australian Defense Force which will be here in mass in the morning. Here's the question? Do you want to take them on, I mean the locals, customs officials, the Australian Army, and whatever magic they have here? Now, I do know another group was sent here to do what we're supposed to do, and they were never heard from again. Since I'm senior leadership, I thought I would bring you information on this concern. We all joined this mission for the money; we're mercs. However, I'm convinced this mission will be conclusive if we attempt to achieve the objectives."

Two shots rang out and hit the Colonel. Bernstein and Brown saw where the flash came from and fired automatically in that area. Seven men were killed and three were injured.

The Sarge said, "Son-of-bitch! Fire indiscriminately into the crowd and see what happens."

Five or so minutes later, white materials were being waved in the air. The Sarge called the long guns and said, "Keep an eye on the back of the group. If they look suspicious, fire on them and make it permanent."

In that short period, thirty-one people had been severely wounded or killed. He saw a megaphone in the building, got it, walked to the side of the building, and began repeating himself. "Do not advance with a weapon of any kind or you will be immediately fired upon and terminated. Do not advance with a weapon of any kind or you will be forthwith fired upon and terminated."

Approximately, five to six minutes later, two thirds of the force had left the area with their hands on their heads. Suddenly there was the violent whirling sounds of twin Gatlin guns firing on the men from the rear. The Sarge commanded his people to open fire on the machine gun positions, but to no avail. The weapons were being fired automatically from afar. When the Sarge realized the guns were being fired automatically, it was too late. In front of him lay eighty to one hundred men, cut to shreds by twin Gatlin guns firing three hundred rounds per minute. He asked for a roll call after the firing subsided and was relieved that his people on duty were unharmed.

Those responsible for the concentrated gunfire that senselessly murdered the mercs, had made their way from the compound and were speeding towards a boat that would take them across a billabong with four large trunks full of money to a truck that would transport them to a private airport.

Later, as everyone in the nearby vicinity emerged from hugging the ground to escape catching a bullet, there was a quiet, no gunfire, and no engine noise. However, in another part of the outback, only screams of men being devoured by crocs could be heard.

On the water where Larry, Zanthius, and Mike were, they saw a speeding boat be thrown high in the air, but never saw what propelled it.

Zanthius asked, "What on earth happened to that boat? Maybe it hit a rock or something? Let's go over there and see if we can help?"

Larry responded, "Are you sure you're a Beckmire? You know damn well what caused that boat to be thrown into the air. This place is full of things that are unexplainable."

After the chaos had subsided, those who had come to lay claim for Walter on Aborigine territory where massive diamonds were discovered, met the fate that was befitting people who murder for pay. The entire system designed by Walter was layered with deception, false leaders, and trigger-happy machine gunners who indiscriminately fired on their comrades for the benefit of the cash boxes. The true number of people murdered in this operation would always be a mystery to the Beckmire group because people died in different ways, places, and by various means. What he did know was that it was apparent that treachery was in the mix from the beginning.   Those fleeing in the boat had predetermined they were going to execute everyone who was not a part of their conspiracy and ride off with the payroll to an awaiting truck, that would transport them to an awaiting jet, which would extract them from the place that God may have forgotten about.

In the morning, the Sarge and his people were well removed from the area and allowed the locals and customs officials to try to make sense of the murdered mercs.

CHAPTER SIXTEEN

The land, the articulating quadrants, as well as the principal individuals, the longitude and latitude, and every other possible description and annotation of ownership, of the land, had been registered in digital format. An application for excavation and/or mining had been filed and all permits listed the names of the Aborigine clans, the leaders, a long list of families entitled to benefit from any removal, processing and sale of any precious materials coming out of the aforementioned quadrants. Monica and Luana believed they wove a tight knit web around the property and most lawyers would understand what process they used and could argue their case in relationship to the doctrines for centuries. It was a continuous loop of information that would never conclude.

#

Two days later, and prior to leaving the outback, the Sarge saw his sons and said, "I need you guys to do me a favor. Do you trust me?"

Larry looked at Zanthius, then back at the Sarge and asked, "Dad, why wouldn't I trust you? You're not making sense to me."

"What I'm about to ask you two to do, is above and beyond trust. I want you two to take a dive in the billabong and tie those four cases of money up so that we can put it to use before it gets soggy and withers away."

Zanthius's head dropped. He asked in almost a whisper, "Pops, you want me and Larry to dive where that boat went down and tie lines on trunks of money? That is a correct interpretation, right?"

"Son, nothing will bother you or come near you. I promise you."

Larry looked at the Sarge intently and bellowed out, "Okay. When do you want this done?"

"How about now?"

The two men walked over to a skiff and the Sarge started to walk away. Larry yelled, "Yo! You got to come with us."

"I know, I was just teasing you. I wouldn't let you do this alone. I'll be right there."

Zanthius asked, "Can't you just have your relatives who live in the water latch on to the things and drag them ashore?"

"Funny man, they only eat things."

"Yeah, and why do you think we're hesitant to assist in this matter?"

#

At lunch, Sue Lyn and Darryl reported that two of the four trunks contained $18 million, and assumed the other two contained the same amount. The Sarge looked at Jong and asked, "Should we do an equal split?" He nodded his head, and the deal was done.

He then looked at Darryl and said, "Put $18 million in those accounts we opened and sit tight. I'm not sure how much it's going to take to get the extraction process going. Everyone wants to participate for a share. I say, we cut the middleman out and pay for it with our own money. We buy expertise and security and then we lease the mining and drilling machines. Darryl walked over to his uncle and said, "Can we show you something? People, excuse us for a few minutes."

Ten minutes later, in the back of the cave where most had sought shelter, there was a deep drop-off. Darryl, Sue Lyn, and the Sarge, picked up lanterns and followed the naturally circular path for approximately sixty feet. The base of the cave floor was covered with 'Hope' size diamonds. Darryl said, "We discovered this the other night, but we were consumed with the assault. This will pay for all of the drilling issues and beyond as well as enrich the Aborigine people handsomely."

The Sarge asked, "Are these really diamonds?"

Darryl said, I'm no gemologist, but I think they're some kind of precious stones."

"Yeah, but so many of them, just laying around. Our people never ventured down here?"

"Uncle, it was our people who told us about the place and indicated it was only safe for a spirit of the people to be here and to remove anything. Of course, we didn't remove anything and played along with the story."

Ben Beckmire looked at Darryl and said, "What's your last name? And who was Andy Beckmire? You are a spirit of sorts—a living one just like I am when I'm here. Don't discount ancient tales."

#

Beckmire, Sue Lyn, and Darryl, later rejoined the group for lunch and he said, "People, my nephew and his wife just showed me billions of dollars in precious stones."

Asiram yelled, "I thought we were a team. Why can't we see them?"

The Sarge looked at her and said, "You're wrong. We're more than a team; we're family. Okay, everyone come with me, but let me remind you of one thing. Only a spirit may sanction the removal of stones from where they are. I implore you not to tempt fate for a bauble. Is that clear, do not remove anything from the place I'm going to take you."

As the group made the trek down the path, prior to going to the bottom, the Sarge, Darryl, and Sue Lyn turned on powerful flashlights and illuminated the floor. Everyone was taken aback at the sight of the diamonds resting on the floor seemingly available for the take. Ben Beckmire heard a hissing noise and turned his light to the perimeter of the cave, and it was covered with snakes. He looked at Darryl and Sue Lyn and said, "This is what I meant by not discounting ancient tales. When we were here alone, there wasn't a snake anywhere near this place."

"Uncle, I know my calling and I know what it means. We're on the same page, but remember my wife is not from the world that we're associated with and sometimes is a little skeptical of things I say and feel."

Courtney yelled, "Honey, I think we got the point. Let's get out of here."

Topside, the Sarge said, "That was a massive display of security. Whew! And those guys are not my favorite species.

Did you guys see how many were there? Anyway, I think we have solved our mining and extraction expenses problem. Darryl and Sue Lyn have a helluva job in front of them. And let me say one more thing, I want to formally introduce Harold, Jasper, Windom, Earther, Desmond and Isaiah. You guys already know Michael. They will be assisting Darryl and Sue Lyn in developing the relationships necessary to extract and market the stones. Oh, by the way, I want to make it very clear our diamonds are from Australia, and they don't have blood on them and they're not mined by indigent minors and slaves. They will be mined by the people who own them—the Australian Aborigine."

The Sarge paused for a second and then continued, "We have searched their souls and have found they are true to the cause and will help my nephew in the completion of this massive undertaking. I think there are literally billions upon billions of dollars' worth of precious stones in that place and beyond. Sue Lyn, while your husband is trying to figure out how to extract them, I want you to figure out how to brand our diamonds and make sure they're more exclusive than anything coming out of our sister continent."

Michael raised his hand and asked for permission to speak. The Sarge acknowledged him, and he asked, "What about those snakes? Do they come up to the surface?"

The Sarge and the group laughed, and he said, "Michael, your family is connected to my family. We're all one and what I have, you have. We just don't buy stupid; you know Rolls Royce and things like that. We buy what the family needs jets, trucks, that are armor plated, and businesses that need a boost like your fathers. You and your people will make a lot of money and I hope you spend it wisely, and if not, then you'll get a pay cut. We don't do stupid, and the snakes will not attack you or even show up when you're there unless your heart is not pure. It's an awesome relationship where the animals are the value judges."

As the Sarge was speaking, two trucks appeared in the foreground making their way to the village. He spoke softer and said, "They're coming to ask if we know anything about the carnage. Of course, the answer is no, we don't. They might want to talk to you individually, but that's okay. We're all on the same page and many of you didn't see anything or join in the fire fight."

# # #

After a few pleasantries, the customs officials asked Beckmire if he was aware of what happened in town, and he told the men that he had heard that a group of people had planned to torch the House of Records to complicate the process of proving ownership of a certain area known to have some expensive natural resources. The official asked if he was aware of the area in question and Beckmire told him that he was. He then asked Ben Beckmire, what was his relationship with the clan that was there and Beckmire told him they were family. One of the agents said, "Mr. Beckmire, you're more than family in these parts. Your ancestors made their mark on this land in a good way. We're not accusing you, but we did happen to find some paperwork that is associated with one of the people in your group. Is there a John Lee Jones here?"

Everyone was stunned, and John Lee stood up and said, "Did you find my money too?"

The official asked, "What do you mean did we find your money?"

"I reported that to the local magistrate. My wallet was misplaced, and I had a thousand or so in cash in it. Did you find it and was my money there?"

The agent looked at him and realized he was full of shit and said, "Naw, mate. No money was in sight. Just your id."

He looked at Ben Beckmire and asked, "Can you and I walk down to the billabong for a moment and "ave" a chat?"

Later as the two men sat near the billabong, the man asked, "Do you see those huge crocs looking at us and easing their way towards us?"

"I do, and you don't seem to be concerned."

"Mr. Beckmire, it is alleged your ancestor left my ancestor without legs, arms and the ability to see."

Beckmire jerked his head and asked, "Mate, are you related to Mr. Cheeks?"

"I am a direct descendant of his."

"Do you realize you have a relative working with me?"

"No, that couldn't be possible because my people are indigenous to the continent."

"I need you to sit tight and don't let the crocs bite, for one minute."

Ben Beckmire hustled back through the bush and yelled, "Where is Chakes? I need him right now. Where the hell is he?" Chakes came running and said, "What's going on? What the hell did I do wrong?"

"Son, you just saved our asses. Come with me. I want you to meet someone."

When they approached the billabong, the Sarge looked at the spot where he had left the customs official, and he wasn't there. There was a large wake and splash in the billabong and the Sarge said, "Oh shit, oh shit!"

Chakes said, "What the hell was that and who do you want me to meet?"

As the Sarge descended to his knees and said, "I thought he was a good person."

From the bush, the official walked out and said, "Your extended family got too close, and I decided to abandon my position."

The Sarge looked at him and said, "Shit, I thought you were a snack. Damn I'm glad you moved, but they wouldn't have bothered you. You just have the smell of your ancestor. You will not be harmed by them. Wow, anyway, meet Maurice Chakes, I think he's related to you."

The two men shook hands, and it was obvious there was a connection. As they attempted to manage the handshake, visions, latent memories, the demise of their ancestor and his wicked friends became obvious to both. When Ben Beckmire broke the bond, he said, "I'll leave you guys to figure out how to relate to what you just experienced. I suggest you don't go near the water. My extended family as you state, is now confused about the double source of historic energy. Stay safe, my friends."

# # #

Later at dinner the Sarge announced they should head back to St. Thomas for a few days. He said he would solicit from the group, where they thought a final battle ground with his cousin should take place. As people were about to respond, he held up his hand and said, "I need you people to consider where you might want to possibly die. I'm assuming after this event our next appointment will be with one of the forces that constitute the military.

CHAPTER SEVENTEEN

Ben Beckmire told his nephew his team would be leaving in a day or so and asked if he was alright assuming control over seasoned-ex-soldiers and running an empire? His nephew told his uncle he was up to the task, and that he would have a final discussion with Michael about his ever-changing role and his expectations of the group. Ben Beckmire told him that Earther and Windom's people were strong and crafty and to use them rather than let them become bored. He told him that everyone that was extracted from Minnesota was to be given a task and supervised by his other two lieutenants, Earther and Windom. He also told Darryl that at dinner, he would speak to the entire village and explain what was going to happen and the risks that are involved when word gets out that a bunch of darkies have discovered diamonds in their village.

Ben Beckmire said to Darryl, "This is going to be your coming out party. You're going to oversee this entire enterprise. Everything that happens from the point I put my feet on that plane and I'm no longer on this soil, becomes an event that will have your footprint on every aspect of it. You're a Beckmire and, therefore, I know you can handle it."

"Your team now has weapons and lots of them, and until you figure out how you're going to secure this place and the people, I suggest that they're always armed. Now, nephew, I frankly don't know much about starting a business or valuing diamonds and the gold that's in the billabong, but you and Sue Lyn are the next generation of leaders of this group. You'll figure it out, you'll hire people from afar and meet them somewhere else. You should bid for a security firm and then lure the good ones away. You guys have a shitload of stuff to get done and you don't have all year to make it happen. More important, you have this entire village to think of, protect, and enrich. You have schools to build both academic and technical.

The Sarge paused and said, "I prefer that our young men from across the continent, be trained by seasoned security people and then interviewed by you, your people, along with Wajickee and other spirits looking into the fabric of their souls. Yes, nephew, you and your lady have your work cut out for you."

Darryl stared at his uncle while expecting him to continue to scare the mess out of him some more. He finally asked, "Uncle, I need you to honestly tell me if you think I can meet all of the expectations you've laid out?"

"Darryl, you're a Beckmire. I wouldn't have given you this opportunity if I thought you weren't up to the task. You have good people assisting you, start by figuring out their strengths. You might be pleasantly surprised at what they bring to the table. I love you and remember, you're a Beckmire and nothing I've asked, is impossible to accomplish by you and your team. You have all my trust, faith, financing, and everything else. Do your thing and I'll come back in a few months after we settle this mess with your other uncle."

# # #

Darryl told Sue Lyn he needed to take a walk and clear his head about some things he discussed with his uncle. She inquired about the nature of the discussion, and he told her what had transpired. Sue Lyn quickly cut him off and said, "Your uncle is letting you know that he's here for you now but will not be in a few days. He certainly is not second guessing your abilities. He wants you to use him while he's here. Once he's gone, the game belongs to you and that includes, extraction, mining, security, banking, investing, and everything else. He just gave you a huge promotion and you're going to need as much help as you can possibly obtain. Also, I think one of the first things you're going to have to do is find a better security system. I don't believe snakes and spiders can adequately and consistently provide security in that cave."

"Sue Lyn, I know you think sometimes I'm an odd brain individual, but please remember this, in this place, there are forces that are hard to reckon with. After my uncle speaks to the entire village at dinner, everyone will understand my anointed role better. I need to find Michael; I have a task for him. I'll catch you later."

# # #

Darryl caught up with Michael and said, "I need everyone to develop a resume showing their jobs, schooling, military service, and everything else. I need you to get our people to do that asap."

"Good as done. I'll have them work on it before dinner and they'll have something for you to look at. I'll ask Earther and Windom as well, and his people that have been assigned tasks."

"Frankly, I know you were assigned to me by my uncle and I'm not quite sure if this is where you want to be," Darryl stated.

Michael after hearing that information, thought that he was being fired. He looked at Darryl straight on and said, "Let me explain who I am. I'm a loyal person who your uncle asked to take care of a disposal problem for him and I did it. Your uncle helped save my father's life. He would have killed himself if he had failed at that business. Your uncle not only saved him but stimulated a situation where my father and mother work together, talk to each other, and laugh. I was not employed or doing very much of anything except trying to help at 'The Sanctuary'. Your uncle helped me and my friends who are good dudes. We owe him, and we owe you. You didn't have to accept us as your team, but you did. We were down on our luck and you people came along and restored our belief in ourselves that we can contribute. I would like to think I'm your Mallory, Jilkes, or John Lee. We are fiercely loyal people who need you to believe in and trust."

"Michael, let me make one thing perfectly clear, I trust each man that's with me. I was just wondering if you preferred to be with my uncle and his people or stuck with me out here in the outback?"

"Darryl, me and the guys are where we want to be, and besides, your uncle has too many people always trying to put a hurting on him. Boss, I'll get the resumes and we are where we want to be and that's with you."

# # #

After dinner and after Ben Beckmire's long speech about support, family, security, location, living arrangements, and other things, his voice changed and deepened. It almost sounded mystical to those listening. He reintroduced Darryl and Sue Lyn and indicated they were his official representatives when he was not on Australian soil. He also introduced Darryl's team as well. He told the clan that members of other clans would be coming here for support and employment and for them to open their arms and hearts. He cautioned everyone about displaying or announcing their new-found wealth and that any such displays would result in a reduction in ownership. He told them that spirits near and far who controlled the small animals in the outback would be watching and would send them to anyone who did not act in the best interest of the village and the Aborigine people.

He finished his long tirade with and in his natural tone, "My nephew and his wife are in full control of the mines, the funding, the products, the investments, and the security. I know some of you are going to tempt your fate and all I can say to you is, you will not be stopped searched or questioned. I also doubt you'll ever come up from that place as well. Nephew, would you like to say a few words?"

"Thanks uncle, and I want to reintroduce my lovely wife, friend, partner and lover, Ms. Sue Lyn Beckmire. As you all know, we were just married a few days ago, here. I want to also introduce you to people who you will see around the village for a long time. Harold, please stand and remain standing, Jasper, Isaiah, Desmond, Earther, Windom, and my right-hand man, Michael. We will be sporting weapons, but they will never be used on any Aborigine. We like to look forward and realize that the word of this place is going to spread like wildfire, and we want to make sure that anyone who comes here with the wrong intent will be fed to the wildlife. Many of you have been officially registered as owners of the mines and those of you who haven't, Sue Lyn will be available tomorrow to assist you in filling out the paperwork. For those of you who can only make your mark, we're going to photograph you making your mark and certify that you are an owner of the mines.

"So, what does all that signing and marking mean? Well, it means you and your family, will for as long as the mine produces a product, be an owner of it, and as such, be entitled to a monthly, quarterly, or annual payment. My uncle told one of my guys if you buy stupid, you will get an automatic pay cut. Y'all know what I mean when I say buy stupid. You don't need a Cadillac in the outback. So, anyway, this is going to be a great adventure for you and us. We have a lot to get done and starting tomorrow, we're going to start listing the kinds of jobs that will be available to everyone in the village. Everyone must work for the benefit of the village and to defend it. Every slick talking con man and crook from all over the world will be coming here trying to get their hands on our booty. As such, and for the protection of everyone, we are going to arm a significant number of you with the goal of having everyone in the village, of age, know how and when to use a weapon. Now, that's an extreme option. The other less volatile option is to move everyone into town, buy up land at the end of town and build condos. We'll leave the security to professionals. Well, that option brings in more hands than needed to remove at some point our profits without us knowing it. I'm going to hold another meeting tomorrow after I go on Walkabout. If you have any suggestions, please be prepared at the breakfast hour to state them. Remember, nothing is too foolish."

Ben Beckmire walked over to Darryl and said, "Nicely done. You're showing them you are in charge, and you know what you're doing. You know the more foreigners find out about this, the more they're going to come here to try and take it from you."

"That's exactly why I'm thinking about hiring our relatives back in Sydney and a few of the guys in charge of customs. Two of them are ex-military and might remember enough to train our people in the basics of securing not only the mines, but the entire village. I was surprised when I didn't get any reaction on the condo notion."

"Nephew, you know these people aren't ready for condos, elevators, doctors, lawyers, judges, police, frozen foods, and all the liquor they can carry."

"Uncle, I'm not trying to be rude, but I had discussed with Sue Lyn the idea of setting up a hospital right here in the village with our own doctors and nurses. Of course, we need a hospital, and I think that's going to be primary on our list. I wish Ms. Courtney could stay awhile and help with that chore."

Ben Beckmire thought about the idea and dismissed it immediately. The two men continued their discussion about other hot topic issues and concluded that it all was an experiment into how to evolve a people who were basically happy living in a cave, into living in the 21st Century.

Darryl stated, "That's exactly why we need to build this village first, with schools, hospitals, markets, restaurants and everything else. I'm afraid we're going to need psychiatrists and psychologists as well as drug and alcohol abuse counselors."

"Darryl, a lot of our people attend the universities. Put an advertisement in the local papers and indicate you're looking for individuals, hopefully indigenous, to take part in an aggressive social experiment, designed to evolve people from the bush into life in the 21st Century. List all that you need. Oh, if you want to build schools and hospitals, I know some Spaniards that are a part of our family who would love to come here and try to help. They owe us big time and I'm sure they could make a difference because they're former con men, crooks, thieves, and some other things that I won't mention. I know they've finished our projects in Valencia and they might want to take on this project. Once we're in the air, I'll give a call and see what they're up to."

Darryl dropped his head and Ben Beckmire said, "Never let your people see you in a defeatist position. When you stop thinking about how big the job is and compartmentalize it, you'll feel better. You have Sue Lyn, Michael, and his crew, along with Earther and Windom. Grow their skill set. Give them a list of things that need to be completed and let them select one or two people to assist. Everyone must select a project and all the projects should be big. Listen, just like I know you'll do fine, so will your people. You and Sue Lyn have the books and the accounts. Everyone must do a budget. I mean, irrigation, plumbing, electrical and on and on—

Nephew you got this. Just don't bundle the process—keep the projects separate and distinct with your people leading the way. All you do is provide oversight. They have to figure out how to make it work and get it done.

"You have all the relevant phone numbers, internet, and satellite connections. I selected you because I know who you are and what you're capable of doing. You, my nephew, have the Herculean task of building a whole new village. You my friend have what is known as the 'Gordian Knot'. Have fun figuring it out and doing it. I love you."

CHAPTER EIGHTEEN

Miles away from Australia and minds even further from there, the group came together and spent their first two days in and around the blue waters of St. Thomas. Asiram asked Zanthius if there were crocs in the water there and he basically laughed at her and said, "No, honey. I think they just have sharks in the waters here. I've heard of shark attacks, but never croc attacks."

Asiram looked out into the water and saw everyone freely swimming and playing and said, "I never saw anyone in the water in Australia, have you?"

"Honey, you have to admit, there were a shitload of crocs in the water and then they talked about that box jellyfish with tentacles 10 feet long that can kill you. Hell no, I'm never going in the water in Australia again. My father had me and Larry dive into the water and tie those trunks together. I was really scared for a moment, but when I saw my father freely swimming without fear or a care, it seemed to relax me and Larry. We saw the cases with the gold in them, but our dad signaled for us to leave them for now. He's a strange and wonderful man. He only cares about the people, his people, and the rest of us. I've never heard him request a single thing. He is so self-sufficient and humble. I heard him tell Courtney that he couldn't wait to get back to John Lee's area and sit on that big porch surrounded by all his grandbabies and no parents. I worry about him. He does it all for everyone else."

"Yeah, I know. My daddy-in-law is a great human being, but I don't know why you worry about him?"

"Darryl told me to keep an eye on his uncle, and to make sure that he's always surrounded by positive vibes. He told me there were forces seeking to find his weak points and exploit them and lead him to his ruin. I don't understand much that happens when we're there, but things rush in and out of my mind and I can't process them. I've seen my father bleeding profusely from the head and not moving. I've seen Courtney bleeding and laying on top of Jilkes who is headless and John Lee who has been gutted to his brain. I've seen this shit while were there this time."

He broke into hysterics and said, "I've seen men lined up to violate you and slam our children against the rocks. I saw my mother tied to a tree and set on fire and Juan's head lying before her with his eyes looking up at her as she burned to death. I've seen our entire group decimated with my uncle pissing down on my father's face. I've been running at night to try to break down these visions, but they keep coming to me every night more violent than before."

Asiram moved quickly to her husband, grabbed and held him tightly and said, "Honey, if your thoughts are not pure then your dreams are multiplied beyond comprehension. Your father has said that on many occasions. What is it you want or who is it you want to be with? And buddy, you had better answer that one correctly or I'm going to kick your ass."

"Asiram, your love returned me from the dead. I mean I was dead and didn't know it. My mother came to my rescue and forced me to take a job unknowingly, as a spy, and the first person I met and who I still love, is you. My dreams are frightening, and I worry about my dad, mom, and stepmom. I am also forced to watch the sordid things that happen to you. Something is not right and I'm afraid to speak to my dad about it, or my mom for that matter. Suppose what I'm dreaming is what happens in the future? I would come back from hell and cut each person's head off who are responsible for these acts, and then kill their families. I would be worse than my uncle could ever be, the evil one that is."

Asiram continued to hug him tightly and realized how important or confusing these messages were to her husband.

# # #

Later, Asiram buzzed Ms. Viola, who after a conversation with her, realized there was an emergency. When she arrived at their room and looked at Zanthius, she said, "Your man be done been bit by a tick and we be needing to get him to the hospital. Is he hallucinating and seeing things or just plain talking crazy?"

"Ms. Viola, he's all over the place. I thought we were protected from the animals in Australia?"

"Ms. Asiram, this no be an Australian tick. This here tick be from the islands. Your man be done lay down between the fresh water and salt water and done caught himself a tick. I need a lighter and a safety pin. How long he be crazy?"

"For as long as I've known him."

"No, Ms. Asiram, how long he be crazy this time?"

"He started talking crazy five minutes ago."

Ms. Viola said, "Get Ms. Courtney up here and have them bring a van to the front. We be having to get him to the hospital in a hurry. I see the tick and I'm going to cut it off so the hospital can know precisely how to handle this thing. This tick only bites a human if it sits on top of its mound. What's up with you people. I think there be a message in this madness."

When Courtney and Ava arrived on the scene, Zanthius was close to unconsciousness. Ava yelled, "What happened to him?"

Ms. Viola said, "Him got bit by a tick and a tick from the islands. He's delirious and we must get him to the hospital and place him on IV fluids immediately. We got to keep him awake and keep trying to make him drink water. If he goes to sleep, he forfeits his life. That tick is so rare, and your husband was too unlucky to find the only place where the tick finds safe harbor."

Courtney said, "We need to move him downstairs and get him to the hospital. Jilkes and John Lee heard the commotion and when Courtney saw them, she yelled, "I need you guys to take Zanthius downstairs and get him in a van. He needs to go to the hospital."

When the Sarge saw the beehive of activity he casually asked, "What on earth is going on?" Courtney gave him the skinny of the issue and he too jumped into action.

# # #

At the hospital, the Sarge realized that his people were separated, and didn't like the idea. He whispered to Jilkes that he wanted him and John Lee to quietly go back to the resort, arm themselves, and bring the entire group to the hospital.

Jilkes looked around and passed off a small pistol to Larry and John Lee gave his to the Sarge who handed it to Asiram.

Asiram said, "Daddy-in-Law, all of the women have weapons on them." He smiled and returned the weapon to John Lee and said, "Seems like they don't leave home without one."

When the two men arrived at the resort, they saw Chakes, Somara, Luana, and Mallory. Jilkes passed the word and told them the group should be ready in ten. The word spread fast, and each member had their little 'out of here bag' and were loaded into the vehicles. Mr. Carter drove one vehicle and his daughter drove the other. Prior to leaving, Mallory took roll call, and everyone was present and accounted for. Mr. Carter's wife appeared in the road, and he rolled down the window and said, "Honey, can you watch the store until I get back?"

"I'll be here waiting on you, lover!" The vehicle he was driving erupted into a loud noise. Everyone was saying, in their own inimical manner, 'I'll be here waiting on you, lover'.

Mr. Carter gave a matter of fact smile and said, "Calm down, we're just testing the waters again." The sound of that gave rise to thunderous clapping by those in his vehicle.

# # #

At the hospital, a place where the group had financed a wing and outfitted it, the group was welcomed. The head nurse stated, "I assume you guys will be staying, and your wing is available. I'll have the carts moved in if you like and I'll get the menu for tonight's meal, and see if it's something you want to experience or if you want to oblige the pizza guy two miles away?"

Mallory said, "We're trying to figure out things right now. Once we find out the status of our mate, we'll let you know. By the way, does the hospital need our help, and if so, our young friends who are in Australia want to do a matching kind of fund raising for you guys that we would silently match? They're going to be there for a while, but I'll have them talk to my wife, Luana and Ms. Viola to figure out what they have in mind and see if you guys want to move forward. As a matter of fact, maybe there is a way to develop a sister relationship with the family in Australia. They are planning on building hospitals, schools, and other things, maybe you guys can be their model."

The nurse looked at the two men and broke into tears. She hastily ran from the room. Mallory and McArthur thought about her actions, independently, but in different manners. McArthur looked at Mallory and cocked his head to the right indicating they needed to understand the nature of that response. Once in the hallway, McArthur said, "That could go one of two ways. I think we need to make sure she hasn't been compromised by the dark side.

When they caught up with the nurse, Mallory said, "You know us and how we operate, and perhaps you have some idea of what we do. I have to ask you a question that may offend you, but it's better to be offended then become shark bait."

Her eyes opened wide, and she said, "I was praying my reaction caused you concern. People were here and threatened me and the head doctor for information about you and we were told if we revealed any information about the inquiry, then they would return and eliminate us. We discussed ways to communicate this information to you and I'm so happy my little drama queen act got your attention. The main character wanted to know about a member of your group who he called the 'idiot spy'. I tried to convince them that neither the doctor nor I ever talked to you people other than about the status of a patient, or thanking you for your contributions to the hospital, or treating you guys. Those people thought we were chums or something, meaning that we dined together and went swimming in the ocean."

McArthur cut her off and asked, "Listen, is anyone in our group in jeopardy?" The nurse looked at him and said, "We're a healing institution and we do not compromise our services to our clients. In other words, hell no. Those guys were bullies and you guys are, well, the jury is still out, but we prefer to play ball with you without being threatened. We haven't seen them around lately."

Mallory said, "I don't think you'll ever see them again, but I want to show you a picture to see if this guy was here?" He reached into his back pocket and retrieved his cell phone and fumbled through the apps and hit the dot that featured a camera. He then scrolled down and found a picture of Walter. He tapped the screen and enlarged the photo and asked, "Have you ever seen this person?"

The nurse looked at the screen and said, "OMG! That's your puppet master. He's the guy that was pulling the strings."

Mallory's eyes widened and he asked, "Is there any way this guy could have orchestrated the placement of a tick in our compound?"

"Not this tick. Your friend sat his ass in the wrong place at the wrong time. Man cannot control the insects on this island."

A short time later, Mallory and McArthur walked up to the Sarge and told him about their interaction with the nurse. He turned to them and said, "We're out of here in ten. Courtney, gather what you need to stabilize my boy. People you have your 'out of here bags', so prepare to disassociate yourselves with everything that you left at 'The Sanctuary'." I need a roll call and head count. I need medicines and stabilizers for my son. In ten minutes, people, I want everyone on their way to the airport. No phone calls. I repeat, no phone calls. Everyone should be armed and dangerous at this point."

Those who were not with weapons hastily made their way to the vehicles and from the secure storage boxes within each vehicle, picked a weapon. The Sarge looked at Ms. Viola and said, "I need you to make a call. I need everyone on that plane without any delay. So, I need you to make sure we are whisked through customs."

"Mr. Sergeant, sir, you people have guns on you. You can't disembark from here with weapons."

"Ms. Viola, the guns get left in the van once we're at the terminal. Make the call!" the Sarge exclaimed.

# # #

Thirty-five minutes later, everyone was on board the plane including a heavily sedated Zanthius. Mallory stood and took roll call and said, "All present and accounted for, sir."

Twenty minutes later, a previously heavily guarded plane blasted down the runway into the air with the false notion of landing in the Maryland/DC area. Once the plane reached cruising altitude, the Sarge stood up and said, "I know you people are wondering why I ordered us off the island with my son sick as can be? Well, Mallory showed the head nurse a picture of my cousin and she told him that Walter, the puppet master, was the one pulling the strings and bullying everyone on the hospital staff. He came to our sanctuary.

"The manifest that was filed indicates that we're on our way to Maryland. Just so you know, we're going to Wyoming to try to lure Walter out there where we can see him mounting his battle. Asiram, I need you to place a call to Clyde and tell him we're in need of a ride in the bus with the toys. I suggest that everyone keeps a weapon on his or her person from this point forward. We've cost my cousin a lot of money and I know he's as interested in bringing this thing to a head as we are. That's all I have right now, are there any questions?"

The Sarge then went to the back of the plane where Zanthius was resting quietly and all his vital signs were slightly raised, but in the manageable range.

CHAPTER NINETEEN

"Praise be to the heavens. My goodness, it's so good to see you people again and look how big them babies have gotten. Thanks be to the almighty," Clyde bellowed out.

Asiram walked over to him and gave him a hug and said, "Clyde, I've missed you and this place. I'm so glad to be back. You can tell me what's been going on when we get to the ranch. How's your wife?"

"Well, she's not doing all that good, and that thing called arthritis is creating a lot a pain for her. I can't seem to convince her to go to the doctor. She keeps telling me that 'God is telling her to prepare'."

"I'll have Courtney look at her at some point tonight. It's good to be back here and smell that fresh air. Is everything okay with the ranch? Any problems or extra expenses?"

"I had a few additions added that I think you'll like and I had the barn painted and the heater fixed in it. I had a new escape tunnel added that takes you deep in the fields and into the woods. I brought some people up from Mexico to have that done. I kept them here and blindfolded them each time I took them under and brought them up. That new president is making it hard to get good labor, but it's complete. Oh, and one of your neighbors just happened upon one of those new

Gatlin guns. You know the one that whistles and spins while firing hundreds of rounds per minute."

"Clyde, how on earth did he happen to manage that?"

"Ms. Asiram, everyone knows what you people did for us and they all realize we have to protect each other. Well, his brother was the inventory commander at a certain base, and he knew that, well, you people had a problem and that people would show up with all kinds of guns trying to kill you people. Well, that there weapon got misplaced. I mean he plain forgot where it was shipped, and somehow it got shipped out here, fell off that truck, and landed in a ditch. I know this is a convoluted story and every time it's told, it's going to have a different outcome because no one really knows where it came from. In other words, that be a local problem and not to be worried about by you and yours. Oh, and a lot of cases of .50 caliber bullets fell off that same damn truck."

# # #

Once the group reached the ranch, everyone was exhausted and hungry. You know country folk, when they hear about guests coming, and especially company that helped them out, well, everyone pitches in to create a feast within minutes. When Asiram opened her door, the smell of fried chicken and other goodies filled the air. The ladies inside came up and started hugging and kissing everyone and then the feast began.

The group ate themselves into a coma. Clyde and the men folk met with the Sarge and told him they assigned some people to keep a lookout so, don't go shooting at things moving in the woods. Clyde looked around, hesitated, and asked, "Where are those young people who installed that system? The cameras work really well." The Sarge told him that they were in Australia working on a large project that would benefit the Aborigine people.

# # #

Around 2100 hours, the Sarge asked Asiram if she would watch her husband for a few because he wanted to take a walk with his wife. Asiram laughed and said, "Going to make hay in the barn, eh?"

Courtney said, "You're so bad, Daughter-in-Law, but I love you like I love life. To your question, I damn sure hope so."

At exactly 2200 hours, Zanthius woke up and started yelling. Ava tried to restrain her son but was violently pushed to the floor. John Lee heard the commotion as did Jilkes, and two men ran into the room. Zanthius was somewhat restrained on the gurney from his chest down, but his hands and arms were free. He was about to turn the gurney over. John Lee grabbed him and Jilkes slapped him into another stupor.

Much later, when Zanthius woke up, he asked, "Who slapped me?"

Jilkes pointed to John Lee and said, "That pig farmer did it."

Zanthius asked, "Asiram, who slapped me?"

Ava, after remembering picking herself off the floor said, "As soon as your ass can walk, I'm going to slap the shit out of you for throwing me to the floor."

"Mom! What are you talking about? I would never do such a thing."

"Honey, you pushed your mother to the floor and that is when Jilkes slapped you, not John Lee," Asiram clarified.

"That's what you get for intervening in a family squabble. I see why police don't like to do domestic disturbances. I hope we don't have to deal with this later. I was trying to bring you around because you were throwing people around like a mad man," Jilkes announced.

"Why am I on this thing and not in my bed?"

"Honey, you were bit by a tick, and you literally went berserk. I thought that I was going to collect on your life insurance policy, but it looks like you might survive. We're now in Wyoming at the ranch. Your uncle was on the island and your father, got us out of there in a hurry. You were literally in the hospital and was transported from the hospital to the airport. You are truly the 'idiot spy', for who else on earth sits on a venomous tick's house?"

The Sarge walked into the room and over to Zanthius and asked, "What's going on? How are you feeling?"

"I'm fine except my wife wants to collect on my insurance policy, my mother wants to slap the shit out of me, and Jilkes already slapped the piss out of me."

"Wait a minute. That doesn't make sense."

"Daddy-in-Law, you might want to welcome him back to reality and try to figure this slapping and pushing thing out another day. I'm going to cut the restraints off him if you think he's alright Courtney."

#

Approaching 2400 hours, Jilkes, Yeshida, John Lee, and Somara were in the dining room watching Zanthius eat himself back to health.   Jilkes saw that Yeshida was acting a little distant and pre-occupied and asked, "Woman, what's wrong with you? What did I do or say wrong this time?"

Yeshida attempted to get out of her chair, and he held her in it. She screamed, "I'm fucking pregnant again."

Silence prevailed in the room and Zanthius stopped chewing. Jilkes stood up and violently kicked his chair across the room and fell to his knees and said, "I love you more than life and you make me happy with children."

Yeshida crying said, "I didn't think you wanted more children?"

"Baby, we must start talking again like we did in the beginning.   We are all consumed with this family and its security and John Lee and I play important roles. If you want to have five children, I would be happy. Where did you get the idea, I didn't want any more? Am I not a good father? Am I not attentive enough?"

"Big man kiss me and take me to our room. I want to make more love to you."

Zanthius said, "In case you people don't realize it. I'm still in the room and so is John Lee and Somara."

Zanthius looked at Somara, recognized she was crying as well, paused and asked, "Somara why are you crying? Are you pregnant too?"

She screamed at the top of her lungs, and said, "Yes, I'm pregnant again." John Lee looked at her and asked in his own inimical manner, "So, we be having another little boy?"

She looked at him and asked, "What you say if it be a girl?"

"Oh, I like little girls if you like them. I just want you to be happy and in love with me and we can keep making babies forever. How about you and I have a small celebration drink and then go and play footsies?" John Lee inquired.

Zanthius said, "Was I in that coma for a long time, or is all of this a recent manifestation?"

Jilkes smiled and said, "Go ask Asiram the one who really slapped your ass." Jilkes then looked at Yeshida and said, "Baby, we got to talk more often. I need you to tell me what's on your mind and what I need to do to make sure you never stop loving me. My entire world is invested in you and I love you so much. Stop being or dealing with what's common in your culture. Let's make a deal. Let's make up our own rules and culture and not go with any tradition other than the ones we want to."

As the group began to disband, Ava saw Zanthius and walked over to him and said, "Baby, are you alright? I was worried. Your fever was high and then broke in a rush. Are you feeling, okay?"

"Mom, I don't remember much, but I've been having some really bad dreams of late. The tick bite multiplied the intensity of them I suspect. I've seen mayhem wreaked upon us with you, my dad, my wife, and children being brutally murdered. I've had visions of members of our group being gutted, hung, burned, and decapitated. This has not been a good trip."

Ava looked at her son and her eyes began to water. After gaining her composure, she said, "My darling Zanthius, I've had the same dreams. Are they telling us to cut and run. I don't know. The only thing I know, and feel is that I'll die with this group in defense of this family. Nothing has been more fulfilling than being amongst these people, loving them and learning from them. If you and I are the only ones having these kinds of dreams, then I suggest you figure out how to, if that's what you want to do, save your wife and children? I'm going to die with my new family."

"Mom, you resurrected me from the dead. My father accepts and loves me. His wife acknowledges me as her son, as well. You can't be serious when offering me a way out. Me and my family will flourish with this group or die with them. It's been a great existence. Listen, you rescued me and told me about my dad and I met the most wonderful woman on earth. I have two children who I love, a third one on the way, and a group of people who will take a bullet for me and me for them. One for all and all for one. Have you ever heard that before?"

"Please! The Three Musketeers. I have an idea. Why don't we focus on trying to save lives, stay alive, and, when and if the end is near, you realize I love you and I'll know that you love me. As I hear things about your uncle, he'll kill everyone in this community, including the kids, Ava announced."

"Mom, you dated a man by the name of Ben Beckmire. You've seen what he and his crew can do with a little help from his children and his friends. My dad is an amazing human being, and I'm so happy that you fell in love with him and that you're still in love with him. Mom, listen, how can you not love a man like that? Juan is tight, I respect, admire, and refer to him as my stepdad, but Ben Beckmire is the man you'll love forever, you know it, I know it, Courtney knows it and so does he. When we're in Australia, I get strange dreams. Larry gets them as well, and my dads are multiplied by the tenth power. I get things coming and going when we're over there. Larry gets mixed messages, but our dad, his stuff is off the chart. Ben Beckmire is the whistle you blew that was real. Don't get me wrong, so is Juan, he loves and worships you, but I'm just saying, and you know I'm right, my dad is the real deal."

As tears poured from her eyes and descended down her face, Ava said, "Can you imagine how many people would be hurt if I confessed and tried to sway the man back to me?"

"Mom, that ain't going to happen. People are where they're supposed to be, I was reflecting on history--a history that had you with the perfect man that produced the imperfect son; 'the idiot spy'. I just wanted to let you know I knew the turmoil that existed in your life at each encounter with my father. I suggest you not be so accommodating to him and spend more time focusing on Juan. Everyone sees it and have accepted its innocence. Don't complicate things by wishing on a star you've already had."

Ava walked over to her son and hugged him tightly. Asiram stepped in at that very moment and said, "Ah! That's so sweet."

Zanthius told Asiram that he was still a little hungry but didn't want to disturb Clyde's people. He was told that there was a ton of food in the refrigerators. She told him that there were sandwich meats, chicken, steak, fish and loads of vegetables that were cut up. She asked him if he wanted her to fix him something and he declined, indicating he wasn't sure what he wanted and had to go and see what was there.

Zanthius left the room and ran into his father and Mallory. Ben Beckmire asked how he was feeling and was told that he was okay and could not really remember much about the past day or so.

His father said, "Everything happens for a reason. Had you not sat your ass, on a tick's house, we would have been blind to the fact the devil was amongst us. I don't know what he was doing there, but I knew we weren't prepared to do battle with him. So, you got sick and we were informed."

"I'm glad I could help pops. Have you decided how we can end this thing? Is there any chance of flushing him out and capturing him without killing a lot of souls in need of funds?"

"Those are all good questions, Son. I'm of the belief this thing is going to end badly for both sides."

"Yeah, that's what my mother believes. She suggested I take my family and run away and live happily ever after. What she failed to realize is, I'm the reason your people came out of retirement, and saved all of our asses. She was just sounding off because she loves those grandbabies."

"Son, every person in this place is asking the same kind of questions or trying to figure out when they can go and live happily ever after? You know other than when we are on the islands, we're tied to the airplanes, caves, and outdoors living. We're not fortune hunters or adventurers, we're just simple folk who are trying to protect one of our own as well as each other. I'm sure you've heard the adage, 'United we stand, divided we fall'? Anyhow, people need to assess their situation and if they must go, then so be it. I'm just thankful we got this far without any fatalities. God is good."

"Dad, you and Mallory have been together a long time and you never seem to disagree. Are you two that much alike?"

"Nope, you're wrong. We have various ways of communicating just like the guys do. I can look at him and he knows exactly my answer or what I'm thinking. When you've been in as many dog fights as we have, you'd better learn another language. Why do you ask?"

"I'm just trying to figure you guys out as well as thank you for all you've done for me. On our last trip in the outback, I had so many weird dreams and visions that I couldn't discern, fact from fiction. Many in our group were killed in one vision but appeared in another. I saw, and I will not name names, people piled on top of each other, and your cousin standing over them tossing gasoline and fire onto the heap. I saw some really bad shit and when I got bit by that damn tick, I saw things as well, but I can't remember them."

"Son, what do you think we should do to flush my cousin out?"

"Pops, I'm working on that. It's a work in progress as I assemble all these different visions and try to add them together. What really perplexes me is why was he asking about me at the hospital in St. Thomas. I hope it's not about the Carbon Factor. I thought we showed the world our resolve with that. Anyway, I'll catch you guys later."

Zanthius grabbed a pastrami sandwich that mirrored the ones you get in Baltimore. It was piled high, on rye bread with a kosher pickle and funky mustard.

Asiram said, "Wow, that's a lot of meat. Can I have a bite?"

"They make corn beef and pastrami sandwiches like the delis back east. This is tender, tasty, and filling. Did you know my dad's cousin asked about me at the hospital in St. Thomas?" Zanthius continued to eat and Asiram turned pale.

She said, "What did you just say?"

There was a pause in the conversation and Asiram once again asked, "What did you say about St. Thomas?"

"I said, my dad's cousin, asked about me at the hospital?"
"Finish your sandwich. We need to talk."

CHAPTER TWENTY

In the barn, Jilkes, John Lee, Brown, Bernstein, and Jong were admiring the things that fell off a truck. John Lee asked, "How much time you reckon we'll get if we're caught with this here thing, and them there bullet sleeves?"

"I reckon your country ass will be in jail for a long time, probably twenty-five years," Jilkes said.

"Damn, that's a long time in a place full of men looking at each other's butts. I ain't touching that thing," John Lee confessed.

Mike walked into the barn and said, "I saw all you guys heading this way and I knew it meant you were up to no good so, I decided to walk up here." After eyeing the weapon, he exclaimed, "Where the hell did you get that thing from!? That's the new Gatlin gun and buddy this thing can cut down an oak tree. Wow, I've fired it many times."

Jilkes immediately jumped in and said, "Buddy, this is your baby! Get to know it, but don't fire it unless I achieve approval from the leaders. Oh, and please keep those rounds locked securely in that vault and only you know the number. Hell, the vault is large enough to hold this thing as well, put all this mess in there. The Sarge is probably going to have a meeting after dinner tonight and we'll figure out how to deploy this thing."

Jong asked, "So, Mike, can it really cut down an oak tree?"

"At the roots if you want it to," Mike replied.

# # #

At cocktail hour, everyone was pensive, quiet, and the Sarge could sense the tension in the air. He said, "I want to first thank God and our friends here who provided this most amazing food for us. Let's give them a big hand."

The Sarge took a sip of his cubre libre, and said, "Normally I like my beer, but tonight, I want to have this rum and coke. I'm going to cut through the chase and give the skinny of where we are. However, before I do this, I need volunteers to eat with the children in the kitchen."

Ten or so minutes later, the Sarge said, "I know exactly what's on your minds even if you haven't discussed it with your mates. Everyone in this room wants this shit over with-- and today. I know, I know! I wanted it over with yesterday and whose fault, is it? Well, it is Zanthius's fault because he kissed a woman, swallowed a capsule, and got us all involved in some shit that we don't understand. Now, what should we do with him? Should we turn him over to the devil? I think not because he's family.

"Seriously, we have enriched our pockets, put a hurting on a lot of people, saved farmers in the Midwest, hotels, our fellow vets, and restaurants all over the world and funded schemes that help people help themselves. We've done good and we've done bad. Do they balance? I don't know. All I know is that there is a force of evil that pays people, and places them in scenarios to die. I also know who the force of evil is, and he's directly related to me. His name is Walter E. Lassiter and he's my first cousin. He wants us all dead because we exist, and we've taken his stolen funds.

"Okay, please listen to me on this next issue. My son, Zanthius, is unknowingly, still connected to the Carbon Factor formula."

The room became deadly quiet. The Sarge took another sip of his rum and coke and said, "That's right, somewhere between this world and the other, he's the key to the formula for the Carbon Factor. Many of you don't have a clue as to why we blasted out of St. Thomas the way we did. Well, let me officially inform you of what happened. Two of my detectives, Mallory, and McArthur, noticed the reaction of someone at the hospital. They pursued it, and it was announced to them that Diablo himself was indeed on the island. My cousin, Walter was on our island. We were at the hospital, once again with the 'idiot spy', with cap pistols. That's why we always keep those 'out of here bags'. You never know when you must disappear. Anyway, our 'idiot spy' has a lot to deal with. Somewhere in the telling of this story, a small detail was left out and it contains the true formula for the Carbon Factor. I'm just speculating, but that's my belief."

John Lee stood up and said, "I can only remember when you started talking. And, oh yeah, I want to go home with my baby, and oh, my wife is pregnant again and so is Jilkes's wife."

The group broke into a boisterous sound of acknowledgment. When the noise subsided, John Lee said,

"Yeah, I want to sit in my rocker and hold my babies. I also want to make sure them there people who are important to me, are as well as I hope I am. It be time to end this thing, but we be better together than apart, and apart, he can control the outcome. Me and mine ain't going nowhere until this is over. We be prepared to die for this mission."

Jilkes stood up and said, "Ditto." Eight additional men stood up and yelled, 'ditto Sergeant'. The civilians orchestrated their own version and yelled, "We are here to the end."

As things settled down, Clyde stood up and said, "There be fifty armed citizens close by and another forty-eight on call who are committed to making sure you're comfortable and safe. We appreciate you people and can't ignore the fact you didn't know us and you went to bat for us and cleared out a bunch of people who had conspired to take our land at any cost. Oh, we know how this will happen and we're going to be on the outside looking and picking off anybody that has bad intents."

The Sarge hugged him and said, "This is our fight. We can't involve you in this mess."

"Sarge, we were involved the day we met you, for life. It would be more prudent if you included us in the planning of the defenses. You don't know poop about this land. You've been here several times, but you don't know the land. Now, I can tell you where the land slants, about animal holes, and distances. You must calculate that mess. If you include us from the beginning, then we're able to know what to expect and prepare accordingly. Listen, you helped us, and the entire region knows it. Oh, and by the way, we've helped some others with similar problems with the fund that you set up.

This community is growing and is dedicated to assisting those who assisted us. You should stop being stubborn and include us in the defensive and offensive operations. We're going to be here! Enjoy the food."

The Sarge looked at Mallory and he without moving a muscle, or any body part, signaled to the Sarge who said, "Clyde, we need you and I will include you in our planning. Any other questions? If not, then let's enjoy this feast once again."

Clyde said a prayer and the group dug in. Luana saw the way the men were eating and the volumes and whispered to Courtney, "We're going to be beat by our own bodies. Our nemesis won't have to fire a shot. Look at the sizes of the helpings on those plates? I know these women can cook, but we need to start a new regimen, or we'll defeat ourselves."

Courtney looked around the room and saw exactly what Luana was talking about. She walked directly over to where the Sarge was sitting and said, "Unless you want to have a heart attack, you need to leave two thirds of that food on your plate. Sarge, you and your people will defeat yourselves."

He looked around and saw the amount of food that Brown, and Bernstein had on their plates as well as Juan, Jong, John Lee, Mike, and Jilkes. He considered what his wife had pointed out, whipped around and said, "Hold up people. Hold up for one second. God knows these women can cook and we can eat, but if you look at the amount of food that's on your plates, you'll realize we should just capitulate to my cousin.

"Mallory, at 1800 hours, let's meet and take a long walk and then a short run and let's do this after each mealtime. We need to be in shape to beat our common enemy. Guys and girls, consider the amount you're eating and let's ask our hosts to lighten up on the calories and the heavy stuff. That's all, enjoy your dinners."

John Lee said, to Jilkes, "You know he be right. Me and you need to start after dinner and take a long walk. You with me brother?"

"I'll be with your country ass." He turned to Yeshida and asked, "Baby Girl, do you want to join us?"

She looked at Okema and Somara and they spoke in their tongue. They all broke into laughter and Brown said, "I thought we talked about that? You know, when you don't want me to know something, you break into that other language."

Okema said, "I just commented on how round you guys were becoming, husband, nothing offensive."

John Lee said, "My wife be doing that all the time. I be thinking she in a coma or something and is waking for the first time."

Jilkes looked at Yeshida and said, "I'm glad we don't have that as a problem, but I do notice occasionally she breaks into that other language even when there is no one around to understand it. Must be the way they do things. I'm simply happy she's my, mi amante, mi Amado, mi guapa, and mi amor. In case you don't understand Spanish, they are all references to lover."

At 2000 hours, Jilkes, Yeshida, John Lee, Somara, Brown, and Okema, were met by literally every member of the group. They all realized they needed conditioning and decided this was the place to start.

The Sarge, Courtney, Monica, and Mallory showed up and he said, "Is my room bugged? How did you people know we were going to do this?"

Jilkes looked at John Lee and threw his hands into the air and said, "We discussed this at dinner amongst ourselves. I don't know where all these people came from?"

The Sarge said, "Since we're all here, let's engage in a short walk and short run and try to work up a sweat. If you're not connected with a weapon, then you need to make that happen. We don't leave home without one."

He turned to see who was without and the entire group was locked and loaded.

The Sarge said, "You people are incredible, and it is this attention to detail that will make us victors in the end. I need someone to act as a pace car. Are there any volunteers?"

Larry stepped up and said, "I'll accept that assignment."

The groans and moans were extremely loud. Finally, John Lee walked forward and said, "I got underwear older than he is. We need a vintage person not a young whipper snapper."

Asiram said, "I'll do it." Zanthius immediately yelled, "She's in great shape. I would refuse that offer if I were you."

"Why this got to be so hard. Jilkes and me will set this ship right. I know he ain't in no shape and I'm struggling to get in my pants. We be the best pace cars," John Lee stated.

"Well stop all this chatter and let's get with it. Do your thing people," the Sarge indicated.

# # #

The night before, the group walked approximately eight miles to and from the ranch and the road. The next morning, breakfast was a lot different than they had expected. There were no grits, ham, bacon, potatoes, pancakes, and the like.

Nope, the only thing available was oatmeal, 2% milk, coffee, tea, berries, granola bars, and melon.

As the group assembled for their walk/run, the Sarge said, "People listen up. I think the two gentlemen we used as pace cars last night have earned the right to lead us again. Do you agree?"

There was a resounding yes. John Lee and Jilkes did mostly walking and a little running the day before. However, the group was not privy to their private interaction about their performance and the two had decided if they were called upon again to provide the pace car leadership, they would extend themselves above and beyond everyone's expectations.

The group headed out and after a brisk walk of five to seven minutes, the two pace cars turned the trip into a run and for the next one and a half miles, people were struggling to keep up with the two. Once they reached the highway, Jilkes said, "We're going to take a ten-minute break, and then start out with a brisk walk that will turn into a long jog, that will end in a heart busting intermediate run. After that, we'll walk fast and at the one and two tenths-mile marker, it will turn into an all-out blast. We don't want to leave anyone on the road, so pair up and make sure your partner is not attempting to do something his or her body says is impossible."

The Sarge who was winded said, "Who the hell made you two generals? Last night you couldn't do anything but walk, and this morning, you're full of energy and stamina. Are you on steroids or something?"

John Lee said, "Mr. Sarge, you ought to know by now we don't do them drugs. We decided we didn't do anybody any good last night by walking most of the road. We're good to go now. You know he and I do some work every morning before we show up and pig out."

The Sarge said, "Well, we won't use you two as pace cars in the future. I think you just killed the group, physically."

Jilkes said, "We'll accept that as a compliment and we frankly volunteer to lead this group as their pace cars." The moans and groans were earth shattering and the two men laughed and walked into the main dining room.

Jilkes said, "Give me five. We kicked their asses and set the tone for how they should respond and the importance of conditioning."

When Courtney walked into her room with the Sarge, she said, "Oh my God! That was challenging and refreshing. I didn't know I was in bad shape, but now I realize what I must do. Ava, Asiram, Monica, Luana, and I have decided we're going to accept their challenge and beat them at their own game."

The Sarge said, "I hope so. They surprised me, but I wouldn't expect anything less, from those two. The way they did that reminded me of our time in the Nam. They were the best and most reliable. They always had each other's back and the backs of our group. We survived because of their passion for each other. They kept us alive. Their fear, as well as their desire to put a hurting on anyone who would attempt to hurt those who they cared about, was obvious. They're an ominous duo and I love them so much. I pray to God that nothing happens to one of us. I pray exceptionally hard that nothing happens to one of them. That would leave the remaining one available to go on a one-man killing spree. The surviving one would be a force to reckon with and I mean that in a sinister way. They are the ultimate killing machine and they do it well!

"I remember, but I won't share with you how they do things. In that place, we were never expected to come back alive, those two would do the front work and that work in most scenarios always meant sudden death. They were the best and the most precise. They could smell, see, and sense shit I could only dream of accomplishing. Honey, they know how to kill, and they know how to send a message when they get angry. I've had dreams about them and they're not good ones. One dies, and the other one goes on a killing mission to honor his lost mate. One hundred bad people would die before he concludes his own life. They're just that good to accomplish a mission like that. I pray it's just a bad dream."

"Honey, they seem like really nice guys. All your people seem like great guys. I can't imagine there's a dark side to them, but I figured that out when John Lee gutted that woman."

The Sarge jumped to attention and said, "What do you know about a woman being gutted?"

"We stumbled on a camera system that was half functioning in the barn. It had some interesting interactions on it. Juan and Ava, you, and me, and everyone in the group who is married. Listen man, I know you are no angel and I'm no catholic nun. We are human beings, and I swore to preserve life not end it. I've violated all kinds of oaths. Your dreams are usually what they are, portraits of things to come, or not. I pray to God you're wrong this time."

# # #

The Sarge entered a state of soliloquy and asked himself the questions aloud that were troubling him. He flatly asked, "who am I going to have to bury when Diablo himself comes a calling? Every time we change venues, he finds us. I love my people and I don't want to suffer any fatalities. How do I minimize the damage of these encounters? Do I ask for a *mano e mano* confrontation? He'll never accept that concept. He prefers to sacrifice innocent, compromised, and hungry people to achieve his goals. He's a coward and the devil. Why did he ask about Zanthius? That is the most puzzling act he has committed. Did Zanthius forget to divulge certain aspects about his encounters with Helga? I must take him back to that point in time and try to reenact the total encounter. Helga played him all the way to her grave if, in fact, she is truly dead. What else did you give, or send to him; what else?

Zanthius and Asiram took the children for rides in the mule. They drove around their vast property and came to a stop when they came across the skeletal remains of a body with its foot still in its boot. He turned the mule around and headed back to the ranch. Asiram became hysterical and started screaming, "When will this all, end?! My God, when will this all, end?"

When they arrived at the ranch house, Zanthius saw Clyde and told him about what they had come across. Clyde dropped his head and said, "I should have told you we placed that thing out there some time ago. From afar, it looks real, but when you get right up on it, you can tell it's a fake."

Clyde continued doing what he was doing. Zanthius looked at Asiram and they both broke into laughter. Clyde said, "I hope that's okay out there and if not, I'll go and fetch Luther right now."

Zanthius inquired, "Wait, Clyde, you named the thing?"

"Oh yeah, there are several of them around the ranch, Luther, Jake, Wilbur and Clarence. They keep critters away and let others know what to expect."

Asiram asked, "So, Clyde, how on earth did you happen upon a Gatlin gun?"

"Oh, Ms. Asiram, as I indicated to you before, that's a complicated story with a lot of twists and turns and layers of people who refuse to tell how they came upon it, and who they happened to tell as well. It's so complicated, but I thought we could use it just in case those people came back here trying to stir up things again."

"In other words, you ain't telling me nothing because you don't know how and where it came from. Is that correct?"

"Ms. Asiram, I've always said you are a smart cookie."

Clyde excused himself and went about his merry way. Asiram grabbed Zanthius's hand and said, "Honey, have you given any thought as to why your dad's cousin would ask about you in St. Thomas?"

"Baby, it's on my mind, but I can't figure out what he's up to. I mean we publicly destroyed every aspect of that thing on camera. To me, the Carbon Factor is a dead issue."

"To you, perhaps yes, but your uncle is asking about you, and his only awareness of you is in relationship to the Carbon Factor. I doubt if he wants to get to know you especially since you're a part of the group that has undermined his empire. No, honey, I think Helga somehow knew we would destroy it, but perhaps the 'it', is what she wanted us to believe was the true formula. Suppose she sent the final formula to you in the mail? Would people know where to access your mail?"

"Baby, where are you going with this? That mess is dead and over."

"Honey, humor me, after all, I was a spy. If I wanted to send you something in the mail, or to a secret box or a place where you meet women online, how secure would it be, and who would know anything about it?"

Zanthius gave her a look that essentially said, 'don't hassle me with this mess'. Asiram pleaded with him to humor her. He threw his hands up in the air and said, "Why are you taking me back down this road. It is over. So, let it go!"

Asiram said, "Honey, you may think it's over, but since your uncle is inquiring about you, then it probably means it's not over, and more importantly the rest of us are impacted as well."

Zanthius realized what she was saying and said, "Baby you know those people watched my house until I got rid of it."

"What about your first wife, Pamela? Did she have access to a different postal box or website for mail delivery that Helga could have found out about?"

Zanthius fell to the floor and had a blank stare on his face. He pulled out a throwaway phone and dialed Pamela's number. There was no answer, but there was a recording device connected. He started to leave a message, but Asiram waved him off and he hung up the phone. She told him to find his father.

Zanthius didn't need to walk too far to find his dad and said, "I was sent to find you by my investigative wife. She thinks she's on to something."

"What might that be, Son?"

"My wife thinks your cousin asked about me because he believes I have access to information about the Carbon Factor."

"Yeah, I've been asking myself that question as well. She is such a sharp cookie."

The two men walked into his room, and Asiram didn't waste a minute. She said, "Daddy-in-Law, I'm of the opinion that our involvement with the Carbon Factor is not over. I think Helga may have found the smallest piece of information on lover boy here and used it to exploit him. I'm talking about his never, ever mentioned ex-wife, Pamela. I asked him to fetch you when I began to recognize the footprint of Helga. I have two assumptions, but I have no empirical information to back me up. My first assumption is, Helga is not dead. I know, this is all conjecture. My second assumption is, your cousin has been in contact with Helga who has provided him with information about your ex-wife, Romeo. Okay, wait before you disturb my train of thought. I have now considered a third assumption. If your uncle has found Helga and needs information, he will torture her, and if your wife, oh, so sorry, your ex-wife is in the equation, then she is either dead, or soon to be."

"I haven't spoken to Pamela since we split, and I haven't had a need to create a problem for me, or you, by doing so. I am now married to Asiram Beckmire De Lombardo, and we have two wonderful children and she's pregnant again, and my life is complete."

He turned to walk out of the door and Asiram said, "I'm not accusing you of anything. I want to make her safe, if possible, rather than let those people stumble upon her. Perhaps it's time to reach out to her and explain what's happening in your life and see if she's able to disappear for a while until this thing is settled?"

Zanthius replied, "I'll call the number again and see if she will answer my call. You know, when we first moved into that neighborhood, we opened a post office box. I should check to see if it's still active. I totally forgot about it. It wouldn't make a difference because Helga wouldn't and couldn't know anything about it. Only Pamela and I were aware of it, and after I became this well sought-after international spy, I kind of forgot about it. What makes it also impossible to know about, is there is an automatic deduction from one of my accounts I never see. My issue is, Helga never could have known about that. I was always in control of my wallet."

Asiram bellowed out, "Are you fucking kidding me? You can't control a thing about you when it comes to sex. You get that naturally from your father."

Ben Beckmire cleared his throat and said, "I'm not sure if I should take that as a compliment or a slight?"

Ten or so minutes later, Zanthius called the number and a male answered it. He said, "Hi, my name is Zanthius Beckmire De Lombardo, and I would like to speak to Pamela De Lombardo."

The voice on the other end of the phone said, "Hold on asshole, I'll get the bitch."

Zanthius's blood began to boil. Asiram noticed the change in his demeanor and hue, and said, "Baby, I don't know what's happening, but I need you to calm down. What happened? All you did was ask to speak to her."

Zanthius never said a word and his father saw his son was turning colors.

When Pamela came to the phone she said, "Well, hello Mr. Zanthius De Lombardo, I thought you were dead.

Apparently, my prayers weren't heeded. Why are you calling me?"

"Hi Pamela, I hope all is well with you, but I guess that's not possible when the person answering your phone referred to you as a bitch, and me as an asshole. Tell him my name is Mr. Asshole."

"Zanthius, what the hell do you want?"

"Do we still have access to that post office box?"

"I do. I don't know about you."

"Pamela, have you been there lately or ever?"

"Why are you calling me and asking me questions about bullshit? I don't need to go there because I have my mail delivered to my door. Is there something there that is important? Oh, I bet you its related to those people who have been coming by here looking for your ass. I'm in need of money, so I can run the fuck away. I've made another bad decision and I need to get away."

No sooner had Pamela said that Zanthius could hear a pop and a thump. The person that answered the phone, cold cocked Pamela and knocked her out. He picked up the phone and said, "If you want the bitch, come and get her if you can wake her the fuck up, asshole." He hung up the phone. Zanthius in the meantime began to turn red. His father said, "What's going on Son? It's a call, what did she say?"

"Dad, he hit her hard and knocked her out. Honey, I'm heading east for a day or so. Dad, I need two of your guys."

"Son, that's not going to happen, but your cousin is heading that way now to bury his father-in-law. We have the other plane, so you head that way and I'll coordinate your meeting Darryl and his crew. That'll give you lots of back-up and keep me from worrying."

Asiram said, "I need to ask Ms. Viola to do me a huge favor. I'm not letting you go without me. And if you try, I might kill your ass myself."

"Baby, I expect you to come with me. I was just worried about the boys, but I also forgot about Ms. Viola. Okay, Dad can you make the transportation thing happen in a hurry?"

"I can't, but Mr. Amazing can. I have one problem with you guys heading back that way. If that call was orchestrated, then you're going to be walking into firestorm. Hold on, I need to rethink this."

"Dad, I have to do this, with or without your help. I have to do this now."

Ben Beckmire said, "Would you give me a minute to think this thing through without interrupting me? Damn Boy!"

A few minutes later and after consulting his brain trust he said, "We can't splinter our forces. We're all going including the children. I'm getting terrible vibes about this action. It seems too easy to concoct and entrap members of our group. We need our full force in place. It'll be a quick trip. Okay, somebody find me Jong. We'll need his DC family as well."

# # #

Less than two hours later, the group boarded their plane and headed to the east coast. Everyone dreaded the trip but sided with the Sarge when it came to the notion of splintering the group.

Usually on their plane trips, there is lots of noise and someone overindulging. The Sarge recognized everyone was pensive. He thought to himself, "my son has been the cause of many good things and a few bad things. He didn't know what he was doing and expected the world to be honest, with principles and justice."

#

Four hours later, their plane began its descent into an airport in Maryland that handled a lot of large commercial aircraft that transported goods. Carla, who was back in the cockpit, told the group to prepare for landing.

Shortly after making the announcement, she placed the bird on the ground with hardly a bump in the landing.

Jong had ten of his family members planted around the airport. After the plane entered the hangar, Sue Lyn called her uncle and told him they would be landing in about thirty minutes. Jong told her he would meet their plane and offered his condolences about the loss of her father and his cousin.

#

When the second plane pulled into the adjacent hangar, Darryl was first to disembark. At the bottom of the steps, was Jong. Sue Lyn, who was directly behind Darryl, said, "Uncle, how nice of you to meet us. We're here for the moment of transcending my father to the other world."

Jong bowed his head in respect and announced, "He offered the world a lot. So sorry he expired so early. I will assume any honorable role you may require. It will be your request and I will bring all of my resources to you."

Jong looked at Darryl and said, "We have another situation. I must deploy you and your crew to an area that is unfamiliar to you. Other than the children, we have a mission, and it might be the answer to a question that has plagued us and our adversaries. This could be the turning point to this entire saga. Today, however, you should attend to your father, but be prepared to join us immediately following the services. The crew, you and your husband have assumed, will be turned over to us for this situation. In other words, the Sarge will command them and us. I will attend the services for my cousin."

"Thank you, honorable Uncle. In Australia, we've made great strides in developing the infrastructure necessary to begin the mining of the minerals. Legally, we're good to go. Security wise, we have our own people managing and operating it with a ton of cameras, scanners, wands, and the notion of random cavity searches."

Jong looked at her and said, "That's an unnecessary precaution. If anyone tries to smuggle a stone out, then it is that stone that causes their death. I'm convinced there is black magic back there that is more powerful than anything I could ever imagine. I'm not a superstitious person, but I've seen things that don't make sense to me. The Sarge is a wonderful human being who believes in spirts, I've learned if he believes in a thing, then I do as well. The security thing is self-determined—where there is larceny—there is death! "

The Sarge walked over and greeted his nephew and offered his condolences to Sue Lyn. He told Darryl he hoped his trip would be over and done within a matter of a day, and that they would be back on their plane heading west and wanted him airborne as well when the funeral services concluded.

Darryl told his uncle that he was dreaming all kinds of things that did not make sense to him and those dreams would reverse in the morning. His uncle told him all that was happening, was trying to end, and that his other uncle had aligned himself with pure evil. Darryl told him that was impossible, because his other uncle, was pure evil.

# # #

Hours later, Sue Lyn bid her father farewell and wished him the most horrible hell one could endure. She smiled at her new husband and said, "With the help of my new family, we will make the world a better place. I love you Darryl and I never knew what true love and passion was, until I met you.

# # #

Zanthius, Asiram, Michael and his crew approached the house where Zanthius's ex-wife lived. Asiram suggested to Zanthius that he should stand to the side of the door, just in case the person who answered the phone, opened it. She rang the doorbell several times, but to no avail. Zanthius told her to bang on the door and see what happened. Asiram did exactly that and after a minute or so, there still was no reply. Zanthius looked at the corner of the house and saw a large flowerpot and wondered if Pamela maintained old habits—and placed a key under the flowerpot? He walked casually over to it, and not to his surprise, a key was obvious. He smiled and removed it and approached Asiram and said, "I guess some habits don't die easily." He inserted the key into the lock and was happy it turned without a problem. Once he pushed the door open, he saw a man's head that had been decapitated and a woman's body that had been savagely sliced and blood splattered all over the room. He did not recognize the man's head, but he clearly recognized Pamela. Asiram never acknowledged the bodies, but instead drew her pistol and started doing a search of the immediate surroundings. Michael, Isaiah, and Desmond entered and were signaled to check the upstairs rooms.

Each room of the house had been violently disturbed. Pictures pulled off walls, all draws emptied, and everything in the closets thrown on the floors. Zanthius said, "We have to call the police."

Asiram vehemently stated, "We will not commit any stupid acts such as involving the police while we are here. Everyone, out and don't touch anything."

As they left the house, Asiram looked around for cameras and did not see any. Once in the car, she called the police and gave them the address. She called the Sarge and told him what the situation was and that they were heading to the Post Office.

# # #

Once they arrived at the Post Office substation, Zanthius was visibly emotionally upset after finding the woman he once loved and was married to, brutally butchered.

Asiram said, "Honey, if you want, I'll go in and see what if anything is in the box? What's the number?" As he stared out of the window, a van with three men in it pulled up to the Post Office. The thing that caught his eye about the group was that one of the men had what appeared to be blood on the back of his white pants. He mused to himself, "if I had blood on the back of my white pants, I would change them?"

Asiram asked, "What baby?"

"That guy walking towards the Post Office has blood stains on the back of his white pants." Asiram turned to look and saw it was an old KGB comrade she had once worked with. She called Darryl and told him and his crew to break into that van and see what's in it.

In the meantime, the Sarge sent Jilkes and John Lee into the substation with Darryl and his crew as back up. When they went to the area where the boxes were, three men were randomly breaking into boxes.

John Lee yelled, "You move a muscle and I'll blow your head off."

Jilkes and John Lee had their weapons drawn as did Darryl and his crew. Jilkes approached the man with the blood on his pants and asked, "You cut yourself or something? You need to get those pants dry cleaned, but before you do, I need you to ease that pistol from under your belt, and gently place it on the floor. Don't do stupid because my friend will fire first and ask questions later."

Asiram walked in and said, "Hello Vladimir. I thought you gave up breaking into places?"

"Comrade, it is nice to see you again. You do know there is a booty on your head?"

"The word most appropriate is bounty or price, but booty works if you're a pirate. Why are you robbing substations that are only for boxes and machine dispensed stamps?"

"We're looking for my friend's box, but he forgot his number, so we open all the ones he thinks him passport is in."

Asiram said, "Let's cut the bullshit! We followed you by drone here after you left that house in shambles. What on earth were you looking for and whose blood is that on your pants?"

"As you say comrade, let's stop the bullshit. We're on a job, just like you, if you followed me, and you got all these men with guns. Who is your employer?"

"Well, since we have all the guns on you and your friends, then I'll ask the questions. Now, Vladimir, what are you looking for in these boxes?"

"Comrade, as you say, since you have unnecessary guns on us, we're following orders to find a certain item in one of these boxes?"

"Did you have to brutalize those people like that?"

"Comrade, you know the cost of doing business is sometimes messy. It was the man who we hurt. The woman was dead when we got there. He sliced her up bad. He acted tough until we started interrogating and putting him in pain. Was he a comrade of yours?"

Zanthius stood in the background and listened to the dialogue and finally spoke up and said, "This can go very bad for you. Did you touch the woman?"

"Comrade, we did not touch the woman. If you checked her body, you would have noticed she had been dead for some time. We didn't touch the woman."

Asiram walked over to Zanthius and said, "It's a plausible story, but I'll let you judge this one, and figure the outcome. I personally believe him. That's not his style to maliciously kill women."

Zanthius looked at Vladimir and said, "If we let you go today, we might have to fight you again tomorrow. You see our dilemma?"

"I do understand, but we're compromised anyway you look at it. You caught us here, and I'm sure our employer will want to distance himself from us. I'm not agreeing to any suicide missions. Just let us go Comrade, and you won't see us again and that is my word."

Zanthius studied the man's expressions and said, "I hope we're making the right decisions by you."

Asiram sashayed up to Vladimir and whispered something to him in Russian. He immediately said, "Comrade, we are out of here and never to be heard from again."

Once the men were out of sight, Zanthius went to an untouched box, #309 and opened it. Inside of the box, were old advertisements and two packages. One contained four thumb drives that were meticulously numbered, and what appeared to be a manuscript. The other was a letter Helga wrote confessing her love for him and hoping their child would have a good life. It also contained keys to several safety deposit boxes, documents she had forged his name on, a 'Will' leaving him all her earthly goods and monies. He showed it to Asiram who said, "We need to get the hell out of here before someone else comes along looking for this stuff. I thought we had seen the last of the Carbon Factor, but I should have known Helga only plays by her rules and complicates the simple things."

# # #

At the airport, Ben Beckmire huddled with Darryl and Sue Lyn and got a quick and dirty status of what was going on, and if they needed any other resources? They told him they weren't sure of their needs yet because they were still in the process of mapping everything out. Beckmire, once again offered his condolences to Sue Lyn and told the couple he was proud of everything they were doing and that he appreciated them. Darryl told his uncle he and his crew were going to spend a couple of days in San Diego and have the plane serviced.

Beckmire hugged his nephew and told him good luck. Zanthius and Larry were near, and they too gave the couple hugs and best wishes. The couple walked on to the large plane and said their goodbyes to the rest of the crew.

An hour later, both planes taxied onto the runway and Carla told the group to fasten their seatbelts and sit back and get some rest. I got this!"

In the front of the plane, Ben Beckmire looked at Zanthius and knew he was upset and devastated by what had happened to Pamela and knew that he would have to come back this way soon to bury his ex-wife. He began to look at the manuscript that was attached to the four thumb drives. He thought to himself, "people have died over another way for man to kill man. What insanity and I have the essence of it in my hand and don't know how to destroy it".

Asiram saw her husband silently weeping and gathered him gently on to her bosom. She comforted him as if he were one of her children and repeatedly told him she loved him and their family so very much. Five or ten minutes later, Zanthius found himself in dreamland about his current family and friends. Two hours into flight, Asiram received a call from Clyde who told her a lot of unsavory looking people had begun to arrive in town and wanted to know if she wanted to switch their pickup place. She asked him to hold while she spoke with the Sarge.

The Sarge got on the phone and told Clyde it might be good if they landed on the converted farmland that was near the ranch. Clyde told him that was an excellent idea, but he had not been out there lately to check it out to make sure it was an approachable site. The Sarge told him if the ILS worked, he was confident that Carla could land this thing anywhere.

Clyde asked Asiram if the group had ever practiced anything before attempting? She told him no. He indicated to her he would take a group out to the farm and walk the runway to make sure it was safe.

It was close to 2330 hours when Carla plugged in the coordinates of the airport/farm. Clyde had called Asiram back and told her the strip was clean, and the lights worked from his end. Carla told the group the ground crew had certified the landing strip. She told her passengers she would make the landing as smooth as possible. She reminded them that as soon as she touched down, she would throw the engines in reverse and break extremely hard, but for the group not to worry. She ended her transmission with, "We got this"!

# # #

Later, the group piled into the school buses and armed themselves. Everyone liked the .308s, but felt the weapon was not appropriate for the kind of action they might encounter.

The Sarge spoke with people on both buses and told them once they arrived at the ranch, he wanted them to take care of their immediate needs and then meet with him in the dining/family rooms that were joined. He indicated it was only fair that they knew what had been accomplished and what the most likely next steps were.

It was nearing 0100 hours when the group pulled onto the main access road to the ranch. Clyde's wife and the other ladies had a late-night snack ready for the weary travelers. When Asiram walked into the foyer and smelled the ham and bacon, she said, "Damn, it's good to be home. People, can you smell that yummy stuff?"

After attending to their personal concerns, the group met in the dining area and the Sarge wasted no time informing the group what had happened. He said, "My friends and family, I believe we've taken possession of the complete formula for the Carbon Factor."

There were a lot of moans and sighs. The Sarge said, "I know exactly how you feel. It only occurred to us when my cousin interrogated the hospital staff in St. Thomas about 'idiot spy', that this thing was not over. I'd like to take time to give my condolences to my son on the loss of his first wife. Your extended family is here for you son. Whatever you need, we'll try to help where possible."

"Now, back to my first comment, and yes, we have the actual manuscript and data disk in our possession. We made a statement before when we burned this mess up in front of the world. Will the world believe us if we show that video again? Are we looking for salvation from the world? I think not. I don't think, and many of you agree, the world doesn't need another cheap tool so that man can kill man. Damn, I wish I could figure this one out. Oh, and by the way, Clyde has informed us that mercs are showing up in large numbers. I want to get the children out of here because we will extend no quarter and we will not ask for any. Is anyone else pregnant beside Yesida, Asiram, Mary Alice, Rashida, and Somara?" There was no indication until Okema's little hand went into the air. Brown stood up and said, "Honey, really?" She smiled and dropped her head. Brown dropped to his knees and asked, "When were you going to tell me?"

"My husband, I just found out when I did the test in our room when we landed." Brown smiled and looked towards heaven and said, "I love this woman."

The Sarge congratulated the couple and moved on by saying, "I need you people to think about our next steps. I'm afraid this one is going to be the mother of all battles with both sides suffering significantly."

He paused and looked around the room and then said, "I'm going to hold all questions in abeyance until tomorrow including that of getting the children out of here. Oh, I would like Ms. Viola, Luana, Marisa, as well as the pregnant ladies to consider securing the children. Okay people, that's all until tomorrow. Clyde, how's our security?"

"Well, sir, I checked with your chief of security, and she has all of those automatic weapons online and ready. We have sensors and people stationed throughout the ranch and I feel we're ready for any inconvenience."

"Clyde, should we put people on the payroll who help secure us?"

Clyde turned to him with a look of consternation and replied, "Sergeant sir, if you don't want to insult us, then please understand statements like that hurt people trying to help their friends. I know you mean no malice or undercutting with that statement, but many of us find what we do for you people is pretty much what we can do. You did a lot for us, and this is a small price to pay, if price is the correct vernacular."

"Clyde, forgive my insensitivity. I meant no slight, and I know you and your people have been a God send for us, and we know you have our best interest at heart. I don't know where that question came from, but we need your help. Please forgive me, I did not mean to offend you."

"None taken Sarge."

CHAPTER TWENTY-ONE

The Sarge woke up at 0430 hours and quietly walked out of his room and downstairs. He stepped out on the porch and Clyde muttered, "A man should make some noise unless he be trying to sneak up on a fellow."

"Hey Clyde. What on earth are you doing here?"

"Making sure we have a sense of calm before the storm I heard you speak of."

"You know Clyde, out here at night, and unless it's a full moon, you can't see a thing coming for you. I may have to rethink this confrontation."

"No sir, you got that all wrong. Once the house is darkened and the shields are up, you can't see where you're going, but those automatic weapons that them young people installed, can hit a tick taking a shit."

"Really Clyde? A tick taking a shit?"

"It was a thing of the moment. However, we got people and things in play now, that we didn't have before. We can deploy a few from behind their lines and put a hurting on them. I think this is your best venue. You can tell when they get to town or near town. You can see them coming, and if you can't, you damn sure can hear them. To show you how well the system works, we got three of them sitting in the field about three miles from here getting the shit bit out of them by mosquitoes. Yes sir, they tried to sneak up on you people, but they tripped alarms all over the place. You want to go and see them? Your people McArthur, Jilkes, John Lee, Brown, and Bernstein are already in those trucks over there."

"Clyde, my people are asleep in their beds."

"Sarge, you want to wear your pajamas, or do you want to change?"

"Give me a few minutes."

Fifteen minutes later, ten former enlisted men and two former non-commissioned officers headed into the interior of the ranch. The Sarge asked, "Don't you assholes ever sleep?"

John Lee said, "Naw, we learned how not to from the master asshole." The group broke into hysterics because it had been twenty plus years since the beloved leader had honored them with a joint exclamation of calling them assholes.

The Sarge said, "I'm worried about this one guys, and I need you people to stay sharp, smart, and listen to those you trust and use your strengths. Don't be heroes and cross into a zone you don't know. This is our Nam, here at home. I know we're older and slower, but we learned techniques from the best—each of you. You know who we trusted out front over there, and we know who we trust out front here. Only the landscape has changed. These guys coming for us are just bigger, meaner, hungrier, and doing it for money and not to run foreigners out of their country."

When Clyde flashed his lights to let his people know they were on their way, he got flashed from all over the ranch. The Sarge asked, "How many people do you have out in the fields?"

Clyde responded, "Sarge, that's mission sensitive information. Until we learn your plan, we won't be sharing ours."

The Sarge responded, "Fair enough, Clyde. However, you had lights coming from all over the place. That signifies to me that there are a lot of your people out there."

"That would be a false reading of the temperature of the ranch, Mr. Sarge. What we've constructed is electronic signaling devices for our test run. There will be a significant number of people in the field and in holes that can be covered and tunnels that will allow us to move behind our foes. They're literally bomb proof because once you retreat, a door falls in place and another one allows you time to assume another position. Listen, it's complicated, but we've worked it out and it's getting better day by day. But for now, you have to decide what to do with these vermin who won't talk about their mission."

When Clyde stopped the van and the team exited, Mallory shined his flashlight on the guys and saw that the mosquitoes and other insects were having a feast on their bodies. He asked Clyde if he could get rid of the bugs and Clyde lit a straw fire and the smoke drove everything away.

The Sarge politely asked, "Who is in charge here? There was no answer. He said, "I'm going to ask again, who is in charge?" Again, no answer.

The Sarge looked at John Lee and stated, "Those guys have been bitten by a lot of bugs, can you scratch them with your blade, and I mean deep?"

John Lee looked at the three men and decided to do the biggest one first and work his way down the line. He ran his knife down the man's arm and the man just made a face and yelled, "Is that all you got?"

John Lee said, "You must be related to the president." He plunged his huge blade through the man's hand who yelled and said, "I'm going to stick that knife so far up your ass you're going to wish you had a vagina."

John Lee looked at the Sarge who nodded his head and that is when John Lee pulled the man around so that his comrades could see exactly what was happening. He plunged his knife into the man's chest and reached into it. One of the other men passed out, and the other was regurgitating his last meal. John Lee gave the bloody knife to Jilkes and said, "I bet you can't top that?"

Jilkes wiped the blood on the dead man's head and said, "Really, all you did was kill him. I'm going to make my choice wish his mother was never born so that she couldn't have had him in childbirth. One of the guys said, "Listen, I'll tell you anything you want to know. If you're going to kill me, just make if fast."

The Sarge said, "Now, that we've been properly introduced, who is leading this mission?" Both men indicated it was the dead man and Jilkes looked at John Lee and said, "Leave it to you, my brother."

# # #

The Sarge and his men extracted important numbers and locations from the two men. Neither man could identify the leader because they worked in groups and had a chain of command. It was made clear to the group that men were amassing all over the state. One of the captives told the group how the deceased leader was once heard talking about four hundred plus people on this job. The Sarge said, "I feel as though I'm going to face you again, if I let you go. I can't do that."

One of the guys said, "I assure you that you will never see me again, but I can't speak for my associate." His associate told the Sarge he would not be a problem for his group.

# # #

When the group returned to the ranch, they were met by their women, and other men such as Juan, Mike, and Carlos. As the clock approached 0800, Mallory said, this looks like a royal complaint is about to be lodged. As they exited the vehicles, Ms. Viola said, "Now, Mr. Sarge man, I know sometimes I be watching them babies, but you can't expect me to high tail it out of here with a bunch of screaming babies. My own babies have decided they be staying man, and I no leave them no matter what. So, I recommend to you Mr. Sarge man, you arbitrarily pick some other person. I'm going to stay and protect my own and any near me at the time. But man, I can't be cutting and running. That not be my style, man."

Mary Alice said, "Unless you don't need my husband, he's coming with me when I leave. However, if he's staying then I'm staying and so will my baby. We've all been on this fantastic adventure and if it ends against the will of God for us then so be it, but I am not leaving and will be at the range tomorrow firing a long gun to master that weapon. I got the rest of them down."

The Sarge looked at Mallory and Jilkes and said, "This is insane."

Courtney shouted, "Then we're all insane, and besides if we're insane, then why are you trying to have a rational conversation with us?"

"People, there may be as many as four hundred bad motherfuckers coming to kick our asses for payment. They won't care about your child Mary Alice, or my grandbabies, or Somara, Okema, and Yeshida's babies. They won't give a shit if you're pregnant or delivering when they arrive. You all will be a part of their bonus payment."

Chakes raised his hand and the Sarge acknowledged him. He said, "Sarge, unless you have another message, then this one ain't going to work. These people and I mean every one of these ladies and gentlemen have decided we will all live protecting what is right or die trying. That's why I say, if you don't have a different message, then we all need to get something to eat, and begin our conditioning and target practice."

Marisa who rarely talked, raised her hand and said, "I don't care for guns, but I've become proficient in the use of them, and I will not surrender my children to the devil. We're not leaving, and I suggest you spend your time creating new fighting strategies that will give us a modicum of an advantage. We need miracles, lots of guns, and ammo."

Larry held her tight and asked, "Honey, is that final?"

She smiled at him and whispered, "I want to grow old with you and I have to watch your back and everyone else's."

"So be it! The conclave has elected a new leader and it's Marisa. All hail Marisa!" There was a lot of laughter, but the Sarge abruptly stated, "If that is the way of the group then the group will have to get ready to slap hot iron on the wounds and keep firing until you're out of bullets, then you have to throw bottles and cans at the aggressors. I'm done with it, and I must say, no matter how this thing ends, I need you parents to be aware of the decision you're making relative to your children. These people will give no quarter, and nor will we, but we're not going into their hood, head hunting either, are we?"

Jong rose from his seat and said, "I think we should have your nephew and my niece bring their people here. I'm sure your cousin has calculated our strength and is watching every move we make. If we could smuggle them here that would decrease the odds from approximately 9:1, to 7:1 that's less bullets chasing each person here and more targeting them."

The Sarge seemed to be pre-occupied while watching Mike on the phone outside. He asked Jong to have Mike join them.

When Mike walked into the room, the Sarge asked, "Don't we have a no cell phone policy unless it was an emergency?"

"Sarge, I'll let you decide if you think this is an emergency. Your cousin has wickedly joined forces with two distinct groups, a faction in North Korea, and a splinter group in Iran. Each group is financing a specific feature of the formula with a non-compete/non-aggression pact agreed between the two. In other words, they have financed your cousin and will share equally in the formula and have agreed to not engage each other militarily."

Mike paused for a moment to sneeze. After an ear piercing sneeze, he regrouped and said, "The mercs you encountered were funded by both countries. It is estimated your cousin has made a multi-billion-dollar pact with both countries and has forfeited any consideration for his country— the United States of America. Now, Sarge, I must qualify the origin of this information and say flatly it's out of the sewers in DC, the same sewers that brought you me, and a lot of other reliable information. I place an eighty percent probability on the information. I know this sounds like a cluster fuck with the people from Iran, that nut in North Korea, and his brother as our president. This shit is going to get crazier."

Mallory asked, "Have you considered calling our friends in Spain for backup?" The Sarge looked at him and thought to himself, "those guys would rather drink wine and hustle than get into a real fight and perhaps die".

"I had not thought about them, but thanks for the idea. As a matter of fact, why don't you give ole Franco a call and see how things are coming."

The group began to dine and Zanthius whispered something to Larry, and he nodded in agreement. Ten minutes later, Larry walked over to his father and asked him for a moment outside and told him that it was important. The two men headed for the door and Zanthius told Asiram he would be right back. When the three men huddled outside, Zanthius said, "Dad, I didn't come to you on my own because I wanted Larry to be in on this idea as well. Listen, if they have four hundred or more people coming for us, then why don't we divide the ranch into quadrants and defend it from that perspective. Those guys are probably going to hit us with rocket launchers and whatever else they can smuggle into the area but they won't want to make it so loud that the National Guard is put on alert. We could break your boys into groups of fours, and each would have a seasoned person in command. The only problem I see with that math is that some of your boys won't part company with their soul mates."

The Sarge smiled at them and put his hand over his mouth as if he were trying to refrain from laughing. Each time he attempted to say something, he placed his hand over his mouth and pointed at them. He finally moved forward and held each man tight and said, "You're not going to believe this, but I was thinking the same damn thing when I looked around the room. I tell you something, Beckmires are a special breed, and they focus on the details. Let's go back in and see what kind of reception that notion gets."

The Sarge walked over to his table and told Courtney he loved her. She said to him, "Okay dude, what the hell are you about to do?"

He turned to her, threw her a kiss, and said, "I love my wife. However, I also love my sons who never seemingly cease to think of ways to make things right for us. Okay, some of you are automatically not going to like this idea, but I need to throw it out there. My boys think we should defend the ranch in quadrants."

There was a moment of silence prior to John Lee standing up and asking, "Is that like dividing this here ranch into four parts?"

The Sarge screamed, "That's exactly what it means, and it also means my 10 + 2 will also be divided."

"I don't know if I like that idea. Will my African American friend be with me?"

"There's a strong chance that he won't be."

"Then I be totally against that there plan. We fight well together, and this could be our last hurrah."

"I have the same concern as you do, John Lee. Do you know how long I've been fighting alongside Corporal Mallory? Do you think I want to go out without he and I doing some crazy Audie Murphey shit? Listen people, we haven't decided how this is going to work, but it puts the impetus on each section to hold their own, knowing that if there is a breach, then we're all dead!", the Sarge stridently announced.

He looked at John Lee and asked, "Would you be opposed to a lottery?"

"Sarge, you know I ain't going to agree with anything that separates me from my African American friend."

Brown yelled, "There were two forces that kept our dumb asses alive over in the Nam. It was, if I must remind my colleagues, Jilkes and John Lee, and as long as they're together, we all have a chance."

Bernstein yelled, "Boss, he's right and you know it. Our lucky charm was them and it still is those two dudes. I think the rest of us could learn to be divided, but if you separate them two, then we're doomed. You know we know there is some strange shit going on in Australia, but if we separate those two, then I think we're going to have an insurrection of the verbal kind. However, would never go against your final decision, boss."

"What's with this boss shit? Suddenly, I'm beginning to feel slighted. This is the second time I've heard that boss shit."

"Sarge, we love you to the moon and back. We like the plan, but we need the lovers together. When they're remotely separated, shit happens to the negative side of the equation. You believe in the magic of your homeland, and we believe in our two Chinese dogs by the doors!"

John Lee jumped up and said, "What the hell that mean? We ain't got no Chinese dogs by the door."

Jilkes grabbed his hand and whispered, "They ward off evil spirits. It's' a good thing my brother. It's a good thing."

After considering his initial recommendation, the 'idiot spy' stood up and said, "A better plan might be to divide the ranch into fifths and that way, each of our people are with their soul mates."

There was a long lull, after which the Sarge enthusiastically announced, "The math is perfect. Lets' sleep on it and see how it feels later on."

## CHAPTER TWENTY-TWO

Darryl, Sue Lyn, and their crew never left the west coast. They spent their time at obscure restaurants enjoying each other's company and soliciting dedicated and loyal people from the sewers. Each man was given the opportunity to recommend two or three individuals for hiring who were on the brink of doing stupid. They were also allowed to be non-military.

On the cheapest flight possible, twelve men who vaguely were acquainted flew from DC to San Diego on a flight that offered them peanuts and soda only. When they arrived, they were collected in fours.

At the hotel where the men would be able to sleep in a bed for the first time in a long time, they were presented with room keys and given an appointment time. In each room, the men were presented with a bar full of whiskey. It was perhaps a poor test, but nonetheless, it was presented to them. Two of the twelve immediately flunked the test by getting drunk. A third individual asked an inappropriate question about Sue Lyn—'who's the chink'? The fourth guy asked the desk clerk, 'where can I get some action and get high'? Two were unequivocally hired for their skill sets and another two were selected but were on a watch list—former alcohol/drug consumers.

Sue Lyn and Darryl interviewed the candidates, made their selections, but wanted to see what additional judgements their people would make as well. They decommissioned three others and gave them a handsome per diem and sent them on their way. The group stood at twelve—Michael and his crew of four, five new recruits who were immediately placed on probation with a list of what can be done, and what shouldn't be done, that would fill two typewritten pages in an 8 x 12 document. Of course, Sue Lyn and Darryl made it twelve.

Michael was given the job of weeding out the weak and bringing those guys above ground. Current events were a constant matter for them. They had their ears close to the ground from buddies in agencies with funny names to clergy who received information through confessions.

Darryl made a call to his uncle and told him he had recruited what he considered five trustworthy, informed, ex-soldiers, and a few people who were down on their luck, but were solid. He asked if he could speak with Mike to see if he had any intelligence on the people he had recruited.

When he finally got Mike on the phone, Darryl began to repeat real names and sewer names. He first asked him about Peter the Professor, aka, Bruce Campbell and was given five out of five stars with an emphasis on superior intelligence gathering and sifting through data. The next name was the Tire, aka, John Cheapman and was given five out of five stars with a notation he was extremely loyal and honest. Next, Darryl asked about the Checkbook, aka, Mike Carmichael and was given the notation that he was good with numbers and never shorted a fellow sewer dweller. When Darryl mentioned the name Speedy, aka, Harold Quick, Mike told him he was good, but needed direction and that the 'SOB' owed him $200 from a bet but gave him a three out five rating because he owed him money. Darryl then proceeded to ask Mike if he had heard of the Ear, aka, Giuseppe Harris and was told he's well connected but must be watched because he sells info as well as buys it, and that he would give him a four out of five rating.

Finally, Darryl asked him about a man called Horse, aka, Arnold Nikelson, and was told that he was the kind of guy you needed in a fire fight and offered the man a five out of five rating. In conclusion, Mike said, "With the crew you have and the ones you've assembled, you could start your own war. I would not be concerned about their domestication abilities, but rather their ability to protect each other, you, and Sue Lyn. I only know these guys from the sewers. I've never seen one of them pull the trigger on another human being. You might want to experiment with that aspect of your recruitment program and see if they have the balls to point a weapon at another human being and pull the damn trigger. No small feat for anyone who calls themselves a human." Darryl thanked him and said goodbye.

Darryl turned to Michael and told him to gather the men and put them through the basics and see what kind of shape they were in both physically and mentally. He told Michael to push them to the limits because he had a bad feeling that bad winds were heading toward the ranch where his family was.

When Darryl reconnected with his uncle, he was told Armageddon was around the corner and it was preparing to wipe them out. Darryl said, "Uncle I know. How can I help? Sue Lyn has improved the pop-up shooters and they can now be fired much more efficiently and remotely."

He began to explain the system when the Sarge said, "Nephew, I don't think that's going to help us. We need a miracle."

Darryl said, "Uncle, may I call you back. I have a bit of a situation here. Get back to you."

Darryl hung up the phone and went to where Sue Lyn was sitting and said, "My uncle the devil, is about to massacre my uncle the almost devil. I have to go to Wyoming now."

"Not without me. Where you go, I go." Darryl hugged her and said, "I would've been heartbroken had you not said what you said. I love you girlfriend. I know we have to take Michael and his crew, what's your opinion on the new guys?"

"Baby, I think you need to tell them what you're up against and let them decide if they want to take a chance on getting their heads blown off."

"Oh my, so graphic darling. However, I feel where you're coming from on this one. By the way, can you deploy the pop-up system? Is it ready and have you selected a weapon? Anyway, grab your bag, we're out of here in one hour."

Darryl called the crew together and had each man introduce himself. Most of them knew of each other, but it was good for Michael to hear who they were, what was their specialty and whether they could pull the trigger.

As a matter of fact, Michael apologized to Darryl for interrupting him and said to the new guys, "Darryl and Sue Lyn are our employers and on occasion, he will turn us over to his uncle who will direct us. Now, let me be very clear and make sure you hear exactly what I'm about to say. Sometimes bad guys come gunning for his uncle, and lately for Darryl and Sue Lyn. You will have a wonderful career if you can follow orders, stay alert, be honest, and be willing to kill another human being. I mean, if Darryl or Sue Lyn direct me to put a bullet in your head, then consider it done. What we need to know is whether you're willing to shoot another human being, and I mean execution style, in the performance of your duty? If not, then you need to take that per diem and head home and forget about this rendezvous. The Ear/Guiseppe raised his hand and said, "You pulled me out of the sewers and the money I got I sent to my ex-wife for my children. I need this job, but I want to make sure if I get into a jam doing my job, will you come to my assistance?"

Sue Lyn stood up and said, "If you do your job, you will be welcomed into this group as a part of the family. You will make more money than you can count and if you want, we'll even help you gain custody of your children. You do your job and you become family. This is a big family."

Darryl said, "My uncle is about to face over four hundred mercs in the mid-west. There is going to be a lot of blood spilled, but we have weapons they don't know about. The choice is yours. We leave here in twenty minutes, and I want to be airborne in forty minutes. Sue Lyn, call the pilots and tell them we must head east to Wyoming."

The new guys huddled with Michael's people and asked a thousand questions. It was apparent that what they heard, allowed them to feel whole again and contribute.

Darryl asked Sue Lyn to give a call to that special friend that they had in Wyoming and see if he could discreetly meet them at the airport. He told her they would need a ride to the ranch and hoped he could pick them up without the kingpin's knowledge.

At the airport, ten employees and two employers entered the private lounge at the airport and walked to a hangar that held their jet. The Tire/John Cheapman asked, "Is this on that time share stuff?"

Michael said, "Naw, the group owns three jets and have pilots on call 24/7."

As the group began to board the plane, a single individual could be seen at the base of the steps, Speedy/Harold Quick. Darryl said, "I guess he doesn't want to join us on this adventure. Michael, tell him it's okay and to take care."

Michael went out to talk to the guy and he said, "Listen, we understand. You got a good per diem, so enjoy it, but don't blow it."

"You got it all wrong. I've been in one helicopter crash and a plane crash. I'm terrified of flying unless I'm full of Ambient."

Michael calmly looked at the man's hands shaking, and said, "Listen, if we hit the ground running and firing, you won't do me much good, now will you, if you're all drugged up? You take the money and stay safe. Maybe catch the train back east?"

"No sir. I want and I need this job. I need this job and I got to have this job because I have two babies who need my help. Please, give me a minute to figure this shit, out."

Speedy began to run around the hangar at full and blinding speeds until he was exhausted. He walked to the base of the steps and said, "Let's get this thing in the air before I change my mind."

Once in the air, the attendant/co-captain, offered the group a snack which consisted of shrimp cocktail, beef sliders and a salad with a choice of wine. Everyone was hesitant to accept a cocktail until Darryl said, "Listen guys, we're on a plane going on a mission, and we have no intelligence about what we're going to face. I want you to enjoy as many drinks as you can tolerate and still function. I always say, don't do stupid because stupid will definitely do you."

In flight, the group began to relax and bond and get a sense of who the players were. After the first drink, they seemingly started to bond by talking about their individual experiences. A member of the group said, "When Mr. Darryl talks, I sometimes can't understand him. He talks like a foreigner."

Michael smiled and said, "Mr. Darryl as you call him is from Australia and that's the way they talk. We just left there a few days ago mate, and it took me a long time to figure out what the hell they were saying over there. Oh, and by the way, you blokes had better go to the post office and apply for a passport as soon as we get situated. Most of our work will be done in the US Virgin Islands, Spain and Australia."

"They seem awful young," the Tire stated.

Michael smiled and said, "Those two, from what I've heard have put down more people than I would like to think about. They, in addition to running the diamond mines in Australia, also develop advanced weapon systems."

Everyone's eyes opened as wide as possible at the mention of diamonds.

The Tire asked, "Can you give us an idea of what you're talking about when referring to diamonds?"

Once again Michael smiled and then asked, "How many of you believe in demons, magic, and beasts? The diamond mines are being guarded by snakes, dingoes, wombats, huge roos, saltwater crocs, and the 'Great Saltie'. That story is too long to tell or to explain on this flight. However, once we head that way, you'll be told the most exciting story you'll ever hear or believe until you see those things in action."

"What the hell is a dingo and a who bat?" the Ear asked.

"It's called a wombat and the dingoes are animals that look like dogs but have massive jaws. I must tell you this, the animals over there make ours look like playthings. I mean the spiders, snakes, box jellyfish, and other strange things kill on contact. The damn box jellyfish can sting you from over ten yards away and there is no antivenom."

Michael paused and looked at the guys, and then said, "You know what, we're only going to call each other by our given names. If I were to go into a bank and try to open an account for you, and all I remembered was the name Ear or Throat, business wouldn't be conducted, and you wouldn't be paid, which would present a problem for you and me. From this point forward, only given names," he declared.

Giuseppe asked, "Are the rumors true?"

Michael inquired, "What rumors?"

"The guy in charge of this whole thing is Sergeant Beckmire? The same dude and his people who put a hurting on the Cong in the Nam? Is it true or some horseshit to get us riled up?"

Michael smiled and said, "Why don't you save that question until we land and then perhaps Darryl or Sue Lyn will deal with it. Listen, I'm a hired hand that is dedicated to these people because they helped my father out of a situation that would have surely caused the man to commit a crime and suicide. I trust these people and believe me when I say it, there are not many people on earth like this group."

Giuseppe looked afar and realized he was on a private jet heading to the Midwest, in clean clothes, nothing was crawling

on him, with people who seemed normal and friendly. He
paused for a moment and thanked God for the intervention.

## CHAPTER TWENTY-THREE

Clyde met the plane, saw Sue Lyn and Darryl, and gave them huge hugs. He said, "You know your uncle is going to be, how you say it, pissed-off because he didn't sanction this trip. He's a stubborn old man who doesn't realize the people of this town are going to be involved in the defense of the ranch from all levels including tainting food, water, and placing things in their rooms."

At the ranch, the Sarge was standing in the turnaround waiting as if he knew they were coming. Darryl stepped out of the bus and his uncle said, "Nephew, what took you so long? I was expecting you six hours ago. Come and give me a hug."

After the two men hugged, and the Sarge welcomed Sue Lyn back to the ranch he then said, "So, who the hell are these vagabonds? Anyway, don't answer now, we'll have plenty of time to meet and greet. However, for now, I'm Ben Beckmire, but most people who know me, call me Sarge. So, you can call me Mr. Beckmire. So, nephew, what's going on in Australia? Have you secured the mines, the villages and the people?"

"Uncle, you do realize we did not go back to Australia. Instead, my people and I recruited what I consider a good group of assistants who are versed in various aspects of life sustaining ventures and understand the nature of our work. I know you told me to continue on my way to Australia, but you can't expect me to do that when there are winds blowing, and signs indicating that the final dance is about to happen. Is it true you have encountered the true version of the Carbon Factor formula, with printed descriptive materials that detail how to assemble it?"

"Nephew, I don't know what we have and neither does anyone else in our group. It's all foreign to us, but it seems and feels as though this is the real deal. My son's former lover went through a lot of machinations to throw people off and deceive everyone at each turn. She didn't place this thing in his box for the purpose of further deceiving everyone. This is the real deal, and I don't know what on earth to do with it."

"I think it's time you called on your faith. When is the last time you've spoken with the elders? Have you asked for help in dealing with your cousin?" Darryl asked.

"Nephew, I ask God for help every night and morning when I wake up."

"Uncle, I didn't say God! I said the elders and the spirits?"

#

Rashida, thanks to the drones, had an accurate description of the entire ranch as well as the adjacent properties. It showed the property lines, and she was able to view the placement of automatic weapons, pop-up weapons and the areas that needed long gun coverage and the layout of the towns people. When she and her dad got together, she showed him the layout of the ranch and the areas that were well covered and those that needed beefing up. Ben Beckmire told her they had twelve new guns on the ground, but he wasn't sure about their abilities. Rashida told her father to test them. He told her if he did that, those people looking from afar would know the strength of their resistance. She told her father to come into the 21st century. She handed him a pair of Oculus Rift glasses.

She said, "Dad, sit down and let your imagination run wild with help from virtual reality."

After fifteen minutes, Ben Beckmire came up for air and said, "Oh my God! Everything seemed so real. I mean the blood splatter and the entry and exit wounds. Wow, that's some pretty sick shit, Darling."

"It's as real as it can get without literally killing another human being. With your twelve new guns I just want to see if they are accurate and the amount of time it takes them to identify a target and to terminate it. There are scenarios where I can insert them in an area filled with friendlies and hostiles and give them facial recognition tests on the hostiles and let them have a go at it."

"Darling, you are truly in charge of the on the ground security. What impresses me the most about you and your development, is you will forever remain my little lost baby who has a wonderful little girl of her own and now a new son. Just between the two of us. Has this moving around and shooting people played negatively on your mind?"

"Dad, killing someone is not an easy thing to do. However, if it is me or them or my extended family, then it just happens. It's not an automatic task because the feeling lasts forever it seems like. How about with you? I know you have done a lot of this sort of thing. Does it ever get easy?"

"Baby girl, it will never get easy, but as long as people are trying to kill you, LaGina, Juan, and everyone else, it will make it easy for me. You're all my family and I believe what we do is for the right purpose. We don't set out to kill people, they try to kill us in the commission of our human responsibilities—not to give up a formula that makes it easy for men to kill men. However, to answer that question about ease, it never gets easy. I know there are a lot of souls awaiting my arrival in that dark place. I can only say I did them before they had a chance to do me, my men, or my family. Okay, let's stop talking about this subject. What do you need to fortify the unmanned areas?"

"I spoke with Sue Lyn briefly and we're going to get together after lunch to discuss a few ideas I have and check out some designs she has been flirting with. Before we move on and I forget, I want those new people to do a virtual tour with me this afternoon to check on their skill sets."

"Baby girl, I know you're in control, but I need you to be management and discuss any failures with Darryl or Michael prior to busting someone's bubble."

"Dad, I would never go straight at them like that. Believe it or not, I've matured since marrying Juan, having a new baby, and realizing this is the greatest family on this side of heaven. No drama, no beauty queens, no poor girls with braids, and no "I got more than you have". This is a man-made family that is functional, with purpose, and I love everyone here and most of all I love you, Ben Beckmire, the man that saved my soul and that of Larry's."

Ben Beckmire's eyes began to water, and he hugged Rashida and said, "I'll love you throughout time. You are so special to me and Courtney. Okay, enough of this, get busy and I'll track you down to see what you recommend for those loosely covered areas."

# # #

Darryl and Michael took their new crew around to meet the people in the family. When they happened upon Mike, someone said, "The brains in the sewers who rescued a few good roommates."

Mike slowly turned around and saw men who were good, but down on their luck. Men who were smart but no one would give them a chance. Men who were dedicated; men who were over-looked; who had lost their families and had to retreat to the dark side of the equation. He sharply snapped to attention and saluted the people facing him and said, "Gentlemen, this is a family situation with rules and mores. I was asked to give an opinion of each of you. I welcome you and caution you at the same time. You guys know how much I love you. If you screw up here, since I recommended you to the group, I will have to put you down like a sick dog or cat. I will escort you into the field and place a round in your head. Your body will be consumed by the animals of the land. Is that crystal clear?"

The men snapped to attention and Bruce Campbell took the lead and said, "Sir, we're happy to be above ground, where the water is clear, the soap is useable, the food has not been left over, and where brotherhood and friendship apparently matter until the end."

"Welcome to your new world and life. I'm sure your boss has told you a lot, but when you get to visit the soil, the legends operate on, I felt it was my duty to make you understand this is some serious shit. Follow the directives and you'll be fine.

Ask an inappropriate question and you'll be sent packing. I put my stamp on each of you. A stamp that is not casually offered. You people know what I used to do when I was on the sunny side of the street. Hey, I'm just making it real. Better me than one of the highlanders. This is the real world, and the pay is phenomenal if you do the right thing, and hey, I'm not even your boss, but as a newcomer, we all have the opportunity to direct your services to less than menial tasks."

# # #

It was less than fifteen minutes when the Sarge walked into the room and said, "Hey guys, we met briefly. Once again, I'm Sergeant Ben Beckmire, but most people call me Sarge. My daughter needs your services. She wants you guys to participate in some twenty-first century technology game using virtual reality. So, Darryl, can you have them all in the barn around 1300 hours? Is that good with you guys? Do you have another engagement that would require you to disappoint my daughter?"

Mike said, "Sarge, I was just giving them another perspective. If they had another appointment, I'm sure they just cancelled it. They'll be there."

Mike walked over to Darryl and said, "I did it by the script. Did I leave out anything?"

"Mike, you did well. Now, we will all keep an eye on these guys until we're sure they aren't playing both sides of the road. My, Michael is confident in the selection, but I have to be like my uncle—if I don't know you, then I don't trust you."

There is an old adage that says, 'Never leave an enemy in a position to heal and come back later and inflict you with pain'.

#

Because of their failure to obtain the information on the Carbon Factor at the substation of the post office, Vladimir, and his partner who were captured and released, were sent to perform covert operations at the ranch including sniper killing of prime subjects and other targets.

At the ranch, simulations were being conducted, but everyone was on alert and carrying at minimum, a pistol. From 900 to 1000 yards away, two shots rang out and hit targets that looked like Zanthius from that distance. Two new members of Darryl's contingency were the recipients of the rounds fired and they were dead before they hit the ground. Two frontal head shots. Everyone knew the drill and hit the ground and stayed where they were until someone gave an all-clear signal.

Rashida frantically tried to bring the systems online. Sue Lyn told her to hit the button on the console that was labeled gas. She hit it and saw a dissipating vapor trail concluding but projecting its origin. She checked to make sure the emergency systems were online and then hit the button to fire. Within ten feet of where the shots came from, the ground was pummeled. She knew information could only be obtained from the living unless they were researching DNA. She fired a burst of twenty rounds and then halted realizing a smart assassin unless he or she was on a suicide mission, would wave a flag. As calculated, two men raised their hands and proceeded out of the rough area.

Later as the Sarge entered the security room, he looked at the camera and said to Rashida and Sue Lyn, "This is exactly why you don't give quarters. We let them go on the east coast, and here they are in the role of the assassins. They took out two of our people who were the same size as my son and favored him. Tell our people I want them alive and well."

Rashida on the loudspeaker stated, "We need them alive and without injury. I repeat, we need them alive and well."

The Sarge and Mallory were having a conversation about security when the two men were led into the barn blindfolded. Once the blindfolds were removed, the Sarge looked at one individual, then at the other, and said, "You shot two of my new guys. Were you targeting the 'idiot spy'?"

Vladimir said, "I have nothing to fear. I know my fate and let me tell you what I know. The two people we hit were on our list. Our mission and the four others at the hotel in town, was to hit precisely those two targets because they are CIA and play both sides of the road. They are the people who it is believed, have a quid pro quo relationship with Mr. Mike. He offers them something and they tell him something. We were selected, and our families are being watched because we failed that mission at the post office. Our families will be destroyed. I know, you say, we have families, too. Their mission was purely related to the diamond mines in Australia."

The Sarge said, "What diamond mines in Australia?"

Vladimir looked askance at the Sarge, but said, "Come now, Sarge. You know where the mines are and what allegedly protects them. We're looking for salvation for us and our families. I think we picked the side that will not be obliterated. I know you're going to ask the question about giving quarters, but in our case, it adds up to a half? Let me say, we have essentially pulled the trigger on our own families unless you let us go back and say we have been successful in concluding the life of the CIA informants. I have no idea who is constructing their battle plan, but I can assure you, they are going to fall into a firestorm. My associate hacked your defenses, and we know exactly where you have weapons. We are familiar with your pop-ups, and your automated gun racks. The people that will be facing them will have no clue of this and, therefore, we know this is going to be a firestorm. What do we want in return? We want the opportunity to try to save our families. I know you're still thinking of that no quarter thing that's turned into a half."

The Sarge studied them long. He asked Juan to secure them until he returned.

# # #

When the Sarge returned, he said to the two men, "Unfortunately, my people don't trust what you say and what you do. You killed two guys and claimed they were CIA. I asked Mr. Mike as you call him about the quid pro quo relationship, and he laughed. Mike told me the only thing he offered people was a few bucks and depending on the information, a thousand or so. I also asked Mr. Mike if he had given anyone information about the diamond mines you spoke of, and he looked at me, and laughed again. Now, I can't have my people laughing at me. Now, can I? Oh, I also asked him about the two guys having ties with the CIA and he told me he did suspect them but could not confirm or deny it. He said he never got any information from them because he had a seasoned source who is still in play. Now, that Mr. Mike guy, I trust and believe him. We talked about the idea of me letting you go and then having to face you again. This time you killed two of my personnel, regardless of their affiliation to any group or agency. I'm sorry, we'll try to make your demise quick and painless."

Vladimir said, "Wait, I can narrow their arrival to this ranch."

Mallory looked at him and said, "That won't buy you much. Oh, and by the way, so that you know, the information hacked by your friend is information we want to share. The hacked configuration is from a drone layout of the ranch and it's as bogus as the bullshit you're trying to give us."

Vladimir said, "That may be true, but the goal of that elaborate gun placement is to inflict heavy casualties on an advancing force. This enemy is coming in armor plated personnel carriers that are capable of withstanding multiple rounds from a .50 caliber machine gun."

The Sarge, with his back facing the two men, stopped in his tracks and thought, "what if that crazy guy has captured a couple of those things. He would only need two of them to get right up in our face and slaughter us. If he had three or even four, they could pummel that heavily plated ranch house until it gave way".

The Sarge turned towards the two men and asked, "Why didn't you use this information at the outset?"

"You gave us a quarter that has turned, so far, into a half. I will sell out my mother's hideout if she was a bandit and I was facing death. I have three little ones and he has two. We're trying to save them and our wives, but we need you to believe what I'm saying is the truth. We're at the end and you're our salvation. Also, they know the ranch has been fortified with bullet proof glass and metal all around it. They're afraid to us heavy armaments, but they're not opposed to using a limited amount of chemical warfare. I'm telling you I don't know what you did to this guy, but he is pissed at you, he wants everyone, and everything related to you, dead!"

"Your employer is the nearest thing to a living demon on earth. We hope to return him to the darkest side of hell from which he comes. He is no ordinary demon. He is connected at the highest levels with those who are as evil as he is, and he has only one interest on this agenda—amassing massive fortunes at any cost. Where did he get the personnel carriers from? Are they local or are they being trucked in?"

"Sarge, look at us. Do we look like the man's brain trust? We were sent on a one-way mission. We don't have any additional critical information other than when they plan on making their way here."

"When is that supposed to be?" Mallory asked.

"We were conveniently placed outside of one of the command centers when certain so-called classified information was broadcasted. According to them, they're coming in four days. That's the information they wanted us to convey when we were captured. I'll take bets they'll be here in force and attacking by tonight or no later than tomorrow night. The announcement was void of any concern that we were outside of the office, and it seemed so matter of fact, which made me figure it was bogus and that we were definitely going on a one-way trip."

The Sarge huddled with Mallory and then had him call Juan, Rashida, Darryl, and Sue Lyn. When the group arrived in the barn, the Sarge said, out loud and in front of the captives, "So, Sergie, or Sergov and Vladimir, say they hacked your weapon systems, and they know exactly where everything is."

Rashida looked at Sue Lyn, who looked at Juan, who looked at Darryl, and instantaneously, they broke into laughter.

Rashida asked, "Dad, this is a joke, right?"

"No, baby girl, they say they know where the gun placements and pop-ups are."

Rashida walked over to Vladimir and asked, "Is this a plea deal? I mean, are you going to get spanked when you get back home?"

"No, our families are going to be killed."

A silence came over the room and Juan said, "You were given quarters a while ago from the botched job at the substation. Can you tell me what it is you think you hacked, and what proof exists you were able to accomplish that?"

Vladimir thought about his next move and said, "You have permission to look in my left shirt pocket."

Juan smiled and thanked him for the permission. He reached into the man's pocket and pulled out a piece of paper and opened it. It was a close facsimile of Asiram's ranch, and it had "x" marks the gun placements. He looked at Sue Lyn and Rashida and said, "You know what, you have a replica of where the placements were at 2200 hours two days ago. Just for your edification, here is where the guns were forty minutes ago, and this is your, juxtapose placement. I'm assuming you're already dead, so let me be clear, I want you to send that picture to your bosses. The guns are randomly rotated according to heat signatures and a host of other factors. They're solar powered, backed-up and sourced from three different generators. The power is infinite, but of course, all guns run out of ammunition."

The Sarge said, "We're free with information when the curtain has been pulled back on a subject. I'm willing to make you an offer. You go back to town and take care of those people who are there, and then come back here. We will let you fight for your freedom. It won't be in a good spot, but if you survive, you get to live, and we fly you east or wherever on a private plane, never to be heard from or seen again. Just remember one thing, we will eliminate your entire family, if my cousin doesn't, if you screw this one up. We will find them through our bounty system, and we will summarily execute women, children, and old folks. So, if I were you, I would consider the pickle you're in, and decide later. Tell us where your people are, and we'll move them to a secure place. You decide but let us know in the next hour or so."

The Sarge left the barn with his group and asked, "Is it or was it possible for him to hack our system?"

"Dad, a good hacker can do his thing, but our protocols are changed every hour and the rotation of the active weapons is a factor. It's random assignment and placement."

"Mr. Sarge, sir, anything is possible. However, we have sophisticated protocols that are hard to track, isolate, and configure in a few seconds before they change again and, therefore, hacking is almost impossible. What they hacked if anything at all, is likely the picture, but not the picture frame. The frame is where the data are, not the picture. The picture is like a video game that recycles repeatedly and into a loop that changes factors every five seconds creating a false hack. Mr. Sarge, sir, that person only caught the picture. He didn't see the coming attractions," Juan stated.

"Okay, people, I need every weapon online and ready to fire in the next hour. I need the additional drums examined, lubricated, loaded, and ready to fire. Now, that is what I want hacked. I want you people to automate this ranch and be ready to push that button that alerts us, our allies, and shoots with precision. This is no drill. If we manage to enter the evening without conflict, I will alert the general body at dinner, but in the meantime, I expect you people to canvas the ranch from the extreme limits to determine how those two in the barn slipped right the hell up on us."

"Dad, they didn't slip up on us. I thought it was a training mission. I didn't engage because I was reassembling the firing patterns. Once I shut the system down, it takes at least three and a half minutes to reboot." I feel sorry for the loss of life that I caused. I didn't know, and I assumed wrongly. That makes an ass of you and me, and it did."

The Sarge hugged her and said, "We were all lax. They had specific targets and they accomplished their mission. How can we improve our defenses especially if those assaulting us are in armored personnel carriers?"

"Dad, that's easy. Their bellies and tops are vulnerable. If they want to use armored vehicles against us, then we should use the drones to drop ordinances on top of them. It's no different than the way Amazon wants to deliver food from Whole Foods. Once we paint the targets for the drones and hit the engage button it becomes an automatic operation. They will follow the laser beam and deliver any kind of package you want. That seems a little desperate, doesn't it? I mean to use armored personnel carriers. Where did they get them from?"

"Baby girl, if I knew that answer, I would go and disable the entire lot. Now, all we need are explosives that will force them out of the vehicles and give them an opportunity to surrender. I don't want to slaughter people, but I will commit murder if they do stupid."

#

As that subgroup was ending the briefing on the automatic weapons, Mallory said, "You need to decide if you're going to give those people the half. We gave them a quarter at the post office, and now they are asking for consideration again. Personally, I would rather conclude the relationship than give them the opportunity to shoot one of us next time."

"I'm with you a hundred percent, but you know we don't just summarily kill people. The two individuals they killed could turn out to be to our advantage if in fact they were both CIA operatives who were playing on a three-way street if that's possible. I mean, they could have established information on us and the mines, fed it to Walter and then connived to destroy us all. That's the three-way street."

The two men entered the barn and found Michael, Isaiah, and Desmond watching the two men. Desmond worked for NSA until his wife became an embarrassment to him and the agency by having salacious discussions and rendezvouses with his work associates and supervisors. Desmond, also spoke, wrote, and understood the Russian language. Michael was aware of this and let the two captives talk.

The Sarge asked Michael, "Did you have any idea those two men could have worked for the CIA?"

"Mr. Beckmire sir, we recruited them and ran them past Mike. He gave us his best guestimate of the guys but wouldn't vouch one hundred percent for those two. I wouldn't know an agent if he slapped me, but if they were, then I guess things worked out for the best. We will do due diligence on everyone else. It all happened so fast, and we probably should have taken the time to look under their fingernails." Michael then whispered something into the Sarge's ear.

The Sarge looked at Desmond and asked, "You got anything worth telling?" He smiled at the two men and began to speak to them in fluent Russian. He turned to the Sarge and said, "The one that talks the most asked the other one if he was game? They agreed that your offer was solid, and respectful. They admitted they wouldn't have given you guys a second chance but are happy you yanks are civil. They agreed to eliminating those in town and taking up any position to fight on your side."

Vladimir asked in Russian, where Desmond learned his language so flawlessly?" Desmond insisted all discussions be held in English from that point forward. He dismissed Vladimir's question and suggested any action against those in town might signal and/or create a diversion for the incoming forces. He suggested they place those miniature receivers under the skins of the two men, and if they did stupid, then engage the GPS system, and discharge them.

The Sarge asked Vladimir, "What were you being paid for this job?"

"Our payment was, if we succeeded, we could enjoy life with our families. If we failed, then all of us would be sent to hell," Vladimir stated.

"How much were you paid for the post office debacle?" The Sarge asked.

"We were to make $15k each if we retrieved the information and nothing if we failed."

The Sarge smiled and asked, "Did Diablo himself tell you that or one of his henchmen?"

"Who is this diablo you speak of? The man who gave us the job, we owed work to from another job. He was from the communist block and was a radical."

The Sarge looked at Desmond and asked, "Is that it? Did they say anything else?"

"No sir. That is the full content of their discussion before you and Mr. Mallory came into the barn."

In front of the Russians, the Sarge looked at Desmond and Isaiah and said, "I know Michael and I know his family. I don't know nothing about you guys including the fact, you as a black man, Desmond, is fluent in Russian. I will not undermine Michael or my nephew, but if you're playing the field on us, our resolve will be horrific and final. So, before we baptize these two into our ranks, if you have something to tell me, you'd better let it out now. We're doing the DNA thing on you guys from glasses and other methods. If you're not who you say you are then I will personally gut you, from your dick to your brain. Is that perfectly clear?"

Both men nodded their heads. Mallory yelled, "We can't hear your shaking heads answer."

Desmond said, "I'm here, and hopefully, I'm with family. And Mr. Sarge sir, because I'm black doesn't mean I can't speak another language. You speak Australian, don't you?"

The Sarge laughed and said, "They speak English in Australia."

"No sir. That's not English, but perhaps some aberration of it."

Isaiah cleared his throat and said, "I'm here and I report to Michael, Darryl, and Sue Lyn when required. I have no outside agenda other than growing with this group and enjoying the benefits of being a part of it."

The Sarge shook his head and said, "Well stated son. Now, insofar as you Vladimir and Sergov are concerned, you will stay bound, but you will be free to move about the barn under the supervision of Isaiah and Desmond."

Outside of the barn, the Sarge called Clyde on his cellphone. When he answered, he asked him if there had been any large people movement in town lately and was told they had people all over the place and no one had reported anything. The Sarge thanked him and told him to keep him abreast of anything that deviated from the norm.

The Sarge told Mallory that everything seemed too damn relaxed and that he was concerned. He indicated it all seemed too nonchalant and that something was happening, and he was missing the big picture. Mallory told him their defenses were pretty much in place and there was nothing more to be done.

In the meantime, Juan, Darryl, Sue Lyn, Rashida, and Larry were connecting an additional automatic weapon and ammo drum to each of the platforms. Ten platforms now had double the firing capacity with large and small caliber weapons.

At dinner, Rashida asked Clyde if he had access to explosives and he told her there was C-4 buried in the field as well as detonators. He told her it was too late to go looking tonight, but that they could go early in the morning if she wanted to. He asked her about the placement of the Gatlin gun, and she told him Sue Lyn was working on a remote switch to engage it. Clyde said, "I don't mean to sound glib when I say this, but you and Ms. Sue Lyn be perfecting some serious killing machines. I know you would rather play with your children, but what you do is important. Me and your brother and those Asian ladies saw what those people can do. I'm a man of God, but in this case, I will do his work by ridding this land of evil in any way possible."

Rashida looked at him and said, "Mr. Clyde, you are absolutely correct. I would much rather be playing with my children at this moment rather than planning to kill large numbers of people."

# # #

Prior to dinner being served, Clyde asked for everyone's attention and once he obtained it, he said, "You know people, we often eat without giving thanks to the Almighty. This evening, I'm demanding that you take a few minutes of your time and thank God for all he has given you, your friends, and the families that he has placed in your life. I'm not going to give a sermon, but I do ask you to oblige me and mine and do this small thing and pray silently and thank him as well. In the coming hours or days, this land is going to be transformed once again into a killing field. I want this group to be on the winning side of that equation and, therefore, I beg you to take a few minutes before you chow down and thank God almighty."

A true leader leads by example. Ben Beckmire grabbed Courtney's hand and descended to his knees. The two of them closed their eyes and only God knows what they asked for, but it was probably the same thing everyone else asked for— peace, and an end to the endless killing, and travel. They prayed for the ability to live life like normal human beings and do the Almighty's work by helping people help themselves.

Approximately three minutes later, Clyde said, "I believe God heard all of those prayers for ending this issue without senseless bloodshed. In the name of Jesus Christ, please bless this food, the hands that prepared it, and may each bite give us strength, wisdom, and the ability to know right from wrong. Amen!"

Rashida and Juan asked Darryl and Sue Lyn to attend to the war room while they got something to eat. Sue Lyn asked her husband, "Where are we going to live? I like Australia, but I also like LA, New York, Baltimore, and Washington, DC. Can we live in all of those places, but do due diligence in Australia for six to nine months a year or less, if in fact we don't encounter any problems exercising our responsibilities?"

Darryl thought for a long time about the questions and said, "We can live anywhere you want, but you know I have a responsibility to my people that is not based upon our whims or desires. It is what the people need to have their freedom, become educated, own their homes, and make decisions based upon facts and knowledge, and not circumstances or mythology. As your husband and lover, I will do whatever it is you want me to do if you consider the things that I'm charged with doing. I mean, we'll have our own plane and will probably have to get a bigger one to carry the guys, and their families just like my uncle did. He didn't intend to expand his group, but the guys fell in love and, therefore, they needed a bigger plane. Oh, I forgot to tell you. My uncle wants us to take over the operations in Valencia. Have you ever been there?"

"Darryl, when were you going to tell me?" Sue Lyn asked.

"Sweetheart, I was going to tell you once he officially told me. He's going to ask me in two days to do this thing."

"You and your uncle are very strange people. I think Spain could be a good place for us to go."

Darryl feeling amorous after her response backed her up against the wall and kissed her feverishly. She began to respond and attempted to undo his belt. He whisked her around and her posterior hit the console and specifically the alert button; not the this is a drill button.

In the control room the only indication was flashing colors. Throughout the ranch and the additions, it was a full call to arms. When Darryl realized what had happened, he said, "Oh shit, your bottom sat on the alert button. When Juan and Rashida ran into the war room, they could sense what had happened and proceeded to take control of the systems.

Rashida asked, "Did you see something or was this a complete function of another kind of vision?"

Sue Lyn looked at her and dropped her head. Rashida said, "Duly noted. I'll send the all-clear signal once I've scanned the entire ranch."

After that event, Rashida realized that Clyde and his people were not on the buzz system and, therefore, they needed to correct that oversight. She turned to Sue Lyn and said, "We've got to put Clyde and his people on this system. This could turn into a nightmare if we aren't careful."

"I'm on it. Give me an hour or so and I'll have it programmed. In the meantime, perhaps I need to program the buzz button for two hits instead of one long acknowledgment," Sue Lyn stated.

Rashida walk over to Sue Lyn and said, "Perhaps you need to learn some new positions so you can monitor where lover boy places that ass of yours." The two women laughed and dismissed any notions of unfriendly innuendoes.

The Sarge walked into the war room and said, "People, a lot of lives are at stake." Rashida was about to respond when Sue Lyn stepped up and said, "It was my fault because I've become clumsy since becoming pregnant. You must admit though, it was good to see how people respond. Right?"

"You just scared the be-Jesus out of us. I'm not sure you know the history of this place, either one of you. Anyway, this is the place where your uncle placed suicide vests on the children. My son Larry, Somara, Yeshida, and Okema along with Clyde made their way to the place and saved our lives. This place is where most of us were captured and sentenced to death, including the children. So, when an alarm goes off, we're up, armed and ready to do battle."

Darryl said, "Uncle, we got it, and we'll be more careful in the future."

As Rashida ran diagnostics on the system, one area kept coming up with a fault signal. She asked Juan to re-run the diagnostics and he too came up with a fault signal. Sue Lyn looked at the report and said, "There is a large contingency of bodies in that area. The extreme heat signatures caused the diagnostics to report a fault."

She turned to the Sarge and said, "I think it makes sense to keep the ranch on alert until we can figure out what's going on."

Sue Lyn stated, "Rashida, you need to target that area and send a high-flying drone over there with a zoom lens." Juan ran a second diagnostic and agreed with Sue Lyn's assessment.

Rashida launched a high-flying drone with a zoom lens. Five minutes later, it showed several men digging fox holes and large caliber weapons with muzzles on them. Rashida said, "Dad, they must be wearing clothing that's not detected by our system. I guess they don't think we can detect their movements. It appears as though they're setting up a battery."

On another part of the ranch, the sensors picked up movement. Juan said, "It has the same characteristics. Honey, can you fly the drone over that area?"

Rashida re-directed the drone, but painted the initial area, and assigned the long guns to every moving target. Once the drone was over the new area, Rashida concluded that holes were being dug. She also could see that the people there had long guns. Rashida painted each target and initialized them into the firing sequence.

Rashida said, "Dad, we need to know what they're wearing since our sensors don't acknowledge them. We need to know this asap so that we can correct this oversight. They literally can walk up to the front door with the outfits they're wearing because we can't detect their movements. We need to evaluate one of those outfits."

The Sarge considered what his daughter had just said and asked, "Can you hit those people without alarming the others?"

"Dad, unfortunately for them, the weapons trained on them are subsonic meaning they are fired through two sets of mufflers and from inside a self-contained environment. They won't hear the shots, and neither will we."

Rashida hit the engage button and eight men were immediately dispatched.

"Michael, I need you and your guys to retrieve a body or two so that we can figure out how they're walking up on us without our knowledge," the Sarge stated.

"Got it Sarge. Guys, lock, and load. This is no drill. This is the thing that makes men into who they are--or widowers! I am not married so I will not have to worry about that. Let's go and show the Sarge we're not neophytes at this work."

The Sarge asked Mallory to find a placement for Vladimir and his friend, but always in front of them. He also asked Mallory did he trust the two men and was told that he did, as long, as they were in front of him.

## CHAPTER TWENTY-FOUR

In Washington, DC, investigations were underway by the CIA, FBI, NSA, and committees of the House and Senate. The primary focus of the investigations was the demise of two sitting US Senators, the personal use of men and materials, the misappropriation of billions of US dollars, and the connection of one individual in particular, to all of the aforementioned issues--Walter E. Lassiter.

Walter E. Lassiter's empire was beginning to disintegrate before his eyes. He no longer had the luxury to publicly show his face and had to retreat to the sewers where he sent so many people packing and hiding. When it was made clear to the residents of the sewers that the man himself was coming down there, people began to move above ground and disappear into the night. His loyal following included his longtime henchmen who would literally do anything the man asked. Walter decided that he would have to be more active on jobs that needed to be completed, including the conflict with his cousin and the ownership of the diamond mines. He realized he spent too much time on trying to gain access of the Carbon Factor formula and should have straightaway concluded his cousin instead of playing games with him. He said to his henchman, "If it's the last thing I do on earth, I will kill my

cousin, his friends, and family. You know what, he has a child
at the Naval Academy. Tomorrow, let's discuss how we get
to him and film his demise on camera."

Marvin, his henchman said, "Boss, the fish you're frying
and the oil they're trying to put you in might be more
important than a family grudge. You have the entire United
States Government looking for you. Perhaps we should focus
on that problem first and then if we have some down time, pay
particular attention to the other matters."

Walter looked at him and said, "You're a close confidant,
and you know I've put billions in places that only you and I
know about. Therefore, I trust the living hell out of you. I
respect what you just said to me, and I agree, we need to focus
on getting the hell out of dodge. Any ideas?"

"I'm working on a few things, but it just might require
you to dress up as a dame. I know just the people to do the
work and who won't run their damn mouths. More perplexing
is getting you out of the country. I think if we can get you
back to your home, and I do mean your home in the outback,
you can run the empire from afar with direct access and control
of the funds, the personnel, and the targets. Once you
consummate ownership of the mines, that are guarded by
animals, I think you will own the country."

"Marvin, you've never been to my country, have you?"

Marvin shrugged his shoulders and replied, "No, I
haven't."

"It is a wonderful place full of folklore, strange animals,
and allegedly spirits as well. I don't really believe in that
bullshit, but there is something to the notion of magic and
larger than life animals. I never discount the place and when
I'm there, I try to abide by customs, at least sometimes.

Anyway, right now, there are no formal charges against me, just people wanting an opportunity to question me about two dead senators and missing government money, which I know absolutely nothing about. How about sending one of our guys up to Starbucks, I want one of those lattes. Make sure you give him a small bill and not a hundred. When you come back, I want to talk to those mercs in the Midwest to see when they can begin the assault."

# # #

In the Midwest, the Sarge had concluded that his cousin would send people on suicide missions, so that he could evaluate their defensive situation. He walked into the war room, and asked Rashida what was the dimensions between the first hole being dug and the second. She calculated the distance and told him it was approximately one mile apart. He asked her had they made any rhyme or reason why the systems weren't picking up the mercs and she told him they're using a combination of silver and iron in their materials. I googled it. I'm not sure that's it. It was developed by a company that is owned by that old football player, Franco Parris."

"Watch your mouth young lady, he's almost a contemporary of mine and was a great football player. I recall he and his company experimented with silver to kill germs and went so far as to develop a paint that was washable that also killed mole, mildew, and other bacteria."

"Anyway, Dad, there is something about the combination of the two elements that has found a way to bypass our systems. Sue Lyn is working on trying to analyze the issue. Until she finds out what's causing the disconnect, I suggest you keep the ranch on full alert. I mean, Juan and I have turned up the sensors, but I'm not sure if there is a general problem with the entire system and until I'm convinced, we can easily detect advancing people, regardless of their outfits, we should be on full alert. It's an anomaly and we haven't figured it out yet."

"Damn, child. What happened to that scared little girl I rescued from hell? What's your plan if they have armored personnel carriers?"

"Clyde and I went into the field with Darryl's team providing backup and retrieved a lot of C-4. Some of Michael's people are making smart bombs that I can trigger remotely. Unless they come with more than eight of those vehicles, we should be okay. To your first question, she grew up to be a wonderful princess, but hasn't had the time to practice it because she has a life altering job of being chief of security for a bunch of renegade family members."

# # #

As the drone began to weaken in power and send signals it had a certain percentage of battery life remaining, she recalled it and witnessed it fly directly into another object. The Sarge asked, "What happened to it?" Rashida didn't respond initially, until the object and the drone hit the ground.

To Rashida's amazement, she saw people parachuting onto the property in suits that were oblivious to the motion sensors. She yelled, "Dad, they're parachuting onto the property. There's hundreds of them in the sky landing precisely on the fringes of the ranch."

Without saying a word, he hit the red alert button. Everyone knew what that signal meant. John Lee and Jilkes kissed their wives and sent them to the sniper cages. Ms. Viola, Mary Alice, and Marisa gathered the children and went to the nearest bunker that was secure and safe. Chakes told his wife he would be back, and she yelled, "You don't know that. Hug me like you love me, man!"

He held her, she cried, he cried as well and said, "Baby, you're with a group of magicians. If there is a way out of this mess, one of our guys will figure it out. Trust me and believe in the magic we felt in that cave in Australia. I love you, Ms. Viola, and Beatrice. Please, have faith. Some may perish, or all may. It's in God's hands. You're so special to me. I love you so very much. I must go. I have to go."

Okema, Somara, and Yeshida were in an almost impenetrable place in the house. Courtney, Ava, Asiram, Monica, Yvette, and Carla, were all attached to sawed-off shot guns, .308s, and machine pistols. The Fab 10 plus 2 knew exactly where they had to be and that was in the middle of the action after Rashida pushed that fatal button. Zanthius, Mike, Carlos, and his guys were in place and ready to fire. The Sarge sent Darryl and his crew to the eastern side of the ranch and split their forces equally to the north and south on the eastern flank. Sue Lyn told Larry and Mike she needed their help. When Larry saw the Gatlin gun, he asked, "Where the hell did you get this thing?"

"I didn't get it. It fell off a truck and some of Clyde's friends found it."

"Did they find the magazines as well?"

"Mr. Larry, we don't have time for this thing you seek to know. People are dropping out of the sky at this moment to kill all that are dear to you and me. Now, do you want to help me move this thing or interrogate me?"

"Sorry, Sue Lyn. Where do you want it to go?"

"I want to do a 180-degree sweep from the southwest to the northwest, refuel it, and do a 180-degree sweep from the southeast to the northeast. After that, we're either dead or there are a lot of bodies in the fields, and they will be left for Rashida to dispatch of."

The Sarge sent out an order—no quarters. He specifically told Mallory to keep Vladimir and his associate in his sights. He called Rashida and asked if Sue Lyn had programmed a remote firing sequence for the Gatlin gun. She told him she wasn't sure. He told her to check and let him know the exact moment when and if it came online. The Sarge said, "I sure am proud of you and your brothers. You've been that juice that makes me want to live forever. Love you baby girl. When it's time to hit that button, please don't hesitate."

"Dad, I'm on it. Make sure your people don't cross my firing line and if they do, they had better have their ID tags on. Once I hit the firing sequence, it will hit everything that slightly moves." As she scanned the monitors, she said, "Oh shit Dad, there are vehicles turning onto the access road and more people flying in the sky. Give me the signal and I'll start this party."

The Sarge evaluated the placement of his people and told Rashida he needed that Gatlin gun up and running in the next two minutes or they all were going to be toast. Rashida called Sue Lyn and told her it was now or never, and she told Rashida that it might be never, but for now, it was now. Rashida called her father and told him the news and he told her to hit the engage button.

Once she started firing remotely, the ladies in their perches began to pick targets off from a thousand yards and beyond. Sue Lyn told Rashida that she controlled the Gatlin gun and wanted to know if she could use it. Rashida told her to hit the fucking button and be done with it.

Without thinking about the consequences, Sue Lyn hit her remote button and the Gatlin gun began to cut down people in a vicious manner. With the intercom system open, one could hear Rashida say repeatedly, "OMG, OMG!"

Rashida was witnessing firsthand the impact of the Gatlin gun. From the west, it tore through as many as eighty-five men and women in an instant, in foxholes, behind trees and with their heads buried in the grass. Once the drum had emptied and was refueled, it was turned to the east and again repeated its abominable, monstrous, and macabre job of destroying life as one knows it.

The Gatlin gun was developed to inflict huge casualties on opposing forces. It has no conscience and prays to neither God nor man. The pop-up weapons, automatic long-range guns, and people perched in a secure environment picking people off is a function of man's inability to relate to man. It is the definition of survival at any cost. The impact of the Carbon Factor formula would pale this episode of stupidity by five hundred thousand-fold.

The Sarge made his way to the war room and saw the potential breaches by people who were scaling down lines out of helicopters, and in other quadrants of the ranch, parachuting precisely to the points on their GPSs. He said to Rashida, "Can you use the drone to disable those people coming in on the main road as well as those in the armored personnel carriers?"

Rashida responded, "Dad, I need you to shut the hell up. If you haven't noticed, we're rather busy targeting and sending signals to our allies where we need input. The roads to the ranch are treacherous and there is a point where a portion of it is hydraulically controlled. They will find themselves in a deep ditch in 5-4-3-2-1!

It was as though the earth sank and the vehicles rushing to assault the ranch were suddenly stacked on top of each other killing men and women who were trying to earn a dollar—the wrong way!

Rashida said, "It's your call. I can have the drone drop C-4 on them and the deal is sealed."

Her dad looked at her and said, "Honey, where is your humanity? Is there any way we can force them to surrender?"

"Dad, you said no quarters. Is it or isn't it, the directive? I have six thousand acres to secure. Okay, you take care of that glitch and let me know how you want to handle it."

It was less than five milliseconds when an errant round found its way through the crack in the door, onto a wall, then ricocheted off a metal panel and into the back of the Sarge's head.

Rashida said, "I don't mean to be disrespectful, but you're scaring me with this vacillation factor." When she turned around, she saw the blood splatter and witnessed her father fall face forward into a wall and collapse. She yelled at Juan, "Kill every fucking thing that moves beyond the yellow line."

She screamed at the top of her lungs, "Mom, Mom, dad has been shot. Mom, I need you."

Over the intercom system, Courtney heard that her husband had been shot. When she got to the war room with Ava and Asiram in tow, she saw the blood splatter first, and thought to herself no one could survive that kind of trauma and blood loss. She kneeled beside her husband and began to cradle him.

Asiram, in her own inimical way yelled, "He's not dead. Get busy fixing and stop that rocking shit."

Courtney realized what she was doing, and began to demand towels, her medical kit, hot water, and lights. In the middle of the war room a hysterical and incoherent daughter and her husband were summarily targeting everyone that moved including those waving white flags.

Asiram yelled, "Rashida, stop and think. Tell those who want to live to drop their weapons and backtrack or they will feel the wrath of the Gatlin gun."

Marisa and Ms. Viola showed up with her bag and towels. Courtney began to wade through the blood and tried to figure out where the bullet was since there was no exit wound. She probed with her flashlight and happened to notice a point on the Sarge's neck where there was additional trauma. She told Asiram and Ava to put gloves on and to follow her instructions to the letter.

Rashida yelled, "We have a breach behind the barn."

She was comforted by the fact that Okema, Somara, and Yeshida had it covered. Mallory called on the open channel and asked, "How is our leader?"

Like a true Beckmire, Rashida said, "Too soon to give an update. Will let you people know as soon as I know. His wife is here and is performing surgery on the floor behind me. What I need, or what we need, is for you people to attend to your business as though this event didn't happen. My dad is counting on you and so am I."

Mallory converted the intercom system so that he was the focal voice and said, "You heard the lady, I need you people to stay focused and ready. We made a dent in their forces, but I think they have a lot more to give up, after all, his cousin is a mad man. Until further notice, you will acknowledge me as the leader of the group with Jilkes, John Lee, Brown, Bernstein, and McArthur in succession. That's the game, now let's play it people. Stay sharp and let's do this for the Sarge."

Mallory looked at Jilkes and said, "We have two additional drums for the Gatlin gun. Let's just spray the east and the west and let the people in the field know this is the end and that we can do this all day until they're cut into little pieces."

Jilkes asked, "How did they get a shot off at the Sarge? I know he's targeted, but they never played that way before."

Mallory said, "Listen, where the Sarge was standing and got hit, that bullet had to be a shot intended for someone else. The round found its way through an unobstructed cracked door, hit a wall, and ricocheted of a metal panel and into the war room. I only know one person who could make that shot, his name is Jesus."

"Mallory don't blow smoke up my ass. Is that the way it happened?" Jilkes asked.

"Jilkes, how long have we been together?"

"I'm sorry, Corporal Mallory. I'm having a hard time accepting the fact that the Sarge has a bullet in his head and will probably not be with us again."

"You and me both, Jilkes. I've spent my entire adult life with that man, but I understand where you're coming from. A bullet to the head is conclusive, even for a giant like the Sarge. You and I must hold this thing together until we get rid of that

Carbon Factor formula and put controls over the mines in Australia and elect members of this group to oversee our vast holdings. This is not going to be easy and I'm going to need you and John Lee to anchor what you think his beliefs and directions were. And wait a minute, I haven't heard his wife announce the time of his death yet. Let's see how that goes before we implement any new actions."

# # #

Meanwhile on the floor of the hallway before reaching the war room, massive amounts of blood, literally were running down the sides of the hallway. Asiram kept saying, "You're a doctor first, a wife second, and unless he was a no-good husband, then don't slack off. But we all know that's not true. We need you to focus totally as a doctor and see if you can save him."

Courtney was in the zone and was visualizing the contents of the head including muscles, veins, nerves, and everything else. She saw the amount of blood and yelled, "I'm going to need blood and plasma. Rashida, you're his type and I'm going to need you to prep. I can't seal the source of the blood loss and, therefore, I'm going to need a lot. Ava, go to the locker in the basement and get two bags of plasma. Asiram, I'm going to need more ice."

# # #

Approximately, twenty-five minutes later, Courtney retrieved fragments of the bullet from the base of the Sarge's skull and cauterized the entry wound. He was in shock and was being assisted with a portable breathing apparatus. She decided against moving his massive frame and got blankets and pillows to keep him comfortable. Fortunately for the Sarge, he was in a part of the ranch that had marble floors that were heated.

Courtney connected the heart monitoring machine and blood pressure devices to the Sarge. As soon as she had the opportunity to recap what she had done, to her own husband, the distress call came in once again. McArthur and Gladstone had been shot and needed immediate attention. Courtney directed Mallory to bring them to the war room and that way, she could monitor her husband and attend to the wounded.

Seven minutes later, Mallory helped transport the two men to the war room area. He called Jilkes and asked, "Do you have the drum connected to that Gatlin gun?"

Jilkes said, "Corporal, I just cocked that bastard."

"Son, face it to the east and cover 180 degrees. Once it is empty, face it to the west and cover the remaining 180 degrees. Here are my standing orders, if you have a weapon then you must not be in the surrendering mode and, therefore, you are still on your mission. On my mark, fire that bastard. Three, two, one and mark!"

Jilkes hit the switch and that gun ripped up trees and individuals and left a blood trail that would seduce the animals of the land for weeks to come.

On the other side of the ranch, Rashida pumped blood and monitored the screens with Juan. She saw that Mercs were regrouping from the vehicles in the trenches and decided to send a drone with two well timed packs of C-4. The resulting factors were horrific, loud, and brightened the night sky. The vehicles exploded adding fuel to the fire and everyone in them met their maker. Those who managed to escape the vehicles were without delay, fired upon by the pop-up weapons.

Miles away from the ranch house, single shots rang out and people from far away fell to the ground. Clyde and his forces fired randomly at targets moving towards the ranch. They would fire from different positions, therefore, throwing the advancing mercs off balance. In addition, the pop-up guns would randomly target groups of mercs and inflict death on them.

Darryl made his way to the ranch house to check on his uncle. As he approached the doorway, a shot rang out and hit him in the side. The bullet went clean through, but nonetheless, there was a sniper making shots that would only diminish the number of people who could respond to their final assault. Juan cut on the gas tracking system that was overwhelmed with gunfire. The first image it captured, once online, was the shot that hit Darryl.

Juan yelled, "I see you motherfucker, and take this as a response." He opened the floodgates of weapons in that quadrant and the sniper was hit by more than twenty rounds.

Jilkes and John Lee reloaded the Gatlin gun. Jilkes called Mallory and said, "The gun is ready to fire again. We're waiting on your instructions."

Suddenly, John Lee said, "I'll be damn. Hit the deck."

From the outskirts of the ranch, mortar rounds were being fired in the direction of the Gatlin gun. Jilkes said, "Get a hold of that line and let's get this thing down range and out of their sights.

Juan saw the flash and painted the area for the drones. He sent two drones packed with C-4 to the area and from five hundred feet in the air, they dropped their explosive devices on the target area.

Mary Alice assisted Darryl to the triage area and Courtney simultaneously, attended to McArthur, Gladstone, and Darryl. When she looked at Darryl she said, "Oh my, it went straight through. How lucky for you. Asiram, can you place some gauze on both sides of the wound and pour a lot of hydrogen peroxide on and around it?"

She looked at Darryl and said, "Your uncle is in a bad place and if you can do some of that stuff that I find hard to believe to save him, I would greatly appreciate it because I love that man more than life."

"In our country, many things can be done. Here, we cannot summon the collective powers of our people. You are a very special woman, and doctor. I need you to believe me and just do as I ask. Rashida is his blood type, but she is not a Beckmire. I'm his blood relative and may be able to help him. I need you to connect that device to me that is running between Rashida and him and let me see if I can summon our lifeline from across the sea. If you trust me and don't believe everything that you read, then this must happen now. He has begun his journey to the other side. Only a blood relative can help him find his way back."

Courtney looked at Darryl and considered her education that was being refuted by what she considered folklore from the outback. She calmly said, "Darryl, he'll probably never be the man we know because the bullet did impact his brain and I only have first century tools to work with out here and three other people to attend to. I'll have Ava make the switch. I have to attend to the other people."

She looked at Asiram and said, "Get up Ms. Lady. You don't have time to cry. I need you to help Ava suck blood from Darryl and feed it into my husband. Come on people, this is a life and death room. Life happens if we do the right things. Death occurs if we don't investigate the real and the surreal. I'm betting on magic and not science in this matter. Hook him up and I mean now."

Rashida staggered back into the cubicle and called Clyde. They had worked out a signal for when to hit and run. Clyde said, "I can't talk. There is a force of fifty to sixty Mercs exiting a trailer and its one that's owned by a farmer we helped. Well, that son-of-a-bitch is going to be mine when this is over."

Rashida calmly said, "Tell your people to play the Ostrich game in sixty seconds."

After the men came out of the trailer, a ramp was lowered and a mechanized robot with huge lights and a shield rolled down it. Once in the field the robot's shield expanded to cover a ten-foot area. Each man also had a shield and they advanced in synchronized steps. The robot was equipped with infrared beams and was disabling the pop-up weaponry. Rashida said to Clyde, "I can't get a beam on that thing because it's using infrared against our setup."

Sue Lyn watching the robot said, "Shut the lights off the weapons system in that area."

Rashida doused the lights and bingo, the mercs became a well-lit target by using their own technology. Rashida yelled, "Clyde, fire in the hole." She hit the engage button and four pop-up guns and four assault weapons fired mercilessly on the mercs. The weapons system destroyed the robot, and pummeled the mercs into submission, terminating many of them and allowing the others to give a tacit notion of surrender.

Rashida called Clyde and said, "I think they are trying to surrender. I'll call that quadrant and tell them to dispose of all weapons and sit with their hands on their heads. We have a lot going on at the ranch and I want everyone to remain in their positions. If by chance any one of those people attempts to leave or disobey a command, don't negotiate; terminate."

Juan and Rashida scanned the ranch thoroughly. There was light movement in the outer areas that didn't present a threat. Rashida hesitated to fire on the area because it would be over-kill. Instead, she called Mallory and asked him to come to the war room as soon as possible.

A few minutes later, Mallory, Jilkes, and John Lee showed up. His priority was to find out how the injured were doing. He saw that Darryl was connected to the Sarge and chanting some strange chant. He saw the blood and asked Jilkes and John Lee if they could hose down the area. He checked on Gladstone and McArthur and was encouraged by what he saw. When he saw the Sarge sprawled on the floor with tubes and bandages on him and around him he broke into tears. He fell to his knees and began to pray."

In the outer room with McArthur and Gladstone, Courtney began to cry and Asiram saw her. She walked over to her and said, "If I had a mother, I would want her to be like you. You represent everything that is good in humans. You don't do drama, you don't do no sniping, and you don't take no shit. You're smart, pretty, and funny. Yes Courtney, if I had a mother, I would want her to be you."

Asiram hugged her and said, "I think your husband and my father-in-law, is too stubborn to leave us. I don't know much about magic, but I think they got something going on between him and Darryl. I pray that he'll be alright. Now, I need to shift your thoughts and I need to ask you a serious question. When people get caught with their drawls down, that's usually because they think they're invincible. Do you agree with that?"

"I guess so," Courtney replied.

"Mom, you're working with second century tools. It's most likely that someone in this group is going to get shot daily because of the very definition of what we do as a group. If we pull through this, we need to consider our existence and survival. We need to have more than one ventilating machine and multiple means to extract blood as well as x-ray machines and vital signs monitors. We find ourselves in this predicament because we think our shit don't stink and we're just that good. Well, we ain't, and the stench is starting to catch up to us. I just wanted to distract you in a positive way. You attend to the Sarge and Darryl, Ava and I got McArthur and Gladstone."

At the helm of the war room, two alarms went off. Juan tried to figure it out and when Rashida looked at the monitors, she yelled, "There's a breach in tunnel # 2 where the children are. There are four armed men racing towards the safe room that's not locked. Mallory yelled, "Jilkes, you and John Lee take care of that mess. Mike and Carla, provide back up."

As the assigned members headed down the steps, one could hear gunfire—shotguns and machine pistols. Jilkes yelled, "You know the code and if you don't, we're going to seal this area in fifteen seconds."

Marisa said, "If you do, I will kick-your-ass."

Everyone laughed and when they got near the safe room, four bodies were sprawled in the tunnel. They had been over-killed by shotgun and machine pistol bullets.

Ms. Viola said, "These people must be from the damn islands. You can't come running up in somebody's bathroom while they be bathing their babies or taking a dump. I mean that's just plain damn dumb, man."

Jilkes called ahead and told Mallory that all was secure in the tunnel but was curious as to how they found out about it. With an earpiece in his ear, Clyde dominated the airwaves and said, "I'm afraid that one of us betrayed you guys. This is Clyde and I have to substantiate the matter, but I think it was one of us."

Rashida said, "This is command, I need the people in the tunnel to secure the children in the room and to report to your commander immediately."

The monitor showed four large personnel carriers approaching the boundaries of the ranch. Mallory asked, "Where the hell, did they get those damn things?"

"I don't know, but we have eight drones loaded with a welcoming package. The bellies and roofs of those things are not armor plated," Rashida announced.

"You are your father's daughter. He would be so proud of you thinking out of the box to protect us all. Rashida, you are so special to me and the group."

When Jilkes and John Lee came upstairs, John Lee asked, "What be happening now?"

Mallory pointed to the screen and said, "These fucking guys aren't going to quit until they kill all of us, or we kill all of them."

John Lee looked at what Sue Lyn was doing and what Rashida was attending to and said, "If'n we get out of this mess, I want you people to teach me as much as you can about how to do this remote-control warfare. I be getting too damn old to do that conventional mess. I think my African American friend agrees as well."

Sue Lyn asked, "Who is your African American friend and why don't you call him by his name?"

"Ms. Sue Lyn, he prefers that I call him that. It's a long feud, but I'm close to convincing him to see it my way."

"Oh, I see! Rashida, I need to quickly check on my husband. I've painted each vehicle, and I want to do the honors. You've concluded a lot of humans tonight. You need to share this burden with a friend and that would be me."

Rashida said, "It looks like they're trying a flanking maneuver with those vehicles." She looked at the cameras in the rear and said, "Holy shit, they have two of those vehicles running at us from the roadside."

Jilkes looked at the screens and said, "John Lee, we need to separate. I need you to handle those two coming off the road towards us and I'll work with Rashida and Sue Lyn on the two attempting to flank us. Is that okay with you Corporal Mallory?"

"You must see something that I don't, so follow your instincts, but be careful."

Jilkes asked Rashida, "How much fire power do we have left in the weapons system?" She hit a button and it showed the number of rounds remaining in each individual weapon.

Jilkes said to Sue Lyn, "We need to show them our resolve. I need you to strategically place the drone on top of the personnel carrier with a timer that I can detonate from here. Is that possible?

"Oh, I see, destroy one and the rest should bail out of them, is that correct? I have just the one to make it look like a nuclear detonation just happened."

Jilkes asked, "What do you mean?"

Sue Lyn studied the cameras and said, "Precisely! I want to send drone number five to the lead carrier and drone number four, one hundred yards in front of it. I want this to happen now."

Two minutes later, a drone landed on top of the lead carrier and left its ordinances. Drone four descended in the field and left its package and took off. One and a half minutes later, the package that drone # 4 placed in the field detonated. It almost appeared as if there was a nuclear explosion because the C-4 was accompanied by hydrogen peroxide, gunpowder, sulfur, and various other volatile and colorful chemicals. When the explosion happened in the field, it shook the earth.

Mallory hailed the advancing Mercs on Channel 16 on the VHF radio and said, "Your persistence to be annihilated is admirable. The personnel carriers you're riding in, although armor plated, cannot withstand our ordinances. The explosion in the field is an example of what is affixed to the top of the vehicle you're in. I will only make this announcement once. Stop your hostilities, exit the vehicles with your hands on your heads or witness our resolve to watch you burn to death like eggs in a pot being boiled."

The mercs had an alternate channel to communicate and the leader told the others cryptically to switch and answer channel 68. Once on channel 68, he told them that they have a job to do, and the carriers could withstand that kind of explosion.

Jilkes heard every word that was said on channel 68 and said, "I commend your grit."

As the lead vehicle started towards the ranch house, Jilkes hit the remote switch and watched as the vehicle and those inside, disappeared into the night and into small pieces. He asked Sue Lyn how many bars of C-4 were attached, and she told him four bars. He looked at her and said, "Sue Lyn, you use four bars of C-4 to level ten floors of a building. One bar in the future is sufficient."

She looked at him with tears in her eyes and asked, "Where is the vehicle and the people?"

"Everything that was attached to the carrier has been obliterated. We might find a deep hole in the ground with some remnants of man and machine, but you'd have a hard time trying to identify body parts. Listen, they would have deployed the same kind of strategy on us. We gave them an opportunity to retreat, and they decided that the pay was more important than their lives. As you can see, the others have abandoned their vehicles and are stripping themselves of their weapons. I don't know how many people were in that vehicle, but our actions saved those who are sitting in the field with their hands on their heads. You saved them, and you saved us."

Rashida said, "Damn girl! We'll have to keep an eye on you on the 4th of July."

Rashida hugged her and said, "It's them or us! I still wake up with the image of LaGina being strapped into a suicide vest by a merc who just laughed and said, "little girl, you won't feel a thing".

From inside of the firing range, two RPGs were fired at the ranch both hitting the concussion wall that was built and worked well. Rashida followed the gaseous signature of the rocket and sprayed the field gratuitously until the Gatlin gun just whistled in the night. The four men in charge of firing the RPGs were unsparingly cut to shreds.

On the loudspeaker, Mallory said, "If one man makes a stupid mistake to try to escape or bring harm on our forces, every man in that group will be cut to pieces by an old fashion Gatlin gun with a modernized firing system that spots movement in the night. Now, for your safety, each person will deposit their weapons at your current location. You will then walk twenty feet from where you're standing to the east, where you will disrobe. If a weapon of any kind is detected on you, you will be expeditiously shot by a machine. People in a mule will bring blankets and fire sticks to keep the indigenous and carnivorous animals away from you."

In the background, the sound of wolves could be heard fighting over the remains of people slaughtered on the ranch. Mallory said, "I guess you can hear that commentary in action. People, I suggest that you move quickly and efficiently. That is a call to dinner that you're listening to."

No sooner had Mallory made that comment, the roar of bears could be heard in the distance. Mallory took the opportunity to inform the uninvited guests, that this is the land of the Brown Bear, Grisly, and occasionally, a Kodiak bear could be found in these parts. I'm not going to endanger our forces and you'll have to fend for yourselves until first light since we were just attacked by RPGs. We will attempt to keep the animals at bay. I suggest when you reach the no weapons zone that you huddle close together and keep those fire sticks waving in the air."

John Lee walked into the war room area, stared at a pale looking Darryl and then at the Sarge and said, "Corporal, we have to find that demon and dispatch his ass all over the earth so that he'll never appear again. I'm convinced he can't mount this kind of task force again. Him be hunted by his own government now. He has to be in hiding and I think I know where we might find his ass."

Mallory said, "Let's complete one task at a time. Right now, I need you to take Michael and his people, along with Brown and Bernstein, to secure the no weapons zone." He looked at Rashida and asked, "How's your weaponry in that quadrant?"

Rashida ran a diagnostics test and realized that they were down to the twenty percent level. She then refocused the long guns with the bump stock modifications on the area and said, "We're pretty low on ammunition, but the long guns have been directed to the area and are prepared to make a rapid response."

Courtney in the meantime along with Ava, Asiram, and Luana, used the crudest methods possible to attend to those who were injured. Darryl continued to share his blood with the Sarge and chant. Although his voice was deteriorating from donating a lot of blood, he continued to slowly chant unknown phrases to the group. The Sarge looked as if he was resting comfortably or what others didn't want to acknowledge, that he was in a coma. Darryl had given two pints of blood and was beginning a third. Courtney looked at him and said, "You cannot do this any longer. I know you want to help, but it's up to him and what he believes in. I'm unable to evaluate the wound to his head and I'm hoping that by sunrise, if he's still with us, we might be able to head to the hospital and get real medical attention as opposed this medieval stuff that I'm doing. You can't give any more blood Darryl, and that's all I'm going to say."

John Lee and his crew slowly and methodically approached the captives who had their hands on their heads. John Lee said, "Okay, we be trying to keep you people alive. If you have anything that looks like a weapon, including them there blades, you will be shot without any questions being asked. Now, if you move your hands off your head, that automation shit is going to hit you hard and splatter that head of yours all over the place. I hope you understand that message. We don't be repeating it again."

John Lee walked into the center of the circle and said, "I hope we can do this without anyone getting their head blown off. Keep them hands on your head until my people signal that you're okay and clean. If you be having to sneeze or cough, then I would sneeze, cough, and say my last wishes all at once. You be making any sudden moves you will have your head blown off. You all be painted and monitored by the computer. If you think you're faster than the computer, by all means you should just drop those hands off that there head of yours and we'll see. That's all I be saying."

The team members slowly approached the area and knew to stay to the side of the captives. Bernstein out of the blue said, "I know you. You were in the Nam with us. What the hell are you doing with this group?" The guy lowered his hands to begin a conversation, and instantaneously, a shot was fired, and a round entered the man's head. Bernstein yelled, "No, back down, he was one of us in the Nam."

John Lee looked at what was left of the man and said, "Bernstein, the little shit was here to kill you and me. Now, you people had better keep those damn hands on your heads. Shit, I be done told them three times the same shit, now his head got a big hole in it."

As the night began to turn into day, Clyde entered the property driving the special school bus. He had people stationed on both sides with weapons locked, loaded, and ready. He pulled up to the front door and the wounded were ushered in. Clyde saw the Sarge and began to cry. He saw his buddy was barely breathing and appeared to have expired. He asked, "Who's my back up on this trip?"

Mallory called Chakes and told him to pick three people. He picked Montomie, Mike, and Jong. A weak Darryl said he was going as well. He asked Sue Lyn to remain at the ranch and keep a vigilant eye out for the bad guys.

John Lee, Bernstein, Brown, and Jilkes oversaw the prisoners. John Lee proclaimed, "If any of my people die in that hospital, I'm gonna take that Gatlin gun and empty it on you fools. That be a promise. By the way, you people get paid immediately after a job, right? Who is the paymaster?"

# # #

Jilkes called Rashida and told her to put the targets on passive so that the people could rest their arms and scratch whatever itches. He said to John Lee, "I had the war room put the targets on passive. He turned to the twenty-three men and women and said, "We're going to step back and let you do whatever relieving you have to do. Ladies, I can only offer you those trees as cover, but remember, if you try to make a dash, you'll be cut down. I'm giving you people five minutes and then I'll have water and food brought out there."

John Lee said, "Wait a minute. Delay that order. I need to know who the paymaster is?"

One of the women said, "We don't know. All we know is that our cash was supposed to be waiting for us at the hospital." Jilkes heard the information and basically in his mind dismissed it.

John Lee said to Jilkes, "That be a strange place to make payment, don't you think?"

Jilkes pondered the inquiry and felt weak when he put the pieces together in his mind. He grabbed John Lee and said, "The Sarge is in danger. They have a plant in the hospital. Bernstein and Brown, I need you guys to handle this situation until we get back."

Jilkes called Rashida and told her to place the targets on active. He looked at John Lee and said, "I need you to trust me on this one and do exactly what I ask of you." Jilkes looked at the responding woman and asked innocently, "Why would you get paid at the hospital?"

The woman responded, "The hospital is where the instructions and everything else that we're supposed to follow came from."

Jilkes asked, "Do you know the name of the person who was responsible for making payment to you?"

The woman responded, "I don't want to be a snitch, but he's the guy who runs the hospital, he's the head doctor."

Jilkes threw his head to the left and asked, "Come now, why are you putting him in that position?"

"His role was to set the stage and make things happen. He was on the payroll for $1 million if he killed a certain Sergeant with a bonus package of $2 million if everyone including the children were not able to create a problem for our employer. He told us our employer mentioned that those who wanted full time employment could serve as his security team once he took over diamond mines in Australia.

"Most of us didn't believe that, but he insisted the financier of this event had access to diamond mines. The doctor at the hospital has significant reasons to do exactly as this guy says, his wife and two kids have been kidnapped and will be terminated if the assault isn't successful. He's between a rock and a hard place. Listen, anyone you take to the hospital will more than likely die a slow death from being poisoned."

Jilkes said, "If our leader dies, that crazy redneck is going to kill all of you. I'm going to give you time to think about how you can make this right or the way you're willing to die. It's all about choices."

# # #

Jilkes and John Lee made their way to the ranch house and retrieved a vehicle. Once in the vehicle, Jilkes called Rashida and told her to call Courtney and tell her to keep everyone except family out of the Sarge's room.

Rashida called Jong instead of Courtney and told him what Jilkes had instructed her to tell Courtney. Jong told her he would handle it and let Courtney focus on her husband, and the other two guys, and not his security. Jong asked her if she knew the nature of the threat and she told him she did not. She asked him to be vigilant because the big man was her dad.

# # #

Jilkes and John Lee arrived at the hospital and went directly to the Sarge's room where they were met by Jong, Mike, and Chakes. Chakes said, "We've been here, and no one has attempted to enter the room." No sooner had he made that statement, the hospital administrator turned the corner with a nurse carrying a tray with a syringe on it. Jilkes asked, "So Doc, what's the needle for?"

"Oh, it just something that will make him rest comfortably."

John Lee looked at the tray and said, "Well, I hope that's exactly what it is, but I don't be believing you. You know what? I think I be giving you a shot of this until we ratify some information we got from a prisoner. Where be your family?"

The doctor tried to turn and run, but was body kicked by Jong. As he rolled around the floor, he began to cry and told them exactly what had happened to his family and what he had to do to guarantee their survival. The doctor told them his job was to kill everyone who came from the ranch with an injury. They didn't tell those people you came with your own doctor. They promised me millions once they found out that Mr. Beckmire was wounded. I was offered two million plus five additional million to kill Mr. Beckmire and if I didn't succeed, my daughter would be violated by the five men that are holding my family hostage. Insofar as the needle is concerned, you can give it to me because it's only saline. I'm trying to preserve him not kill him. Go ahead, inject me with it. Better still, inject me with some of it and give the rest to Dr. Beckmire to confirm. I'm trying to buy time to figure out how to save my family."

John Lee studied the man and took the needle off the tray. Courtney walked into the room and saw the doctor on the floor and asked, "What in the world is going on in here?"

Jilkes pulled her aside and gave her the skinny on the issue and she asked the doctor, "Is what he said the truth?"

"Dr. Beckmire, I'm afraid it is. Insofar as the needle is concerned, please inject me, and save some for analysis. It's saline to hydrate your husband, but not bring him out of that coma until we know how to approach the issue. The money they offered me was never a consideration. What you people have done for this community is simply remarkable. I have never violated the Hippocratic Oath. I was trying to figure out how to save my family and your husband."

John Lee asked, "If'n you be telling the truth, how do they be contacting you?"

"Sir, they call me on my cell phone?"

"You be having that phone on you right now?"

"I do," the doctor indicated. He handed John Lee the phone and he asked, "Where is the Sarge's nephew?"

Chakes responded, "He's feeding his face in the cafeteria and saying some chants."

"Chakes, can you fetch him for me? I need to ask him some questions about this here phone."

Three minutes later, Chakes ushered a chanting and wounded Darryl into the outer room where the Sarge was. John Lee said, "I know you be knowing how to find out where this phone got a call from. That be correct, right?"

Darryl looked at him, turned to Jilkes and asked, "Jilkes, can you translate what he said?"

Jilkes laughed and said, "You see country bumpkin, people don't understand that foreign language you speak.

Darryl, we're trying to trace the last call on the Doc's phone. Can you manifest that information?"

He handed Darryl the phone and he immediately asked the doctor for his password. Once he received the password, he looked at the call list and saw that it was blocked, but that it was local. He went to settings and manipulated several apps and downloaded one.

Five minutes later he said, "Your phone sure is slow. You might want to think about switching to another provider."

Once he checked the last number, it gave him a GPS reading. He read the coordinates out loud and Jilkes read them to Siri and she told him that the call came from the hotel .35 miles away.

Jilkes called Mallory and gave him the skinny on the involvement of the doctor, his reasons for being seduced, and the potential location of his family. Jilkes asked Mallory to hold on a second. Jilkes looked at the doctor and said, "We were told you were the paymaster. Is that true?"

"Paymaster? I don't think so. My secondary instructions were to provide the two huge machine boxes to anyone on the list that I was given. I don't pay people. The hospital does that.

Jilkes smiled and asked, "Doctor, where are these two boxes?"

"They're in my office taking up a lot of space."

Jilkes apologized for asking Mallory to hold the phone and indicated to him he was going to go to the doctor's office to survey two mysterious boxes. He and John Lee went to the office and saw two enormous cases that appeared to be custom made.

John Lee said, "I guess it makes sense. You kidnap a man's family, make him do your bidding and if he doesn't, you let five willing freaks have their way with his wife, teenage daughter, and son."

Jilkes called Mallory and told him, he thought they found the paymaster and the payroll. He told him they would secure it but wouldn't open it until it was x-rayed and cleared by Darryl or Sue Lyn. Mallory asked him about the family of the doctor and was told that they may be in a hotel down the street. Mallory told Jilkes to send Michael and his crew to figure out how to extract the man's family.

# # #

After initial discussions about the nature of the location, Jilkes received a call from Michael who told him the pizza place was delivering a lot of pies to room 456. Jilkes asked him to ask the pizza guy if he used the same delivery people and was told he uses the mailman, sometimes a policeman, and firefighters. Jilkes asked him are any of them black and was told no. Michael looked at his people and decided that Jason was the most likely candidate.

At the pizza parlor, the men huddled with the owner and asked had any of his guys noticed anything suspicious and was told they never gained access to the room but that a guy would come out to pay for the order and disappear. Michael called Jilkes back and told him he needed to speak to someone in the hotel and wanted to know if they had a contact? Jilkes called Clyde and was told that everyone there was related to the people providing protection. Michael told Jilkes he wanted to go to the main desk as if he was checking into a room and get a layout of the room and any that adjoined it. Jilkes told him that they didn't need any heroes or innocent bystanders injured and if he didn't have a feasible plan then to abort until full force could be applied.

# # #

An order for pizza had come in the store. One of the occupants in room 456 called to check on the pies and was told the guy should be there in five minutes. Michael hit his watch and assigned Desmond and Isaiah to breach room 458 and for Harold to cause a distraction in room 454 that adjoined the room that allegedly held the family of the doctor. Michael had obtained a master key from the desk clerk as well as chain cutters for night locks.

The clock was ticking and according to his watch, they had less than ninety seconds to execute a half thought out breaching operation. He told his people the announcement that the pizza man was there was the signal to breach.

With thirty seconds left on his timer, he thought about all the things that could go wrong and prayed for everyone's safety. On his mark, Jasper knocked on the door and yelled, "Pizza man." Someone looked through the peep hole and unchained the night lock. The person as he opened the door asked, "What took you so long?" He was surprised by the weapon that was placed to the side of his head. Michael instructed him to take the pizzas and walk back into the room. When he walked into the room, the men were surprised as Michael's team approached from both adjoining rooms. It was apparent the men had their way with the wife and the daughter. Michael looked at the doctor's wife and told her to take her family into the other room. He asked her, "Did they all participate?" She started crying and said "Yes".

Michael asked, "So, who is in charge?" There was no answer. He looked at Jason and nodded. Jason randomly selected one of the men and shot him in the head.

The man beside him said, "It don't take a real man to shoot an unarmed man, it takes a coward." No sooner had he finished speaking, Isaiah put a round in his head. The 'puff' sound was the only thing heard since the weapons were fired with the suppressors attached.

Michael asked, "Why would you defile that child? I can't imagine why you would rape her. She's probably going to be scarred for the rest of her life."

The guy who had the pizzas said, "They weren't ever going to leave this room alive. That was the deal, no matter what the doctor did, they were already dead."

Michael put three rounds into his head. He said to Isaiah, "Go into that room and tell them to clean themselves up and that nobody has to know what happened to them. I want to keep these two alive in case Jilkes wants to question them."

Michael called Jilkes and told him the breach was successful, but there was a body count. Jilkes asked if it was theirs, or ours, and was told it was theirs. Jilkes asked about the status of the hostages and was told they had been defiled. Michael told him he needed one of their people to come over and secure clothing because he was going to try to clean the hostages up and let them decide if they needed to tell what happened to them. He said to Jilkes it is not our call. Jilkes pondered the request and asked Monica and Mary Alice to attend to the matter as discretely as possible. Michael told Jilkes two of the scumbags were alive and wanted to know if

he had any use for them. Jilkes told him no, and Michael asked
him to hold the phone for a minute. He walked up to each man
and said, "Had you violated the mother, I would let her decide.
You guys forced your way on her child and for that, I'm going
to send you straight to hell." He shot each man twice in the
head.

When he re-engaged the phone, he told Jilkes they needed
a cleaning crew over there. Jilkes told him to secure the room
and that he would have the bodies removed later that night and
the rooms re-decorated. He told Michael good work and to
stay sharp.

# # #

Mallory called Darryl and told him that he needed him to
x-ray two containers. Darryl smartly asked, "The hospital
doesn't have any x-ray machines?"

Mallory considered his statement and his response to
Darryl, was, "You know Darryl, it's good thing your last name
is Beckmire."

He started to hang-up when Darryl said, "Mallory, I was
not being flippant. They have tons of machines here. Why do
you want me to do that?"

Mallory realized exactly what he had asked him to do and
said, "Darryl, I think we all could use two good nights of sleep.
As I recall what I asked, it certainly sounded a little moronic."

CHAPTER TWENTY-FIVE

One week later, Ben Beckmire remained in critical condition. Courtney and the group took turns monitoring and protecting him. Clyde had his people assigned around the clock. His people flatly believed they would be there until hell freezes over. After all, Ben Beckmire and his band of merry associates helped people they didn't know with no expectation of remuneration. The people in the area were aware of the importance of the man who was in a coma. Prayer vigils were held nightly, and that good old-time religion was spread amongst the believers.

Courtney had specialists flown into town to look at her husband. She also had video conferences to show the X-rays and the positions of the bullet fragments, as well as the vital body controlling functions, that had been shattered. Every specialist that viewed the frames was afraid to consider the operation because it looked as if the fragments were in places where if they were removed, the collateral damage would be too great. It was as though the bullet fragments were producing far more challenging problems. Each specialist told her it was crap shoot and the damage to date was beyond repair. She was told at best, his chances for living a normal life were slim to none and that time was not a friend.

Darryl called upon his family members to honor and pray for his uncle. He knew the Beckmire clan was strong. He prayed to the 'Great Saltie' and asked him to guide the hands of Courtney who would have to remove toxic metal fragments from her husband's head.

Courtney had consulted doctors near and far and each was skeptical of her husband living once the bullet fragments were removed. As she cried, she said to herself, "I must believe in magic and spirits to save my husband—not science".

Two weeks later and running out of options, Courtney asked the head doctor of the hospital to assist her with the operation. He reminded her he didn't have the necessary skill sets to assist in such a delicate operation. Courtney looked the man square on and asked, "Do you believe in magic?"

"That's a strange question. Why do you ask?" The doctor inquired.

Courtney insisted on staying the course with the question and said, "I need you to answer the question."

"I don't disbelieve in it. I'm often amazed at how sometimes things happen that are on the brink of a miracle."

Courtney cut him off and asked, "Can we start at 0700 hours? I want to get a good night's sleep and review the situation as many times as necessary until I feel the best way to approach the problem."

Darryl saw Courtney coming out of the doctor's office and said, "I will be in your dreams tonight and the 'Great Saltie' will help you as well."

She looked at him and said, "I can use all the help I can get." To herself she said, "that kid is really weird. He sounds like a clone of my dear husband—weird".

Courtney told Monica she was going to go back to the ranch and for her to call her if there was any change in his condition. Monica told her she would stay in the room until it was Asiram's turn in about four hours.

Monica called Mallory and told him she peeked in on the Sarge and that he didn't look good at all. She told him he looked pale, his eyes were sunken and that he just didn't look like their friend. He told her he would come to the hospital once he transferred the chain of command.

#

Darryl x-rayed the containers and told Mallory there was no evidence of explosives or chemicals. He told him there were just shadows that looked like Franklin. Mallory asked, "Who the hell is Franklin?"

Darryl said, "Dah—one of the past presidents of your country." He told Mallory that he and Sue Lyn were going to be in the middle of the field surrounded by fire and magic, and that it would be best that everyone, including those who provide long-distance surveillance, go home and pray or cut their televisions up loud. He said, the animals of this great country would roar. Mallory told him to do what you must do but save his friend and bring him back whole.

As Courtney wrestled with the notion of trying to not only save her husband, but preserve his mind, she thought to herself, "he helped so many without a price. I sure hope he has at least one coin in the fountain and the spirits will shine down on it.

Prior to falling into a semi-unconscious state, she visited the aspects of her life that needed consoling and attention in her dream state. Courtney fell into a place where the mind controls pleasure and pure rest is guaranteed. She entered a space where the Sarge was providing her with atomic reactions and nuclear explosions. Her body writhed as though the act was real. Her movements and contortions were in memory of the man who taught her how to make and enjoy love. She tossed and turned until what appeared to be an angel revealed itself and showed her the wisdom and patience, she would need to save her husband—it was Darryl with his boyish smile and his understanding nature guiding her from the frivolous mindset to the exact operation in the morning. Courtney was confused. In her dream-state, she wondered how her husband's nephew appeared in a dream that was so real and sensual. It was all about distraction as his appearance would be the last thing she remembered for the balance of the night.

People were stretched thin and the normal security precautions were left to automation. Rashida and Juan literally took up residence in the war room. LaGina would come in the middle of the night and stay with her parents. Ms. Viola kept the baby and secured him along with the other children who needed to stay with her. She was such a wizard in the sense she could hum them to sleep, sing to them to wake up and demand they take a nap daily. Indeed, Ms. Viola was a wizard.

By 0500 hours, Courtney had showered, had her first cup of coffee and was in the main dining room talking to Clyde and his wife. They held a prayer service, but it felt incomplete to Courtney.

At 0515 hours, it appeared, in her mind, as if Darryl had walked through the door and said, "I know what you dreamt about last night. Some aspects of your dream were blocked from my viewing. I know you don't believe in a lot of things other than pure science, but please listen to me and listen to your training and your heart. Today, you'll be presented with choices. Each one will have an epic result. Your medicine and training will help you a lot, but it is your heart and the love you feel for that man that will allow you to make the correct decisions. Some things will absolutely refute what you've learned through those many years of schooling. I will say this once again, trust your heart and you'll save a great man in his entirety".

Courtney started to say something and realized there was no one there, but Clyde who was escorting her along with his people to the hospital. He said, "I didn't quite get that question you asked, Mrs. Beckmire."

As though in a daze, Courtney said, "Sorry, Clyde, I was asking myself a question. I'm going to rest until we get to the hospital. Oh, what did the doctor's wife and daughter decide to do?"

Clyde said, "They're trusting in the Lord. They've decided not to admit and deflect conversation about it unless forced. He wouldn't care."

Mallory had assigned Michael and Mike to shadow Mrs. Beckmire to and from the hospital. The men spoke to her, gave the chase car the proceed sign and headed down the long stretch of road leading to the main highway. The men let her sit in the middle of the bus, and they were close enough to react if necessary. Michael whispered, "I have a flask full of that coffee from the island you like. Would you like a cup?"

"I'll take you up on that once we get to the hospital. It's not spiked, is it?"

"Oh, no ma'am. It's just been prayed over by me, Ms. Viola, and Luana."

"In that case, I'll have a little now and a little before I go into the operating room."

# # #

After the bodies had been removed from room 456, a cleaning crew spent the night removing all traces of blood from the room. Once that was done, the local cleaner that had been engaged by the group entered the room with an ultraviolet lamp and checked behind his people. There was no indication of a spot of blood anywhere in the two rooms.

At the hospital, the head doctor met Courtney and told her he was ready to assist in any way possible. He thanked her and the people for intervening in the matter surrounding his family. He said, "I know they were abused, but they're trusting in the Lord, and that's good enough for me. I think this sad event is going to make us a stronger family."

Courtney smiled at him and said, "I'm happy for you guys. Let's get scrubbed and figure out how to save my husband."

The operation was scheduled to start at 0700. Ben Beckmire had been prepped and was about to be put under medically. Courtney was about to enter the room when Michael said, "Doc, before you go in there, I must secure that door on the other side. I didn't take that into consideration.

Please, hold here for two minutes. He directed Isaiah and Desmond to find their way around to that location. He called Clyde and asked him to station his people on the lower floors in case there was a problem. Without any further delay, Courtney was in the room with her husband, with two specialists on video and audio, and the necessary doctors and nurses to handle their specific tasks.

Courtney said, "Good morning. I'm Dr. Beckmire and I'll be assisted by people on audio and video, and your good hospital administrator, Dr. Bernard Wallace. Shall we begin? The patient as you well know has bullet fragments lodged in the base of his skull that has both been a life saver and a curse. I removed a significant part of the bullet, but pieces are resting against his hypothalamus and has cauterized certain bruised or damaged arteries and nerves. Our job is to extract them and be prepared to do repair on the fly. I've never done this before, but if I don't do it now, he will probably not last the week. He is my husband and I love him. I'm going to do this correctly with your help."

#

For those on the outside waiting on word of the Sarge's condition, it seemed like an eternity. Six and one-half hours had passed and there wasn't any movement from the doors that the doctors and nurses were behind. Mallory called every hour and worried Jilkes about making sure there wasn't a plant in the room and that all exits were secured. Jilkes told him that Michael was charged with security and from what he could see, the guy was doing a great job.

John Lee sat up against the wall and rested his eyes as he laid his head in the lap of Somara. There was a ruckus occurring in the street. Clyde called Jilkes and said, "I need you people down in the lobby. The State Police are here with an arrest warrant for Benjamin Beckmire."

Jilkes told him he was on the way. He pointed to Michael and said, "No living person enters that room. If they try, and I mean police, priest, or angels, you shoot them. If anyone breaches that room, you'll have me and him to deal with."

Michael called Isaiah and told him that the State Police were outside and that under no circumstance are they to enter the operating room.

Jilkes and John Lee walked outside and saw the local people pointing weapons at ten State Police Officers who also were pointing guns at the locals.

Jilkes said, "I need everyone to relax and lower those weapons. In our society, we usually figure out why we want to shoot each other before we do it. Can someone tell me what's going on?"

Clyde said, "These rustlers came blowing into town like they're generals or something and were going to try to arrest the Sarge. We told that guy there, the one with the captain bars, that the man was in surgery and he said, "He don't give a shit if he's talking to God."

John Lee walked towards the man and Jilkes, forced him back and said, "I need everyone to calm down. Now, Captain, was that John Wayne shit necessary? Can you and me and one of yours walk away for a minute and figure out what's going on and how we can fix it? Can we do that? As you can see, the locals aren't going to let you have him and neither are we. Let's figure this out. What is Ben Beckmire charged with?"

"Your man is charged with murder in the first degree."

John Lee said, "That be sounding serious. Who did he kill and where is the body?"

"Listen, we're serving a warrant that accuses your man of shooting two individuals in the hotel down the street."

"And when did this here murder take place?" John Lee inquired.

"It's alleged your man killed two New York types, last week."

Jilkes said, "Last week, are you nuts? He's been in a coma for the last fifteen days and under heavy surveillance by his family members, by the way we all are related to him. Obviously, there is a mistake. Will the evaluation of his hospital stay clear this mess up? I mean, the head doctor for this hospital is assisting in the operation. I'm sure, once it's over, he will attest that there is a mistake."

"Listen, we're serving a warrant on Ben Beckmire. We're not here to hold a kangaroo court."

Jilkes looked at him and said, "That's a little harsh."

John Lee nudged him and said, "What kind of court is that? One of those courts back in the outback?"

No sooner had he said that, Sue Lyn and Darryl walked outside, and Darryl said, "My uncle expired five minutes ago. Ben Beckmire is dead. He lowered his head and beckoned Jilkes over and whispered in his ear, "How can three of these cops have the same damn badge number? We got up close and personal with them from the window with a new device that we're trying to perfect?"

The captain said, "Well, I guess this was all for nothing. Our perp is deceased and once we verify the body, we'll be on our way, fair enough?"

John Lee looked at the captain and said, "You want to know something?"

"Not particularly, if it's got nothing to do with why we're here."

Jilkes said, "John Lee, we need to go and console his wife the lawyer."

The captain said, "I thought his wife was a doctor?" That statement caught everyone by surprise. Jilkes looked at John Lee, ran his hands through his hair and pulled his weapon. Jilkes shot the captain in the arm and John Lee, Sue Lyn, and Darryl provided clean up on the rest of the crew. Clyde yelled, "What have you done? You murdered police officers. What the hell is wrong with you people?"

Jilkes looked at him and said, "Clyde, since when do cops have the same badge number and name?" After a thorough evaluation of the bodies, Clyde yelled, "They all have the same name and badge number."

John Lee turned to Darryl and asked, "Is it true? I mean is the Sarge really dead?"

Darryl, with a serious look on his face turned to John Lee and said, "I know what that man meant to you guys and, therefore, it saddens me to admit that it was a lie. My uncle is in recovery and his wife is being heralded as a genius. She did some magical stuff in that operating room and reconnected things that are so small you can't see with the naked eye. Anyway, he's in recovery and the prognosis is positive. He will live, but his quality of life is the question."

Darryl hugged each man and said in a voice they had never heard, "Loyalty amongst family members, seals the unit until time is no more."

At that point in time, no one from the operating room had made a statement. When Courtney walked out of the operating room, eight and a half hours later, she said, "I'm not sure about the success of the operation, but I'm confident my husband will have some measure of life, and I'm hoping its qualitative. I want to thank each one of you and the people back at the ranch for praying for the Sarge. I especially want to thank my nephew for his magical manifestation of my belief in things other than those proven by science. I'm tired and I've invited the entire medical staff for dinner at the hospital tomorrow. I'm hoping some of the ladies I know and love, will assist me in providing a thank you dinner for the staff. Listen, I'm not sure what God has in store for my husband, but I can tell you we tried to extend his life because he's a good man who loves everyone. I personally want to thank everyone in this town, and tell you what this town, Asiram's ranch, Clyde, and his wife, and all of you have meant to us. My husband often would say to me at night, "we should be able to help these people. They don't know us, and we don't know them, but we're all God's children"."

CHAPTER TWENTY-SIX

Four and a half days later, in a bed with his wife by his side, a groggy and confused Ben Beckmire woke up and said, "Why on earth are we in the hospital. Did you fall and break something?" Courtney screamed at the top of her lungs and Michael and Isaiah rushed into the room with guns drawn only to witness Ben Beckmire, aka the Sarge, sitting up in the bed questioning his wife about why they were in the hospital. Jilkes and John Lee came from the other side of the hospital and blew through the door with weapons in the ready position. John Lee fell to his knees and started to pray. Jilkes walked over to the man and kissed him on his lips and said, "I love you so very much, dude."

"Why the hell are you kissing me on my lips. Did you leave that beautiful wife of yours, and find your true calling? What happened here and why is my head all bandaged up?"

Jilkes said, "Breathe for a minute and ask that beautiful and talented wife of yours. Oh my God! We're so lucky and you're lucky your wife is an excellent surgeon. Damn you're a lucky man in all respects. Get some rest, and we'll talk later. Welcome back Sarge!"

Jilkes pulled out his phone and called the ranch and told Rashida, that her dad was alive, well, and talking. He asked her to pass the message on to Mallory and have him make an official announcement and schedule, starting tomorrow, three-minute visits. He then said, "It's a glorious day, Rashida."

Darryl and Sue Lyn came out of Dr. Bernard Wallace's office and saw the smile on the face of Jilkes. He said, "We know my uncle is okay and that he was sitting up and talking to you guys. On another note, there is between $36 and $42 million dollars in those cases. What are we going to do with that much cash?"

Jilkes said, "I'm sure we'll think of something to do with it. It's' not like we are short on projects that need funding."

That afternoon, a video of Dr. Courtney Beckmire and her team was circulating around hospitals and throughout medical schools. It was shown without her approval and was released by the staff of the specialist that she had assisting in the operation from afar. The video elicited calls for speaking and publishing rights. She called Monica and told her what had happened, who in turn sent out an email indicating that privacy issues had been violated, and that pirating and modification of the video had occurred. From that point on, it became the Monica show who vehemently indicated she would seek damages from any institution knowingly showing the video of doctors, nurses, and patient without their express written consent.

Monica later told Courtney, "I guess I'll get a chance to practice law again because of this unauthorized event. I wonder if Luana would want to assist in this matter. Also, if you had a choice, what medical institution would you designate as the beneficiary of any proceeds that are netted from this situation."

Courtney looked at Monica and said, "Perhaps we could endow the Benjamin Beckmire School of Head Trauma?"

Monica responded, "Girl, I'm on it. What a marvelous idea and a needed one at that."

# # #

The Sarge said, "Honey, can you keep people out of the room until I fully understand what happened to me? Oh, and did you really operate on me? Where did I get shot? Oh, I see—dah! Don't answer, I know it's a head wound. Wow, how long have I been in here and why, can't I move my legs?"

Courtney called for a nurse to assist her and realized her worse fear was in the making. She thought that the nerve damage could impact any part of his massive body but was thankful it wasn't his legs. His muscles had atrophied, and it became hard for him to move them.

All the simple neurological tests for movement, Ben Beckmire passed. He said, "I need to stand up." Courtney looked at him and said, "Do you love me? I mean do you really love me?"

"Don't be silly. You know I love you. What does that have to do with me standing?"

"Honey, I spent eight plus hours operating on your head and trying to reconnect nerves, membranes, and everything else that makes your body function. You, my love, have been in a coma for nearly three weeks without any muscle movement, exercise, or brain work. You jumped up and started asking questions which gives me hope that your brain might be working fine but is that short or long term. There are a thousand tests that you'll have to undergo to make sure you can stand on your own, urinate and defecate without help, as well as eating, swallowing, digesting, and a thousand other functions that people take for granted. My question about love is simple. If you attempt to do that macho thing that you do, and something happens, I will feel as though I failed my most precious patient. I need you to stay in that bed, and let the doctors run various tests to make sure everything is functioning properly, and if not figure out what needs to be done? That's when we start therapy once we've diagnosed the issues that we need to concentrate on."

Ben looked at her and said, "Have I really been out for almost three weeks, and where is my nephew? He tormented me in my dreams each time I thought I was slipping into a deep unconsciousness."

"Yeah, he was in my dreams as well and at some very inappropriate moments when I was being seduced by you+."

"Wait till I see that little freak. I'm going to hug him, thank him, and all the Beckmire clan for their sacrifice, so that I can continue to do the work that God and the Spirits have designed for all of us. I told you that magic was powerful."

"Dude, I need you to stay still and slowly use me and the orderly to recline. I do not want you to use any muscles, just trust us."

He looked out of the door and saw Michael and asked, "Michael is my main security?"

"No. He is mine. I don't have a clue as to who is watching you Mr. Man, but I got the young bucks checking my flanks."

# # #

Two weeks later, and after a series of neurological and physical tests and exams by the best in the business, Ben Beckmire was allowed to go home after nearly seven weeks in the hospital. It was as though he was transmogrified into Shirley McLain in the movie *Guarding Tess*. He refused to ride in a wheelchair, until he realized that he could get some mileage out of it.

When the elevator stopped on the first floor, there were locals with flowers and cards to present to him. Ben Beckmire milked the moment for all it was worth. He enjoyed all the attention. He pretended to be in pain, but he wasn't, and again, it was his moment, and he embraced every second of it. Being a very smart man, he turned to his wife and raised her hand in the air and kissed it. What a player!

In the bus he said, "That was very special, and it made me feel at home. You know what, I have an idea I would like to share with the group."

Courtney said, "Honey, I need you to continue to rest and avoid stressful encounters."

"What's stressful about communing with my family? I like that idea about building another wing onto the hospital and naming it, not with my name, but with the names of all the members of our group. Also, we need a name for our group, don't you think?"

Darryl came forward and said, "Uncle, I neglected to tell you, but we have two containers with anywhere from $36 to $42 million in each. Sue Lyn and I cleaned them to make sure they were not wired. The cases had C-4 in them, but we eliminated that and found two dummy GPS units and one sophisticated one. It is our assumption that once things settle down and these cases have been moved inside for counting, an ordnance will be fired at the system we did not disarm. I guess it's to make sure that whoever wound up with these cases if all had failed, well, they could kiss their butts adios. Our plan is to place it in the field. We counter-balanced the weight with hotdogs, beef patties, chicken parts, and anything else that animals will eat."

"Nephew, are you telling me you have placed us all in danger?"

"Uncle, I'm telling you that Sue Lyn and I control the code on this thing as well as the jamming of signals within a three-mile radius. We got this Uncle."

Beckmire looked at Sue Lyn and said, "I just got out of the hospital. What are my chances of seeing my family on the ranch?"

"Dear Mr. Sarge, your nephew, my husband, is a brilliant individual. He and I calculated the survivability of this event, and it is greater than ninety-five percent. We do calculations often and usually, we're in the normal range of + or – factors, and when we miss, we miss by large margins."

"That's extremely comforting to know." He looked at Courtney and said, "All of your good work is now dependent upon their mathematical abilities. Wow, aren't we lucky they both can count to ten?"

# # #

When the group reached the ranch, Darryl had called ahead to have one of the mules meet them at the threshold of the property with a lot of aluminum foil and duct tape. As the bus slowed to a stop at the turn off point, the mule was positioned and driven towards the rear of the bus by one of the locals. Darryl kissed Sue Lyn and told her he would see her soon. Darryl attached a trailer hitch to the two cases and pulled them out of the back of the bus and down a slide with the mule. He then drove the mule to a place where it appeared that an explosion would have no collateral damage.

Exactly one hour after disconnecting the mule and hastily getting away from the cases, the real GPS came to life and broadcasted a strong signal. At the house Darryl, Sue Lyn, Rashida, and Juan watched the radar scope. Ten miles away from the ranch, a large high-speed military style drone was launched and carried an explosive device. Rashida saw it first and said, "People, we have incoming."

The Sarge asked her to broadcast it on the monitors throughout the ranch. As the group watched the drone hover over the cases without a clear picture to broadcast because of the foil, the package was dropped and two minutes later the earth shook. The Sarge asked Rashida, "Can you track where that came from?"

"I'm already on it Dad. It came from the next farm over."

Clyde asked, "Are you sure about that?"

A puzzled Rashida said, "I'm pretty sure."

Clyde looked at his wife and said, "We'll be back, and we'll handle that person. It's a local matter and we don't want you people getting involved in local stuff. We got this one."

Mallory waltzed up to the Sarge and said, "You know we still have Vladimir and his friend living out of the barn. How do you want to handle them?"

"Did you place them in a hotspot, and did they shoot at their fellow mercs?"

"Sarge, I placed them right in front of the ranch in that foxhole. They used up a lot of ammo and I saw them fighting three guys when they ran out of bullets. I think we should have one of our local friends drive them to that far away airport and send them on their way with maybe $100k each. They did deliver."

The Sarge gave Mallory an incredulous look. He said, "I guess that's a good move. Tell them if they ever come at us again, we'll gut them like hogs. Also tell them if they can get us any credible intel on their employer, it would sit well with us, and they would be granted a significant bonus."

Mallory started to walk away when the Sarge said, "Yo, Mallory, I'm really tired of this killing and people trying to kill us. Once I'm cleared to fly, I would like to head down south and check on our homes and develop a real action plan to find, seduce, and murder my cousin!"

"I'm with that. The sooner the better," Mallory said.

Once again, Mallory started to walk away and the Sarge said, "Hey, one more thing? How did the new guys do?"

"Sarge they are a bunch of ruthless sons-of-bitches. The mercs that abused the doctor's wife and daughter, well they executed three of them, kept two for us to cross examine, and Jilkes told them that I didn't want to talk to the scum. They called Jilkes back and indicated they needed a cleaner. They're not to be crossed. I feel good giving them assignments that we would give to any of our guys. I mean, they're just that good and methodical."

"Wow! How is the doc's family doing?" The Sarge inquired.

"They're trusting in the Lord. Those young guys went out and got the wife and daughter outfits and cleaned them up and told them that no one needed to know what happened to them. They have the same moral fiber we have. They're compassionate and thoughtful. I really like them especially since Vladimir took care of the two suspected plants."

"One more thing, how did things go after I got hit? I mean was there chaos or what?"

"Naw, Sarge. You run an independent, well-oiled machine where those involved understand the risks and step up to any task, and I do mean any task to support the collective. I was proud of how your daughter never abandoned her post. She cried like a baby after you got hit, but she didn't deviate from her role. Larry walked in for a moment, gave her a hug, told her he loved her, and for her to focus on keeping us all safe. I mean it was somber, but it worked, and worked well. I sent people on missions, some appeared one way, but they all did their job. And by the way, some of the most renowned specialists in the world wrote you off and told your wife that time wasn't your friend. They said, the placement of the projectiles had cauterized impacted nerves, and organs that controlled vital functions. That wife of yours along with those chants your nephew made, created a successful journey into the back of your head. She went against science and used common sense. You owe her an awful lot my friend."

The Sarge started to cry, and Mallory patted him on his shoulder and told him that he'll catch him later. He summoned Jong and told him that he needed $200k for the guys in the barn.

From afar, the group could hear gunfire. As they went on semi-alert, Clyde called Rashida and told her that him and some of the boys were cleaning up some foreign snakes and a few local ones. He told her not to worry, they had all the local mess under control. Rashida broadcasted that Clyde, and his associates were cleaning up some foreign and local snakes they found hiding in the grass.

Three days later, the group decided they should head to Alabama and check on their properties, but not before the Sarge asked Clyde to check on that property, that became available after that errant missile strike. He asked Clyde to get the particulars on the land, and to consider placing a bid on the property in Ms. Asiram's name.

Ms. Viola said, "If you be getting me that close to home, then I be catching a commercial flight to feel that blue saltwater run between my toes."

Monica said to Mallory, "Honey, tell the Sarge we all need to feel those healing waters and a few days will give everyone time to relax before we begin this final adventure. We had a lot of blood flowing at the ranch and it will do us all some good to get some silly drinks, relax, and plus, you know how we get it on down there."

An excited Mallory said, "Honey, I'll be right back."

Courtney threw a wrench in the engine when she told the group that Mac, the Sarge and Gladstone all had appointments tomorrow at the hospital. She said, "If the hospital releases them to her then she'll make sure Ben Beckmire will want to head to that warm and beautiful island.

# # #

Three days later, Vladimir called Mallory and told him that the man executed his wife and children as well as Sergov's, and that they wanted to join up with their group to hunt him down. Mallory said, "You have our condolences, but we don't operate like that. A few months ago, you tried to kill us."

Sergov said, "You yanks, are too consumed within. Read the newspaper now, and then and you will see. It is on all major news stations. We can do this with or without you." He hung up the phone.

Mallory went to the Sarge and told him what he had been told and asked how he wanted to proceed with this one? The Sarge said, "Can you summon Sue Lyn and Darryl and let's discuss our options. I want their group to become more active so that we can plan to retire. I want to be there at the end, but I need some young foot soldiers. Do you trust Vladimir?"

"Sarge, I trust us and the new guys, but I keep one eye on their asses."

"Smart move, but I can tell you that Darryl was aware of the two double agents and was going to utilize them, you know giving a little, and expecting a lot. You know the next time you're in the outback, you really should listen to the sounds that are made and messages that are communicated," the Sarge indicated.

"Yeah, yeah! I believe in you and your nephew. I believe in spirits and a whole lot of shit I can't explain or describe. So, I listen Mr. Man. I listen, and carefully. But, back to Vladimir and Sergov, we need to check the news and see if there are any mass murders of women and children."

"Ask Larry, he watches the news every day. He'll be able to tell you if that is fake news or real. Even if it's real, did they kill everyone or are they holding a hostage? Walter is a demon and he'll play every card possible."

Mallory looked at the Sarge and wondered, "is the Sarge as devious as his cousin to consider such a thing"?

The Sarge unexpectedly asked, "You think I'm like him, don't you? Well, I hope so because that jerk has hurt a lot of people. I'm just trying to figure out new ways to catch his ass. Thinking honorably does not catch a thief who is determined to steal your heart. I have decided to transmogrify myself into the likes of my cousin, so that I can minimize the pain and suffering he will place upon us and those he controls like a puppeteer if he is successful in this long battle. Mallory, I'm afraid of him because he apparently has access to never ending resources and now new weaponry. I'm afraid of what he'll do to my children, your children, my grandchildren, my friends, and your friends, and their children, and what the hell he'll do to us. He knows I know how to go on Walkabout. He can't, you can't, and they can't. Only Darryl and I can, and that makes me eager to think like that asshole and find the hole the conejo lives in and pour hydrochloric acid down it until he meets his father, Lucifer."

Mallory looked at the Sarge and said, "You know what, you're absolutely correct. He had those suicide vests placed on the children without any afterthought. You know Sarge, I'm getting tired as well as old from this most exciting adventure. I considered you were parlaying us to get to him. I'm human and I know, and you know betrayal, but that does not excuse my momentary lapse in judgement."

"Mallory, I must become a monster to catch the most vicious human on earth. After all, who else would pay people to investigate a situation knowing they were going to die and for what?"

After a brief pause, the Sarge said, "Our clan has grown and continues to. I want to die naturally and watch my friends go that way as well. Only with you will I share my dark thoughts, and you must keep them between the two of us. You must also listen to them and decipher the true meaning. I must travel to a dark place, and I'll need your kindness and devotion to bring me back. I don't want to get stuck on the other side of hell. The world is bigger than the internet or the cloud. There are foul factions and good ones. I need my friend to be there if I need another bullet to the head. This is beyond us Mallory. I have some very bad, as well good spirits, in me and I sometimes don't know which one has the floor. Darryl's chanting was to summon both sides to bid for my soul, or to control my earthly actions. I know you don't believe this, but I'm from a place where they tell me my relative is a saltie and the biggest of them all and who can't die. I know, it's a lot to digest, but trust me, I may need you to place a round in my head if the bad ones take over. You have to promise me that."

"Sarge, I'm not going to shoot you. Have you lost your damn mind? Ask your wife to do it. You must be drugging or something."

"Let me ask you a question my friend? When you saw my ancestor in the billabong, did you think it was real or a mirage of some sorts?

"I thought it was an anomaly just like I think you are sometimes. It was a big fucking crocodile."

"Your first mistake was not identifying it properly. It was a saltwater croc and it measured more than forty-two feet when I last saw him. I hear he has grown another eight feet. All these small details are important in the bush. You're the next in line in leadership of this band. If I need that shot and if you don't do it then the whole clan will be slaughtered including Monica and those babies, you adopted. The issue is whether the bid package went north or south. If it went north, then I'll be back. Otherwise, I'll see you in hell. You have time to process this information, but it would not be in your best interest to discuss it with anyone, including Monica."

Mallory threw his hands in the air and said, "You know what Sarge? I'm just going to see you later. No more talk. I'll see you later."

Mallory walked out of the room and ran into Courtney. He looked distressed and she asked, "Is everything okay?"

Mallory turned away from her and said, "I'm not sure. Listen, I must ask Monica a few things. I'll catch you later."

As he walked through the dining area, he saw Darryl and Sue Lyn. He asked Darryl if he could have a word with him. Mallory told Darryl about the exchange he had with the Sarge and asked for his advice. Darryl, with a serious look on his face asked Mallory to excuse him for a second. He walked back to where Sue Lyn was sitting and took a drink of his Bloody Mary and proceeded back towards Mallory. He put his arm around Mallory and asked, "My uncle shared that information with you?"

"Yes, he sounded crazy. He wants me to shoot him in the head if the bad spirits compromise him."

Darryl said, "That action would be the resolve. However, if I were you, I would go back to where my uncle is and slap the shit out of him for messing with you like that. There ain't no bad spirits in the man, and if there were, he would be dead because the energy around him is honest and pure. You're pure and, therefore, he's just having fun at your expense about things you don't understand. If I, were you, I would go back in there and say, "I got on my knees to pray, and the image of that huge croc came to my mind. I bowed and asked him for guidance and he told me to slap the shit out of your crazy ass". He's messing with you Mallory. He's probably laughing his ass off at this moment."

Mallory took leave of Darryl and walked near the area where the Sarge was and found him talking to Jilkes and John Lee and everyone in the room was laughing. Mallory walked into the room and yelled, "I fell to my knees and confronted the 'Great Saltie'. I will honor your request, but I will do it now. He pulled his weapon out and cocked it and aimed it at the Sarge's head and said, "I love you man, I will see you in hell."

Jilkes and John Lee jumped up and realized that this thing had gone south, and that Mallory was prepared to put another bullet in the Sarge's head. Mallory broke into laughter and said, I unloaded it after I found out you're so full of shit. How could you do me that way?"

After laughing hard, the Sarge said, "You must admit, I was convincing, wasn't I? I told these two nuts and they're still laughing about it."

Mallory laughed for a few minutes and said, "I'll tell you the truth. Every time we go into the outback, I experience something different. I mean think about it. How natural is it to see a croc that big, or better still to see a lot of them providing protection over what they would normally see as a delightful meal—the children. That ain't no normal shit. Or think about how the animals came together for that feast of bodies that were caught in a sort of no-fly zone. Things aren't what they seem like there, and for anyone to discount spirits, demons, and enormous animals, they would be in for a rude awakening. Australia, my friends, has spooked me and I won't make light of it. I will however, the next time I have a loaded gun, place another round in that moron's head."

The Sarge looked at him and burst into tears. He cried for a couple of minutes before Courtney came into the room. She said, "Guys, that's a sign he's tired. He attempts to fight it, but when he gets tired, he cries. Until he's completely healed, this might go on for a while. He's embarrassed, but I'm sure he's happy it's just you guys and not the whole village seeing him like this."

# # #

The following day, the Sarge, McArthur, and Gladstone were cleared for travel and the group boarded their plane. They decided to head to Alabama for two nights and spend the balance of the weekend in St. Thomas, but they hadn't decided to tell Ms. Viola yet.

Three hours later, the group began to prepare the cabin for landing. Carla came on the intercom and told the group they would make this stop over for two days and then take Ms. Viola to them there islands so that she can run that there saltwater through them there feet of hers. Ms. Viola was happy and thanked everyone.

John Lee had called his people before landing and told them he was coming home for a short visit and asked if they could send that special bus for them?

An hour later, a modified school bus pulled up to the hangar and John Lee saw his friends and had a brief conversation with them. He was told that all the houses were complete and built exactly to specifications with the furniture that the ladies picked out. He asked about the special windows and was once again told that things were to specifications.

When the group entered the bus, Jasper began calling out names and handed attractive boxes to the recipients that contained gold-plated keys to their homes. Jasper told the group he inspected each home each day of the construction process and signed off on the completion phases. He indicated the landscaping was only a week or so old and that this was the best time to make any changes that the group may want. He also assigned house guest status to those who were not in on the initial offerings.

Juan asked Rashida, "Have you ever had your own house before?"

"I did, but this thing is five times as big as my little place we still own in DC. What about you?"

"No, mi amor. We lived where we could and with anyone who would let us in. My mother always attempted to find single men with homes and would apply herself, so that we would have a place to stay."

"Well, my husband, we have a home and two wonderful children. We'll fill this place with love and any family that you want. I love you."

Juan gave her a suggestive look and said, "We should put the children to sleep early and have a full night of enjoying each other without pushing buttons to kill people. I know that sometimes weighs heavy on me and I never ask you about it. However, if you ever want to discuss it in detail, I'm here to listen."

"Honey, I don't enjoy it, but I remember those suicide vests that were placed on the children. If they're into hurting innocent babies, then I'm into terminating them without consideration or hesitation. Anyhow, I think it's going to be nice to stay in our house, in our bed, by ourselves, without everyone listening through the walls at the sounds being made in the next room. People will probably scream their lungs off after recognizing this kind of freedom and privacy."

McArthur said to Gladstone, "We should talk to that country dude about selling us some land. What's your thoughts?"

"You know, we should ask Montomie and Whitmore to join us in the conversation. I mean here we are being assigned rooms, like linen. We should've jumped on that equation when they first proposed it. You know, if we decided to do that, we could hire crews around the clock like we did in Valencia. I need to get back there. You remember those two ladies we met? Well, I talked to my friend the other day and she was wondering when we were coming back. She said her girlfriend often asked about you. Just a thought. We could take one of the planes and no one will miss us," Gladstone said.

The problem is we leave the group exposed. I think we must conclude this mess with the Sarge's cousin first. Maybe we could drop the dime that we should check on our holdings in Spain. I'm sure they'll get the hint and decide to join us because, after all, we go where they go and never ask questions," McArthur stated.

"I wouldn't state it like that. We're family, they will understand our need to check on our holdings. You want to go into town and have a drink?" Gladstone asked.

"Naw, I'm going to camp in my designated room in the Sarge's house and have a lone drink and try to figure out what I want to do and if I want to do it with another woman dictating. I do not plan on yielding to peer pressure. Those people are happy because they're in love with seemingly, the right people. You, me, Montomie, and Whitmore apparently haven't been that lucky or foolish enough to make that commitment again. Why don't we find Montomie and Whitmore and see if they want to have a drink with us? I mean, they're lone wolves as well."

The four men got together and realized they were like a third wheel but knew everyone loved them and vice versa. McArthur said, "I will not follow a crowd unless it's led by my true friends. There is no pretense for us to consider joining their club. I'll say it again, they're happy with who they have as mates."

The discussion lasted for most of the night and concluded with no conclusions. The four men fell asleep in the Sarge's man cave without concluding or resolving a damn thing.

# # #

At breakfast in John Lee's home, the Sarge asked, "How did everyone sleep last night?"

Jilkes said, "I didn't really sleep. I kept looking out of the window for the boogie man."

Rashida said, "I was the same way. Juan never moved a muscle, but I kept looking for someone and waited for something to jump off. It was unsettling, to say the least."

Ava looked at her Juan and said, "He's so sweet. I had him put a chair to back up the lock on the door."

Asiram looked at Zanthius and said, "Well, boyfriend didn't move a muscle and neither did the kids. I kept them in our room and I had to stand guard all night long while they snored."

Courtney looked around the room and asked, "Guys, what message do you think that sends us?"

Mary Alice said, "That we can't seem to adjust to living alone in homes even if they're close by. We're like a tribe. We're like the villagers in the outback, they're always communing together, and if you think about it, that's what we've been doing for a lot of years now."

The Sarge asked, "Has anyone seen McArthur, Montomie, Whitmore, and Gladstone?"

Courtney leaned over to him and said, "They're drunk as skunks in our basement."

He looked at her and smiled. "Thanks for that info, babe."

Later, after rousing the four men from his man cave, the Sarge said, "You guys need to take a shower and become a part of the solution. We need to consider some serious moves in the next day or so, and I need you guys to have your wits about you."

McArthur asked, "Are we leaving today?"

"Naw, we're leaving for the islands tomorrow for a few days of vacation and then we begin a strategic hunt for Diablo," the Sarge said.

"We're going to head into town tonight and hang out in the islands as well. Do you think we need to have an escort?" McArthur asked.

"Of course, until we take care of the demon. I can't let you guys get blindsided. No, tell me when and I'm sure some of the married guys are going to fight to escort you."

At that moment, Jilkes and John Lee heard the Sarge talking. They went to the basement steps and called out the Sarge's name. He responded and told the men to come on down. When they got to the bottom of the steps, he stated, "These guys want to head to town tonight and hang out. They also want to go playing once we get to the islands. My question is, do you think they need escorts?"

John Lee yelled, "Hell, yeah! At least four of us to cover the four of them. I volunteer and so does my African American friend."

Jilkes looked at him and said, "I want to be with my wife and child. I'd rather you took another partner and count me out."

John Lee's eyes literally swelled up and he asked, "What did I do wrong? Why you be mad at me?"

"Country man, I'm not mad at you, but if you call me your African American friend again, I'm going to beat the shit out of you."

"Deal! I'll just call you my black friend. Okay, that was easy? Oh, and I know exactly where we should go tonight for a few beers and to watch you guys try your magic."

# # #

It was approximately noon when an old phone of Asiram's began to ring. She hesitated to answer it because it was the instrument she used back in the day when she was doing a lot of dastardly deeds. She answered it and asked, "Who is using my private number?"

The person on the other end of the phone said, "It's a two-time loser that needs to talk to your boss."

"And just who is my boss?" Asiram asked.

"It's the big fellow. This is Vladimir and I need your help to catch that son-of-a-bitch that killed my family."

Asiram hesitated a minute and said, "I'll call you back on another phone." She hung up the phone. She looked at Zanthius and said, "Honey, that was Vladimir the guy who we let go twice. He said your uncle killed his family and he wants to speak with your dad. I hung up so that if he was trying to track me, he would need more time. Watch the boys for a minute. I'm going to go find your father."

In the dining room of John Lee's place, the Sarge was busy exercising his brain by doing word puzzles. When Asiram walked in he asked, "Where are the babies. I need to see babies when I see you. Anyway, what's up?"

"Dad, I just got a call on my spy phone from Vladimir. He said your cousin killed his family and he wants to speak to you." The Sarge shook his head and inquired if anyone had a throw-away phone that couldn't be tracked?

Asiram said, "Where is Darryl and Sue Lyn, I'm sure they have such a thing."

A few minutes later, the duo showed up and Sue Lyn offered her phone that would show she was in Hong Kong.

She gave it to Asiram who dialed the number and gave it to the Sarge. When Vladimir answered the phone, the Sarge said, "Vlad, as I said a while ago, I'm sorry to hear about your families. I'm going to put you on speaker. Is that a problem?"

"No, comrade, no problem," Vladimir stated.

"How can I help you?" The Sarge asked.

"First of all, Sergov and I would like to thank you guys for that care package. That was really human of you people. Secondly, we want to join forces in the hunt for your cousin. We know who his henchmen are who murdered our people, and we're going to get them real soon. However, they be puppets to the man. We think we can help you and you can help us."

The Sarge paused briefly and then said, "Our hunt for him is personal and family based. You want revenge, and by the way, so do we, but we want him for ourselves."

There was silence on the other end of the phone and Vladimir and Sergov discussed a few things and he then said, "Why can't we locate and monitor, and we all share in his demise. We just want to put a bullet in his head and be done with it."

"Vladimir, that is entirely too quick. We have promised to gut him from his dick to his brain and then eat his heart before he fucking dies. After that, we're going to roast his ass and gather his ashes and distribute them all over the earth so that there is no way in hell, another monster like this one will ever be a part of humankind again."

Vladimir said, "Then the rumors are true. You people did this kind of thing to a double agent of ours by the name Scottie."

"We don't discuss clients or activities, but we are specialists at certain things. I must go, but I will call you tomorrow at the same time after I discuss your proposed arrangement with my people. You know they're going to have little faith in you and Sergov because after all, you did try to kill us twice."

"No, Sarge! We had the CIA as targets, and you, if you happened in our scopes and that you did a lot of, showing up in our scopes. The first time you caught us, we were breaking into lockers. That sure shouldn't count as an attempted assassination."

"Tomorrow, I will call you."

"One more thing, we will do this thing with you or without you. Have a good day, comrades."

# # #

That evening, Mallory held a feast of pizza, chicken wings, and beer. All the houses had a footprint that embodied space, few walls, and a Zen like décor. Monica's house, however, was spacious but more traditional with a library full of legal books, a huge mahogany desk and a separate entrance for clients. After all, she is a lawyer.

As in a tribal gathering, the men talked mess and the women talked about the children. A few of the men, who were Johnnies come lately, asked about the opportunity to gain space in the community and that's when Jilkes and John Lee held court.

John Lee began the discussion by letting the group know that he and his partner, Mr. Jilkes, had acquired an additional five thousand acres with the option to buy ten thousand more.

He told the group they made those purchases so that people couldn't build strip malls in their community and they could control the traffic footprint. He told them that when they were fully retired, he wanted their kids to be able to ride their bikes until they be needing to call an Uber, or something to get home."

Gladstone said, "That must have set you guys back a pretty penny. Why don't you let some of us buy-in and reduce your costs and your liability?"

Jilkes looked at John Lee and asked, "May I take the floor?"

John Lee nodded and Jilkes said, "We made this investment for the group. We did this for the twelve of us and we added a few others like Larry, Rashida, and the two Juans, etc. We've also set aside an option for some newbies to buy in if they want to wisely invest their money. This is prime real estate we're talking about. My partner, Mr. John Lee and I saw this opportunity after a friend of his told him that a group of Miami developers were looking to build a middle to low income shopping mall in the area. Now, listen, we didn't buy this for your buy-in, we bought this to make sure we are somewhat insulated and that our kids have free range to make smart decisions. If anything, it might be a great place for a technical school or college, but not a damn strip mall."

John Lee said, "Speaking of money, how many of you know how much you have in the bank?" Only Jong raised his hand. He said, "I know because I'm the keeper of the money and I get mine first."

Everyone laughed and called him the name of several famous thieves and Ponzi masters. He then said in a serious voice, "I've tried to get the Sarge to check behind me and to have audits and he keeps saying that we're family. In real life, who screws you the worst, and first? Family, right?"

Chakes bellowed out and said, "I'm not sure family would go against armed men and secure you from harm's way. I'm not sure family understands the commitment we made in the Nam. I am sure they wouldn't understand what Bernstein and Brown did for us and for damn sure they wouldn't understand the love affair between Jilkes and John Lee. This is my family and you are the keeper of the records. Keep them and we trust you because you are us and we are you." Jong started crying and finally threw his hands up in the air and said, "In that case, you won't be concerned that I charge forty percent on each transaction."

## CHAPTER TWENTY-SEVEN

As the magnificent plane ascended into the air, Courtney looked at her husband and realized that he was under stress. She slowly pulled the mask from his side panel and affixed it to his face. She opened her bag and prepared an adrenaline shot but did not administer it because she was not sure what had caused the sudden increase in his heart rate and the profuse sweating. Mallory saw that she was trying to monitor and secure the Sarge at the same time. He unbuckled his seat belt and crawled over to where the Sarge and Courtney were sitting to assist her. Monica replicated his movement and found herself in a helping position as well. Monica yelled, "Courtney until you know what caused this, I wouldn't administer any drugs."

Courtney snidely remarked, "When did you get your fucking medical degree?" She then said, "I'm keeping this shot ready in case he appears to be heading into shock. Doctor, of course I'm not going to give him a shot."

Monica made her way back across the aisle and Courtney realized she had offended her friend and needed to find a way to amend her remarks.

After stabilizing the Sarge, she unbuckled her seatbelt and walked over to Monica who was glaring out of the window and said, "I screwed up. You're my dearest friend, but he was in a place I didn't understand, and you offered me medical advice. I would never offer you legal advice because I know you're the best lawyer on earth. I thought, you would have at least given me some professional courtesy and realize that I am bonified."

There was a stillness and Courtney turned to walk away when Monica grabbed her and said, "I really screwed up as well. You are by far the best doctor I know. I was feeling too much of myself when I said that. Please, and I do mean please, let that shit go. We've been in worse places than words can take us."

Courtney leaned forward and hugged Monica. The two women cried for a few seconds while embracing in front of the entire group.

Later as the Sarge began to rejoin the group, Courtney said, "Monica, you were right. He's back and without any juice." The two women gave each other the bird and laughed.

The Sarge said, "I've had this feeling before, but I can't explain it. It feels as though my heart begins to race when I'm sitting still with a blank mind, no stress, no one shooting at us or anything that would cause my heart rate to elevate. I became excited because I've never experienced this sensation before and in all honesty, when my own mortality comes into play. I've become afraid of dying and, therefore, I panic easily."

"Honey, why didn't you tell me about his?"

"I'm tired of worrying you about every little thing that happens to me. You're my wife, not my wet nurse."

Courtney grabbed his hand and held it tight as she attempted to fight back the tears. He looked at her and knew he had taken her to her limit again, with that last comment. After Courtney calmed down, she looked at Ben Beckmire, and said, "If you ever demean our marriage like that again, I will leave you to your selfish thoughts. I'm your wife for better or worse. Do you remember that? Do you? I must say, Ben Beckmire, that is the most hurtful thing you've ever said to me. Right now, I need you to do me a single favor and that is not to speak to me until I speak to you or you need medical attention."

The Sarge sat in his seat trying to figure out how to mend this terrible situation he found himself in, when his phone rang. It was Vladimir. The Sarge said, "I'll call you back on a secure line."

He summoned Mallory over and told him that Vladimir had just called and he needed a secure phone to talk to him on. Mallory gave the Sarge his phone and told him he had fifteen minutes before he had to hang up and that he was in Bora Bora.

Vladimir said, "We were waiting on your call Mr. Sarge and thought perhaps you forgot, so we decided to call you. We realize you only react to the man when he shows up to kill you. Our alliance would net you the situation you currently find yourselves in plus our outside intelligence. We have a lot of resources to bear. This is not a hustle as you call it, this is us trying to avenge our families, and disappear into the night."

The Sarge listened to him and thought, Darryl lost two men, why not see if these blokes could be of use in the outback. The Sarge said, "Have you blokes ever been to Australia?"

Vladimir shrugged his shoulders at Sergov and answered timidly, "No. We've not been to that world. Why do you ask such a strange question, Mr. Sarge?"

"Well, you said you didn't have any resources, and you wanted to disappear. After this mess is settled with my cousin, I might need two slick talking crooks like you two to do some mining for me and my people." There was silence on both ends of the phone.

Vladimir said, "If we called for a meeting, you'd probably think we were setting you up. Is that not right, Mr. Sarge?"

"Damn, you're smart. Did you attend Harvard?"

"Mr. Sarge let me be straight for both of us. We don't plan on living and have agreed to a death pack. We're planning to strap C-4 on when we locate him and detonate ourselves."

The Sarge frowned at the thought and paused. He softly stated, "I wouldn't call that heroic, smart, or modern. I would call that suicidal. Do you think you're just going to waltz up to him and shake his hand? First, he has mysophobia and it's probably gotten worse over the years. More importantly, suppose he's in a place where my grandkids or anyone's grands are, and you detonate. What impact do you think you're going to have on innocent families? Guys, you haven't thought this thing out because your focus is revenge and only revenge. Let me take you back a bit."

The Sarge paused for a few seconds and then announced, "We have caught you twice and we were seduced by your rhetoric and, therefore, we let you go, both times. If you have a death wish, then you can't associate with us. My friends, we're about trying to live a normal life and it doesn't include people who have witnessed a tragedy, who want revenge, and who are planning an event that could possibly hurt other innocent people."

"Mr. Sarge, what would you do if it were your family?"

"Sergov, he strapped suicide vests on my grandchildren and other children. He has killed people all over the world including members of his own family in Australia. Tell you what, this conversation is not what I thought it would be and, therefore, I'm going to have to deny access to our resources. When you guys realize that his death is not going to bring your families back, give me a call on my daughter's phone. If you can relate honestly to what we do, including our work in the outback, then give me a call. Don't call with any more harebrained schemes. We don't want martyrs, we want people who want to live a long life and who realize that eventually, death consumes us all."

The Sarge abruptly hung up the phone and asked, Asiram, "Do you trust them?"

"Dad, that's a lot of pressure. I barely knew Vladimir and only saw Sergov once or twice. I can't say I trust them because I don't know them. Did you trust Mary Alice, Yvette, Carla, Luana, Ms. Viola, Mike, and Michael and his crew? That is the only thing that separates us from your cousin, our ability to trust people and pray that they are who they present themselves to be."

He rose and said, "Baby Girl, I'm going to abdicate my position and put you in charge. We need new leadership; leadership that is not tainted by the tragic things me and my band of merry men have done."

"Dad, stop the horseshit. You're the only leader we need because you see beyond the hills and most of us aren't capable of doing that."

At that very moment, Asiram's phone rang and she showed it to the Sarge. He told her to answer it and when she did, Vladimir said, "I know where your cousin will be next week and from that point in time every meeting that is scheduled for him, I will know. We want in and we will follow your rules."

The Sarge said, "We're at a funeral. If you're still interested in three days, then call my daughter and we'll see where your heads are. I must go."

Ms. Viola didn't waste time placing her feet into the blue salty water. After the vans pulled into 'The Sanctuary', she walked directly to the water and said, "You Yanks had better come and get healed from whatever be ailing you. My soul is tender from all that we've had to do to protect each other. Come now, forget those clothes. Come and be healed by the waters of the islands."

At a late lunch, Mr. Carter was happy and proud to see his son. He walked up to Michael and hugged him, a thing that he hadn't done in a long time. He said, "Your new life seems to be good to you. You look fit, alert, and focused. Will you be going back to Australia?"

"Yes, Pop. We're trying to figure out a schedule so that we can spend time there and come back home as well. The main guys are still with me and we all have proven to some degree that we're loyal, honest, and can follow instructions."

His father hugged him again and said, "Please be careful. Keep them safe and keep yourself safe. Oh, and by the way, your mother and I are spending quality time together and have discussed the idea of finding a small place on a trial basis to see if we can manage it."

"Pops, you either want to be with her and she with you, or not. Don't waste your time and money on an experiment that makes you act a certain way because you don't want to fail. If you love her and she loves you, then stop screwing around and make it happen. She is a great asset to this place and you know she is an honest woman."

"I know son, I just don't want to rush her into something she may not really want to be in," Mr. Carter lamented.

"Trust me, she wants to be in it. But the two of you are pig headed, but there's hope for you guys especially, if you been taking walks on the beach at night."

"How you know about that?"

"A little birdie told me. It's good to see you and be home."

# # #

That evening everyone gathered near the beach. Michael, Jasper, Harold, Desmond, and Isaiah had guard duty along with the security personnel from the other properties in 'The Sanctuary'. The children swam in the wonderful waters while Michael and Isaiah watched the landscape from the dingy that MacArthur had purchased. It had become common practice that members of the group would always be with, or near a weapon.

Mrs. Carter cooked a pig in the sand that drove John Lee nuts. It was a Kalua feast and Mrs. Carter knew how to prepare the pit, check the soil, and layer it against anything that might be drawn to heat and the smell of the meat. John Lee said, "I think I'm going to have a chicken sandwich. I can't eat no pig that be cooked in the sand. It just ain't right."

Jilkes said, "Stop being nutty. Where's your sense of adventure? Let's have a drink at the bar and come back and have a meal. You can't offend Mrs. Carter, after all, she went through a lot of stuff to make this thing happen. Your pig is in pigshit heaven. Don't worry, this one is fresh and new, that she's cooking."

The two men walked into the hotel lobby and saw the rear view of six women checking in. Jilkes said, "Oh my, if only we were single."

John Lee smiled and said, "It ain't never killed nobody to say hello. Why don't we be the welcoming wagon, and invite them down for that there pig in the sand feast?"

Jilkes looked at John Lee and asked, "Do you want your wife to kill your ass?"

"I be thinking about Gladstone, Whitmore, Mac, and Montomie. We can act like we're the magic men and hook them up. I mean these girls ain't no teenagers and they ain't as old as them boys, so it might be worth a notion."

The two men walked over to the front desk and introduced themselves to the women and John Lee took the lead by saying, "We be noticing you ladies and it done occurred to us that you might want to join our pig in the sand dinner. We have some friends down there who are as single as the Pope. They ain't no priest or nothing, they just be wholesome men who know how to treat a lady."

The women smiled, but indicated they were expecting their husbands in a minute or so.

Jilkes said, "Well, as long as they aren't terrorists, all of you can come down to the water and have a meal, and I do mean a meal on us."

One of the ladies asked, "So, who are you and where are your wives?" John Lee smiled and said, "They be down there on the beach about to eat that pig in the sand food."

Another lady said, "We don't want any trouble, we just want to relax and get something to eat."

John Lee said, "Oh, there be no trouble around here. There is lots of security about tonight. You be safe as a baby in a rocker in heaven."

Another woman smiled and said, "I like the way you talk. You seem to tell a story when you speak. Okay, we might come down for a drink and we might bring our husbands as well. Is that okay?"

"Absolutely!" Jilkes retorted.

The day was about to roll over into the night when Montomie and McArthur swam to shore. As the two men walked onto the beach, they couldn't help noticing six statuesque women walking towards the beach where the Kalua was taking place. Montomie asked McArthur, "Are you seeing what I'm seeing or are we dead or something?"

"No man, I see exactly what you're looking at and they're looking in this direction and there ain't nobody over here but me, you, and a sleeping Gladstone."

McArthur said, "Gladstone, wake your sorry ass up. I think we might have company on the way." Gladstone yawned and turned his head around and was captivated by the view of six magnificent looking women. McArthur said, "Good evening. Are you ladies lost?"

One of the married women said, "No, we were invited here by the tall, big guy who talks funny."

"You mean talks in tongue, or is real country sounding? Is that who invited you guys down here?"

The married lady said, "Yes, that's the one." McArthur realized he and Montomie were standing there in swim attire and pretty much everything else was announcing itself. He grabbed a couple of towels and threw one to Montomie and the men began to dry off.

Meanwhile, the rest of the group had eyes on the three single men and watched as they flexed their muscles and smiled innocently at those wonderful looking ladies.

Zanthius said to Asiram, "Perhaps I should go over and give the guys a hand? What's your take on the idea?"

Asiram smiled and asked, "Do you want to live through the night, darling?"

She wandered over to the group and introduced herself and threw a protective shield around the guys because she knew they weren't thinking with their largest head.

Asiram asked basic questions and realized that they were not a physical threat to her or the guys. She inquired whether they were taking a stroll or just coming down to check out the events on the beach? She was told that the funny talking guy and his friend invited them down to the pig in the sand affair. She smiled and said, "Ladies, please forgive my directness, but when six beauties walk up on my friends, I know their real brains have seized up, and it's that other thing doing the negotiating and that's when we have to provide security for these blokes."

Everyone laughed except for one who said, "You use the word bloke as if you have some familiarity with its origin?"

Asiram half smiled and said, "It's not a mysterious word and is used often by people I know. Why do you find my use of the word curious?"

The woman smiled and said, "I'm from down-under and was surprised to hear you use it. Anyway, can we see how this pig in the sand thing is going?" Asiram looked at McArthur and pointed to his clothes.

As the women approached the group, a stillness grew, and John Lee said, "Guys, these ladies have just checked into our hotel and are expecting their husbands, and in the meantime, my, ah friend, Jilkes invited them down to the feast. He asked me if it was okay and I told him that I didn't see any reason why such nice ladies couldn't come to our party."

McArthur and Montomie in their shorts and shirts walked over and eyed the women more closely. Gladstone who was still recovering from his wound eventually showed up.

The Sarge stood up and said, "Hi ladies, "I'm Ben Beckmire and this beautiful lady to my left is my wife, Dr. Courtney Beckmire, and that good-looking guy in the yellow shirt is my son Larry and that's his wife Marisa and their children, and next to them is my daughter Rashida and her husband Juan with their children, and you met John Lee and Jilkes and those two ladies walking this way are their wives. This good-looking guy next to me is Mallory, and his wife Monica and their children and that Spaniard is Ava and her husband Juan and this guy holding the two boys is Asiram's husband, Zanthius. Oh, the guy holding that beautiful lady's hand is Jong and his wife Mary Alice and their kids, Carla is our pilot who is standing next to Jong and that guy is Mike, her old man. Now, those two guys, Brown and Bernstein and their wives, Yvette and Okema and their children are standing in front of me. Oh, Mr. Carter is the owner of this property and Mrs. Carter is about to serve up her pig in the sand, better known as a Kalua, I think. Last, but not least are McArthur, Montomie, Whitmore, and Gladstone and they don't at this time have wives, children, prospects, or girlfriends. So, that's who we are. Who are you people and how did you find out about our special getaway place?"

The married woman who spoke before took it upon herself to introduce the group. She said, "Hi guys, my name is Barbara Ann, that's Daniela, next to her is Alvara, PJ, and Gerri. We're from DC, Maryland, Philly, and New York respectively. Okay, how we found this place is simple. Alvara, PJ, and Gerri have been by here on the ferry. They investigated it and found out it was owned outright and wasn't a front for some large corporate conglomerate. We found the prices to be a bit steep until that taxi turned off the road and into this magical place. Oh, Alvara, PJ, and Gerri, are the single ones amongst us." McArthur rolled his head from side to side and dead-reckoned on PJ.

Gerri gave Montomie a look that sealed that deal and Gladstone, still on pain killers, asked Alvara if she would like to fetch a drink and sit by the fire and talk? Whitmore had assumed the security detail and was out of sight. He saw a person of interest approaching the property from a different direction. He viewed the person through his binoculars and said, "OMG! Who the hell is that woman?"

Someone in the group said, "You really should have a conversation with Michael. He can lead you to that jewel, but she is one hard person to get along with."

# # #

Life is full of adventures, heartbreak, pain, misery, and the ultimate--death! One day you're on top of the world and the next, you're trying to figure out how to hustle a meal. Everyone has a story and these ladies were no different.

PJ inquired of McArthur, "Who were you eyeing when we walked up on you half-naked? Are you people wholesome and who were you targeting?"

He stumbled a bit with his words and said frankly, "It wasn't you. I assumed you all were married, and I liked Barbara Ann because she appeared to be the leader."

PJ's head dropped for a moment and she then asked McArthur if she could tell him a little story? He agreed, and PJ said, "When I woke up this morning at around 4 am, I knew something wonderful was going to happen and here you are."

"How do you know I'm something wonderful?"

PJ touched his arm lightly and said, "You could have lied and said I was who you had your sights on, but you didn't. You told me the truth and you didn't care if it hurt or not. You told me the truth. I've been lied to, cheated on, deceived, and tormented by issues I didn't know existed. You told me the truth and for as many days as I'm here, I hope you can at least continue that rare activity."

McArthur smiled and said, "Our group is all about people. Some of us were in the Nam together and others happen to assist in our mission to help people help themselves. I don't want to talk about the group, I'd rather spend my time talking about who you are and you trying to figure out who I am."

#

Gladstone had settled in with Alvara and they appeared to be engaged in conversation that was funny and seemingly with a little flirtatiousness involved. Alvara leaned over and told him that he was a sexy, an almost middle-aged man, and wondered how he had managed to escape the rope of marriage. She told him she had once tried it, but her husband was consumed with the streets. He wanted to be married and maintain his ball playing relationships with his friends.

Montomie and Gerri were a natural. He was quiet and reserved and so was she, but they felt the attraction and wanted to figure out how to consummate it without giving up one's soul. Gerri asked him, "Do you believe in love at first sight? I'm not saying that applies to anything going on here. I'm just wondering do you believe in magic and fantasy?"

Montomie said, "Sheila, when you asked about Asiram's use of the word bloke, my senses jumped your bones."

"My name is Gerri."

"I know your name, but I also thought you knew what Sheila meant down-under. It means girl or female and that's how I started the sentence by thinking you knew more words than bloke."

"She smiled at him and said, "Can we put our feet in the water and promise to be completely honest?"

Montomie smiled and said, "We can do whatever you want to do. Why do you think, I'm not being honest? Because I used the name Sheila?"

"No, Montomie. This is about me. I'm fresh out of an abusive relationship and I have scars to prove it. When we walked down to the beach, and I saw you, I said to myself, "if that guy isn't married or into same sex relationships, I'm going to test his water". She went on to say, "I've been beaten badly, and left on the side of the road. I've been humiliated in public, demeaned, and cursed. I don't want to waste another minute with you if you've ever mistreated a woman."

Montomie lowered his head and said, "Those are things that happened to me. My woman had a child by her lover, used my money to support his habits, and fled to a village in Mexico to avoid prosecution. My experience with women since then has been pretty much carnal—emotionless!

#

Mrs. Carter rung her bell and every living soul in 'The Sanctuary' came down for a taste of that pig in the sand, as John Lee termed it. He was probably third in line and when he bit into the food as he walked away, he stopped in his tracks and said, "Damn, that be good. Hold up, I'm still in line and I need some more of this here pig in the sand. Mrs. Carter, I be wanting to learn how to do that. Will you promise to teach me?" She nodded yes.

Michael and Isaiah rotated with Jasper and Harold. When they came to shore, the other two men entered the dingy and drove out to a place where they could see vessels coming from afar. Once in line, Michael asked Isaiah, "Who are those ladies?"

Isaiah looked at him and said, "Dah! I've been with you for the last two hours, how the hell would I know?"

Barbara Ann turned around to introduce herself. When her eyes met Michael's, the chemistry had already been mixed. She stuttered, and he was speechless. Barbara Ann finally composed herself and said, "My name is Barbara Ann, what's yours?"

Michael stumbled with his thoughts and manifested the fact that his name was Michael and that he had been on the boat. Barbara Ann asked, "What boat are you talking about?"

"My name is Michael. What's your name?" Barbara Ann looked at him and thought to herself, "what's wrong with these people".

She said, "So, Michael, which one of these ladies is your wife?"

"I don't have a wife. Do you have a husband?"

"I do, but he won't be coming here. We're in the middle of a nasty divorce. He wants me to move out of my house in a hurry so that he can move his mistress/bitch into it," Barbara Ann announced.

"Sorry to hear that. What brings you ladies down here and how did you find out about this place?"

"Everyone keeps asking me how we found out about this place. One of us saw it being constructed so, we thought we would give it a try. I must say, it is exquisite. Who was the designer?"

"Those ladies got together when they were in foreign places and picked things out and the results are what you see," Michael said.

"Okay, exactly who are those ladies? Are they part-owners?"

"Yes and no. They are the wives of the group that invested in the gutting, rebuilding, and for that matter, the other properties that make up what is called 'The Sanctuary'."

"So those guys are the owners?" Barbara Ann asked.

Michael smiled and said, "They saw the place when it was in disrepair and met my father who was being kicked off the property by the bank. They had a conversation with him, went to the bank with him, paid off the loan, and sent an architect down to create a high-end place. They funded the entire project and left it in my dad's and the other owners' names. They come when they want and stay as long as they like. The don't create a fuss, they just act like normal tourists."

"Wait, so they built this and then gave it to your father without any rights whatsoever?"

"They have a few edicts, such as the property must remain in the family. So, essentially, this property is mine, my mother's, and sister's according to the legal documents. I currently work for that young guy over there in the funny shirt that has billabong on it. He's in charge of other properties. We'll be leaving here in a few days I think."

Barbara Ann asked, "So, do you swim?"

Michael looked at the water and replied, "Not at night. The water predators enjoy snacks at night. Swimming at night, is not a safe activity."

"So, when you leave here, where will you go next?"

"I think we're off to Valencia for a week or so. The group has a resort there and from what I hear, a fabulous restaurant that takes up to five weeks to get a reservation. Can you imagine? I think it's all about the show. How can food be that good that you'll wait five weeks to get a seat. I don't think so, and besides, I don't have the kind of taste buds that can discriminate between what's good, fancy, or what's better— pig in the sand, if you ask me?"

The evening went on into the wee small hours of the morning until their conversation was interrupted by Gerri who said, "Ladies, you know we have a rule when we travel, and as we see it, you are over the limit. Please say your good nights and we'll see you back in the room. Good night, ah, Michael."

Michael checked his watch and said, "Time just flew right by us, I hope you were having a great time? At least I know I was. Let me walk you to your room." As they began to walk, Barbara Ann asked, "Who are those men just strolling around the property?"

Michael looked around and saw two men and said, "What's important to the management here is your safety. These guys will stroll as you say until they're relieved. We don't have trouble here, but this is a high-end area, and people who have nothing sometimes venture onto the property."

As they walked up the steps leading into the resort, Barbara Ann turned to Michael and asked, "Is this a totally legitimate operation or should we be fearful?"

Michael thought about her question and said, "You know something, there is a little larceny in all of us. However, for the most part, this group is legitimate, and they spend a lot of time and money helping other people. Now, in the process of doing good, evil always finds you and wants to stomp you down and out.

"It was good to meet you and I enjoyed our worldwide discussion of everything under the sun. You are incredible in so many ways and I hope you and I can continue this dialogue until we find out what makes us smile at each other." He kissed her hand and walked away.

When Barbara Ann entered the room, Gerri told her she didn't want them making no crazy decisions on their first night here. The ladies laughed and talked about the people they met.

Alvara asked Barbara Ann if she told Michael that she was married and she indicated that she had, as well as that she had given him information about her impending divorce proceedings.

# # #

The following morning, at 0800 hours the main group met outside of the resort office and started their exercise routine. They walked slowly at first, gradually increasing their strides until they were in a full run. As they rounded the bend leading up to the other properties, six color coordinated, good looking women, were making their way back to the resort. They waved and never missed a step. Asiram yelled, "I don't like those women. They are a threat to our very fabric."

An hour later when the group returned to the main resort, the ladies were enjoying fresh orange juice and fruit. Michael saw Barbara Ann and said, "If you would like to take that swim, I'll accompany you."

Barbara Ann looked at him, took off running, and yelled, "Last one in the water buys dinner."

Michael not opposed to that suggestion poured himself an orange juice and leisurely strolled to the water."

The Sarge said to Courtney, "Now, that's a smart boy. He wants to have dinner at any cost so he's willing to pay for it."

Barbara Ann considered what had transpired and said, "I need to watch what I say to you, Mr. Guy. Looks like you'll be buying dinner."

Michael laughed and said, "I didn't think you were that interested in seeing me again after my boring conversation. I'm not a real aggressive kind of fellow. Me and my guys haven't worked that long for the group and we're trying to make sure we live up to their expectations and their sense of morality. At some point this evening, if we're on for dinner, I want to talk in hypotheticals. I think this allows people to raise questions about things they like and dislike, from food to cars, to clothes to music, from love to hate, and to honesty and loyalty. I think it'll give you a sense of who I am while I try to gather the same about you. I will say one thing now, when you turned around while we were in line and introduced yourself to me and I saw your face and that look on it, I knew I wanted to have a go at learning who you are, Ms. Lady."

"You talk too much. Come in the water."

Courtney, Asiram, Zanthius, Mallory, Monica, and the Sarge were sitting at the water's edge watching the babies splash and play. A cell phone began to ring, and everyone tried to figure out whose phone it was. It was Asiram's phone and on the other end was Vladimir who said, "I need to talk to Mr. Sarge." She told him to hold on and told the Sarge it was Vladimir. The Sarge got up and walked away from the group. He motioned to Mallory and Zanthius to accompany him. He walked towards the bend in the road when Vladimir said, "I have someone on the line who wants to talk to you."

The Sarge hung up the phone and asked Mallory for his phone which would show they were in Australia. He called the number back and said, "What happened to you? I guess I lost you, we're out of the country. What were you saying before we were disconnected?"

A booming voice came on the phone and said, "First of all, I want you to hear this traitorous son-of-a-bitch scream." The muffled sound on the other end of the phone clearly indicated that someone was being tortured.

The voice came back on and said, "That's Sergov having his heart cut out. I'll save Vladimir for last. Anyway, hey Couz, how the hell are you? You know you people owe me close to a billion fucking dollars and I want it back since that fucking cowardly government of mine has sent Russian operatives after me. I hear these two had you in their sights several times but didn't have the balls to pull the trigger."

There was a silence on the phone and the Sarge said, "As smart as you think you may be, you continue to show people how insignificant and paranoid you really are. Just so that you know the facts, your people killed Sergov's and Vladimir's families after giving them the assignment of killing two dumb ass CIA types. Are you stupid? Do you put morons in charge of all your operations? We like doing business against you because you can't deliver a product. Vladimir is worth a lot of money in another dimension that your dumb ass couldn't conceive of. If you kill him like you supposedly killed Sergov, the entire Russian government will be looking for your ass. The man you're looking at screwed the nut that runs that country's wife and more than once. Sergov and Vladimir performed double duty on her for four straight hours. Oh, and by the way, I'm recording this shit and I do have a direct access to that funny place in Europe. Have a nice day and you can bet your sweet ass that I'm coming for you, freak." Beckmire hung up the phone and looked at Mallory and said, "I want to be airborne in ninety minutes."

# # #

Protocol states to call the pilot first and make sure the planes are ready. Mallory called Carla and said, "We have to do the dash in ninety minutes, will both planes be ready? Is that a problem?

She replied, "Not at all. I'll have my people file papers that we're off to Miami or somewhere and then change the orders."

Mallory next called Rashida and Juan and told them the group was out in ninety. Rashida broadcasted the message that stated the planes would be airborne in ninety minutes.

Montomie, Gladstone, and McArthur had made plans for the evening, but when that text came in, the first family became the priority of each man. When Michael got the text, he forwarded it to his people and each man knew they were a part of the extraction/protection team.

McArthur passed Michael and said, "You know what, I really like that woman. How did you make out with the one you met?"

"We were supposed to have dinner tonight," Michael announced.

"Damn! Montomie, Gladstone, and I were supposed to take them to dinner as well. You're the extraction security detail, you know we shouldn't get caught up with strangers, but we're human. I need you and your boys to cover our asses and give us at least five minutes to speak to our dates. In return, I'll give you ten," McArthur stated.

# # #

Montomie, Gladstone, and McArthur presented themselves at the double suite that the ladies had reserved. McArthur knocked on the door and when Barbara Ann opened it, he said, "I trust that Michael explained the nature of our business to you. Look at my phone, this is what was broadcasted ten minutes ago. Barbara Ann looked sideways and thought that once again she threw her heart out there and it was trampled on.

McArthur said, "Michael will be here to represent himself. We need to speak to Alvara, PJ, and of course Gerri."

Michael gave them ten minutes to express themselves and to gain future contact information if they were truly interested. As the three men were leaving with numbers and other information, they ran into the Sarge who said, "I thought you guys had security assignments?"

McArthur said, "Sarge, we're men first and we had to make a connection because we all felt a bond. Take any issue out with me and not with Michael. He did what we were going to do with or without our consent."

The Sarge smiled and said, "I must admit, I saw six beautiful women. You could close your eyes and come up with a winner that's good on the eyes and morals. Guys, we're good. Just don't miss the fucking plane."

Michael, who barely spent time with his mom, went to her room. When she answered the door, she said, "Oh my! I saw you with that lovely lady last night. Son, she had rings on her finger."

"Mom, I'll tell you all about that if it's something I want to pursue. I just wanted to say, I'm happy you and dad are civil to each other and that God does work in mysterious ways. Dad was about to be kicked out and these people, and I do mean different people, showed up and paid for everything. They hired me and now I'm making more money than I can count or spend. We must leave the island in a few. I'll probably be gone for a while, but I just wanted to say, I love you so much and I'm so happy you're not as stubborn as that pig-headed man you married."

From behind a closed door, a voice said, "I'll come out there and slap you crazy."

"I knew you were here. Ask me how I knew?"

"How did you know I was here?"

"Dad, you're the only man that still wears that cologne-- Old something or the other. Listen, we're off again. I love you and I must say, the two of you have turned this place into a huge money maker."

"Son, do those people ever talk about expecting something in return or a payment?"

"Dad, that would insult them. The rule of thumb is that it must remain in the family and if not, then they have the right to appoint overseers and direct the proceeds to well defined charities. Dad, every lawyer from here to the mainland has told you that if they challenged your ownership, they don't have a leg to stand on. Monica, their lawyer wrote it so that you and only immediate family members have rights unless stupid shows up. Listen, I'll call you when I can. I love you both and just try to respect each other and you both will have a partner for life. Oh, those six ladies, let them have the run of the place and upgrade their rooms to suites with an ocean view. When they check out, tell them the pleasure was ours and we hope that things work out."

Isaiah and Desmond were at the bottom of the steps when Michael came out of his parent's room and they directed his attention to the beach and showed him their watches. Michael walked down to the beach where he found a red-eyed Barbara Ann crying her heart out. He slowly slid down beside her and touched her hand that she violently jerked away. He softly said, "Do you remember when I told you I work for the group. They have some business to take care of. I don't know where and they don't consult me for my input unless I have intel. Now, Barbara Ann, I like you a lot. My mother told me she liked you as well, but that you had rings on your finger. I will fly you to where I am if it's safe. Will you accept a ticket from a stranger who feels he's so close to telling you he cares for you? I mean, it's only been thirty-six hours or so, but I feel as though I want to get to know you. If I were to make a guess, it appears that you might want the same thing. Listen, the guys have your friend's information, if you want me to have it then let one of your girlfriends know and they will get it to me. I must leave."

Michael stood up and extended his hand to Barbara Ann. He gently pulled her close to him and said, "I know what I like and what I want. They're both you." He kissed her on the cheek and ran off.

CHAPTER TWENTY-EIGHT

Captain Carla approached the small runway and told her passengers she was going to blast this bird into the air. She told them to prepare for take-off. She approached the runway and was given permission to take-off. The crew throttled the engines up, released the brakes, and the plane went screaming down the runway. In a matter of minutes, the plane was in the air and everyone was looking at the marvelous blue water they had just left. The group could also see Darryl's plane taking off on the runway. Carla announced that the little guy was also in the air.

The Sarge looked out of the window and thought about Vladimir and Sergov. He leaned over the aisle and asked Mallory if a phone number can be traced after the call is over? Mallory looked at him and said, "You've got to get rid of that flip-phone. He looked towards the mid-section of the plane and saw Rashida snoozing. He stumbled back to her and woke her up. He motioned for her to come forward.

When they arrived at the Sarge's seat, they got on their knees and the Sarge explained what he was trying to do. Mallory gave her the phone and she told him they might be able to call the number and get a general location within five to ten miles.

Rashida knocked on the cockpit door and informed Carla about what she was trying to do, and Carla plugged her into the satellite phone. Rashida called the number and it rang, rang, and once it went to voice mail, she zeroed in on the location of the phone. When she came out of the cockpit, she said, "Dad, I guess we're going back to Virginia."

The Sarge told Carla to make it happen.

# # #

A few hours later, the planes were descending into the Maryland. While the plane was on descent, Courtney held the Sarge's hand and said, "Honey, are we over-extended?"

He looked at her and asked, "In what sense baby?"

She said, "I mean we have two planes landing at the same time and another one sitting somewhere. Darryl and Sue Lyn should be in Australia handling that project for the people. It just seems like we have a lot going on and more importantly, your cousin is still trying to kill us." The Sarge smiled and continued to look out of the window.

He squeezed her hand and said, "I'm thinking we can get a lot done this trip. I've had contact with a legitimate authority to rid ourselves of the Carbon Factor and I think we've narrowed down my cousin's window of operation. I think we are short-timers in this adventure."

In the meantime, Rashida and Juan were looking at their iPads and scanning the camera systems. They switched to the Ring system that can be monitored and record remotely. Rashida said, "Juan, look at this dude."

Juan said, "I'm looking at the northern quadrant and there is a guy checking the locks on the front door. Let's scare the shit out of them." They both hit the panic buttons and alarms went off and an automatic voice began to announce, 'intruder, intruder! Police have been alerted and subjects have been photographed and targeted'. Rashida fired a round at the huge wooden pillow in the front of the house and everyone began to scamper away from the doors. Still photos were made of everyone. Once they played the camera back and sequenced all videos of human movement on the property, they were surprised that other than the immediate intrusion, the property had been void of trespassers other than the keeper and his family. Rashida and Juan ran weapons checks remotely and all systems were in the go position. She went back to Asiram and said, "My lady, your palace has been inspected and is safe to inhabit."

Asiram looked at her and wondered what the hell that meant?

# # #

It was approaching dusk when members of the group made a physical inspection of the weapons systems. They scoured the grounds in threes and decided the probability of corruption was minimal. A group of six went to the property where the senator once lived and found signs that someone had been there looking around. This was reported to Rashida who told Juan to check the camera system in that area.

As Juan reviewed the log, he noticed an independent camera that was fully motion oriented detected the movement of cases into the ex-senator's house that was now owned by Asiram. When Michael and his crew arrived, Rashida said, "I need you people to prepare to go on perhaps a suicide mission. Is that a problem?"

Michael looked at her and asked, "No disrespect intended ma'am, but do we look like we're suicidal?"

Rashida said, "No, you don't. I want you to review some video and decide how to handle what you see or make recommendations."

As the men watched the video, they were convinced that whatever was in those boxes, it wasn't explosive the way they were bounced around. Isaiah, said, "I don't think what's in the cases are explosive. Watch carefully when this thing hits the ground, no one concerns themselves. Watch their reactions. Exactly, no reaction, whatsoever."

Darryl said, "Okay, let's take a closer look at it and let me take that hand x-ray unit and check it out."

Michael said, "With all due respect, sir. This is what you hired us to do. Is that correct?"

Darryl said, "Dude, at this point in time, if we're not a team, then we'll never be. What say you?"

Michael looked at him and saw that the Darryl was going to lead this evaluation, no matter what, and said, "You're the boss."

Darryl turned around and said, "I may be the boss, but if you neglect to give me critical input, then you won't have a boss or a job."

Michael thought about what had just been said and stated, "If you're the boss then it's me and my team that has to approach this situation. No disrespect intended boss, but we don't need you leading us on operations like this that we've trained for."

Darryl looked at Michael who thought for sure he had crossed the line. Darryl asked, "Did I abdicate my position? Did I say to you I now need Michael to make sure that me and my wife are safe and secure? No, I don't think so. You know what you're talking about and what you need to say to me is simple. Boss, we got this. Don't play word games with me when it comes to your security or mine. Be direct, damnit!"

# # #

Rashida casually looked at the telephone that Mallory had given her. When she glanced at it, the coordinates seemed to be near. She continued to evaluate the farm to make sure there were no unknown incursions.

Mary Alice had ordered her company to prepare a heavy dinner for the group. It was less than two hours later, when her company vans pulled up with a dynamic spread of food stuff. Rashida saw her and asked, "What's on the menu tonight?"

Without thinking, Mary Alice said, "I'm glad my business is near the farm." Rashida stared at her and realized that the location of Vladimir's phone was in close proximity to the farm. Her body shuddered for a moment and she yelled, "The devil is close by. Silent alert. Silent alert."

Rashida broadcasted 'Code Red' and everyone knew what that meant.

Marisa, Ms. Viola, Yvett, and Mary Alice, ushered the children into the basement and into the bunker. They grabbed weapons on their way and knew the drill. Ms. Viola took a head count and realized she couldn't seal the door because the Beckmire children were missing. She also knew the system would seal the door automatically once the time had expired and indicated that it should be shut and locked. As she stood at the threshold of the doorway, she could hear someone descending the steps. It was Asiram in full battle gear and apologizing for being late with the babies.

The Sarge made his way to the war room and asked Rashida what was going on and she showed him the last place Vladimir's phone had registered. The Sarge said, "That's pretty damn close. If you had to guess, how far away is that?"

"Dad, I don't have to guess. It's six plus miles away, but it's moving slowly and heading this way."

The Sarge looked at her and asked, "How can you track a phone that no one is talking on? How can you do that?"

Rashida laughed and said, "Your nephew had Michael put a plastic locator inside of the charging hole. It's almost like, a liquid-antennae. You've got to leave the seventeenth century and slide into the twenty first."

The Sarge mumbled something under his breath and Rashida said, "I heard that. Oh, that phone is now exactly six miles away."

"What, are they walking here? Let me know when it's three miles out, honey."

Mallory was waiting outside and said, "Do you think we want to send the young bucks on a recon mission? I mean they're fast, quiet, and most of all, they're appreciative of what we did for them. What are your thoughts?"

The Sarge mulled over the thought for a minute or so, and then said, "My nephew is a neophyte. He doesn't have a clue about what we're into."

"I think you're underestimating him and Sue Lyn. Everyone here has blood on their hands including the newcomers. Also, they don't have to go with them. You have operational control over the men when they're in our midst."

"You know, I forgot about that. Find Michael and have him report to me, asap!"

# # #

When Michael appeared in the war room, the Sarge said, "I need you guys to go on a little recon mission."

John Lee and Jilkes were donning their vests when Jilkes after hearing the word recon, said, "Sarge, this is their first time here and they don't know the boundaries. Me and John Lee can handle it because we still have munitions buried in the field and can provide a double threat to anyone crossing the threshold of the farm. All you must do is make sure we're not targeted, and no one fires in that direction. Put Somara, Yeshida, and Okema on the roof in our stead and have these guys provide backup for us. Once the automatic weapons are engaged, they'll be mowed down because they don't have coded ID tags from Rashida."

Mallory said, "He's right. I guess it's been a while since we had to defend ourselves here. Those two know the ranch and layout. The rookies don't have a clue."

Michael raised his hand and said, "We ran to the road and split our team into twos and I'm comfortable we know this place and besides, we studied the picture on the wall over there."

Jilkes said, "What you saw was what we wanted you to see. There are pop-up weapons all over the farm and if you're not coded, then you're a target. Follow our command and you can hang with us. No macho shit."

Meanwhile, Rashida yelled, "Dad, that phone is four and a half miles out and moving as if it were a turtle or something."

"Do you have any other movement on the property?"

"Absolutely not, other than a bunch of deer, one bear and coyotes."

He looked at the screen and said, could they fool us like they did in the mid-west?"

Rashida smiled and said, "Fool me once and you make me smart. Try to fool me twice and I'll have a surprise for you. The motion detectors are on high alert, and the cameras are showing everything that moves. I'm hoping they aren't invisible, and if so, then we're in for a long night."

John Lee looked at the monitors and asked, "How far can we go before you be not seeing us?"

Rashida showed him the monitored area near the road and said, "I can track you all the way to road. Now, if they have signal jamming equipment, your card will vibrate like your phone and if that happens stay on the ground and bury your face and ass in it or you'll be cut down like the enemy."

"That be real comforting, Ms. Rashida. Any other way me and my friend can approach this here problem?"

Rashida laughed and responded, "Stay the hell home."

The Sarge chimed in and asked, "Is it necessary for us to have an offensive rear position?"

Mallory who was studying the monitors said, "Hell, yeah! If you're taking fire from the front and rear at the same time, then it can be discombobulating. However, in the past when we did that, the guys were subject to friendly fire either directly or ricocheting. I don't like them being exposed like before and if they're injured, we have to wait to try to help them."

The Sarge looked at Jilkes and said, "Each time we do this, the layout and the siege are different even though we're on the same land. They change strategies and we try to adapt."

Jilkes was about to say something when Rashida bellowed out, "three miles exactly and still dead reckoning for the property. Sorry Dad, you told me to let you know."

He turned to her and said, "Thanks Baby Girl. You have any ideas about deploying seven of our people to the rear to come up on the enemies' ass and let them have it both ways."

Rashida looked at Jilkes and then at John Lee and pointed to two areas where she felt they would be extremely safe, but on the western side of her picture, the land borders and belongs to a member of some right-wing group, that flies the confederate and Nazi flags. I think he's also a congressman on the local level from what I can discern. He'll probably turn his dogs on you if you violate his land now that I think about it, that's probably the perfect place to sit and wait for whatever is coming our way at a snail's pace. If I'm not miscalculating your cousin, he probably has this guy in his pocket as well, and as a matter of fact, a lot of the assaults against us, emanated from the west, where his property is. We should bankrupt him and give him an ultimatum he can't refuse. Each attack began from that direction. Think about it. He's in this, based upon his location and where everything has started, since the beginning. I need to contact Mary Alice in the bunker to see if she knows anything about this guy."

There was a hiatus in the discussion when the Sarge asked John Lee, "Do we have any doggie treats here?"

Jilkes mused and said, "He's into pigs Sarge. He doesn't know shit about dogs."

The room broke into hysterics and the Sarge said, "People, I need your best intelligence because apparently something is coming our way that's big and slow."

Rashida looked at the screen and announced, "2.4 miles out. It's now or never. I figure whatever is coming this way, is traveling approximately five to eight miles per hour. Even I could run up to the road by then."

The Sarge looked at Michael and asked, "Are your people fully loaded for a long incursion?"

Michael threw his neck from left to right and said, "Sir, each man has four weapons. Two double loaded clips for the assault weapons, three double loaded clips for the machine pistols and three double loaded clips for their main weapon, plus four clips for the nines and bush blades for close work."

John Lee said, "Well, I'll be damn, that's a shit load of munitions and weapons. Can you run to the top of the road carrying all that shit?"

Michael once again threw his neck from left to right and said, "We did it earlier in a matter of minutes."

Jilkes looked at the Sarge and said, "We'll decide our point of reference. Most likely, we'll breach that farm to the west and figure out how to protect from afar. My problem is we don't have any long guns with us."

Michael asked, "What's the range you're interested in compromising? What we picked up in the armory downstairs and the rounds we have, seem to be enough to hit targets beyond the main farmhouse."

"Okay, we'll try to keep up with you guys. Head southwest towards that dim light in the foreground. Rashida, can you give them temporary locators?"

She looked around the room and said, "Dad, Mallory, Juan, and here's mine. We're one short."

As Asiram walked past the room, Rashida said, "Stop, I need your ID." She then snatched it off her bullet proof vest. She gave Michael the ID cards and told him to make sure his people placed them on the outside of their vests.

Jilkes told Michael and his crew they don't do a lot of running at night because of the holes in the landscape and road. We're going to ride those mules up that hill and from there, we'll strategically place each of you at my direction. He looked the group square on and said, "You do what John Lee and I tell you, or we'll personally make sure you won't participate in this mess again. This is not a drill. This is real, and our lives are at stake as we engage a group of people who we don't know their skill sets. Don't screw this up and don't be a hero, or you'll die young."

As the men loaded into the mule, John Lee said aloud, "I'm not comfortable being with you guys, but I'm going to trust my friend's life and mine in your hands. Don't mess this up and you'll live to see another day. Oh, and by the way, if anything happens to my black friend, I will gut each of you, in public. He's Black Jesus, and, therefore, you'd better make sure you don't compromise him."

Rashida yelled out, "1.6 miles and slowing its approach. Dad, I can't figure out why they would have that phone on. I mean the signal is real, but why would you telegraph your moves by keeping a supposedly dead man's phone on, and in your possession. Perhaps Vladimir and Sergov are not dead, and this is a ruse, and we should be focusing our attention on where the senator once lived. I'm scanning, monitoring, and unless they have some space shit on, I can't capture an image, so therefore, I won't say they're fronting us on this one."

Mallory said, "Rashida, let's start a few controlled barn fires. They work remotely, and we kept them near that property because we didn't want to get caught with our pants down and provide our captives with the fuel to burn us. Both of those pits are active unless the grounds keeper removed the batteries. Give it a shot and anything that's near there will be obvious and can be targeted."

"Mallory, if we light up that area, we also give them directions to the farmhouse. I prefer to try a few other things prior to illuminating the night sky with a fire. I'm going to use that damn racoon hunting music and gunfire that John Lee recorded a year and a half ago."

# # #

Jilkes called the Sarge and said, "Hear me, and obey me! Don't waste any time, get everyone into the bunkers. The people coming for us have two fucking Howitzers. This is a destruction mission."

The Sarge looked at Rashida and yelled, "Broadcast—bunker—bunker—bunker." They have Howitzers out there. Everyone in the bunker now."

As people began to head towards the bunker, Asiram began to cry. The farm was her favorite home and she realized it was going to be destroyed once again.

Juan and Rashida grabbed as many of their tools as possible and headed for the bunker. Once in the bunker, they plugged in monitors to existing Rj-45 plugs and began to focus on the approaching force. She said, "Dad, they've stopped and are a mile out. When Asiram and Mallory crossed the threshold to the bunker, the alarm was sounded—intruder—intruder—intruder. They realized Michael's guys had their badges and, therefore, they weren't recognized. Asiram grabbed the two boys and looked at Rashida and said, "Damn, girl. Last, I heard, I was still on this deed. Fix that shit."

Everyone laughed.

The system began to articulate who was missing from the bunker. It repeated the intruder alert when Darryl and Sue Lyn entered the bunker."

When the Sarge came down, he asked, "Who's missing?"

There was initially silence, Rashida said, Jilkes, John Lee, Michael and his crew."

The Sarge looked at his wife and she knew that look and walked over to him and said, "Handle your business. I'll be here waiting on you. Love you so much!"

Mallory saw the look and so did the rest of the crew. They kissed their wives and armed up.

The Sarge said, "I don't need you. I don't need any of you. I need you to stay with your families."

Mallory yelled, "We're out. Are you coming?"

The Sarge looked at Rashida and said publicly, "I raised you to be a lady, but tonight, I need you to be a bitch and target my foes precisely and permanently." He walked over to her and kissed her on the cheek.

The bunker was sealed. The Sarge split his forces into two groups, realizing that he had seven men in the center of the issue and that he needed to breach the western and eastern flanks and coordinate a superior strike on the aggressors. He texted Jilkes and informed him they were moving to the east and west of him and for him to let his people know that in the east and west, friendly forces were amassing.

In the bunker, Okema, Yeshida, and Somara were having a discussion that ended in them telling Rashida they could protect the group from the roof. Rashida told them that plan had not been approved by the Sarge.

Okema said very clearly, "I'm married to Richard Brown, and he will need my cover fire. By the time they figure out the exact range, we will have their spotter identified and concluded." Rashida looked around the bunker and noticed that Courtney was walking over.

Courtney vehemently announced, "Rashida is in charge. Do not challenge her authority."

Okema bowed, never made eye contact with Courtney, and said, "Was not the intent of our suggestion. They will need long distance spotting and lasers. We can identify that process."

Rashida threw her head from east to west and said, "After two successive rounds from their guns, if you're not here in thirty seconds after that, I'm sealing the bunker and I will presume that I have to adopt some Asian looking children."

Okema bowed lower this time and said, "When in love, one must protect what one really feels and loves. If you no understand that then you are truly not in love."

Rashida smiled and bowed lower and said, "When I say times up, don't fuck around."

Somara laughed and said, "At least I will follow that instruction."

Rashida said, "They're at the top of the hill. Headsets and mouth pieces in the children. All adults brace with your mouth pieces in.

# # #

From the local Congressperson's property, two Howitzers were quietly being maneuvered into place with a significant force to support them. Rashida called Jilkes and asked, "Do you see what's on the horizon?"

Jilkes responded, "They're very casual about this event. However, there must be a spotter trying to place a beam on the farmhouse."

Rashida said, "Your high-spirited wives are on the roof looking for the spotter as well. They have two rounds and thirty seconds to get down to the bunker."

Jilkes looked at John Lee and realized that by sharing that information with him, he would blow their cover and risk being shot. He considered the options and said to himself, "I'll have to buy this one—right or wrong. If I tell him, he's going to run right up to those guns and get shot. I can't have that."

As Okema, Somara, and Yeshida searched for the spotter, Asiram showed up on the roof with a pair of strange looking glasses and said, "Try these on."

Okema put the glasses on and saw where the two spotters were setting up their firing schematics based upon laser assumptions. Asiram asked, "May I?" She then set her sights on the target and fired, but not before he had relayed some coordinates. A round hit forty to fifty yards away. The Sarge communicated with his people that they might be subjected to friendly fire, but they had to stop this assault before a direct hit was made on the farmhouse.

The thunderous explosions rocked the earth, swayed the house, and scared the mess out of the ladies. A second, and third round was fired before Asiram yelled, "Rashida is going to lock the fucking doors. Leave everything and let's get the hell out of here."

As the ladies made their way to the basement, a round hit so close that it knocked them to the floor. When they reached the basement, Rashida, yelled, "One more second and I would've left you people to the stupid ward."

Each lady immediately put her mouthpiece in and braced for the concussion effect. In the meantime, and elsewhere, the Sarge yelled, "No quarter to be given."

From various positions, all affecting the intruders, the Sarge and his crew opened fire. The intruders didn't' have a chance to respond to the voluminous rounds being fired at them. When the Sarge and his people stopped firing, he called Rashida and said, "We're in our holes, complete the mission and fire on anything that moves in this quadrant."

Rashida hit the engage button, but the system did not fire a single shot. The Sarge and his crew had terminated, viciously, thirty-six individuals in less than three minutes.

The Sarge communicated with Rashida that his crew would spend the night in the woods and for her to keep the property on lock down and the weapons systems on high alert. Rashida told him to have his crew fall flat and stay flat in ninety seconds and stay down while she did an active weapons scan of the area to make sure there were no people hiding in the trees. She told him she had placed a call to the cleaners prior to the assault and they were standing by and seeking permission to access the property. The Sarge told her to tell them they might need more people because he believed the use of artillery was going to bring on a new kind of scrutiny in the morning.

The Sarge called Mallory and asked, "How the fuck do you commandeer Howitzers and live shells in this country? Is this a result of the new president and his lack of empathy and perhaps his support of groups that fly the confederate flag and salute that moron Hitler? Is our president involved and does my cousin have evidence of collusion on this guy? Perhaps, we need to capture him and find out what he knows about the president. In the morning, we need to vacate the farm. We're going to get rid of the Carbon Factor again, but this time, we're going to give it to an unsuspecting authority. In a few days my friend, we will test the bonds and fiber of the United States Government and the Constitution. We will provide the alleged, most modern, and dangerous weapon to people who are supposed to legislate the laws of the land. Stay focused and quiet. In less than an hour, the cleaning people will be here to extract the remains.

A police helicopter flew nearby and the Sarge fired warning shots into the air and drove it off.

# # #

At 0450 hours, the Sarge met the head cleaner and told him where the remains were and that his people should be prepared to conclude all inconclusive subjects.

The cleaner told him they had four crews in place, and they should be able to be out of there in two plus hours. The Sarge thanked him and told him payment would be handled in cash and that Mr. Jong was making his way to them with the agreed upon amount.

# # #

Later in the morning, the State Police, people with strange initials on their vests, and other local authorities were gathered at the local Congressman's home where he was remiss in trying to explain the advent of two Howitzers and spent shells on his property. The more he attempted to explain the situation the deeper involved he appeared to be. Those people with the funny initials began inspecting the serial numbers on the weapons and where they were last detailed.

Beckmire and his group were at breakfast when the caravan of black SUVs barreled down the road towards the farmhouse. When the first one came to an abrupt halt in the front of the house, the Sarge was there to greet it. The driver dug up the grass when he engaged in an abrupt turn that threw rocks with its tires at the Sarge. A guy got out of the vehicle with dark glasses on and started brushing his suit off.

The Sarge said, "Don't know who you are, but do you assholes often enter private properties in such an aggressive manner?" The man continued to brush his suit off without acknowledging the Sarge and pulled out a black wallet that had a gold badge in it.

The Sarge snatched it from the guy, threw it to the ground, stepped on it, and said, "This is my home asshole, and your gold pigshit badge don't mean shit out here."

At that point in time, his people were out of their vehicles with weapons drawn. The Sarge said, "That is not a wise move by your people. Do you want to die here?"

Members from the group began to slowly walk out of the farmhouse, and from other vantage points, with weapons in their hands. The Sarge said, "I suggest you head back to the top of the road and slowly back your pretentious ass down our private road and beg to speak to those in charge of this property."

# # #

Twenty-five minutes later, a group of black SUVs were backing down the road at a slow pace. When the Sarge saw what was happening, he said to Mallory "I'm sure that son-of-a-bitch is pissed at the reception he received."

He instructed, "Tell Rashida to record all conversations and to scan them for wires. By the way, did the cleaner repatriate our property?"

Mallory smiled at the Sarge and replied, "If they didn't, then as John Lee would say, 'we be screwed'."

As the SUVs backed onto the property and found their way to the front of the farm, the Sarge stood stoically awaiting a grand apology from people who had violated the groups' space. The guy in the suit, rather than brushing his clothes off, said, "Sir, my name is Agent Utz and I need to ask you questions about the detonation of explosives in your backyard. Is that something we can discuss?"

The Sarge looked at him and said, "How on earth do people get control of two Howitzers, live rounds and fire them at a commune of people of all colors and faith? Suddenly racists, are being empowered by this president and they feel they can do whatever they want to do to people who are not of their persuasion. Did you catch those people who commandeered the Howitzers and live rounds, and unless you have specific answers to those questions, then there is nothing for you to ask any member of our household? Is the government supplying hate groups with military grade weapons to silence or destroy people of color?"

Agent Utz said, "I want to first tuck my ego up my ass and ask you to take a walk with me so that I can speak to you about a certain individual by the name of Walter E. Lassiter."

The Sarge flinched and said, "I need my main man with me."

Mr. Utz said, "Do you mean Mr. Mallory and if so, I gladly welcome his participation."

As the men began to walk towards a deep hole left by one of the ordnances, Agent Utz said, "Your people in the field fired at the correct time. They had apparently narrowed the coordinates down to a pinpoint strike. We artificially threw off their calculations by corrupting their firing sequences. Listen, that move on Ms. Asiram's property was to throw my guys off. We want your cousin in the worst possible way. You asked how did he commandeer those Howitzers? Well, he did because he has dirt on every crooked asshole in our government. I have a personal interest in capturing him because he used my brother as a throw-away in Australia. He set him up to be killed. Your people or something over there ended his life. I want who killed him, and I so desperately want to apprehend your cousin."

The Sarge said, "You can't have him because he's mine to conclude. Before I say another word, who do you work for?"

"Oh, now you ask. You didn't take time to look at my badge?"

"Frankly, at that point in time when your man cocked those wheels and threw stones at me, I wanted to grab his ass out of that truck and beat the shit out of him."

"I'm sorry about that, but I wanted an excuse for you to back us down and give us the opportunity to have this frank conversation. I work for the NSA, but I'm cautious because I think I have a mole in my group. I'm sure your daughter, Rashida is running interference on this conversation by disrupting any recording signals. Listen, your cousin is a powerful man, but not too powerful to fail. He has been accused of the deaths of senators, a couple of congressmen, his employees, and countless numbers of other human beings. He has an open checkbook that we can't seem to close. There are literally billions upon billions of dollars that were supposed to be shipped to Iraq and other places, that never reached there and his signature was the only one on those documents. Sometimes if you raise a question, you had better be prepared to leave the country and disappear at the same time. Anything related to your cousin was classified and required White House type security clearance to access. He's a bad man. We know everything there is to know about you guys, as well, and as a matter of fact, I'm prepared to offer you guys a grant to explore the wilderness in foreign lands, i.e., we need your expertise around the world to do due diligence where we can't. Before you respond, let me say once again, we know everything about you and your group or let me be really specific, only the guy you're talking to has this knowledge, of what I would call, millions of dollars ending up in various trackable accounts."

Mr. Utz looked around and then continued, "I'm prepared to give you a set of numbers that no one can decipher and realize that it's your group. I know about your activities in Valencia, St. Thomas, and what you did for those poor farmers in the Midwest. I know everything you've done, and this is my opportunity to show and let you know I was the quote, unquote, 'the unknown main man'. I know, I screwed that up on arrival. I humbled myself in front of my people as we backed into your domain indicating to them and to you that I am essentially your cunt."

The Sarge said, "Find another word. We don't use that word around our ladies, and we certainly don't want to own one. How about I call you my 'conejo'?

Mr. Utz asked, "What the heck is that?"

The Sarge responded, "A conejo, is a rabbit."

Utz laughed and said, "I'm glad you didn't select croc as my title."

Mallory said, "Before we start naming our relationship, can you tell me why we need to have a rabbit in our midst?"

"Mallory, how many people have you people cleaned. Your cleaner works for me and always has. We own him lock, stock, and barrel. Now, your question is how many bodies can we attach to this property, Australia, the Midwest, Europe, and other places? Listen, this is not a blackmail session. I'm reaching out to you because what we need done on a periodic basis does not sit well with those who run our country. I can acquire for you and your people get out of jail cards for life with no possible opportunity to be questioned in a court of law. I can have that in writing and in your hands in twenty-four hours. This world is full of corrupt people and your cousin is in charge of most of them. We need to bury him and soon, because he has files on congressmen, senators, the president, the pope, and virtually, everyone else."

The Sarge looked at Utz and said, "I don't know you and your answer to Mallory was suspicious."

Utz fired back and said, "Man, you people have a body count that exceeds thousands. Are you fucking kidding me? I could call the National Guard and have this place decimated for cause. For cause means that I'm in control. In other words, Ben Beckmire, you're between a rock and a hard place. Tell me, do you have some illusion you're still in the Nam?"

The Sarge looked at Mallory who was fondling his weapon and asked, "Why are you kissing that gun?"

"Because at the nod of your head, I will blow his head off."

The Sarge laughed and said, "There are probably eight people in the woods who are probably lining up to get shots off at us. Perhaps they'll miss me and hit our so-called, want to be handler. So, Mr. Handler, there have been three long guns on you since you entered our property, as well as your elite sniper group, in the woods. Tell me, do you care about those men in the field? My daughter thinks they're hostile and I just need to say one word and your eight men will be blasted beyond recognition.

Utz looked at Mallory and then at the Sarge and asked, "Can I show you some pictures and give you information that might help solidify our relationship?"

The Sarge glanced at Mallory and without looking at Utz asked, "If I could be so bold, what could you offer as security if you have the correct group? We're intrigued by these assumptions you insist are real about our group. We are philanthropists, we don't rob Peter to pay Paul, we give money to help people help themselves."

"Quid pro quo. You've had guns on me during all this and I've had a reciprocal relationship on you. Can we all just get along together?"

The Sarge said, "You and your people were tracked once you turned on the access road. I suggest that you issue a stand-down order to your people in the field, or they will be fired upon mercilessly by our automated weapons systems."

Mr. Utz looked at the Sarge and knew not to play dominoes with the man. He moved his left arm to his mouth and told everyone to stand-down and extract themselves from the property. He walked close to the two men and said, "I can deliver your cousin to you. I can obtain you and your people get out of jail cards. I can make that big cash problem go away. I can make the National Guard and the FBI attack this place. I can make Christmas a very merry thing or a nightmare. Who do you think your cousin stole that money from to engage all those mercs you slaughtered? Listen, you have three jets and pilots to accompany them. You've ordered a new jet. There ain't much I don't know about you guys, and I mean the names of babies as well."

The Sarge's face contorted, and he said, "Never mention our babies, if you my friend, want to walk away from here."

"I didn't say it in a bad way, but I realize they are a touchy subject especially after your cousin dressed them in suicide vests. Listen, the way you guys operate, it's as if you have your own army, laws, and you just enjoy American virtues when they suit you. By the way, what are you going to do with the Carbon Factor formula? If he gets his hands on that formula, he'll sell it to every rogue regime there is in the world to sort of wreak havoc on the balance of power, notion."

The Sarge looked at Utz and said, "You've been rather busy. I hope you realize we pay top dollars on our contracts."

"Mr. Beckmire, I'm trying to work a deal. You guys are smart, but you must realize when your cousin broke out the

Howitzers, all bets were off. We kept the local boys out of here for now, but you and I know they're going to make their way to this farmhouse eventually. Listen, that fool fired live rounds at you in Virginia. Look at the hole we're standing and talking in. We have our people marshalling the locals and we've instituted a no-fly area including drones. Someone is going to get an aerial of those craters. Can we at least decide to have a conversation tomorrow once you've had an opportunity to speak with your group?"

Beckmire said, "I'm so afraid you have the wrong group and that was a marvelous tale you wove. Do you write fiction?"

Mr. Utz moved his head east to west and said, "If we don't make a deal to communicate tomorrow, I will personally order tanks on this farm. Man, be reasonable, I don't want the money or those newly discovered diamonds in the outback, I just want to put a hurting on your cousin, or watch your man do to him what he did to Scottie."

Mallory jerked and asked, "Who the fuck, are you?"

"I'm the man who admires your work, your patience, and your loyalty to this country. I'm going to tell you something which might make you super suspicious of my objectives."

Mr. Utz disconnected his communication device, and admitted, "It was my father that sent you guys on those suicide missions, the captain. I know, not the same name, but I changed mine after I found out he hated you people because you were honest and somehow, he got wind of your extra-curricular activities that were instituted by the two rich boys in your group. Guys, listen, I know this conversation is silent because of your wonderful daughter. However, a lot of those conversations in the jungle and in the camp were waiting for someone to dial the right channel and my father was that someone. I don't like my father--he beat my mother and he beat me. If you'd like to see something that might make us comrades as opposed to suspicious individuals, I'll show you exactly what I did to him. Do you want to see it?"

"I don't trust you Mr. Utz. I think there is another angle that is not being expressed."

Utz looked at the Sarge and said, "There is! Your cousin killed two guys and their families, that I absolutely loved. He butchered Vladimir and Sergov, two of my confidants and my sisters husbands. Don't worry, the agency knows my sisters were married to Russian operatives. He had them and their children butchered like livestock. I want him, and I don't want him to gain access to the Carbon Factor formula. If that happens, then all bets are off. You know you could give it to the Pope, again, and confess this is the end of this episode."

"Oh, please tell me why you want the Pope dead? That would be the result of us giving the information to him a second time," Beckmire commented.

"I'm going to ask you a simple question? Please answer it in simple terms. Do you know how much money you could earn by selling that thing?" Mr. Utz asked.

"The notion of money is not important to us. The first place that people would detonate that thing would be here in America. We're all Americans, or nearly so. We are patriotic and don't want to see this thing in the hands of any government, individual, or mentally challenged groups. So that you know, there is only one person in command of that product and it ain't me, the Sarge stated."

"Sarge, I know you people tried to give it to people who were pictured as honest public servants, but that turned out to be a dense forest. My job is not the Carbon Factor formula. My job is your cousin, the most wanted man on the planet. Others from agencies you won't even know will come for you about that. I can insulate you for a while, but eventually, conversations will have to be had. Your son made contact with some very bad people, most of them are deceased. His baby momma is suspected to be alive and well. I wouldn't rush out and share that information. And by the way, did you people kill that dude, the former legislator that owned that house on stilts in Poughkeepsie? Just curious because money is being withdrawn from accounts with his name on them, and the DNA, well, it ain't his from the body we recovered from his demolished house."

The Sarge responded, "I don't have a clue as to what and/or who you're talking about."

CHAPTER TWENTY-NINE

That night, prior to the Sarge meeting with his crew, he met separately with Mallory and reflected on the fact that Utz had asked, if they killed that legislator who lived in the house on stilts in Poughkeepsie.

Mallory exclaimed, "We blew him and his funky house to hell!"

"Mallory, did we see him die?" The Sarge asked.

"Sarge, don't go there. How the hell could he have survived that blast?"

"Mallory, we didn't see his ass die. I'm wondering if there is a connection to why Mr. Utz suddenly shows up and is now trying to be our new pimp. You know that guy was paranoid and had tunnels, much like we do, all over the place. We didn't see him die."

# # #

Sarge and Mallory met with the group and laid out their conversation with Mr. Utz. The two men had met prior to the meeting and decided that their backs were against the wall. He told the group the amount of information the guy possessed, including knowledge of the diamond mines. The Sarge said,

"As usual, when people have or think they have something on you, and they need your help, they tend to bargain away your rights by threatening to expose your so-called crimes. All we did was defend our homelands, properties, and each other. If that's a crime, then perhaps we all should surrender. As a compromise situation, he is willing to keep our records sealed if we consider performing international tasks for his agency, allegedly the National Security Administration (NSA). I for one want to end this siege, find my cousin, and this man says he can deliver Walter to us. Mr. Utz states that Sergov and Vladimir worked for him, and my cousin had their families murdered first, and then butchered them."

The Sarge continued to inform the group about Mr. Utz and told them they were supposed to have a conversation with him tomorrow and entertained questions from members of the group. The Sarge said, "I'd like to change the channel for a moment. You know my wife and I stayed in our own home as did many of you. We did happen to extend an invitation to some single guys who got blasted off free booze. I want to express how I feel. I want to tell you guys a short story."

Everyone began to boo and yell stuff like, 'oh please, not tonight'.

The Sarge said, "Guys, I'm going to tell this story, so I need less than five minutes of your time."

The room calmed down and the Sarge said, "Thank you. When I spoke of staying in my own home, I want to express that it was not what I expected. Perhaps it's because we're always in close proximity to each other. That first night was a bear to say the least. I kept looking out of the window, down the road, and realized that I'm not prepared to assume this kind of life yet. This is the first time Courtney is hearing this, but I wanted everyone to know how unsettling it was for me in that house while the rest of you were so far away."

John Lee stood up and said, "I be admitting I watched my black friend and his family's house all night long."

Bernstein was next and mentioned he sat in a chair next to the window watching Brown's, Jong's, and Mallory's houses.

Mallory yelled, "Why you little freak! Thanks brother, I was scared as shit in that house with the kids and Monica and really didn't know how to work any damn thing in it."

Yeshida stood and said, "My, Mr. Jilkes took me, the baby, 308s, and walked around all the properties. We were careful not to be discovered."

Mary Alice stood up and said, "As I mentioned before, we're not use to being without each other. Sarge, if I might suggest something? If the deal is solid, and we're not being blackmailed and find ourselves in a continuous march to serve new masters, then I suggest you exercise the option. After all, if we can't sleep nearby then we need to sleep close by."

#

That night, the group stayed close and enjoyed the music. Rashida and Juan left Darryl and Sue Lyn in charge of surveillance and swam in the pool with LaGina and the other children. Luana and Ms. Viola watched the group. Ms. Viola asked, "Are you happy with that man of yours? I mean, I don't see that there gleam in his eyes when he looks at you."

Luana smiled and said, "That's because you're not in bed with us. Him almost has too much gleam for me and works his magic on me almost every night. Him be a beast."

Ms. Viola laughed and asked, "Does all this gun toting and shooting people bother you?"

"No more than it bothers you. Why you be asking lady? Are you ready to go home and serve rum punch at the airport?"

"No child, this here be really exciting to me. I mean when I shot them fellas in the outback, I felt like Annie Oakley or Bonnie. No, I'm happy with this and what we all do with our money. I mean we've made more money accidently than we could have on purpose at home. I'm just fearful all good things must come to an end, and I don't want anything happening to you, my babies, or any of our adopted family. I'm just curious about your mindset, that's all."

#

Montomie, McArthur, and Gladstone talked with the ladies they met, often. No one knew that Michael was in constant contact with Barbara Ann, the mouthpiece of the group, and no one suspected that Whitmore and Michael's sister were an item.

Michael said to Darryl, "Boss, is there such a thing as time off? I met someone and I would like to have a normal dinner with her soon, if that's possible?"

"Damn, Michael, I'll have to check to see how that's handled. I'm sure it's okay, but I need to ask my uncle. There may be a security issue or something like that. I don't know, but I'll check it out."

As Michael was leaving the area near the pool, Montomie, McArthur, and Gladstone were on their phones. He stood and watched for a moment and saw Montomie hang up his phone first. He walked over to him and asked, "I need to ask you a question that is somewhat confidential."

Montomie, not really knowing much about Michael, stated, "I hope this is not a protocol question and if so, you need to ask the Sarge, Mallory, or our man, Darryl."

Michael looked at him and said, "This isn't about protocol. It's a matter concerning my interest. Listen, do you remember the woman that did most of the talking when we were on the island? Her name is Barbara Ann."

Montomie thought about the question and said, "I do remember her, but what does that have to do with me or my friends?"

"Listen, I know you don't really know me, but I'm feeling really good about getting to know her and wanted to know if you guys stayed in touch with the ladies that you met?"

Montomie looked at him and said, "Dude, when you want to ask about a woman, come straight on. I just hung up talking to the lady I like, and those two nuts are still on their phones speaking to the ones they like."

"How the hell do we get to see them? Is there any way we can get time off and meet them somewhere?"

Montomie arched his chest and said, "The people here are my main family, but I do understand where you're going with this one. You want to leave base camp and rendezvous with your friend. Is that correct?"

"That is precisely correct. Is there any way to do that without leaving a hole in the fence, or the defenses?"

"Michael, that is a situation you'll have to answer. I will not leave my family to satisfy my need to feel love. I will not leave my family for anyone or anything because these are the people who have watched my back, healed me during sickness, changed my underwear, and bathed my soul in brotherhood. We learned to love each other in the Nam. We don't do "see you next weekend"."

Montomie began to laugh and said, "Now that I told you that mess, this is what we're planning. We've asked the group to accompany us on a date in St. Thomas next weekend if our schedules and duties don't conflict. We're going to have one of our jets meet them in a neutral place and fly them to the island. Would you like to include Barbara Ann?"

Michael exclaimed, "Hell, yeah! If she can come, I want to include her."

Montomie looked at Michael, and his attitude, and demeanor changed. He was silent for a moment and after being pressed by Michael about the nature of the change in his attitude, he said, "Your friend has a few broken ribs and a black eye. She allegedly fell down the steps after drinking too much wine."

Michael looked at him and asked, "If I wanted to do a small mission and take care of a problem during the early hours in the morning, do you think anyone would miss me?"

"That is not how we roll. If you have a problem, then we have a problem. You must speak with Darryl, Mallory, or the Sarge, and let them know what you're up against. During this heightened state of siege by his cousin, I'm not sure he's willing to let anyone leave the farm. However, Darryl might be able to convince him that this is a surgical mission--in and out and over with. The other problem the leadership will have is that she is a married woman. Just so you know, my friend told me her husband beat the shit out of her when she returned from the islands. Can I suggest something to you?"

Michael shrugged his shoulders indicating yes. Montomie said, "If you just want to screw her? Then leave it be. If you want to take her out of that abusive relationship and make her happy, then I'll be your point man."

Michael's eyes swelled up and he said, "I would be honored to have you with me on a short mission. I'm going to do it one way or the other. If I could get the support of the group, then it would be an easier mission for me to accomplish."

Montomie said, "Let me talk to my contacts and see what I can come up with. Perhaps an extraction by contract workers might make sense. Let me discuss it and see who we have in the area."

Michael thanked him and walked away.

# # #

As the children were about to exit the pool, Ms. Viola calmly said, "I need everyone to stay in the pool."

She could hear growling sounds. Ms. Viola turned to Luana and said, "I hope you have a weapon because we have company."

Luana saw the four sets of eyes glowing in the dark that were illuminated by the almost full moon, and said, "I have one in the chamber and eight in the sleeve. How about you?"

Ms. Viola kept her eyes on the predators and said, "I have my sawed-off-shotgun in my lap and both barrels are cocked."

She turned to the children and said, "I want to see who can hold their breath the longest on the count of three? One—two—three!"

Ms. Viola blew both barrels of the shotgun and Luana placed five rounds into the uninvited guests. When the main support crew showed up and the large floodlights were illuminated, the group saw, five dead wild dogs looking for an easy meal.

When the Sarge showed up on the scene, he looked at Rashida and asked, "Why didn't the system detect these animals?"

Rashida knew that Darryl and Sue Lyn were in the war room and responded by saying, "Dad, the damn dogs don't carry weapons and ammo."

She walked away and left her dad feeling miserable at chastising his daughter in public.

The Sarge ain't no dummy. He knew that Darryl and Sue Lyn were on duty and that his daughter did not give them up. He was a proud father. He looked at the dogs and realized this was a signal to him from far away. He nudged Mallory and said, "I need to get back to the outback. There are issues that only me and Darryl can attend to."

When Darryl and Sue Lyn completed their union, he felt spent and said, "Oh my God, I need to get back to the bush."

## CHAPTER THIRTY

The Sarge had attempted to divide his forces and let those who were weary of traveling stay at the farm. Needless to say, no one purchased that ticket, and they all were aboard their planes heading to the Outback.

# # #

Once in the Northern Territory, the Sarge realized his cousin had attempted to divide and conquer his group. In the mines that were initially protected by serpents and spiders, the opposing forces set off flash grenades and incendiary devices that destroyed any animal or human in its killing radius. The villagers entered the mines and quickly exited in an area that was quicksand based. Thirty members of the tribe had been captured and were being held by forces loyal to Diablo.

# # #

The Sarge smiled at the results and said to his group, "We're here for two days. We must weed out some local snakes that have been seduced by Diablo's booze and drugs and get them into rehab. But, as you can see, the billabong has placed everything under water and the mines are safe. There are thirty natives being held captive, being abused, and my forefather has sent me a message, ordering me to capture the bad, exonerate the good, and send the evil into the billabong for what will seem like easy diamond picking."

That night, the group was led to the visitor's camp that was heavily guarded and witnessed the captors having their way with whoever they wanted. A man walked over to the captives and fixated his eyes on a woman. He bent down and watched her withdraw from him, and he said, "This Abo is going to be my bitch tonight. He grabbed her by the wrist and two men attempted to rescue her. They were cut down by gunfire by the guards. He took the woman into his tent and that's when Michael went ballistic.

Michael, without anyone having a clue as to what was going on with him, walked into their camp with two automatic weapons and two pistols. His targeting was precise until he ran out of ammo with the automatic weapons. Jasper, Harold, Isaiah, and Desmond disobeyed orders and followed their man into action. Michael dispensed of thirteen individuals by himself and received perimeter fire from his people.

The Sarge held his people in abeyance, and everyone was mesmerized by the precision of the executions by Michael and his crew as well as his nephew and Sue Lyn from the flanks. He said to Mallory, "They may have never been in a war, but they are the real deal. Did you see the way he marched in that camp and executed those people? That was some Wyatt Earp shit! You remember that movie when he walked into the water and began shooting people and Curly Bill ran out of bullets? That was amazing."

In the tent where the man thought he was going to have his way with the woman he selected, Michael and Darryl arrived at the same time to find the man holding his captive and pointing a weapon at her head. Darryl said, "We are coming in, hold your fire."

The guy yelled, "Leave your guns outside."

Darryl yelled, "Do we look suicidal? No, my friend, let the lady go and we can talk about a resolution.

Once inside of the tent, Darryl said, "This is a tough situation for you, my friend. You brought that woman in here to do whatever comes to your mind. You found an Aborigine woman and decided to just take whatever you want. Let me tell you how this is going to end. There are six lights beaming on your head. My suggestion is that you let the woman go and then you decide how you want to end this standoff. However, if any harm comes to her, you will be incapacitated, and you will bear witness to the atrocities that will befall your family. We will find your family and summarily, erase their names from the journal of life."

The man looked at his finger on the trigger and decided to conclude his own life. He kissed the woman on her head and placed the weapon to his head and fired it. Darryl handed the woman off to Sue Lyn, who comforted her.

# # #

Back at base camp, the five Aborigines and four white men that assisted Diablo's mercs and even participated in some of their shenanigans, were marched into the village. The Sarge said to the Aborigine men, "How could you stand by and watch your people be treated like that? What were you thinking?"

He then looked at the four white men and said, "I'm thinking you people were promised riches. Am I right? Don't bother to answer because I'm going to give all of you a sporting chance. Behind you in that cave, is the thing you enslaved your brethren and your countrymen for. Since you guys are good at what you do, I'm going to give you a test and if you pass it, you get to keep the jewels and live. Now, y'all strip down to your skivvies. Go on now, take your clothes off or go in the cave with them on. If you decide to keep them on, then you must keep all of them on including your boots."

Five minutes later, five Aborigines and four white men stood at the entrance to the cave and could see the diamonds sparkling below. The Sarge told the men that on the count of three hit the water and return with a diamond. The men knew that the snakes, spiders, and other creatures had been destroyed by the incendiary devices and thought this was a simple and passable task.

Each man took a deep breath and the Sarge said, "On my mark, one-two-three." The men jumped in the water and were in arms-length of retrieving a stone when they saw the blood red eyes of the 'Great Saltie'. As the men tried to swim to the surface, twenty to thirty crocs of varying sizes, began to rip them apart and gorged themselves. The Sarge walked out of the cave and said, "Let that be a lesson to those who would go against the Aborigine people and try to exploit those things that are inherently theirs."

# # #

As the group sat around the campfire and enjoyed food from nature, Courtney whispered to her husband, "What happened to those men?"

He looked at her and solemnly said, "They were eaten by the 'Great Saltie' and other crocs."

She unassumingly, exclaimed, "Oh!"

At 0600 hours, the group boarded their transportation to the airport only to be met in customs, by of all people, Mr. Utz. He said, "Good day mates. Might I have a word with you in private?"

The Sarge motioned to Mallory and the two stepped away from the group and near Mr. Utz who asked, "What happened to those blokes that went into that cave?"

The Sarge calmly asked, "What blokes and what cave?"

"Come now Mr. Beckmire, I was in the bush all night watching the entire action and plus, you owed me a telephone call. I thought it was rude of you to leave town without calling me or at least acknowledge our conversation."

The Sarge looked at him and said, "Get used to that. I want you to remain very still. I mean I want you to hold your breath and don't even blink your eyes because you have the deadliest spider in the country near your neck. I can save you, but you're going to owe me big time. Do we have an accord?"

Mr. Utz never moved a muscle. The Sarge put on a glove and picked the little spider off his collar.

Mr. Utz said, "You're full of shit. That little thing is harmless."

The Sarge walked the spider over to a customs official and asked, "Is this spider harmless?"

The guy jumped and yelled, "Extremely dangerous and no anti-venom, kill it."

The Sarge looked at the spider and said, "Naw, it's his world and we're intruding. I'll just place him where I found him."

Mr. Utz backed up and said, "Don't bring that thing near me."

"Mr. Utz, I think you need to listen to me and believe what I say to you. In this place called the outback, there are forces here that control things your little brain couldn't possibly fathom. I'm going to give you a quick lesson in survival in this land. These guys usually run-in pairs and I see the other one on you. Now, I asked you, do we have an accord, and you didn't answer. If we do, then just blink your eyes."

Mr. Utz blinked his eyes and the Sarge proceeded to pick a nonvenomous spider off him. The Sarge said, "What you saw while you were peering through glasses in the bush was what happens to people who betray their kind, take advantage of people, and allow themselves to be exploited by drugs and booze. In these lands, Mr. Utz, I'm like royalty because of who my forefathers were to this land and its people. You my friend are an easy prey to me because you're more like a mosquito's buzzing sound—just annoying. You know a lot about us, but you don't know what we're capable of doing to you, your men, and your families from this backwards place. Wait before you start that threatening shit. I gave you fair warning and will not issue it again. If in fact there are bad people that need dispatching and it fits our interest, then we might consider it. If you ever try to force our hand, I promise you there is no sanctuary my little friends can't enter. Do we have an accord?"

Mr. Utz still scared from the spider said, "I don't believe in hocus pocus."

"Oh, my friend, you should have stayed away from here because there is a lot of that here and your DNA has been left. You pissed in the bush and blew your snot as well. The animals know you and everyone with a like DNA. Don't mess with me. We're going to board our plane, but your plane needs repair. Your hydraulics are leaking. You know how to reach me and remember when you're in the hospital with that fever, you will see how magical this land is. Good day Mate!"

# # #

On the plane ride back, Mallory looked across the aisle and inquired, "How did you know his plane had a problem, and when did you start liking spiders to the point that you handle them?"

"You know I'm petrified of those things. Darryl told me his plane had a problem when it landed. His sickness is a combination of bad food and uncooked food, and his symptoms were the swelling at the base of his neck. Nothing magical, just natural observations and recognitions. That's why you call me Sarge because I'm supposed to see the invisible. Good night, Mate!"

CHAPTER THIRTY-ONE

As their beautiful plane descended into St. Thomas once again, their smaller plane had landed, and their guests had been whisked off to 'The Sanctuary'. An anxious McArthur asked Montomie had he heard anything about their guests? He told McArthur that he too had been out of touch and wasn't sure if they would take them up on their invitation. Gladstone still in somewhat of a funk asked if things worked out and was told that no one knew.

From the front of the plane, the Sarge told the group about the mysterious Mr. Utz and his illness. He indicated he would probably call him in two days and try to get a timeframe for when they would make a final assault on their nemesis— Walter E. Lassiter. He also said, "This is going to be a trip of fun, sun, drinks with little umbrellas in them, and lots of food. However, we're going to earn the food because each one of us is going to stay in running shape. Are there any questions? Even if there are, I don't want to hear them."

#

Mr. Carter showed up in the lead vehicle and the Sarge said, "You have all of those people working for you, why do you insist on picking us up?"

"Mr. Sarge don't be stupid, you saved my business, my family, and my marriage. The least I can do is pick you up and feed you some 'BS'."

The two men laughed and the Sarge said, "You did mention marriage, am I to assume you've hit that home run again?"

"Mr. Sarge, they're still trying to find that damn ball."

The Sarge yelled! The two men screamed and banged on the dashboard. Everyone was wondering what was going on. Mr. Carter said, "Don't mind us, just two old guys trying to share fiction."

#

After they arrived at 'The Sanctuary', four men, Montomie, Gladstone, McArthur, and Michael, placed calls to their lady friends who left an impression on them. None of the guys were able to connect because the ladies had turned their phones off and had arranged for a magnificent entrance.

As the vans pulled into the circle of the resort, the four ladies were signaled by the resort staff that their guests were arriving. After hugging his son again, Mr. Carter asked, "Who the hell is that in the water?"

Michael turned around as well as the other three loners and said, "God is good. God is great. God is all empowering." He dropped his bag and high-tailed it down to the water with the other guys in tow. He ran into the water and swam to

Barbara Ann, submerged, reemerged, and kissed her. Gladstone was unable to make that kind of move because he was still in recovery.

Michael said, "OMG! I've been thinking about you so much. He placed his hands on her face where there was still an indication of her being hit and said, "You will never experience that from me. I want you to stay with me and never go back there."

Barbara Ann said, "That's so sweet, but unrealistic. I have a job and I have everything I own back there."

Michael smiled and said, "You don't have anything unless you have love. Those things you speak of, can be replaced. I can afford anything you want; I hope. The next time he hits you, might be your last time on earth and then I would have to avenge your plight in a most horrific manner. I want to save you from the abuse and me from what I would do to your husband. I have two of the smartest lawyers right here. You don't have to live with me or sleep with me until you feel comfortable with who I am and what I'm trying to propose--if you ever do. If you never feel safe or comfortable with me, then I will not pursue you in any manner, but will provide you with enough money to make your way out of the abusive relationship."

"Do you always talk so much. Let's get to know each other and enjoy our time together. I prefer not to focus on my relationship but I do want to understand what I might be subscribing to. Private planes, ownership in fancy hotels, all seems a bit suspicious, but I'm willing to listen to you and try to figure out if I can exist in that world. I will not, and I repeat, be a part of anything that deals pain on any level."

# # #

That evening, Mr. Carter made special preparations for the four couples on the beach with candlelight and nets to keep the bugs away. He managed to order a shipment of John Dory, a fish that is indigenous to the waters around Australia, to the 'The Sanctuary'.

The men took turns telling the ladies about their relationships and how and where they met. Montomie, Gladstone, and McArthur talked briefly about Vietnam, but shied away from details. McArthur said, "I'm going to begin to weave a story about the 'now' and turn it over to each of my comrades."

Two hours later, the men had covered their experiences with relationships to their adventures for the past few years. Barbara Ann said, "Michael, they didn't include you."

"That's because I'm a late comer. What these guys neglected to tell you is they came here to stay and had visions of creating a sanctuary. My father was about to have this place appropriated from him, by the bank. These guys marched him to the bank, secured the loan documents, and paid it off. They also did the same thing for the other properties in 'The Sanctuary'. Something else they didn't tell you is that the contract written for these places, leaves the ownership in the hands of the original owners. They bailed this area out, had the old buildings torn down, the new ones constructed, and they still have no real ownership rights in the property. Their altruism is still suspect to many people. I became involved after completing a minor task for them and was asked to not only work with my father, but to do work for them. Currently, I'm stationed in Australia, and I oversee the security of mines that have been discovered on Aborigine land."

He paused for a moment and said, "Sometimes, people try to kill us. The government attempts to hire us. We're probably never without a weapon and we spend more time in the air than we spend on the ground between here, DC, Wyoming, and Australia. They are extremely rich, frugal, and family oriented. Most of them have homes in Alabama on property that the guy who talks funny, partially owns. We saw you guys on your last trip down here and have had you on our minds since that time, and that's the truth."

Montomie said, "He's not telling the real story. He's a part of this group and an intricate part, at that. Now, I must admit, we help people help themselves and rarely strike deals for repayment. Mr. Carter will offer what he wants to offer us one day, but until then, we don't keep books. Our leader's cousin is our arch enemy and the enemy of the United States Government. He has stolen billions, assassinated two sitting US Senators, just recently commandeered Howitzers and launched live rounds at us on our farm in Virginia. He is a stone-cold killer and will do anything to compromise us, including sending four beautiful women down here to weaken our defenses."

Gerri asked, "That plane we rode on, is that stolen?"

The guys broke out into laughter and Gladstone said, "I'm not sure which one you were on, but we own three, and a big new jet is being constructed. We travel as a family with women who protect us, and children we educate. We're all about family, and for now, as long as we allegedly control the Carbon Factor formula, we'll never be safe.

"I mean, I saw Alvara, and my heart swung to the other side. I want to end this convention and spend time with you and try to figure out who you are while you figure out who I am. Before, I go any further, let me make a few things

extremely clear. We do not do drugs. We don't hurt our
friends, or our ladies, and our group is made up of people of
all races. If you subscribe to us, then our friends will do the
same to you. We're all grounded."

As Gladstone was talking, he noticed that tears were
running down Barbara Ann's face. Gladstone asked, "Barbara
Ann, you seem troubled?"

Michael turned around and said, "Let's take a walk and
put our feet in the water."

"I'd rather go swimming."

"Never at night, my love. You'll become shark food.
What has you so upset? Did we collectively say something to
hurt your feelings, or is it the fact you're still married and here
in a place of temptation?"

"I don't want to go back there, but I can't stay here either.
This is too convenient and tempting."

"You can hang out here for as long as you like. We're out
of here in two days for what we hope will give us peace and
privacy. If you get bored, you can help my mom in the kitchen
or just walk around the four properties and list what's missing
and what would draw, even more people. I mean we're
booked until next year, but we might want to consider building
another venue because we have an extended property line.
You could have fun here and your friends are welcome as well.
There's not much I control with this group, but I do know my
dad wants to make sure I'm attached and to someone he
approves of."

"Your dad doesn't know a thing about me or my issues."

"That would be an understatement, but he likes you and,
therefore, arranged for that show on the beach when we
arrived. People basically think all people are good until they
do something stupid. This isn't about judging you or me, but

about two people trying to figure out if there's a match. Your pain creates pain for me because logically, I should be focusing on a single woman. However, my focus is on you, and if you're willing to take a chance with me then, I'm damn sure willing to embrace you and work towards a more perfect union."

"How old are you, Michael?"

"How old are you, Barbara Ann? I'm not trying to connect to a number, I'm trying to unionize an individual."

"Nicely stated. I'm so confused about this whole thing. Why I'm here? And what I expect to get out of this liaison?"

Michael held her hand and said, "This liaison, as you call it, from my perspective, has the ability to blossom into a wonderful relationship. I know I've not thought of anybody or anything except you since we parted. I saw a man abduct a woman to fulfill his sexual pleasure and I lost it because I envisioned your husband abusing you. I marched into that camp and decimated it and we gave him the option to conclude his own life. My actions were not about the woman, they were centered on you."

Barbara Ann, crying, and acting confused said, "Please don't hurt me, or throw me away like I'm trash. I need to be loved, respected, and wanted. Not abused, battered, and discarded. I'm mentally at my wit's end. I need love and understanding, or I don't want to exist."

Michael kissed her cheek tenderly and said, "This can work, if you trust me and not wait for the other side of the coin to hit the ground. We just met, and before we consummate any relationship, you'll know all that you want to know about me, and I'll know the same about you."

Although her eyes were puffy from crying, Michael said, "You look happy and sad at the same time. My goal is to make you look happy all the time. By the way, one thing that is probably happening as we speak, a background check is being conducted using your DNA and other factors. Don't be alarmed, it protects the group from my emotions."

# # #

At 0545, four people could be viewed on the beach with individual fires simmering and people hovering over them to avoid the night's coolness. McArthur whispered to PJ, "This has been perfect. We didn't talk much, but we expressed our emotions in thoughts, smiles, and touches. Now, we're enjoying the rising sun, a sight I promise you if this works out, you and I will witness from all parts of the world."

PJ smiled and kissed him on his cheek and said, "I don't want any more relationships. I want someone to love, honor, and worship the ground I walk on. Can you attempt to do that?"

McArthur looked at her and then at the rising sun, and said, "I'll best that by light years. I've been around the world twice, and I've seen and played bass fiddle with a lot of people, and from where I am sitting, I can supersede your goals. I have never had a woman to upset my space and create anxiety within it. When I couldn't reach you, I thought I tried to be too cool, and misplaced my emotions and missed the opportunity to show you who I really am. I hope you saw it last night and now this morning."

PJ squeezed his hand, kissed his lips lightly and said, "I'm so impressed, or perhaps disappointed you didn't make a single attempt to take advantage of me. Don't respond because I want to have my private thoughts about that issue." They both laughed.

Gladstone and Alvara were close to the base of the resort and saw lights approaching 'The Sanctuary' at a rapid pace. He pulled out his weapon and fired two rounds into the air and everyone came to attention. He told Alvara to head back to her room and to collect her friends.

When the four vehicles showed up at 'The Sanctuary', the entire group was armed and prepared to do battle. Once in 'The Sanctuary' the vehicles slowed down and created a less than aggressive entrance. As the headlights were dimmed to the parking lights, the door to the first vehicle opened and it was Mr. Utz. He apologized for arriving before the sun had fully risen, but said, "Your cousin has boxed himself in and one of his confidants has concluded his access to funds. He is working on what's in his pockets and whatever bags he has. Also, check this out. You know how banks have that exploding money? Well, your cousin, randomly picked a bale of $100 bills that was destined for Iraq. Not only is it traceable, but it also has an extra code on it that effectively operates in the GPS mode. He screwed up and picked the wrong stack of bills and we had his ass narrowed down to DC and Virginia, but he is now airborne and guess where he's heading?"

A sleepy Sarge said, "Enlighten me."

"He's on his way to Colorado and just a stone's throw away from Ms. Asiram's ranch. You might have a mole out there, or someone might try to sacrifice you, for a loved one."

Mallory slowly approached the scene and said, "Mr. Utz, you're not welcome in our haven. Your illness should have indicated to you this game ain't played fair.

The Sarge said, "First, how the hell are you feeling?"

Mr. Utz smiled and said, "If you want to rid yourself of me, stay in Australia. I ain't never going back there. I suppose

I had a fever because all I dreamt about was crocodiles, and I mean really big ones."

"Do you and your armed caravan have a place to stay?"

"Sarge, we just landed, and I didn't want to waste time because your cousin, believe it or not, is also trying to sell an unproven version of the Carbon Factor formula and is setting up a bid conference via the internet. I need your help and you need mine. Can we attempt to take care of this matter together? My superiors have changed my focus to that of securing the Carbon Factor formula."

"That puts us at odds. We're not going to turn the formula over to you, or anyone else that's aligned with the government. We tried that before and it almost got us killed," Mallory blurted out.

"I'm sorry guys, I don't want you to turn it over to me, I'm to make sure you don't turn it over to your cousin at any cost."

"And what would be your final act in making sure that didn't happen? Would you attempt to murder us?"

"Let's hope we don't have to face that decision. I can't be everywhere you are, but I can arrive eventually and secure outside areas like here. Listen, your cousin is more desperate than ever, especially since access to his cash has been cut off and is being stolen by his confidants, who unsurprisingly, we have our fingers up their asses. Now, those are some people I wouldn't want to be. He will find them, and he will hurt them and their families. However, we still can't figure out who is withdrawing funds from accounts owned by the guy who lived in the house on the stilts, in Poughkeepsie. Our hope is that your cousin continues to use that money we can track. Oh, I've assigned the Coast Guard to patrol these waters and areas leading to your sanctuary. You won't see them, but rest assure, no one can cross those hills on either side or behind this place. Until you make your decision to acknowledge, or destroy the product, we'll be close, but not too close. My superiors feel a new surge is going to come your way and they might use any and all avenues to extract the specifications of the Carbon Factor formula. By the way, you know the Russians are at it again, but they keep blowing up scientists and laboratories trying to manifest the formula."

"Mr. Utz, you're a wealth of information, but mostly stuff that's precautionary. When will you really help us?"

"If your group is prepared to leave soon, we can at least narrow where your cousin is currently, and perhaps reach out and touch him. If I know him, he's probably trying to secure other cash stashes that he has."

"We're not leaving today, but it will be a point of discussion at dinner tonight. As a matter of fact, why don't you and your merry band, join us?"

"Thanks, Sarge, but we're planning on having pizza from down the road. The prices around here are a bit steep for our per diem. If you guys like, we can spring for a beer and pizza if you want to join us?"

# # #

McArthur joined the newly connected and decided to break protocol and tell the ladies exactly who Mr. Utz and his team were, and what he wanted. He explained their connection to the Carbon Factor formula, mines in Australia, restaurants and resorts in Spain, ranches around the country, and three jet planes. He told the ladies every member of their group was rich–minus, Michael who was well on his way and was heir to 'The Sanctuary'. He told them things come up and they have minutes to get their stuff in order and be on the plane. When there is an emergency, we often leave everything we own and head out. He explained that weapons were a part of their uniforms, and they were all proficient in the use of them. He concluded by saying, "We're the good guys who people often try to make into the bad guys. We're going to fly out of here early in the morning. We can try to send for you guys if you like, but by the time you get there, we might have orders to move again. Until we conclude our deal with Diablo, we're going to be moving a lot. What's fortuitous about that event is, it's coming to a climax, one way or the other. Our mission is simple, 'We help people help themselves'."

Michael told Barbara Ann he had to attend to his guys and that he would take a nap and catch her around 1400 hours or so and if she wanted to, they could go for a swim. The other guys concluded their magical night as well and offered the same experience as Michael suggested.

## CHAPTER THIRTY-TWO

Following a marathon night of eating greasy pizza, and drinking beer, the Sarge and most of his guys became familiar with Mr. Utz and his people. The Sarge placed a call to Clyde and asked if there were any suspicious movements or influx of strangers into town and was told there were only a couple and that they didn't look like the threatening type. The Sarge thanked him and told him they would be there in a day or two, but he would let him know once they were airborne.

The Sarge called Brown, Bernstein, Mallory, Jilkes, and John Lee and asked them about their impressions of their new friends. John Lee said, "That Mr. Utz is a good guy with a good heart. I give him a 50=50, but he has a couple of snakes in his bag. That big guy with the small ears and the quiet guy, I'm not sure about them. The big guy got confused when I asked him where he was from. Once he said he was from Ohio and the second time after drinks he was from Virginia. I registered the diametrical remarks and figured out he is not reliable. Now, that quiet guy kept checking his watch. Hell, everybody knows if you don't know the code then you can't tape, hear, and transmit, a damn thing, then it ain't only a watch. I think his watch is his transponder."

The Sarge said, "Mr. Utz told me he felt he had a snake in his bag but couldn't identify it. My jury is still out on Mr. Utz. He indicated that Walter is in Colorado, a few clicks away from Asiram's place. Is that coincidental, or is he trying to do his own work at this point? I'm not sure, but if the government is tracking the money he's using, then they ought to know where he is. I want to switch gears. I want to leave the women and children here and go head-to-head with this guy. What say you?"

Jilkes and Mallory both stated that suggestion was not going to fly. Jilkes said, "If the guy can commandeer Howitzers and live rounds, I want my woman near me in case I meet my maker. And besides, they're our backup. Okema, Somara, and Yeshida are excellent long gun shooters. Rashida, Juan, Darryl, and Sue Lyn are the only ones who understand the total operation of the weapons systems. I don't like your suggestion and I frankly will not support it, Sir."

John Lee rose and said, "I have to agree with my friend, Mr. Jilkes. Don't make sense not to have them women shooting things from afar."

"Let me remind you this is not a command. I just so happen to be the senior person in our group. I made a suggestion and the two of you don't seem to like it."

Mallory raised his hand and said, "Three of us."

Brown and Bernstein slyly raised their hands, and Brown said, "They're a part of this team. We can't exclude them, and I don't want to make a choice at this point. I want my woman near me wherever I go. Sorry, Sarge."

Bernstein yelled, "Ditto."

The Sarge said, "I respect your positions. What about the children? Should we leave them here with Ms. Viola?"

Jilkes responded, "Ms. Viola is our friend and helper. She's not their mother. She would be offended at such a suggestion, knowing we're all in and alive, or all dead and in heaven together, while she keeps babies."

John Lee stated, "I afraid that there might be a lot of casualties. I actually want to do this by myself because I feel that I would not be able to live peacefully if something happened to you people."

After a few moments of reflection, Bernstein said, "Sarge, it's already happened. We survived Vietnam, we had to decimate Gianni and his gang, we've beat your cousin at every turn, we enriched ourselves accidently from funds that were for the purpose of terminating us. We've helped people along the way to build their businesses, save their ranches, keep their resorts, and reinvigorate their restaurants. We've had a helluva run and if our number comes up, then, so be it. Plus, I know you must have hurt like hell to know your relative was in love with me, a white guy. That in itself, will make me smile at the demons or angels' gate."

The Sarge laughed and said, "You know what Mr. Man, I told the guys to stand pat and let you handle that because I was hoping you had that kind of soul to save her from that demon. I was happy you were the chosen one. Ask Courtney if you don't believe me. Anyway, I have bad feelings about this situation and it's going to be a bloody mess on both sides. I've heard your reservations and concerns. I'll give a final review of it tomorrow. I thank you for being loyal and true friends. That means the world to me."

# # #

At 0200 hours, Mr. Carter dropped the Sarge off at the airport and said, "You can't do this alone, but I assume you know what you're doing. God speed and I wish you well. Thank you for giving me my life back and enlisting my son and stimulating my wife to help me as well. I owe you people a lot, but I can't figure out how to pay you back. Each time I try to make a payment, and I do mean sizeable, the bank tells me that the transaction is not sanctioned, ergo, 'The Sanctuary'. I hope it works out for you, Mr. Sarge."

What the Sarge didn't know is that Mr. Carter had driven his main team plus some additional souls to the airport at 0100 hours. Those additional souls would be Mike, Michael, Darryl, Larry, Zanthius, and a few others. When the Sarge arrived at the terminal, the captain was standing outside of the plane and when he saw the Sarge he said, "We'll depart in twenty minutes. Welcome aboard."

The cabin was dark and after ascending the steps, the Sarge stepped into the cabin of the small jet and the lights were cut on. Someone yelled, "Hey, cut the damn lights out."

The Sarge looked around and saw his entire Nam crew plus a few other good souls and asked, "Where is the leak in my command?"

McArthur said, "That Darryl be from down-under, and he can smell a rotten plan before it begins to happen, right Mate? The women and children will board the main plane in forty-five minutes. This is a family, a group, a community, and that is how it will flourish or conclude, together, but never individually."

The Sarge sat in his assigned seat and cried. No one consoled him because he had forgotten what the group meant to each other. John Lee said to him, "You can't pick occasions for us to get together."

Darryl said, "I'm going to make a management decision and delay this flight until the women and children are here and then you guys can take the main plane and me and my crew can take this plane and hopefully head to the outback after we're finished with our work in the Midwest."

No one challenged him and, therefore, he told the pilot to communicate to the tower that the flight would be delayed.

CHAPTER THIRTY-THREE

At 0500 hours, a day later, Captain Carla told the sleepy travelers to prepare for arrival. After the plane landed, Carla pulled into their secure hangar followed by Darryl and his crew in the smaller jet. The men immediately entered the school bus and extracted their weapons of choice. Once they were secure, the women left the plane and began to secure and load their weapons. A harness was constructed for Ms. Viola's sawed-off-shotgun. She retrieved it along with her ammo belt and placed two loads into the barrels.

During the ride to the ranch, Rashida and Juan reviewed the camera systems and checked to see if anyone had entered the property. Those that had entered were sanctioned and, therefore, the alarm system was disengaged once the school bus entered the road leading to the main ranch house.

The Sarge was being comforted by his bride who told him that people loved him and didn't want him sacrificing himself for the sake of the group. She told him in no uncertain terms, to never try that stunt again.

Darryl knew exactly what his uncle was thinking and walked up besides where he was sitting and said, "I must remind you uncle, that family is forbidden from killing family, even if they're not on Australian soil. It would be bad karma and it would affect the entire group."

Ben Beckmire said, "I think our forefathers will forgive me for this one indiscretion."

Darryl looked at him and announced, "Uncle, all that you've done and have built, will be forfeited for your senseless desire for vengeance."

The Sarge paused for a moment, turned around and looked at Darryl and asked, "Are you my elder, or am I yours?"

"Uncle, it doesn't matter. None of us are given all the information. There is always a need for balance and on this one, I am presenting you with an issue that matters most to you and for the sake of all of us who have participated in this adventure. You are prohibited from killing a family member," Darryl walked away.

Courtney asked the Sarge, "What did your nephew want?"

"He wants to be my father, their father, and all the fathers that make up the Beckmire clan. He grounded me with simple truisms and guidelines. He is truly a modern Beckmire, and I've forgotten a lot of things that have guided me in life, like hating my cousin with a passion. He told me to abandon my notion of revenge and reminded me that family cannot kill family, no matter their location or cause."

"That's an easy thing to handle. Let John Lee or Jilkes do the work. You know they will enjoy it and take pictures if you like."

"Why Dr. Beckmire, you're supposed to be the one who saves lives, not find alternative ways of ending them."

"Well, Ben Beckmire, if you want to know my true feelings, then let me have a go at him, and then I can assure you he'll die slowly, horrifically, and in a helluva lot of pain, but conscious to the very end."

"Sorry, dear, I am forbidden, you are as well, and so is any member of the group that is considered immediate family. Once we have him, I will try to figure out how to test the limits of my clan. However, right now, I'm just happy my people have found peace, love, and happiness, not to mention a massive fortune. We have three issues that we must reconcile, before we can become normal human beings, my cousin, the Carbon Factor formula, and now Mr. Utz. After all we've been through, nothing seems insurmountable for this group."

# # #

Clyde answered his phone while driving the bus and decided to pull over to the side of the road to talk. He told the Sarge a plane landed with strange looking people wearing sunglasses and that they unloaded large containers. The Sarge asked Clyde to ask his people to take pictures and send them to him.

A few minutes later, Clyde's phone buzzed. Clyde opened his email and told the Sarge that it is the same guy. It was the mysterious, Mr. Utz. The Sarge told Clyde to tell his people to keep an eye on them, but to otherwise be hospitable to them.

A few hours later at the ranch house, everyone settled in and began to wonder if this was their Armageddon. People moved slowly, and love and emotions were in the air. A lot of hugs and kisses were shared, and everyone felt as if this might be the day when 'the death dealer' would visit the ranch.

As usual, Clyde's people always prepared a helluva table for the group. As the Sarge was about to speak, Clyde cleared his throat and whispered the word prayer.

As he was about to pray, his cell phone rang, and his people indicated that people with sunglasses were trying to gain access to the ranch. He told the Sarge, who indicated to let them in. The Sarge asked Clyde if he could hold the prayer in abeyance until the real sinners showed up.

Minutes later, Mr. Utz and his crew showed up with vests and sidearms on them. The Sarge said, "We're about to eat. Would you guys like a real meal and indicated that he would need two of Mr. Utz's team to monitor the gate?"

Mr. Utz ordered the big guy and the quiet guy to handle the initial watch and told them he would send two people down once they finished eating.

The Sarge whispered, "Those are your two leaks."

"How do you know that?"

"Because two of my guys sorted them out. My guys have never been wrong. They can smell a rat a mile away and foreign cologne five miles if the wind is blowing in the right direction. We can handle them, but you need to know who they're reporting to and what's their take."

Utz thought about it for a moment and asked, "When you say handle, do you mean permanently?"

The Sarge laughed and asked, "Do you like to have a complete session when you have sex, or go away still full of vim and vigor? We don't do halves. We finish what we start, and we're great at extracting information from people."

Again, Utz considered the options and said, "I need my people alive, even if your cousin may be in control of them. My problem is trying to figure out if they're assassins and if they will attempt to put a hit on you."

# # #

Rashida signaled to Mallory to have the Sarge come into the war room.

When the Sarge walked in, Rashida said, "Dad, I need you to listen to a conversation that just took place."

"Honey, I'll be right back."

Rashida looked at him and said, "Dad, I need you to hear this conversation now."

She turned the volume up and said, "This is the conversation those two men at the beginning of the road just had with another man."

The Sarge listened to the conversation and asked Juan to summon Mr. Utz. When Utz came into the room, he was surprised at the equipment and communications systems. The Sarge asked Rashida to rewind the conversation and play it back. The Sarge then handed Utz a headset and told him to listen.

Mr. Utz could hear the two men having a conversation with another man who instructed them to take a shot at the target once you're back in the ranch house. Utz also heard the other person say, "You will do this or attend funerals for your entire family".

The Sarge looked at Utz and said, "Now, that's who you're dealing with. Diablo is apparently holding the families of those men hostage. How do you want to play this?"

Utz looked down the road and said, "I'll send two of my guys to relieve them, so they can eat. Once they're in the ranch house, we'll disarm them and let them know we are on to them and their mandate."

Thirty minutes later, two men drove a mule to the access road and relieved the two men in question. When the two men got back to the ranch and out of the mule they were riding in, Utz and his other team members, drew weapons on them and held up a sign that read, "if you speak, I will blow your fucking head off".

Off to the infamous barn, the two were escorted and once in it, they were presented with a video of some of the horrific events that had taken place in the barn. Jilkes taped their mouths and examined their bodies. Both men were wired. He removed the wires and decided they needed to be placed on someone eating.

Once convinced they were out of communication range, Utz said, "What are you willing to do for your life? Who is your handler? And how did you get corrupted? Was it, money?"

Jilkes removed the tape from the first guy's mouth and said, "Answer in the order asked."

Two hours later, both men explained their situations and how they were seduced by Diablo who provided them with gambling money, confiscated high end jewelry, fur coats, and multiple cars. Utz asked, "So in essence, your families are basically worth a lot of bullshit, right? I mean if you sell your soul for bangles and baubles, then your families must be worth cotton balls to you. Here's what I'm going to do. I'm going to let you turn yourselves in when you get back to Washington and explain how you are being blackmailed."

The Sarge waltzed up beside him and asked, "May I have a word with you in private?"

The two men walked outside and the Sarge said, "I don't know about you, but if my wife and kids were being held hostage, I would try to settle whatever debt I obligated myself to. If they go back to DC, then he'll surely kill their families. He has committed that atrocity with many others, including your family members. Try to figure out if they're willing to play ball while we try to pinpoint his location. This is time management at its best. We know that he's within a seventy to eighty-mile radius and it gets smaller and smaller by the minute. Right now, those two are allegedly eating. They just flew in, and I wasn't in the room and plus we have a no weapons doctrine for meals in the house. Think on your feet man. You can't castrate a man for trying to save his family, no matter his affliction. Let's figure out how to slow time down, locate precisely where my cousin is, then load up with state, local, federal, NSA, FBI, CIA, and every fucking body else. I can't kill him, but I sure as hell hope he'll want to go out in a blaze of glory and then I'm justified in putting a cannon size bullet through his head."

"You really hate this guy don't you."

"Hate is too subtle! I want to turn his ass into ashes," the Sarge adamantly stated.

# # #

While using a combination of information from the team of Mr. Utz, Rashida and Juan narrowed the location of Walter E. Lassiter.

Rashida yelled, "Hey dad, we have tracked your cousin within a ten-mile radius of where the signals indicate he is. We can do this tracking from the road, but we also need a strong contingency to support the ranch. I say, we go and end this. We can leave Darryl and Sue Lyn to man the machines, and Juan and I can do and be wherever you want us. This ain't about safety, this is about concluding some shit that has haunted us for years. Let's do this and get it done."

The Sarge looked at his beautiful daughter and calmly said, "Have my team mount up, fully loaded."

CHAPTER THIRTY-FOUR

When the Sarge entered the bus in full battle gear, he saw Clyde sitting behind the steering wheel. He said, "Clyde, I love you, but I can't allow you to do this."

"Mr. Sarge, you don't have a choice. Once you cross that state line, you'll be in harm's way. Now, my cousin is the local Sheriff there and is expecting me and a bunch of school children. You can't get into Colorado with this armament and I'm the only one who can get you to where your cousin is."

# # #

Rashida yelled, "Dad, I have him in a two-mile radius. He's in Loveland, Colorado at a Days Inn motel."

The Sarge said, "I need confirmation of that baby girl."

Five minutes later, Rashida said, "Dad, he's in Loveland, Colorado, at the Days Inn, in room number 234."

# # #

The Sarge warned Utz not to show up in a macho fashion or he and his men would be considered hostile, and his people would open fire on them if necessary. Utz indicated that he and his crew would cover the back of the building and the Sarge and his men had control of the front.

Rashida and Juan entered the rental office, showed a picture of Walter, and asked the clerk for the register of who was in what rooms. The clerk vehemently, declined to acquiesce to their demands, until Rashida put her .308 in his mouth. He obliged and told them everything that was happening in the hotel including the fact that the man in room number 234 liked men, women, sometimes together, but that he was a strong tipper.

The Sarge laid against the wall and recalled his dreams and began to sweat.

Mallory recognized that the Sarge was under stress, and said, "You need to fall to the rear. You're too close to this."

Darryl saw his uncle and said, "This is a family affair, I should lead this matter."

The Sarge said, "I'll cover you from behind that truck parked thirty yards away. Nephew, he's in the midst of a ménage trois, with a man and a woman."

Darryl looked at Michael and said, "I need you to hit that door hard and follow it to the floor, remain there with your hands over your ears and your eyes shut tight. I'm going to throw a stun grenade into the room. Isaiah and Desmond, fire shotgun rounds into the ceiling, Jasper and Harold blow out the windows with snake rounds. I don't want to hurt the occupants of that room, but a little buckshot won't kill them, and the impact of being disoriented, will keep them and us safe."

Like clockwork, the prescription went off without a hitch. Walter E. Lassiter, without any fanfare, surrendered without incident, and was handcuffed in room 234, with only his birthday suit on. The Sarge had a beam on his cousin's head through the open door. Walter knew it and essentially sneered at him and dared the Sarge to shoot him. The Sarge lowered his weapon and remembered family can't kill family and made his way to the room.

Once in the room the Sarge exclaimed, "I see you're still a freak! One question? What do you do with that little pecker of yours? It's so tiny!"

The Sarge smiled, paused, and said, to himself, "they didn't say shit about shooting family". He considered shooting his cousin, 'just because'. He said to himself, "fuck it—I'm going to hurt his ass because he has willingly killed people for no good reasons". He unholstered his pistol and strategically fired a round into both of his cousin's shoulder blades, and then shot him in both kneecaps. The Sarge, raised his weapon in the air and yelled, "Friendly fire—friendly fire! An accident that I'll remember for the balance of my life."

Meanwhile, two buses pulled up at the Days Inn and people began to scamper out of them with weapons. Jilkes radioed the Sarge, told him they had company on the way, and that they were armed to the teeth.

Jilkes sent out the alarm, Mr. Utz saw the group from afar and then the firefight began. As the groups fired round after round at each other, Clyde maneuvered the bus so that it was facing the opposing forces. Once in position, and thanks to Rashida and Sue Lyn, he hit a button and a rear panel was lowered that exposed a Gatlin gun. Clyde hit the engage button and the gun began to cut down men and destroy machines until the remaining opposing forces threw their weapons to the ground and raised a white flag.

Those who were lucky enough to survive, were arrested by federal officials on a variety of weapons charges, endangerment, and other sundry offenses. Mr. Utz, on this day, turned out to be a good guy. After lengthy discussions with local and state officials, his people gathered the spent shells from the Gatlin gun and gave them to Clyde who was allowed to leave.

Mr. Utz and his crew read Walter his rights, arrested him on the spot, and whisked him off to the local hospital in Loveland. He was attended to, sedated, and chained to the bed. Walter was operated on, and the damage done by the bullets were significant and strategic. It would take 6-hours and 3-follow-up surgeries to stabilize his condition. The placement of the rounds were tactical and would require conversations relative to amputation.

Forty-eight hours later, the Sarge stood over Walter as he gained consciousness. He said, "By Aborigine law, family cannot kill family. They didn't say shit about me shooting your stank ass. Listen, asshole, when you get out of here, and after you're arraigned and sentenced to prison, our people are going to send the smallest of creatures to entertain you each night. Enjoy the drugs because once you're situated in jail, our people from the bush are going to come for you in a way that will be cruel, violent, intrusive, and mentally exhausting. Your days of sleep are limited, asshole!"

Walter looked at the Sarge and mumbled, "I'm not dead yet. See you in hell!"

The Sarge looked at his lower extremities and said, "It's a shame the doctors couldn't save your right lower leg or your left arm. Perhaps gangrene will also cause the left leg and right arm to be amputated. Enjoy learning how not to walk. Oh, and by the way, you remember the stories about Mr. Chakes from our forefathers? Well cousin, you're on your way to being without arms and legs. I assure you, as soon as your body can withstand the intrusions, the other arm will be severed. Then of course, that other leg will be banished as well. Enjoy the drugs and your conscious time. Life is about to change for you, cousin. Oh, it slipped my mind, within thirty days, you will develop a fever that will cause you to forfeit sight in both eyes. Bad day mate! Bad day mate!"

Walter was drugged and couldn't feel his lower extremities. He panicked and began to yell and scream at the top of his lungs, "I will kill you and everyone that you know."

Ben Beckmire responded, "The only thing you'll do, is beg for coins to cover your miserable needs. Oh, and I will find out who your so-called loyal associates are, and then barter with them for their lives for your stolen loot. I will often appear before you and give alms. However, I will extract minutes from your time on earth for those you needlessly sent to their death. I will, however, attempt to be civil in approaching your new-found life. You must tell me who your puppet master is? In the giving of this information, I will allow you to self-conclude. You were once on top and controlled many people and the entire government bank. Soon you will be without all limbs, resources, and you will be begging on the streets. Give me your master and banker, and I will give you a quick demise, after I allow you to track, discover, and annihilate those who betrayed you by stealing a fortune that you stole!"

Walter without hesitating said, "If there is such a person, and if I gave you that kind of information, I would be committing you and your group to an immediate hell. The only thing you've been able to do, is buy time before their reign of fire comes down on you and your people. I'm going to die. You my cousin, are going to live a miserable life knowing that your ego was the cause of your family being terminated from this earth."

"Yes Couz, you are going to die, as well as all my people. However, not before you experience the hell you placed innocent, desperate people in. No, Couz, your ass will suffer long after I am dead and gone!   In a loud and demonic sounding voice, the Sarge exclaimed, "HAHAHAHAHAHA!

CHAPTER THIRTY-FIVE

Two weeks later, in an elaborate and staged video, Zanthius could be seen sitting in an outdoor venue with a laptop, a burning kettle, and with six people behind him, allegedly acting as witnesses. Also surrounding this venue, was a group of people who had been through skirmishes on five of the seven continents. Parked in the field was a blue school bus that happened to be outfitted with a Gatlin gun.

During the night, Mr. Utz and his six men were hijacked, bound, and gagged. The Sarge apologized to him and said, "In the end, we believe the world will be a safer place, and if not, it will not be because of some product that we controlled."

Mr. Utz mumbled something and the Sarge pulled the tape from his mouth and said, "You got thirty seconds."

"Sarge, please don't do this. You will set everyone against you and there is no way I can protect you."

The Sarge smiled and patted him on the shoulder and said, "We know you can't protect us on any level. However, we can attempt to protect the world from a bomb that is supposedly deadlier than a nuclear weapon, cheap as hell to make, fits in a milk carton, and we have the specs for it. Naw, my friend, we'll burn in hell first before we turn this over to any government including the one, we love."

On Clyde's farm, a random group of witnesses, who were selected through a lottery, were seated in front of a makeshift stage. Zanthius took the lead seat and said, "Thank you all for coming to this event. What you're about to attest to is our burning of the schematics and specifications for a product that is called the Carbon Factor. The Carbon Factor is a new cheap weapon that can be nuclearized, we think, and is sought by every government in existence and every corrupt organization that has terror as its main objective. I am known as the 'idiot spy'. In some circles, I'm still considered the idiot, but hopefully, no longer a spy. Several years ago, I was thrust into the dark world of espionage and didn't know it—hence my title, the 'idiot spy'. That led to my receiving critical information about the Carbon Factor formula as well as assassination attempts on my mother, my father, and his wife. I had been told that my father died in the police action in Vietnam. Since that time, I've been hunted along with my family that is providing security for us at this moment. My nieces and nephews have been strapped in suicide vests on our ranch. Literally, thousands of people have died seeking control of this product including two sitting United States Senators. Me, and my family believe the world has far too many ways of annihilating itself and, therefore, a cheap, easily manufactured, carbon-based weapon, would only lead to horrific terroristic events around the world."

"My family and I have been shot, poisoned, stabbed, and chased from one end of the world to the other. We feel the world is not ready for a weapon that can be produced using the by-products of coal and, therefore, it is for that reason we want you to witness our actions. I know you have seen us declare this deed before in the presence of the Pope and a pledge to God. We didn't start this campaign and in front of the Pope we thought we had the relevant parts of the formula to exonerate us from this evil project. We were wrong. We ask that you realize that we played the hand that was dealt to us. It was not done with any chicanery in mind but those who involved us played us until the very end."

Zanthius teared up and took a swig of water. He said, "I'm going to open each file and show a portion of its content and then I'm going to throw the data disk into the burning flame. The author of these thumb-drives is presumed dead and made sure these thumb-drives could not be copied. I'm going to open this first drive and attempt to transfer it and copy it."

Zanthius went through the process, and it was obvious the drives had been locked. He then showed a random portion of the drive and then closed the screen. He then dropped the thumb-drive into the burning kettle. He repeated his actions four times. He took his laptop and placed it in the fire as well. Mr. Utz and his men were near the burning kettle and witnessed Zanthius drop the drives and laptop into the flames.

The Sarge took the gag off Mr. Utz and freed his hands. Mr. Utz said, "I'm glad your video will show us bound and gagged. I think you've made a mistake, but I'm not the one who has been hunted like a wild animal. I'm on your side as long as you'll help me do some wet work overseas in a couple of weeks. I really need your expertise. You can't train people to respond to events the way you and your people take care of issues. I'm so sorry my father was such an asshole and couldn't realize you guys could have been his route to his first star. Besides, the master puppeteer, as well as spy, who won't die, is allegedly, still out there. Believe it or not, your cousin had someone pulling his strings."

Zanthius said, "Mr. Utz, the kettle is yours to do with what you want."

Utz, immediately grabbed the bottle of water that Zanthius had seemingly drank out of and that was conveniently near. He emptied the contents onto the flames. The flames shot high in the air and Zanthius smiled at Mr. Utz. The bottle he drank out of had a false top that was removed once he consumed what was pure water. The remaining contents of the bottle was an accelerant.

# # #

Later, after a lot of posturing on both sides, Mr. Utz said, "Ben Beckmire, it's been a real pleasure. I'll call you in a few weeks. I'm not sure if I like your son. I think you owe me at least two outings. I won't show up anywhere you are unless the entire world is at risk, and I give you my word, but I need you to tell me you'll at least broach my request with the rest of your group and get back to me. That's all I ask, Sarge."

The Sarge said, "Mr. Utz, I'll broach that idea with my people and get back to you in two weeks, or so. However, if we see you, your people, or feel we're being watched, we will forfeit any notions of helping you. From this point forward, trust has to be the operative word as well as full disclosure."

Utz held out his hand and the Sarge said, "Man, give me a hug and seal our fates."

# # #

Darryl who had been silent on his uncle's actions approached him and said, "It's a good thing that some Abos follow tradition, even if the older ones don't. You really took that no killing thing, divided it into sections, and decided to shoot my other uncle, but not kill him. How on earth did you know he wouldn't die from an infection or something?"

"Darryl, your sources of information are more spiritual than mine. My sources attempt to circumscribe the barriers and find ways around the verbal laws yet stay within the intent of them. We don't attempt to break laws--we intend to enhance them and make them apropos to the circumstances that we face in the 21st century."

Darryl smiled and said, "One day, perhaps you'll teach me your magic, oh great one, who knows all and sees all."

"Perhaps!' Ben Beckmire stated. "Perhaps!"

the end!

also in the 'idiot spy' series

Available at Amazon and BarnesandNoble.com

www.ingramcontent.com/pod-product-compliance
Lightning Source LLC
Chambersburg PA
CBHW030754260626
47169CB00001B/42